Tea Cooper is an Australian author of historical and contemporary fiction. In a past life she was a teacher, a journalist and a farmer. These days she haunts museums and indulges her passion for storytelling.

The HORSE Thief

TEA COOPER

First Published 2015
Second Australian Paperback Edition 2017
ISBN 978 1 489 23742 2

Published by
HQ Fiction
An imprint of Harlequin Enterprises (Australia) Pty Ltd.
Level 13, 201 Elizabeth St,
SYDNEY NSW 2000
AUSTRALIA

Printed and bound in Australia by McPherson's Printing Group

To Katy,
the little girl who loved 'the horses' and
the beautiful woman who always picks the Cup winner!
All my love, always.

One

August 1865
The Hunter, New South Wales

Bold black handwriting sprawled across the envelope:

> *Alexander Kilhampton Esq.,*
> *Helligen Stud.*

The flourish beneath the writing stopped at a small spot of ink as if the author had prevaricated then come to a sudden decision.

'Off you go.' India Kilhampton clutched the letter and dropped a penny into the young boy's hand. She tore open the envelope before he'd even turned to leave. Her fingers trembled as she extracted the paper and unfolded it.

'Peggy! Peggy!' Grasping her skirts in one hand she flew across the flagstone courtyard, the letter held high above her head. 'I have a response.' Skidding to a halt on the threshold of the kitchen, she brandished the letter under her housekeeper's nose.

A sceptical look flashed across Peggy's round, pink face. 'That's mighty fine news.'

'I never believed we'd hear from anyone.' She tapped the envelope against her lips, relishing the scent of ink and new prospects. 'I placed the advertisement over a month ago.'

'What does it say?'

She glanced at the paper again, elation and tension blurring the words. 'Not as much as I hoped. His name is Jim Mawgan and he'll be in the area during the week of fourteenth of August and will …'

So much depended on this advertisement. Twelve months to prove a point and perform a miracle. The fourteenth of August … the knot in her stomach tightened. 'Wasn't that yesterday?' Too late. The date had passed. Why hadn't he turned up? She slumped down at the kitchen table. 'Maybe he changed his mind.'

A cloud of white flour settled over India's precious letter as Peggy dusted her hands. 'Calm down. Read me the letter.'

Shaking the paper clean India cleared her throat and adopted her most businesslike tone. It was one she intended to practise, and use, if she ever got the chance.

'Dear Sir,

In reply to your advertisement in The Maitland Mercury, I wish to make application for the position of Stud Master. I will be in the area during the week of fourteenth of August and beg your permission to call to discuss said position.

Respectfully,

Jim Mawgan.'

'There you are.' Peggy's rolling pin thumped the table. 'You're supposed to be the educated one. The *week* of the fourteenth of August means anytime during the week. Today's Monday. It could be any day until the weekend.'

The simple script floated in front of India's eyes, the neat lines merging and drifting. 'Oh, Peggy, I think you're right. I hope so.' It wasn't too late, he hadn't changed his mind, he just hadn't arrived yet. Somewhere in her chest a bubble of elation burst. Unable to stay still a moment longer she leapt to her feet and spun around and around, clasping the precious letter tight.

'Stop cavorting and carrying on. Come and sit down while I finish these scones.'

More from habit than agreement India plopped down again at the scrubbed pine table. Neat circles of dough fell from Peggy's hands and lined up like soldiers on parade. India's thoughts were less cooperative. It was such an outside chance. Some might call her idea reckless and foolish. No-one advertised for a stud master. There was no point. No reputable stud parted with the one man who knew all their secrets. No-one would apply for the job. It simply wasn't done. *Well!* She sat back and indulged in a smug smile. She'd done it.

'Are you going to tell your father?'

As usual, Peggy discovered the hair in the icing.

Telling Papa wasn't necessary. After all, he might not even be in Sydney. He could be anywhere. Sailing the seven seas, trading his goods, anything to keep him away from Helligen. She chewed on her lip. 'No. Not yet. He agreed in principle. I'll wait and see if the man can do the job before I let Papa know. And anyway, he agreed matters were in my hands for twelve months.'

With a long-suffering sigh Peggy swung the oven door open. 'Morning tea. Who's here today?'

The smell of freshly baked scones compensated for Peggy's lack of enthusiasm. India knew her plan would work—she didn't need Peggy's approval. 'Only Fred, Jilly in the scullery, and the men working on the back fences with Tom Bludge. I'm going to tell them it's their last day today. I'll just keep Fred and Jilly on until I discover what this new man is like.'

'Don't get your hopes up. You advertised for a stud master not a labourer. He won't be sweating it out in the paddocks. He'll have other things on his mind.' The corners of Peggy's mouth twitched and her eyes twinkled as she let out a loud chortle.

India had lived most of her life on Helligen Stud and she had no doubt about the direction the housekeeper's thoughts had taken. 'Peggy!'

'Well, I don't know. Putting an advertisement in the paper for a man to do your breeding.' She slammed the oven door. 'Hardly ladylike.'

'Not *my* breeding.' India laughed and pushed the chair back. She stretched her legs under the table and wiggled her feet. 'I can't wait. It'll breathe new life into the place having some foals around again. I've missed the rhythm of the seasons so much. I'm never going back to Sydney or Melbourne again.' She lifted her hands and pulled her heavy hair off the nape of her neck. 'Except to race Helligen's first champion in the Melbourne Cup.'

'And will you be taking your sister?' Peggy's caterpillar eyebrows twitched.

Violet! Heaven forbid. There'd be no chance of leaving without her. She'd made the most awful fuss about returning home to Helligen. 'She'll do as she's told. Until she marries she has to do as Papa says, and right now I'm in charge so she'll have to learn to live with it.'

'Those are brave words, my girl.'

India jumped to her feet. 'I feel brave, audacious and adventurous.' For too long she'd plotted and schemed, wondering how to get things moving. 'It's a new beginning for Helligen—for all of us.'

Two

Heat radiated from the dry bush, carrying a pungent blend of eucalyptus and the almond scent of wattle flowers. And on the rising breeze, the promise of rain. A long overdue promise. The ground crackled beneath the stallion's hooves and puffs of sandy dirt billowed with every step.

Jim Mawgan ran his tongue over his parched lips as he searched the track. The boundary of the property couldn't be much further. According to his father a change in the terrain would mark his arrival. In the old days the fertile wetlands provided year-round tucker for the natives.

He dug his heels into Jefferson's flanks to urge him on. After a full day on the road both of them could do with a drink and something to eat. They'd covered over fifty dry, dusty miles since first light.

An expanse of shimmering water came into view, the long afternoon rays of the sun turning the surface of the lagoon to gold. Smelling water Jefferson whinnied. In response a flight of birds took to the wing, their cries breaking the silence of the tinder-dry bush.

The ground vibrated and a horse thundered past. It shuddered to a halt beneath a solitary stand of trees. A cry drowned out the sounds of the waterbirds. The rider fell forwards, arms dangling free, slumped against the buckskin's neck.

Guttural gasps reached a crescendo and turned to rasping sobs. Jim jumped from his saddle, tethered Jefferson and edged closer. The figure sobbed and groaned. Flowing white robes cast an ethereal glow over the silhouette.

'Ma'am, allow me. Are you hurt?'

She lifted her head, her face barely visible through the heavy curtain of tangled hair. The horse shied. Jim darted closer and grabbed the bridle. 'Ma'am?'

With hands whiter than her cobweb gown she pulled back her hair. He smothered a gasp. Pain etched her ravaged face and her eyes blazed; her mouth stretched wide by her wracking sobs.

'I've searched … I've searched high and low.' She threw back her head, exposing the frail column of her neck. 'I can't find him.'

Her mournful keening sent prickles skittering across his sweat-soaked skin. Uttering a pathetic moan she slipped sideways. He caught her as she toppled to the ground and with his arms tight around her waist he steadied her.

She stared at him with a look of total confusion. 'Have you found him?' Her demented gaze scanned the edges of the paper-bark forest, as though at any moment she would pull free and run.

In an attempt to pacify her he dropped his hands and spread his palms. 'Ssh! Ssh!'

Her thin fingers bruised the bare skin of his forearms as she clung to him. 'You must find him.'

'Indeed I shall, ma'am, but first let me help you.'

At his words her head snapped up and her stormy eyes flashed a warning. With unexpected force she pushed him aside and vaulted back onto her horse. She gave one last agonising cry and took off in the direction of the lagoon, sending another flurry of waterbirds soaring upwards.

Loose white material billowed behind her. A long shawl trailed over her shoulders and tangled with her dappled hair, blending with the pale colour of her horse's coat. As he peered after her she disappeared into the last rays of the setting sun.

The hairs on the back of his neck prickled and he ran his hands up and down his arms to chase away the strange sense of foreboding. Should he chase after her? She rode without a saddle and in her distressed state could easily injure herself. Then again, she'd mounted and galloped off as confident as any seasoned rider.

Unable to countenance leaving the woman alone he headed for the lagoon at a gallop. The ground softened, forcing Jefferson to pick his way along the edge of the lagoon, his feet sinking into the damp grass. The slanting sun threw tangled shadows across their path and Jim shaded his eyes as he scanned the foreshore.

She'd vanished. Only the two red brick chimneys his father had said pinpointed the house marred the pristine landscape. He shrugged his shoulders and turned his horse.

Within minutes an impressive set of double gates came into view. Jim dismounted. His heart beat hard and fast against his rib cage as he ran his fingers over the weathered words engraved on the timber sign. *Helligen Stud.*

He took one last look back at the lagoon, but there was no sign of the woman so he swung the gates open and entered the property, taking his first step towards avenging the past and securing his future.

A long meandering driveway curved up to the house, which dominated the landscape. It perched, master of all it surveyed, atop a small incline. Tangible proof of the power of the Kilhamptons. Pillars of Australian society, leaders of business, and the owners of a fleet of trading vessels that roamed the globe. Timber fences as solid as the family's reputation ran the length of the treed driveway and marked out a series of lush green paddocks. Cattle grazed lazily and horses ambled along the river flats.

Dusk had settled by the time he entered the flagstone courtyard. How long since Kilhampton had bundled them off the property? Close on fifteen years. Not a lot had changed. A new dovecot sat in the middle of the vegetable garden and the massive barn was complete. The temptation to turn tail and run coiled in his gut but that would solve nothing. The top storey of the stables, the hay storage beckoned. That's where he'd throw his swag, the perfect spot to keep an ear open and an eye on all the comings and goings.

He cast a surreptitious glance in the direction of the house and slid from the saddle, easing his cramped muscles. No tangible difference, yet everything seemed smaller, less impressive, and a little colourless. He inhaled the warm, heavy air redolent with the odour of hay and dung. A couple of stable doors swung loose on their hinges. The water barrel beneath the eaves wallowed in a damp puddle. Weeds clustered at the base making the most of the seeping moisture. A few chickens picked and plucked their way around the stable doors. More than anything the silence struck him—the heart had been ripped from the place.

Jim led Jefferson into an empty stall in the stable block. He removed his pack saddle then searched around for something to rub down his horse. A tousled head, cocked to one side, appeared around the half-door. Toffee-coloured eyes twinkled a sheepish welcome.

'This your job?' Jim inclined his head towards his horse.

'Yep.' The boy brandished a piece of sackcloth. 'I'll rub him down and see to his feed. They're expecting you. Been waiting since your letter came. Miss India says you're to be treated proper, with respect.' An impish grin lit his face. 'Sir.'

Jim ruffled the boy's hair. The kid reminded him of a time and a person long gone. 'What's your name?'

'Fred.'

'Well, Fred, you can drop the sir. Jim will do. And this is Jefferson. *He* should be treated with respect.'

Fred ran a practised hand over the horse. 'Nice animal.' His fingers reached up to trace the brand on his shoulder. 'A Munmurra animal.'

'That's right. Know your horses, do you?'

'Could say that. Jockey needs to know his horses.'

'Oh, you're a jockey, are you?' Jim grinned; the boy's cockiness impressed him.

'Not yet. I will be, one day, if I'm ever allowed to race.'

'Patience. You're young, you've got all the time in the world.'

Lucky. He hadn't a moment to waste and so much to achieve. In a matter of weeks registration for the Flemington Races opened and by then he intended to be ready.

'Go and see Peggy in the kitchen and she'll tell you what's what.' Fred clambered onto an upturned bucket and reached for Jefferson's neck.

Jim ruffled the boy's hair again and slung his saddlebags over his shoulder. Pushing aside his discomfort he made for the kitchen. The door stood ajar and he poked his head around the corner half expecting to see his mother standing at the stove. Disgusted by his sentimentality he rapped on the open door. 'Jim Mawgan. I'm looking for Mr Kilhampton.'

'Are you?' The woman stood, hands on hips, guarding her range.

Jim dropped his bags to the ground and removed his hat. 'I'm here about the job advertised in *The Maitland Mercury*.'

Small flurries of flour flew up into the air as she brushed her hands together. Her eyes danced with welcome, and she grasped his hand in her plump fingers. 'I'm Peggy. Nice to meet you. We've been expecting you.' She took a step back and examined him from head to toe. 'You'll do.'

Jim gave a quick nod; he'd passed the first test.

'I'll tell Miss India you're here. Dinner's on in an hour.'

'Right. Good. I need to check on my horse. The young boy in the stable is sorting him out. And then find somewhere to bunk down.'

'The stud master's house is across the way. Ready and waiting.'

Jim peered through the window across the courtyard, past the two rows of stables, to his birthplace. He'd played in the dust in front of the old cottage, split his head falling from the verandah roof. He blew out a breath of air and raked his fingers across his scalp, scratching the scar where the sweat and damp hair irritated. That house held too many ghosts. 'That's too big for me. I can doss down above the stables.'

'You'll do no such thing. That's the stud master's house and that's the job you're after, isn't it?' Not giving him time to draw breath, Peggy continued, 'And that's where you'll be staying. You'll eat over here with Fred, Jilly, the boys and me in the kitchen. Miss India will see you tomorrow. She'll be pleased. She's got big plans.'

Not half as big as his own, he'd put money on that. 'What about Mr Kilhampton? Ought I have a word with him, tell him I've arrived?'

'Nope. He's not here. Miss India's running the show.'

That wasn't included in the advertisement. Jim shrugged off the memory of the mischievous pampered child who had hared around under everyone's feet. Fifteen years of privilege added into the mix would make for a sight to see. Maybe his task would be easier with Kilhampton out of the way.

She dug a key out of a pocket in her voluminous apron and offered it to him. 'Off you go then.'

The key nestled warm and familiar in his palm. He stooped and lifted his saddlebags, then stopped. 'By the way, I saw a woman out by the lagoon. She looked upset and took off before I could help. I wondered if ...'

The housekeeper's eyes widened then she shook her head. 'Nah. Take no notice. She's from over the way. Rides at sunset most days. Dressed in white, was she?'

Jim nodded.

Peggy dusted her hands again, tut-tutting and wrinkling her nose at the mess she'd made of the table. 'Grub in an hour. Don't be late.'

'Right. Won't be long.' With his bags slung over his shoulder he followed the path to the cottage door, his footsteps dragging and the bitter taste of the past coating his tongue.

He counted his steps. Not one hundred and fifty-four anymore, less than half that. The date etched above the door loomed large. He lifted a heavy hand and ran his fingers over the worn sandstone. He no longer needed to jump to reach the initials he'd carved beneath the lintel.

The key slipped into the lock with ease and he opened the door and ducked inside. Two overstuffed armchairs, both a touch moth-eaten and faded, greeted him. He blinked away the vision of his father sitting in front of the fire. He'd buried him little more than two months ago.

The cottage was smaller than he remembered, the ceiling lower, the walls closer together. The skeletal coat rack by the door stood empty. He wandered down the hallway and peered into the first bedroom. The patchwork quilt his mother used to bundle him up in covered the simple iron bedstead. Next door the spartan room he'd shared with his brother still housed two narrow single beds. He chucked his saddlebags down and made his way out the back, looking for signs of the diamond python that once lived in the roof trusses. The cottage looked and smelled as though it had stood empty for a long time.

Outside the old pump hunched against the wall. With a practised kick and a jiggle of the lever he coaxed it into action. It grunted and groaned and spat a damp, rusty cloud over the dirt before a thin stream of tea-coloured water trickled out—ground water, brackish and bitter, not the best. They needed rain, same as the rest of the country. In the old days they pumped up from the lagoon in a dry spell. Regardless he stripped down and sluiced his head and body, then dried off before pacing back into the house and donning a clean shirt. Once he'd fastened the buttons he pulled the door closed behind him and heeded the clanging of Peggy's bell.

Three

'Morning, Peggy.' India wandered into the kitchen and poured a cup of tea from the teapot standing next to the range.

'Mornin', my sweet. And how are you this fine morning?'

'Well, but I have a list as long as my arm of things to do. I'll have to chase up Fred. The stables are a mess. I want everything spic and span. I suspect Jim Mawgan will arrive today and I don't want him thinking we don't run a decent show.'

'You might just have left it a bit late.' Peggy's face broke into a knowing grin and she winked. 'He arrived last night.'

'Last night! Why didn't you tell me?'

'It was getting late and you and Violet were going hell for leather in the dining room. I didn't want to interrupt.'

'Oh dear.' India sighed. Despite her best attempts to be congenial and agreeable, nothing went according to plan. Last night Violet's behaviour had almost driven her to distraction. Her sister couldn't get it through her pretty head that living alone and unchaperoned in Sydney wasn't feasible. They could hope for a suitable marriage offer but as Violet pointed out, stuck in the Hunter it was an outside chance. Helligen wasn't the back of beyond yet it was a good ride to Morpeth and then six hours on the steamer to Sydney. Newcastle was closer, but the company Violet sought wouldn't dwell in the coal mining port.

Some days the responsibility was all too much and Violet's tantrums only added to her difficulties. 'I wish you'd told me last night.'

'Well.' Peggy stuck her hands on her hips, her chin jutting. 'I thought I was doing the right thing.'

'I'm sorry.' India curled her arm around Peggy's shoulder. 'You're right. It's far better if I meet him this morning. The last thing we want is for him to become embroiled in family problems. He's here to manage the horses. I need to be businesslike. And anyway, it's probably better to give the poor man a chance to settle in before I bombard him with my plans.'

Her new-found independence was both a blessing and a curse. There were days when she could do with a hand in running the place and a different viewpoint would be a godsend. Maybe Mr Jim Mawgan would provide that—not that she intended to hand over her hard-won right to make decisions, just as a second opinion.

'Here.' Peggy pushed the round breadboard across the table. 'You'd better have something to eat. Can't work on an empty stomach. The loaf's just out of the oven and there's some of that strawberry jam you like.'

India hacked off the crust. More than anything else in the world she wanted Helligen to flourish. Make it the vibrant family home it had once been. Bring it back to the time when any horse carrying the *HK* brand commanded the highest of prices.

When she'd stood at the rail at Flemington with four thousand others and watched Archer thunder down the two-mile track she'd made up her mind. Her heart skipped every time she relived the excitement, the clamour, and the thundering hooves. She would breed Helligen's first champion racehorse and win the coveted prize. To present Papa with the winner's purse would compensate for all their suffering, and prove she was capable. When Archer won for the second year running she'd nearly died of jealousy. The prize belonged to Helligen but for the string of misfortunes over the past years.

That single fact had firmed her resolve and after months of cajoling and pleading Papa had agreed—to give her a year once she turned twenty-one. One year to prove her capabilities. Before long the first Thursday of November would be a day in the history of the Kilhamptons, not just Flemington.

'People say when Archer won the Melbourne Cup they walked him all the way from New South Wales to Melbourne. And he went on to win by eight lengths. That's stamina, but our bloodlines are just as good.'

'Are you still harbouring that little fantasy of yours?'

'I might be. It takes time and hard work for dreams to become reality.'

Before Mama's accident the stables had been full of mares awaiting service and the property supported an energetic and vibrant community. Papa had tried but he'd sunk into such despair he retreated to his shipping business in Sydney. When he decided to drag her and her sister off to a school for young ladies in Sydney, Helligen and their mother had withered and become mere shadows.

In the time they'd been away so much had changed. Mama's health had declined further and Papa, out of his depth and unable to cope, rarely set foot on the property.

'This is just the beginning.'

To achieve her dreams she needed help, and a stud master would provide it. Jim Mawgan's arrival marked the first step on the long journey to Flemington and the prize she coveted more than any jewel. Today was an auspicious day on more than one count. Employing a stud master marked her first independent act in restoring the Kilhampton family fortunes.

The bread, dry as the sawdust spread on the stable floors, churned in her mouth. She chewed fast. Peggy wouldn't let her out of the kitchen until she swallowed it and there was so much to do. The stable doors dangled and the water barrels were a disgrace. They leaked liked Peggy's kitchen sieves and smelt almost as bad as the boiled cabbage she crushed in them. India tossed back the last drop of scalding tea, swallowed, picked up her hat and made for the door.

'Oh, before you go—just a word of warning.' Peggy's tone stopped her in her tracks. 'Jim, Mr Mawgan, said he saw a woman on a horse over by the lagoon last evening when he arrived.'

A bruised silence descended on the warm kitchen. India replaced her hat on the dresser and sighed. 'Have you spoken to Anya?'

'I haven't seen her this morning. I'll have a word when she comes down to get the trays. Your mother must have got back safe last night otherwise Anya would have raised the alarm.'

India's puff of exasperation echoed. 'I really don't want to deal with it right now. I want to get everything started in a business-like fashion—no echoes of the past.'

'If you didn't want "echoes of the past", why try and get the horse breeding back on track?'

'Because we're the best in the business and …' At the light rap on the half-closed door she clamped her lips together and crossed the floor. 'Mr Mawgan.'

Four

Jim made an effort to close his mouth then blinked twice at the vision before him.

'Mr Mawgan?' she repeated.

Clearing his throat he held out his hand, quite why he didn't know. It wasn't customary or proper. 'Yes.' His chest tightened and the hairs on his forearms rose.

'I'm India Kilhampton.' Her hand was warm, not cool like the pale hands of yesterday.

For a long moment he stared into her charcoal eyes: thunder-clouds chasing across a stormy sky. She raised an eyebrow and tugged her hand back.

'I wrote. The job. I'm here about the job.'

A smile hovered on the edge of her lips and she pulled back her sun-kissed hair against the nape of her neck. His skin prickled in response to the gesture, so like the woman yesterday. They could be one and the same but for the light of laughter in India's eyes and her taut, flawless skin tanned from hours in the fresh air.

'I am so happy to see you. Let me show you around and perhaps you can tell me a little about yourself.'

They stepped out into the morning sun. Countless colours, threads of gold and red danced in her hair and snatched his breath away. The same streaked tresses, the same eyes, and the same skin. All painted in a brighter hue, not washed out by the frenzied agony he'd seen last night.

'I'll take you for a tour of the property, and we'll discuss the job.'

Jim raked back his hair and scratched at the scar on the back of his neck. He tried to concentrate on her words as he planted his hat back on his head. The likeness between the two women was remarkable and yet the difference—watercolours to oils.

Miss Kilhampton didn't appear to notice his pensive silence, simply strode out and expected him to follow. Her self-assurance was no doubt a reflection of the confidence that privilege and security brought. He was thankful as it gave him time to gather his thoughts. He'd mentioned the woman on the horse to Peggy and she'd dismissed it. The resemblance was uncanny. He followed, forcing the image of the troubled woman to the back of his mind. Instead he searched the stylish skirt and buttoned boots, looking for some inkling of the precocious child he remembered.

'And so, in this area around the house we have two stable blocks, here and here.' She raised her arm and indicated to the two buildings framing the courtyard. 'The hayloft is above these stables, the stallion yard next to the vegetable garden. Over here is the new barn. I say new—we completed it about fourteen years ago.'

Last night he was too caught up in his own memories and hadn't noticed the aura of neglect about the place. In daylight it became tangible, a physical presence, forlorn and forgotten. Although nothing was falling down an air of decay and despondency pervaded every building. To see the once-thriving property standing idle made him want to turn back the clock. Helligen was his childhood home and his father's life work. Once it was full of laughter and hope. Bloody Kilhampton and his high-handed notions.

'Over there is the blacksmith's shop, the dairy, old barn and slaughter house. We lease them out to local farmers.' Miss Kilhampton's hands waved, her gestures as fluid as a dancer against the hazy morning sky. He didn't need the buildings pointed out; he remembered every one of them only too well.

They completed a loop of the driveway and ended up in front of the big house, majestic in the sunlight. Two brick chimneys soared above a grey-blue slate roof. A wide verandah skirted the front and sides of the building and tall double-hung windows flanked the impressive front door.

The more he saw of the place the more he remembered. His roots were here, his heritage. From humble beginnings, with hard work and determination his father had put his convict status behind him. He earned his reputation as the best stud master in the area. Once, Helligen was home to some of the most sought-after thoroughbred sires in the country, until Kilhampton destroyed all those years of work. And now she wanted to start over.

'Can you tell me something of your experience?' she asked.

He'd been expecting the question. He paused for a moment, picking his words from his practised response. 'My father was a stud master so I grew up around horses. He worked for some of the more reputable studs in New South Wales.'

And some of the least.

'Was?'

'He died a few months ago.' A broken man, his reputation ruined and his dreams shattered by a colonial upstart. Someone who thought money could buy his entry into a life he didn't deserve.

'I'm so sorry.'

So she should be. So easy to say. The sins of the father. 'I've been working in the Upper Hunter on a stud called Munmurra, you might have heard of it.'

'Indeed I have. They have a fine reputation for breeding remounts for the Indian Army.'

And other bloodlines, but that was another story and nothing he would ever share with a Kilhampton. For all her city manners and gentrified airs the woman seemed to know the business.

'Please don't think me impertinent but why are you looking for work if you have a job at Munmurra. It's a thriving stud.'

'This was a thriving property once. My father maintained it carried some of the best stock in the country.' Jim turned from her, the colour burning his cheeks. He'd said too much. Let his mouth run away with him, allowed his prejudices to show.

'I agree with you. It's a huge waste and a terrible pity.'

Like a kick in the guts her words snatched his breath away. She agreed with him!

'That's why I want to restore Helligen. It's sitting here like some shipwreck thrown aground on the rocks and left to rot.'

'And what does your father think of your ideas?'

'Papa is involved with his other business interests.'

'And the rest of your family?'

'My mother lives here. It's her home. She wouldn't be happy anywhere else. My sister Violet also lives here, although she believes Sydney is where she belongs. Helligen deserves more.' Her face paled and she quaked with undisguised passion.

The spectacle of the heartbroken woman yesterday came to his mind. 'Your mother lives here?'

A shuttered look crossed her face and she folded her arms. 'My mother is an invalid. She rarely leaves her rooms.' She glared out over the empty paddocks, her brow as furrowed as a newly ploughed paddock.

Scuffing his feet in the dirt, Jim followed her gaze. The paddocks were once full of mares and prancing foals. To squander such opportunity. Some people didn't appreciate what they had and cared even less for the lives of others. He'd spoken more freely than he intended, and she had too, if the faraway look in her eye was anything to go by.

She recovered faster than he did. 'And so, that's why I need your help. I want to rebuild Helligen's reputation as a horse stud. Will you help me?'

Despite his best intentions, Jim answered, 'Yes.'

Five

With that one word India's dreams became real. For the first time her ideas and plans weren't scoffed at. Placing the advertisement was the right decision. Never mind Peggy's throwaway remark about raking up the past, this was the path to the future. Quite what Papa would say when he discovered she'd taken his name in vain, she wasn't sure. That problem could wait until another day. Tempted to crow with delight she reached her arms up to the sky, allowing the tension to leach away through her fingertips. She clambered onto the top rail of the fence, tucked her skirt under her knees and surveyed the property.

As he swung up next to her she cast an appreciative glance at his strong shoulders. Having someone on hand to manage the heavier jobs would be a godsend. Fred was a good kid and did his best in the stables but there was so much work. This man would be far more capable than a mere boy. Most of the work she left for the itinerant labourers they employed when there was a need. When Helligen was in its prime it was home to several families and everyone contributed to the smooth running of the place. Nowadays they lived in the village and were forced to find the bulk of their income elsewhere.

'So where are you going to start?' He chewed on a blade of grass and spun his hat on his finger. 'What stock have you got here? And what are you planning on doing?' His dark hair fell across his forehead, black and glossy as the cockatoos that heralded rain.

'We still have about a dozen mares but none of them are in foal. Some animals were sold off to keep money coming in.'

'What about sires? Are they unrelated?'

'We have two working sires. A bay that carries the bloodlines of Theorem and Emigrant, and a black bred from Boiardo. He also sired The Banker who you'll know won the Melbourne a couple of years ago. And there are two younger animals related to these stallions on the mare's side.'

'You'll need some fresh blood from somewhere. Have you thought about that?'

She'd thought about it but with what little money there was, the last thing she wanted was to spend it paying for service fees.

'Have you got the stud records?' A strange intensity lit his eyes, sparks of gold flaring in their hazel depths, as though he expected her to fall short in some way.

'Yes. Of course I have.' All the paperwork was in the library and everything had been recorded. Mind you, she hadn't seen hide or hair of the studbooks since she returned from Sydney. That would be a job for this evening, after dinner.

'There's also the possibility of trading a service here and there if you want to broaden your scope.'

'I'm uncertain, as yet.'

'We'll see.' With a clean break, Mr Mawgan vaulted down from the fence and turned to face her. 'Come on. Show me the worst.' He held out his hands to help her down from the fence.

For a moment she hesitated, his gesture overfamiliar. She studied his long fingers and broad palms then threw caution aside and placed her hands in his. His clasp tightened, and with it a jolt of something new and entirely different seized her. She slipped to the ground. 'Thank you.' A masculine mix of leather, sweat and saddle-soap enveloped her. Striving to fight off her confusion, she withdrew her hands, smoothed her skirt and batted away the flush staining her cheeks.

Lifting her hem above the tops of her short boots she trudged through the grass that was still damp from the welcome shower overnight.

The quiver of a smile flickering on his face unsettled her.

'What's so amusing?' It was almost as though the man was toying with her. Testing her.

'Nothing really. How long have you been away?'

'My sister and I spent several years in Sydney and Melbourne completing our education. According to Papa it was essential. He wanted to broaden our horizons. He'd lost interest in the place and thought we needed a change. Violet blossomed. She loves being in town and loathes the indignity of coming home to the Hunter. I was glad to return. I don't think I'm destined to live anywhere but here.'

His gaze roamed her face then sank lower.

'You look like a city person.'

India stopped. 'I beg your pardon?' His comment implied she wasn't capable.

'Don't take it as an insult. It's a compliment. The way you're dressed. You look very … very … metropolitan. Those boots …'

She stared down and wriggled her toes. The dew from the grass had seeped into the pointed toes and dampened her feet. The soft leather would stain beyond repair. 'That is hardly your concern.' Why hadn't she thought to put on her riding boots when she'd dressed that morning? A serviceable skirt and pintucked blouse were hardly metropolitan compared to Violet's frills and ruffles.

'I intend to employ you, Mr Mawgan, to assist me on the property, not as my *couturier.* I'd appreciate it if you would keep your opinions to yourself.' The fact he'd managed to get under her skin was worse than his apt comment and she changed the subject. 'I'll take you to the back paddock and we'll look at the mares.' She stomped off across the long grass ignoring the dripping hem of her skirt flapping against her legs.

Jim followed her, chuckling under his breath as he curbed his amusement. Despite her clothes and her pretentious attitude he could still see the little girl he remembered. He'd always thought of her as a firecracker, like the ones Mr Kilhampton brought home and let off to celebrate the birth of his son. They were the good days, before Kilhampton turned and bundled them off the place with such high-handed disdain.

When he'd answered the newspaper advertisement he wondered if he would have to admit to his family's history. Except for his small slip-up about his father's experience it seemed no-one remembered the Cobb family. Using his mother's name helped and, of course, the fact Kilhampton wasn't on the property. There was no-one who remembered the little boy who'd spent his time hanging around the stables dreaming of a future. No-one who knew or cared about the family who had given their all and lost it on the whim of an irrational and disappointed man. How he wished he could remember more. His parents tempered their stories with so much regret and misery. No matter. He'd set the record straight and right the past wrongs. Kilhampton would live to rue the day he'd tossed his stud master off the property without a second thought.

Pulling his hands out of his pockets he picked up his pace and caught up with Miss Kilhampton. 'How should I address you?'

She stopped and frowned at him. 'By my name. How else?'

'Miss Kilhampton?'

'Yes … well … no … that's not really necessary under the circumstances.'

'Miss India?'

'Goodness. No! It makes me sound like an old maid.'

Anything less like an old maid he'd yet to see. 'I don't think I'd classify you as that.' With her hair hanging down her back in a delightful tumble she resembled a somewhat dishevelled princess.

'India will do just fine.' A smile played at the corners of her lips. 'After all, we'll be working together.' She rested her arms along the top rail of the fence. 'The mares are in here.'

At the sound of her voice the group of grazing horses lifted their heads and ambled over. He cast a practised eye over the animals he'd glimpsed on his arrival last night. Although the stables and outbuildings were decrepit there was nothing run-down about the horseflesh.

The animals ranged from black to bay and at the back of the group two beautiful buckskin mares frolicked. Their pale coats shimmered in the sun contrasting with their dark manes. As they drew nearer they gave an arrogant flick of their tails and his breath caught as the memory of the woman yesterday surfaced. 'Buckskins.'

'Yes, they're glorious, aren't they? We used to have quite a reputation for them. They were always in high demand in Sydney as carriage horses and elite riding mounts. We only have these two left now. They were my mother's favourites.'

Beautiful animals. In the early days buckskin stockhorses had been a hallmark of the Hunter, but it was difficult to maintain the colour when breeding back to thoroughbreds for elegance. Breed two together and you were likely to end up with a bay or even a black. His breath caught. 'So you sold them to the neighbours, then?'

'No. I don't believe any of them stayed this end of the Hunter. Why do you ask?'

The buckskins hadn't stolen his breath. It was the thudding certainty the two women were connected. 'Because I saw someone riding a buckskin yesterday, on my way here. I mentioned it to your housekeeper. She said it was a woman from a neighbouring property. I was worried. The woman seemed panicked, disturbed …'

'It's time we went back to the stables. I have a list of things that need doing and I'd like to make a start.' India pushed back from the fence rail and a muscle flickered under the skin of her cheek. She turned on her heel and set off for the house.

Jim took one last look at the mares and followed. He couldn't get the woman from last night out of his mind. This was the second time someone had brushed aside his concerns. He ran a couple of steps and caught up.

'Does your mother ride?'

India's face darkened. 'No. I told you. She doesn't. She's an invalid who rarely leaves her room. Anya cares for her. Not that it's any of your business. The horses are your business. Not my family.'

The horses were his business. Keeping that in mind Jim trudged after India, watching the rise and fall of her hair against the back of her shirt. Never a fanciful person he wondered if he'd seen an apparition yesterday. Some ghostly being haunting the fringes of the once-famed Helligen Park. Despite the warmth of the day a shiver traced his spine. The air of dejection about the place was getting to him.

'If I may make a suggestion,' he said, 'I would like to go over the stables. It's the hub of any breeding enterprise and without wishing to put too fine a point on it, there's work to be done there.'

She shot him a look down her pert nose. The woman was so damn prickly. The sooner he got into the stables, the sooner he could start looking for the stud records. That was his first priority. Find what he'd come for. After that he could worry about whether he wanted to fulfil the ludicrous commitment he'd made to her in a moment of foolishness.

India's lips curved into a smile. Like the sun coming from behind a cloud her aggravation of a moment ago dissipated. 'That's an excellent idea. And Fred could do with a few pointers. He tries his best. Unfortunately I don't think anyone has ever shown him what he should be doing. I remember as a child the stables were always as neat as a pin. The original stud master had his office in there.' She took off almost at a gallop and headed back to the courtyard.

Jim curbed a smile. That's where he'd find the information he needed to register Jefferson and take their first step to the winning post.

'Fred, where are you?' India stood in the middle of the courtyard shading her eyes. The lad appeared from the barn. 'I'm here, miss.' He dragged his feet while humping a bundle of straw wider than his scrawny shoulders.

'Mr Jim. Good morning, sir.'

India's eyebrows rose and Jim smothered a laugh. Kilhampton might have bundled his family off the place, but the mere fact he was a male commanded a degree of respect around here. 'Good morning, Fred. I told you, no need to call me sir. Jim is fine. How's my boy this morning?'

'Just about to go and fix up his stable—that's what this is for.' He tossed the straw onto the ground.

At the sound of Jim's voice the stallion's head appeared over the half-door, his ears pricked.

'India, come and meet Jefferson. He's the apple of my eye.'

'Your horse?'

'Yes, a Munmurra animal.' He unlatched the barred gate to release Jefferson then slipped a rope around his neck and led him out into the courtyard.

The expression on India's face changed from appraisal to appreciation as she examined his horse. She reached and touched the warm velvet of his muzzle. Jefferson pushed his big head into her hair, snuffling and snorting as she ran her fingers through his mane.

Concerned she'd object Jim pulled back on the lead rope and brought Jefferson around.

'I was enjoying it.' Pushing up from the tips of her absurd boots she stretched out her hand and rubbed the horse behind the ears. A quiver of delight rippled Jefferson's glossy hide from the top of his neck to the tip of his black tail.

Unable to drag his gaze away, Jim stared, a vicarious thrill shooting down his spine. In the next life he might come back as a horse and ask to be stabled here, particularly if one India Kilhampton ran the show. Chance would be a fine thing. He didn't belong in a place like this, definitely not if they twigged to his dubious lineage. Jefferson—now that was another matter.

'Would you like to put him in the mating yard?' India gestured to a small well-grassed paddock next to the stables. 'All the horses love being in there. Lots of treats on the other side of the fence in Peggy's vegetable garden.'

She led Jefferson away and Jim waited to see what would come next. Hoping for a conducted tour of the entire stable block he walked to the first door and gave it a gentle push. It swung free, dangling crookedly on one hinge. All the doors could do with a fresh coat of paint. A distinct odour of poorly mucked-out stalls permeated the air. Not wanting to get young Fred in trouble by mentioning it he took a closer look.

Once inside the smell intensified and Jim peered over the barrier to see Fred spreading fresh straw on top of the old. He leant over the half-door. 'Hey, Fred.'

The boy dropped the remaining straw and gave it a quick kick before looking up. 'Yep?'

'Fancy a ride on Jefferson this afternoon?'

The boy's eyes grew round and his face flushed. 'Do I ever!'

'I think we can arrange that. Let me know when all the stables and yards are spic and span and I'll see what I can organise.'

Fred took off as though the bunyip from hell was after him, grabbed a rake and started removing the urine-soaked straw.

Jim winked at India when she appeared beside him. Her lips pursed and she stepped closer to him. 'Why didn't I think of that?' she whispered.

A cloud of something far more enticing than the soaked straw wafted in the breeze. It reminded him of newly slashed grass and spring flowers. 'Probably because *I know* what lies closest to a boy's heart, especially a boy who thinks he's cut out to be a jockey.'

'He might make a jockey one day. He has the build for it.' She turned, her hair flaring behind her and catching the light. 'We have eight stalls here. Four and four.' She nodded her head into the shadowy interior.

Jim swallowed, his throat dry as he controlled the impulse to reach out. He wanted to run his fingers through her hair as she'd done to Jefferson's mane.

'And down there is the tack room and the old office.'

The word 'office' brought him crashing back to his purpose. Old office. Of course, how could he have forgotten? He willed his memory into sharper focus. Running through the darkness. Throwing the door open. Seeing his father sitting, pencil tucked behind his ear, poring over the large leather-bound book. *The studbook.*

Clenching his fists against the thrill of anticipation coursing through him he quickened his pace. She led him around the corner and into a cool shadowed passageway running the length of the stable block.

'There's nothing to see really, just a lot of old tack and …'

The door sported a small enamelled plate that read 'Stud Master'. He flung the door open and his heart sank. An assortment of trunks and old furniture filled the room. A broken mirror leant against one wall reflecting an old cedar table, home to a series of wicker baskets, all stuffed full of discarded knick-knacks. A large wooden bucket, a broken lampshade, a bedhead, some faded cushions and folded curtains lay in a pile against one wall.

India mistook his sigh for disapproval. 'I know it's a bit of a mess. We just use it for storage now.' Her voice carried a hint of apology.

'You don't have an office anymore?'

From the pinched expression on her face she'd taken his words as criticism. 'Yes, of course. When Papa took over management of the stud he moved everything to the library, in the house.'

Jim muttered a curse under his breath. So close and such a disappointment. He'd imagined walking into his father's office and finding all his paperwork filed away with the neatness and precision he'd always demanded. The disappointment made his shoulders slump.

'I have to admit I have been a little less than diligent with the paperwork since I returned home. It's one of the jobs I intend to deal with now you're here. I will have more time if I don't have to chase up Fred and worry about the horses.'

Given the perfect opportunity Jim took it. 'In that case I think it's time I got to work. Why don't you go back up to the house and attend to your paperwork? I have plenty to keep me occupied here. I'll keep an eye on Fred and make sure he's not slacking. Fix those doors for you and get myself acquainted with the place.'

India held out her hand. 'Then I take it you would like the job.'

'Indeed I would.' He took her hand and shook it, trying not to contemplate her firm grip and the way her tiny hand sat so comfortably in his.

Six

'Makes a nice change to see you with a grin on your face.'

India sank onto the kitchen chair and heaped sugar into the cup of tea Peggy dumped in front of her. 'I'm thrilled and exhausted.' She pulled off her hat and dropped it to the floor, wiping her damp forehead with the back of her hand. The decision to hire Jim was right.

'And you've got the dirtiest face I've seen in a long time.'

'I don't care.' She fingered the three-corner rip in her skirt where it had snagged on the broken hinge. 'Do you think Jilly could fix this?' She'd caught it as she climbed up to peer over the stall to see what Jim was up to. Her escapade hadn't revealed much other than the fact he could use a hammer. She'd ended up in a heap in the pile of hay Fred had raked out of the stables.

Peggy peered down at her skirt and wrinkled her nose. 'And wash it as well.'

Tomorrow she'd make sure she wore something more appropriate. 'Have you had a look outside? Jim is a marvel. He's fixed the doors, the water barrels are replaced, the stables mucked out properly for the first time in weeks. Fred has worked like a Trojan and all because Jim offered him a ride on his stallion. Why didn't I think of that?'

Peggy sniffed. 'You can't be expected to think of everything and besides, Jim has experience.'

It appeared he did have experience and right now she couldn't believe her luck. 'Which is why I offered him the job. Do you still think it was a mistake?'

'I never said it was a mistake. Just so long as your plan to restart the stud doesn't open old wounds.'

The room resounded with the tick of the clock and memories better forgotten. Peering through the window she half expected to see Mama vault onto her handsome buckskin. Instead, Fred led Jefferson into the pristine stables.

Ignoring Peggy's disapproving glance India slurped down the last drops of her tea. 'I'm going to get cleaned up before dinner and I'll check on Mama.' She stood, unable to control the sigh that always seemed to accompany thoughts of her mother.

'You've got about half an hour. Is that long enough or do you want me to stall dinner?'

'No, it's plenty. I could eat a horse.'

'Probably not such a good idea, eating the profits. You'll have to settle for corned beef.'

'Wonderful. It smells delicious and I don't suppose there's …'

'Jam roll and custard? Yes.'

Smacking her lips India left, hurried along the covered walkway and through the back door to the main house. At the bottom of the stairs she paused and ran her hand over the smooth cedar banister. She inhaled the lingering scent of beeswax and lavender then trudged upwards, the pleasure of the day leaching away with every creak of the steps. Each afternoon she made the trip to her mother's room hoping for a change, yet she always left disappointed.

Knowing better than to enter the suite of rooms without permission she knocked and waited. The door opened a crack and Anya's dark face peered around the corner.

'Good afternoon, Anya. I've come to see Mama and tell her about my day.' India repeated the words like an incantation. The same words she'd spoken every day she'd been at home since that fateful evening fifteen years ago when everyone's life changed.

'Good afternoon, Miss India. Please come in.'

The door swung open and India stepped over the threshold into the darkened room. The familiar fragrance of roses and dust greeted her. Such an old smell, and Mama wasn't old; just trapped in the misery of the past, unable to move on.

Anya did her best to keep the rooms clean while Mama insisted everything should remain untouched. She sat statue-like in the bath chair, her profile gaunt and her body frail beneath the white gown and shawl. Staring out of the window she swung the old metal cradle and fingered the mourning locket she wore on a chain around her neck.

'Good afternoon, Mama.' India walked over to the bath chair and dropped a light kiss on her smooth, pale cheek.

Mama's eyes flickered although her attention remained fixed beyond the window. India could clearly remember the last time she'd held her mother's attention. The occasion of her fifth birthday. The cook, the old stud master's wife, had baked a cake for her birthday, full of blueberries from the garden. No-one had ever had their own cake before, made especially for them. It had made her feel so special, so loved. Mama looked straight into her eyes across the table, then stood and brought the knife tied with a ribbon to her. They'd allowed her to cut it, and everyone had clapped.

'Mama, we've had a very successful day. The new man has arrived and we've spent hours working around the stables. We've even given the inside walls a lime wash. They're sparkling like new.' The false joviality she forced into her voice snatched at her throat, competing with the memories.

She understood Papa's despair. In one fell swoop everything he'd cherished and worked for had vanished. Misery had gouged the heart out of the homestead and the property, sucking every ounce of life from him until he became as much a shadow as her mother.

It wasn't until she returned from school in Sydney that the enormity of Papa's despair had become apparent, her home reduced to such a shell of despondency. It made her heart bleed. Encouraging Papa to return to the city and his shipping business, she pledged to return Helligen to the home it had once been. Besides, she had a responsibility to Mama. One day she would regain her senses and return to the vibrant woman of India's childhood.

Receiving no answer India turned, as always, to Anya, the one person who understood. 'Have you everything you need? Is there anything I can do?'

Anya's hand grazed her shoulder and she shook her head. 'It has been a pleasant day. We have talked of past times and remembered old friends.'

India listened to the words, knowing them by heart. Tears stung her eyes; there were so many conversations she wished she could have with Mama, so much she'd missed. Thank goodness Anya had the patience to deal with Mama's delusions. Day after day they sat staring out of the window recreating the events that had changed everyone's lives forever.

'I saw Goodfellow.'

India jumped at the unexpected words. Anya's hand tightened on her shoulder before reaching out to smooth her mother's greying hair. 'There, there, Miss Laila. Hush now. Don't concern yourself.'

For a reason India didn't understand she stilled Anya's hand. 'Did you, Mama?' Her voice snagged; she didn't want to upset her mother but all the same she couldn't let the first inkling of communication between them pass. The granite slab marking Goodfellow's grave stood alongside Oliver's beneath the fig trees. Mama often sat on the stone bench there, staring into the distance.

'A man was riding him near the lagoon.' Mama ran her finger and thumb over the chain around her neck, the constant reminder of all she'd lost.

India met Anya's dark gaze. 'Were you out riding?'

Her mother nodded. Her neck was so thin India feared she might damage herself with the movement.

'Don't go alone. It's dangerous, you might fall again.' As the words left her lips India realised her mistake.

Mama's frail body crumpled, her hands cradling her head, and her loud heart-rending sob filled the room.

Anya's eyes blazed, the she-cat protecting her ward. 'See what you have done? Go, Miss India. Go now.'

Slamming her hands against her ears to block the sound of her mother's keening, India backed to the door. Goosebumps flecked her skin and threw her back to the past. To the time when these same cries rent the night and she burrowed under a pillow, unable to assuage her conscience and her heartache. Fumbling, she found the door handle and turned it. As she left the room Anya held the small glass of laudanum to her mother's lips. The drug offered its release almost before she closed the door.

After a bath and a change of clothes, India made her way into the dining room hoping Violet's company might erase the sound of Mama's cries still ringing in her ears. Violet stood at the tall sash window, arms clasped around her waist, staring out into the fading light.

'Hello. Have you had a good day?'

'Not particularly.' Violet grunted and turned. 'As I've told you I find it insufferably boring here.' She rolled her eyes. When she was happy they were the colour of the tiny violets that grew between the sandstone pavers in the walled garden. Tonight they resembled the purple Paterson's Curse that overtook the paddocks in autumn. 'What have you been doing? I haven't seen you since yesterday.'

'Well, I have excellent news.' India forced a cheerful tone into her voice. Since her visit to her mother she'd been trying to devise ways of keeping her in the house. The thought she might have another riding accident made India's stomach turn. Anya did her very best to keep her safe, but the belief someone had stolen her child while she lay insensible was her sole reality. Her twilight sojourns had become difficult to monitor. In the time it took Anya to rush downstairs to the kitchen her mother could be out of the house and astride a horse. Her ability to ride without a saddle made it easy for her to slip away. Perhaps Jim's presence would curtail her jaunts.

'I have employed a new overseer.'

Now she had Violet's attention.

'Oh! Is that who I saw you talking to? He looks charming—in a pastoral sort of way, of course.'

'I didn't employ him for his looks.' However, she didn't find them offensive; his wide grin and straight white teeth were charming. And he appeared very capable and assured. Her mind flashed to the way he'd swept her down from the fence and the lovely scent of saddle-soap and leather. 'You know how much I want to restore Helligen's reputation as a stud. Jim is the first step along that road.'

'Oh! *Jim.*' Violet batted her eyelashes then cocked an eyebrow.

'Don't be so ridiculous. Of course it's Jim. We're employing him. What do you expect me to call him? Mr Mawgan?'

'It would seem a little more appropriate. Have you forgotten all the manners we learned at Miss Wetherington's?'

For a moment India wondered if she had. The man had walked onto the property last night and already it was as if he belonged. 'No, I haven't forgotten my manners. He is simply the perfect candidate for the job and I was lucky enough to find him with the first advertisement.'

'I can't understand why you feel the need to employ the man in the first place. What's the use? We don't need to be here. We'd be far better off in Sydney. If you'd take Cecil Bryce's offer more seriously you wouldn't have to spend your time getting your hands dirty.'

The same old refrain. Violet's ability to turn every subject back to Sydney was a source of constant amazement. Did she think of nothing else?

Violet's pert nose wrinkled. 'Running the property is man's work. By all means employ someone, but for goodness sake let's get back to Sydney and leave it all in Cecil's capable hands. He'd be more than happy to take over control.'

'It's out of the question. Helligen needs people living here, and so for that matter does Mama.'

'Mama?' Violet managed to invest the word with a disdainful sneer, as always.

'Yes, your mother. Did you see her today?'

'No.' Violet pouted as she inspected her fingernails. 'Quite frankly, I don't understand why you even bother. She hasn't been a mother to either of us since the accident and she's not interested in anything except Oliver. Why she can't get it through her shattered head the boy is dead is beyond my comprehension. It's been years.'

India sank down onto the chair and rested her elbows on the dining room table. The same old arguments every day, the same tirade. The accident had taken a toll on Mama but her physical injuries weren't the main cause. It was her mental state. Trapped in the past by a melancholy so strong that some days she could barely lift her head from the pillow.

India took a sip of water. And she was to blame. Although she didn't share Violet's views on Mama she could understand them. Violet had little memory of happier days when Helligen sparkled with life and promise. Before the accident Mama and Papa were the vibrant centre of their universe. 'It would be nice if you could spare a few moments of your day to spend with Mama. Anya would really appreciate it, too.'

'Oh, so now it's Anya.' Violet gave a dramatic sigh. 'It seems everyone comes first, before me. There's Mama, there's Papa, there's you, there's Anya and even Oliver. He reaches out from the grave to taunt us all. It's like a living hell.' She stamped her foot and folded her arms, an ugly scowl marring her china doll perfection. 'It's time to put the past behind us.'

'Come and sit down, Violet. Let's have a nice dinner for a change. Peggy will be along soon.' Receiving no response India searched for something neutral to disperse her sister's miasma. 'We have your favourite for pudding. Jam roll.'

'For goodness sake, India. Please stop trying. I'm not a child anymore.'

Resisting the temptation to tell her sister to stop behaving like one, India offered a conciliatory smile. 'No-one thinks you're a child. You are a very attractive, well-educated young woman …'

'Who wants a husband? I even come last in those stakes. At least someone has proposed to you. I can't understand why you don't accept Cecil. He adores you and he's as rich as Croesus.'

India gave a small shudder. 'Cecil Bryce is not a solution to our problems and he hasn't proposed to me.'

'But he's a solution to *my* problems.'

Not understanding her sister's comment she raised an eyebrow. Surely Violet didn't want to marry Cecil. He was a good twenty years older than she was. He spent half his time in Sydney presiding over the shipping empire he and Papa had created. The rest of it attending every function his mother believed would improve his chances of becoming a politician. Added to that, the man was distinctly unattractive with his receding hairline and arrogant sense of self-importance. 'How is Cecil the answer to your problems?'

Violet flounced out of the chair. 'Sometimes, India, I think you have something missing up here.' She tapped her head with her forefinger. 'If you marry Cecil you will have a Sydney house. I will be able to live there. We will have a position in society. I won't be stuck in this godforsaken mausoleum and, in case you have forgotten, I am your younger sister, so I will then be able to find a husband. If I marry before you, you'll look like an old maid, someone left on the shelf.' She thrust out her chest and thumped her hands onto her hips. 'I have your best interests at heart.' With that Violet spun on her heel and swept out of the room in a flurry of frills and flounces, almost sending Peggy and her trolley flying.

'Dinner's ready.' Peggy eyed Violet as she sashayed up the stairs.

'I don't want anything. I might as well starve myself to death. There's no other way out of this preposterous situation.'

A door slammed.

'Everything progressing as normal, I see.' Peggy removed the serving dishes from the trolley and plonked them on the table.

India indulged in a loud sigh. 'It would appear so. It would appear so.'

Seven

Jim cast a surreptitious glance around the courtyard then slipped through the newly repaired door and into the stable block. Jefferson whickered a welcome as he offered the horse a carrot filched from Peggy's vegetable garden. 'That's bribery. Now keep quiet. I've got business to attend to.'

The path of moonlight slanting across the hard-packed dirt floor led the way to the back room. As he slid back the bolt the grating of the rusted metal put his teeth on edge. With a wrench he pulled the office door open and peered inside. In India's presence he'd only scanned the room, not wanting to appear overinterested in the haphazard contents. Now every nerve ending tingled in anticipation. He'd waited an eternity for this opportunity.

It was as black as pitch. His fingers closed around the small stub of candle he'd purloined from the cottage. With the other hand he rummaged in his back pocket for his battered box of Lucifers. As he struck the match the acrid phosphorous fumes mingled with the dust and mould in the air. Once the candle was alight he snuffed the match out with his damp fingers. One errant spark and the whole room would go up in a moment.

He cupped his hand around the flame. The yellow glow emphasised the thick layer of dust coating every surface. The cloying, musty smell of the air caught in his throat. Debris littered the floor—baskets, crates and boxes, piles of old curtains and cushions. In the flickering shadows a large cupboard tucked into the back corner became visible. One door hung slightly open. He picked his way through the piles of discarded household goods until he reached the back of the room.

The door squeaked as he pulled it open. He reached inside searching for books, papers, anything resembling records. A rat stunned by the unexpected intrusion scurried across his hand. The piles of old cushions made a perfect nesting spot but hid nothing of any use to him. He hadn't enough time to explore every nook and cranny. He swung the door closed. Holding the candle high he eased his way past the rows of shelving containing all manner of items bundled in disarray.

He pulled the lid from a brown box and peered inside. A collection of framed daguerreotypes. Family portraits. India dropping a half curtsy and grinning while a pouting young child looked on, her younger sister, perhaps. A woman sat side-saddle on a buckskin horse dressed in a fashionable riding habit. She peered haughtily into the distance while Kilhampton stood in front of the house, arms folded, master of all he surveyed. Jim slammed the lid back down on the box. None of this was any use to him.

He hadn't time to waste on the Kilhamptons' family affairs. He shifted the candle and resolved to continue his search. The stale smell made his flesh creep. A burial ground, a tomb for decades of discarded lives.

With the palm of his hand placed flat against the sandstock wall he steadied the candle and shone it down the wall. Twisted barley sugar legs poked out from the wall blocking his path. He ran his fingers around the intricate twirls. The smooth timber sparked a vision of boots, of sitting on the floor below the desk—his father's boots, his father's desk.

His heart rate kicked up a notch or two and his body hummed with excitement. Lifting the candle higher he stepped back, crashing against a wicker basket and sending it toppling to the floor. A collection of rusted tins clattered and tumbled to the ground.

The candle shook between his fingers as he stood stock-still, holding his breath and waiting. Jefferson snuffled and snorted in his stall and a mopoke owl hooted somewhere in the distance. He licked his fingers, snuffed out the candle and waited while his eyes adjusted to the darkness.

The scarred desktop scored his palms as he traced the worn timber searching for a drawer. When his fingers closed on the metal handle he tugged. It squeaked and groaned as he wrestled it free, then he reached inside. *Nothing.*

The second drawer slid open without complaint and his fingers closed on a book.

He smoothed the worn leather cover, swallowed the lump lodged in his throat, then tucked the book inside his shirt. Pocketing the extinguished candle he edged his way through the debris of the past to the door and outside.

A solitary light burned brightly in an upstairs window of the house. He slipped into the shadows of the storehouse as the curtain twitched, and accomplished his trip back to the cottage in no time.

Once inside he lit the lamp then sank into the old armchair in front of the empty grate. His eyes fluttered closed and his hand rested on the book still tucked beneath his shirt. As he waited for his breathing to settle he eased it from his shirt and laid it on his lap, running his thumbs across the red pockmarked leather.

Had he really found what he was searching for? The prospect of holding the stud records proving Jefferson's bloodlines stunned him. He'd anticipated spending weeks, if not months, building up enough credibility to allow him access to this book.

His hands shook as he opened the cover and angled the book to the light. Neatly pencilled cursive script filled the pages. He smoothed a dog-eared corner and ran his forefinger down the columns. Every sale, every purchase, every mating. The faded dates continued until 1847. He turned the final page. There was no more.

He yanked the lamp closer and flicked back through the book, even held it by the spine and shook it. The entries began in 1840 and ended in 1847. They hadn't left the property until he was ten, in 1850. Of that he was certain. There were no entries from September 1847 and three blank pages at the end of the book. Why? What could it mean?

It was all a fruitless waste of time. He was a fool to imagine it would be so easy. He dropped the book back onto the small table beside the chair and began pacing the floor. There had to be a second book. What had India said? When his father left Kilhampton took over the management of the property. He'd moved the records to the library, inside the house. He had to get in there, but how?

India woke with the sun and sprang out of bed. Today they would bring the brood mares in from the back paddocks. Housed in the stables below the hayloft they would be on hand and ready. Helligen's two remaining stallions could be stabled with Jefferson, next to the mating yards, and they would assess the young colts.

Nothing would tarnish her excitement. Not Violet's continual complaints, Mama's increasingly strange behaviour or the prospect of the mountain of paperwork covering Papa's desk in the library.

Dressed in sensible work clothes and ready for whatever the day might bring she clattered down the stairs, the solid heels of her riding boots ringing on the timber treads. Before she'd made it halfway across the courtyard Peggy's call stopped her in her tracks.

'You get back here and have some breakfast, missy. No riding without a full stomach, or a hat!'

She skidded to a halt and retraced her steps to the kitchen. 'Just tea, please. I'm not hungry.'

'You'll sit down and eat this and no nonsense.' Peggy pushed a plate with a thick slice of toasted bread and a mound of egg in front of her.

'I don't have time. I want to bring the mares into the home paddock. We're going to check them over and see who is ready.'

'Oh, *we* are, are *we*? That would be you and Mr Mawgan, would it?'

By shovelling a large mouthful of egg into her mouth India managed to hide the flush on her cheeks. She couldn't wait to get outside. Her life had changed so much since Jim arrived. It was wonderful to have someone to work with, someone who understood and shared her interest. 'Yes, *we* are. If you remember that's why I employed Mr Mawgan.' She wiped a piece of egg from the corner of her mouth and put down her knife and fork. Then she picked up a couple of slices of bread and slipped them into her pocket.

'Mawgan! What kind of a name is that? Sounds like some Cornish smuggler. Don't forget to take your hat with you.'

'Yes, Peggy.' India threw the words over her shoulder and rolled her eyes as she escaped into the courtyard.

Jim lounged against the rail, his long, long legs crossed at the ankles and the inevitable piece of grass clamped between his white teeth. Jefferson and her mother's buckskin stood side by side, saddled.

'Morning, Miss Kilhampton.' He lifted his hat a fraction and flashed a grin that instantly increased her pleasure in the day.

'India, I told you.' Unable to resist she returned his friendly smile. 'Good morning.'

'I hope I made the right decision. I thought you'd like to ride the buckskin and she was already in the stable.'

She eyed Mama's horse, took a deep breath and nodded. Violet was right; it was time to put the past behind her and forget her childish superstitions. This was as good a start as any. She gave Jefferson a rub on his velvety nose then ducked under the rail and untied the buckskin's reins. Despite her best intentions, she failed to control the smirk creeping across her face. Jim had indeed saddled the horses and expected her to ride side-saddle. She glanced down at her overskirt, and pressed her lips tightly together to restrain the bubble of laughter building in her throat. She reached for the saddle.

'I've tightened the girth,' he said as she lifted the leather flap.

'I can see that.' She unbuckled the girth, lifted the saddle from the horse and deposited it on a pile of hay resting against the stable door.

Jim followed her every move. She could feel his eyes on her and she smiled up at him, noticing the way his brow creased and the wary look that flickered across his face. Unable to resist she slid her fingers to her waist and unclipped her overskirt. She threw it on top of the saddle. Dressed in her divided skirt or *gauchos,* as Papa insisted on calling them, she vaulted onto the buckskin's bare back.

'I don't ride side-saddle,' she called over her shoulder as she edged the horse into a trot and made for the front of the house. Papa would throw a fit if he saw her riding astride in company, but he was in Sydney and while he was away she called the shots. Releasing a loud bellow of laughter she spurred her mother's horse into a gallop.

—

'Bloody hell.' Jim closed his mouth with a snap. She should barely be in control of the horse she'd taken off so fast; instead they were as one. She guided the animal without any effort down the driveway before disappearing behind the fig trees flanking the house.

'Could've told you that.'

He glanced at the impudent young upstart leaning against the stable door sporting a knowing grin. 'Then why the hell didn't you?' He pulled himself up into the saddle and wheeled Jefferson around. 'I expect those stables mucked out and clean by the time we get back or you're for the high jump.' He dug in his heels and headed down the driveway, Fred's laughter echoing in his ears.

To add insult to his dented ego India sat waiting under the shade of the huge trees in front of the house. She'd pushed her hat back and a smile as broad as Fred's lit her face. Without a saddle her lithe body merged with the horse's back and her hair blew in the breeze mirroring the buckskin's tail. His body tightened. He'd seen women riding astride but never looking so completely at ease on their mount. Loose-fitting pants that covered the top of her polished riding boots accentuated her taut muscles.

He reined in the prancing Jefferson beside the buckskin. 'I'll know next time. Sure you don't need a saddle?'

'No.' She grinned. 'The horses prefer to be ridden like this. My mother taught me to ride and she rarely bothered to saddle a horse. She felt it hampered the horse's enjoyment and sense of freedom—and her own.'

The woman … 'It was your mother I saw riding the day I arrived.' It wasn't a question.

India offered a curt nod.

'I thought you said she was an invalid.'

'She is.'

Before he had time to frame his next question India took off across the paddock. She set a thundering pace, clearing the fence line with ease as she headed down towards the river flats where he'd seen the horses grazing on his arrival.

More than happy to follow he delighted in the rhythm of her body and her unrestrained pleasure. So young Fred wanted to be a jockey—he'd have some stiff competition if India chose to race.

As they rounded a bend in the river the herd came into view, lifting their heads and whinnying as India approached. The buckskin pranced into the shallow water sending a cascade of droplets into the air. When India dismounted the other horses clustered around, nudging and pushing, well used to her presence. She produced a handful of bread from her pocket and rewarded each in turn.

'We can walk them across the paddocks.' She lifted her arm and indicated to her right. A sudden gust of wind blew the hair from her face and her shirt against her body. Jim swallowed a gasp. Surrounded by horses in the bright sunlight—it was the perfect portrait.

What he wouldn't give to spend every day with her and these magnificent horses. He pulled himself up. What was he thinking? He was here for one reason only, not to lust after the daughter of the man who had ruined his family and stood between him and his future.

'We should be able to walk all of the horses up to the home paddock without too much trouble. There are only a couple of gates and if you can take care of those it'll be easy,' she said.

Jim dragged his attention away from her to the horses waiting in a docile group on the river flats. Pulling Jefferson around he rode alongside her and they set off at a slow pace towards the first fence line.

'They're used to being handled although we haven't done any service work for a long time. Since I've been home I make a point of riding out most days and moving them from place to place, just so they don't forget.'

'This is a lot easier than I expected,' he said after the five minutes it had taken for his blood to cool.

Spotting the first gate Jim cantered ahead then leant over in his saddle and swung it open. India walked her buckskin through and as promised every one of the other horses followed.

Keen to catch up Jim latched the gate. She'd dropped back, maybe waiting for him, and was ambling along behind the animals as though she had not a care and all the time in the world.

'Have you got a plan?' he asked after a few moments.

'Oh yes. I have a plan. I want to try and recreate the bloodline that produced these buckskins, although they're difficult to breed. They're always in demand and ladies love them.'

'If you've got the bloodlines it shouldn't be too difficult. Just a question of studying the studbooks and working out a pattern.' Jim looked across at India, searching to see if his comment caused her to pay specific attention. Everything hung on the stud records—his future and Jefferson's. The disappointment still burnt from last night when he realised the book he'd found was incomplete. Somewhere on the property there had to be more sales records and the lineage of all the horses.

'I know it all inside out.'

He chewed on his lower lip. The reason for the records ending could be because no-one had bothered with the details. He tossed the idea aside. There was no chance of that. His father had been too thorough, too committed to the importance of record keeping. He'd had it drummed into him as a child. *Always write it down then there are no mistakes.* 'You must have records somewhere.'

'It's like your own family. I don't need studbooks. What do you need to know?'

Eight

The flicker of annoyance grew in India's chest. Of course there were studbooks. Papa's record keeping was meticulous. A habit ingrained by years at sea and the nightly recording of his logs. The problem lay in the muddle of paperwork in the library. What a fool she was! She should have known any stud master worth his salt would want to see records.

Hoping to buy some time she gave a coy laugh, the kind Violet would employ. 'You wouldn't forget your brother's children, would you?' she said.

'My brother doesn't have children. He's too busy digging for gold.' He screwed up his face making the lines around his eyes crinkle and sparking a dimple she hadn't noticed before in his cheek.

'My point exactly!' she returned with a look of triumph. 'I know every one of these animals and their sires and dams.' She patted the buckskin. 'This is Aura, named after my father's first ship, because she flies like the wind. Her foal is Cirrus, after the clouds that herald rain because we had a storm the day she was born. Her sire was Papa's horse.'

Jim narrowed his eyes. 'All right, all right. You've made your point. However, I think it would be a good idea to record the lineage, especially if you want to produce specific traits, like colour or speed.'

She was caught between the bunyip and the billabong. If she continued down this path Jim would doubt Helligen's credibility as a stud. If she admitted to the mess in the library she would look like an incapable woman unable to run the property. She let out a long drawn-out sigh. More than anything else she wanted to breed for speed. Colour too, but a horse of any colour could win on the race-track. It took an animal bred for speed over a long distance to win the prize she coveted. 'We do have records,' she said. 'To be honest, they're in a bit of a state. Papa moved the office from the stable block to the library when …' When Mama's accident and Oliver's death caused life to unravel. She'd admitted enough. Jim didn't need to know the whole sordid story. Some secrets were better kept.

'Brilliant!' With a blinding smile Jim gave Jefferson his head and galloped to the next gate.

Jim's euphoria was an interesting response to her simple admission that they had stud records. She shook her hair back and dismissed the thought. His enthusiasm and commitment were commendable. She should be pleased she'd found someone who had the best interests of Helligen Stud at heart.

The mob of horses rounded the bend in the driveway and made straight for Peggy's vegetable garden. Fred appeared and swung open the rails to the holding yards. He chased the horses through but not before they'd mangled Peggy's scarlet runner beans. India hoped they weren't intended for tonight's menu. 'Thanks, Fred.' She dismounted and handed him her reins. 'I'll leave you and Jim to sort this mob out. I have some paperwork to do.' Lifting her hand in a brief wave she crossed the courtyard and headed for the kitchen and some advice.

India dropped her hat onto the kitchen table and poured a glass of water from the pitcher in the scullery. 'Peggy?'

'Hmm.' Peggy's brow creased in a frown as she peered at a loose-leafed book.

'What are you doing?' She'd never seen Peggy reading anything other than the name on an envelope or the label on a bottle. Even her collection of homemade jams and preserves, her pride and joy, carried a picture of the main ingredients and a large capital 'P' to denote the maker.

'Reading a recipe. What does it look like?'

It looked as though Peggy couldn't see it clearly. She couldn't be getting any younger. Perhaps her eyesight was going.

'There's something missing. I haven't made it for so long I've forgotten.'

'Here.' India took the scraps of paper from Peggy's hands. 'Let me look. Bread and butter pudding. We haven't had that for ages. Eggs, milk, sultanas, butter. Oh, here it is. Have you remembered three spoons of marmalade?'

'That's it. Good girl.' Peggy bustled into her storeroom.

'Are we celebrating?' India called after her.

'Not so much celebrating, just ringing the changes.' With a deal of clattering and banging Peggy reappeared clutching a large jar decorated with a 'P' intertwined with a number of oranges. 'Change is as good as a rest.'

'You're right. It is. Why don't we all eat in the dining room tonight? It would be a nice change. Violet and I rattle around in there like a couple of old maids.'

As India anticipated Peggy's face broke into a huge grin. 'Lovely. I'll put on a clean pinny and let Mr Mawgan know, too.'

'You do that. I'm heading for the library. Jim wants to see the studbooks and I have absolutely no idea where they are. Have you?'

'Other than in the library, no.' Peggy sighed and turned back to her recipe book. 'All the books from the office are in the cupboards underneath the bookshelves. I've got dinner to finish. I can't spare the time now.'

'Don't worry. I'll go and have a look. I have a couple of hours up my sleeve before I see Mama.'

Humming some long forgotten tune India wandered into the library. She made a quick circuit of the room, running her hand along the polished cedar of the bookshelves. Row upon row of books. When Mama and Papa bought the property they were both keen, after so many years of living aboard ship, to make a home. Both of them had a passion for books and reading and they had indulged it. Some of the leather-bound volumes contained original drawings by Sir Joseph Banks, and somewhere Papa had a set of maps said to be those of Matthew Flinders.

She sat down at the tabletop desk and stared out of the floor to ceiling windows. Reflections of small white clouds littered the surface of the lagoon where a family of black swans cruised. Without reading any of the paperwork scattered across the surface of the desk she scooped it up, shuffled it together and made one large pile. Then she moved the chair to the other end and dusted down the tooled leather surface with her handkerchief.

She pulled open the two desk drawers and rummaged around, finding nothing except a collection of paper and pens, old letters and receipts. Nothing resembling a stud ledger. In the back of her mind an image hovered of red leather-covered books with green reinforced corners. Large books with lined pages and columns. She ran her hand around the back of the drawer and her fingers closed on the ornate handle of a small key.

If the ledgers were in the library the only possible place would be in one of the cupboards beneath the glassed bookshelves. Leaving the desk she paused at the fireplace to gaze at the portrait. Goodfellow—Papa's stallion. The cornerstone of Helligen's reputation.

When Papa bought the property he'd searched high and low for a stallion. The sale had included the house and all the furnishings and it was already a thriving horse breeding business. The army of resident workers made the place more like a small village than an individual property. However, he wanted more. The stud master had arranged the purchase of Goodfellow and the magnificent horse became the symbol of all the Kilhamptons' life would be. Life had a strange way of whisking away promises.

Sitting down on the floor in front of the shelves she inserted the key into the lock and twisted it to the left. With a small clunk the mechanism shifted. She cupped her hand around the smooth knob and pulled. A click and the first set of double doors opened. The musty smell of aged paper and ink wafted from the rolls of neatly stacked maps and plans, most tied with red ribbons and a dob of red sealing wax. Annoyed she turned to the next cupboard. The key wouldn't turn in the lock, and despite a deal of tugging and wrenching the doors refused to yield. Shuffling along the floor she tried the third set of doors. The key slid into place and with a flick to the left the lock released. She tugged the knobs and the doors swung open to reveal a series of books stacked in size order. With a muffled cry of delight she pulled them onto the floor.

Stained with faded smudges of ink the cover of the largest book looked as though it had suffered water damage. She hefted it onto the desk and opened it, her heart in her mouth. Inscribed on the fly page in a neat precise hand were the words 'Helligen Stud' and the date below, '1847'.

Wiping her damp hands down her gauchos she flexed her fingers and turned the first page.

Goodfellow: 17 hands. Bay stallion. Black points. Storm. Buckskin mare. Black points. Offspring female …

She turned the pages one by one until she reached the last entry. Papa's writing sprawled across the page.

May 16th, 1850. Goodfellow. Broken hind leg: shot …

A scratchy flourish and a splatter of ink underscored the entry. Nothing more. One day after her mother's accident, the day of Oliver's death. The day she'd drawn the cover around her brother's tiny body and tucked it tight. The last time before the angels claimed him.

The recollections of those terrible days flooded her. The unnatural silence of the house. The whispered words. The never-ending string of men in tall hats, carrying leather medical bags, and their refusal to let her see her mother. She'd run up the stairs and flung open the door seeking solace. Mama's corpse-like figure, tiny on the four-poster bed. Head swathed in bandages, eyes closed and only the slightest movement of her chest proving she still clung to life. Oliver in his cradle bawling his eyes out. She'd tucked the covers tightly around him and swung his cradle.

Before she'd reached Mama Anya caught her and carried her, kicking and screaming, to her own room. She'd bathed her face and stroked her back until the tears subsided. Then she'd told her to sleep and soon she could tell her mother of her day. And so began the afternoon visits and the words she repeated every day: *I've come to see Mama and tell her about my day.*

The clock on the mantel struck five as if to remind her of her duty. She closed the old book and rearranged the paperwork on the desk. She stood, pushed the leather chair back, squared her shoulders and left the room. The door closed behind her with a gentle click and she made her way up the stairs.

Nine

Jim followed the circular patterns India traced with her fork on the white damask tablecloth.

Eyes the colour of storm clouds studied him. 'Do you have everything you need?'

Her question startled him. A simple inquiry about his accommodation and his wellbeing, or was she hinting at something more? He couldn't tell her he needed the stud records. Then he'd have to admit to his previous association with Helligen and his father's unceremonious departure. Did she remember his family? Taking a punt, influenced by the formality of the dining room, he took her words at face value. 'Yes, thank you. The cottage is far more than I need. It's very comfortable.'

Her gaze narrowed as she completed another circular movement with the prongs of the fork. 'No-one has used the place since the last stud master and his family left. We …' Her words trailed off as Peggy bustled in wheeling a timber trolley laden with steaming bowls of vegetables and a platter piled high with chicken. She parked it next to the table and began unstacking. 'And where's Miss Violet, then? I heard you call her.'

'She'll join us in a moment,' India said. 'I told her dinner was ready on my way downstairs.'

'I'm here.'

Jim shot to his feet, fumbling to steady his chair and prevent it falling. Putting down the silver fork India raised her eyes to his and suppressed a grin. 'Jim, may I introduce my sister, Miss Violet Kilhampton.'

'A pleasure.' Remembering his manners, Jim dropped his napkin onto the table and escorted the girl hovering in the doorway to her seat.

'Thank you.' She sat and lowered her thick lashes then arranged her skirt. 'Please sit down.' Violet folded her hands neatly in her lap and smiled at nothing in particular.

The two sisters were as different as night and day. Where India stood tall and slim, Violet reclined small and soft. She had the palest blonde ringlets he had ever seen and her eyes were, as her name suggested, pure violet. Not the grey-blue of her sister's, but a vivacious purple. Violet was a china doll in a cabinet, painted and perfect, whereas India sparkled, alive as the sun on water.

Only Peggy's huffing and puffing as she served each of them broke the rather uncomfortable silence. Once she'd deposited the two bowls in the centre of the table she sat down. She crossed herself before passing the vegetables to India and the potatoes to Violet who pushed the bowl aside.

As India spooned the beans and carrots onto her plate she met his gaze. 'Violet has just finished school.'

Dragging his thoughts from his contemplation of the two sisters, Jim said the first thing that came into his head. 'I expect you're pleased to be home, Miss Violet.'

India's eyes grew round like the plates on the table before him and her lips twitched.

'You are quite wrong.' Violet's high-pitched voice, scratchy not melodious or lyrical, rang out in the formal room.

In an attempt to continue the conversation Jim plucked an inanity from the air. 'May I say how elegant you look this evening?' His pathetic attempt at social conversation made him cringe. He belonged in the stables not in a dining room with polite company. 'It's a pleasure to make your acquaintance.' He couldn't help himself. Despite the delicious smell of Peggy's roast chicken his appetite deserted him.

Violet gave a little giggle and patted her perfect ringlets. 'You told me you were employing an overseer, India. I didn't expect him to be such a ladies' man.'

India raised her eyebrows, her eyes twinkling as she slipped a slice of carrot between her lips. Taking a sip of water Jim searched for something else to say. In future he'd take his meals in the kitchen with Peggy, or in his own quarters, where words meant what they said. This language of gestures and raised eyebrows was more difficult than the speech of the natives. Right at this moment he'd rather be breaking a fickle filly to the saddle than attempting to entertain the women who sat across the table from him. These squattocracy games were way out of his league.

'Miss Violet will be living at Helligen from now on.' Peggy threw him a lifeline. He owed her.

Giving it one last try, he said, 'I'm sure you're delighted.'

The clatter of silverware hitting fine bone china resounded through the room. 'No! I am not. I have been dragged to the back of beyond by a conspiracy between my father and my sister. They are determined to prevent me from finding a husband.'

At a loss for words Jim cut a piece of chicken and speared it with his fork.

'I might as well be locked up in St Vincent's asylum, or better still Bedlam.'

'That is enough.' India pushed up from the table. 'I will not countenance this appalling behaviour.'

Violet's eyes narrowed and she stumbled to her feet. The air crackled as they glared at each other, their hands flat on the damask tablecloth, their shoulders tensed and their faces flushed.

'Girls!' Peggy's voice cut through the charged atmosphere.

Violet straightened up and flung back her chair. 'If it hadn't been for you and your misbegotten plans we would both be living in Sydney enjoying a far happier life, instead of rattling around in this mausoleum dying of boredom.' She ran from the room, slamming the door behind her.

Jim moved around the table and with exaggerated care lifted the upturned chair from the carpet. The cloying scent of Violet's perfume hovered in the air at odds with the homely aroma of roast chicken.

India sank back into her seat, eyes closed. One elbow rested on the table supporting her chin and her fork dangled loosely from the fingers of her left hand.

Unperturbed Peggy covered a piece of chicken with gravy and popped it into her mouth.

'I apologise. I didn't mean to cause such an upset,' Jim offered. The fraught silence was almost worse than Violet's outburst.

India opened her eyes and with great care placed her fork onto her plate. 'Please don't apologise, Jim. It's nothing of your making.'

'Nothing a good spanking wouldn't cure.' Peggy munched her chicken. 'Coming back from Sydney full of all those highfalutin ideas of her own importance.'

'Peggy, it's not Violet's fault.'

India's wan smile twisted his gut.

'I shouldn't have insisted she came back to Helligen. You know how difficult she finds it here.'

'That's all well and good but who's going to look after her in Sydney? If she wants to live there then she'd better find herself a husband.'

Jim chased the remains of his food around the plate. The small successes of the day and the delight of spending time with India had turned cold and greasy like the chicken on his plate.

'You've hardly eaten anything. Big strapping bloke like you needs his food.' Peggy pushed the platter of meat towards him.

His stomach roiled. The blatant aggression in Violet's display had dissolved his hunger pangs faster than the biggest meal. 'No, thank you, Peggy.' He concentrated on the remaining food on his plate; the congealed gravy and the cold vegetables stared back at him. Following India's lead he placed his knife and fork together on the plate and wiped his mouth on his napkin.

'Perhaps I can tempt you both with a little bread and butter pudding.' Not waiting for an answer Peggy loaded the plates and bowls onto her trolley. 'I'll be right back.' Accompanied by the squeak of the wheels Peggy pushed the contraption out the door and down the hallway.

For a few moments Jim sat motionless. India took several small sips of water, rearranged the remaining cutlery in front of her and eased back in her chair. When she lifted her head her eyes were full of pain and almost black. More than anything else he wanted to assure her everything would be well.

'As you can see—' her raspy voice hid unshed tears and she took another sip of water, '—life at Helligen isn't a bed of roses.'

'Family tiffs happen. Please don't be embarrassed.' The possibility his presence or words had sparked Violet's outburst weighed on his mind. 'I'm mortified to think I caused Violet such distress. Obviously my social skills are lacking.' No wonder Violet would rather be in Sydney, forced to sit at the dinner table with the cook and a stablehand.

'Jim, please don't take it upon yourself, you will only make me feel even worse. Violet is upset, beyond upset, with me. She didn't want to come home, however, I insisted. You've seen for yourself the state of disrepair the property is in. It mirrors our life.'

Jim stood, walked around the table and moved Violet's vacant chair closer to India. He sat and rested his arms on the tablecloth. Her face, usually so alive and animated, was pale and wan and her head slumped. 'I've got broad shoulders and they say a problem shared is a problem halved.'

India gave a watery smile. 'I don't think I'd know where to begin.'

'It doesn't have to be the beginning, just wherever you feel you are at the moment.' The impulse to reach out and touch her was almost more than he could control. She needed consolation but it wasn't for the stablehand to provide.

The incongruity of his situation struck him. Never in his wildest dreams had he imagined he'd find himself concerned for the wellbeing of one of the Kilhamptons. To see India struggling cut him to the bone. He'd returned for one reason and one reason only—to discover Jefferson's lineage. Without it he couldn't enter him in any reputable race, nor could he stand him at stud. As soon as he found the information he needed he intended to leave.

The chair scraped and India sat tall and raked back her long hair. The lamplight caught the amber highlights and returned the colour to her cheeks. 'Thank you. I feel I owe you an explanation. You can't be expected to do a job without knowing what it entails.' Her eyes flashed. 'I am determined to get Helligen back on its feet. In a way Violet is right. This place is like a mausoleum. That's why Papa left. Why he sent Violet and me away to school. I want Helligen to be as it once was—a home and the best horse stud in the area. I want to breed racehorses.'

Jim started. Their dreams were no different. He could only imagine the cost and responsibilities involved in a property of such size and it was unusual for a woman to be taking it on. 'And your father left you to manage the stud?' Kilhampton must have paid scant attention to the effects his actions had on those around him. His own father would have vouched for that.

'Why is that so unusual? Before her accident Mama ran the property while Papa attended to his business matters in Sydney. She's no longer capable and it is my responsibility. It's the obvious solution. Things might look run-down but the structure is here, and as always there's a demand for good horses. We still have the stock, as long as I don't keep selling animals to pay the bills.'

'And that's where I come in.'

'That's where you come in.' She rested her hand flat on the table.

Acting on instinct he covered it with his own. 'We can make this work. Look how much we managed today.'

Peggy's trolley squeaked its way across the polished floorboards of the hallway. He lifted his hand with a sense of regret.

'Bread and butter pudding. Everyone's favourite.' Peggy's lips twitched, and he had no doubt her bright eyes noted their proximity. 'I've taken some up to Miss Violet. She's in her room sulking. I told her to stay there until she learns some manners.'

'That's a bit harsh.' India pushed her chair back. 'I'll go upstairs and talk to her.'

'You'll do no such thing. What that girl needs is to understand she's not the most important person in the world. Besides, you're talking business.' Her face broke into a dubious grin.

'Indeed we are. Tomorrow will be day one of the new breeding program. Give it twelve months and just as I promised Papa, a whole new herd of animals will be frolicking in our paddocks.'

Peggy poured the golden custard over a generous helping of pudding and placed it in front of India. 'Eat up. You've got a busy day ahead of you tomorrow.'

The soothing smell must have restored India's appetite. Once he had his plate in front of him she picked up her spoon, grinned and tucked in.

Perhaps Jim was right. Having shared only a small part of her concerns the future already looked brighter. India sneaked a look at him from under her lashes. Would he have dropped his hand from hers so quickly if Peggy hadn't come bundling into the room? His warm and welcoming touch soothed her. Sitting side by side instead of staring at each other across the table stripped the room of the false formality Violet's presence had created.

Her buoyant mood of the afternoon returned and with it the belief Peggy was right, too. She would stop pandering to Violet's tantrums and leave her to her own devices. If Violet wasn't going to be any help then at least she could ignore her and prevent her being a hindrance. She put down her spoon. 'Thank you, Peggy.' Wiping her mouth she turned to Jim. He was so close the stubble on his tanned cheeks was visible. It gave him a disreputable air she rather liked.

'If you can spare me an hour or so I've located the studbook and perhaps you could give me some advice. I'd like to begin making plans tomorrow. It should be our first priority.'

'I think it's a perfect idea.' Two bright spots of colour flared on his cheekbones as he pushed his chair back from the table and began to rise. 'Thank you for a delicious meal, Peggy.'

'Come with me and I'll show you the library. It's the office now.'

India led the way through the double doors into the library at the front of the house. The scent of Papa's tobacco still hung in the air and the soft light from the desk lamp bathed the room in a comforting glow.

Ten

An enormous hand clenched Jim's heart and a cold sweat peppered his forehead. The massive oil painting hanging over the fireplace dominated his very being. He forced some air into his starved lungs.

The bay horse in the centre of the framed canvas stood proud between the two fig trees leaving no doubt where it had been painted. A perfect anatomical representation of a thoroughbred in his prime. It might have been Jefferson.

He bunched his fists defying the impulse to reach out and touch the painting. The carriage of the animal's head and the proud arch of his neck were as familiar to him as the lines on his own hand. Even the black markings on the legs replicated Jefferson's. There was no doubt. He didn't need to read the small silver plate screwed to the frame. He knew what it would say. Nevertheless, he couldn't resist.

Goodfellow: Sire Helligen Park 1840–1850

'That's Goodfellow, Papa's horse. He was his pride and joy.'

Jim winced and turned, a knot tightening in his stomach. The dates couldn't be right. 'What happened to him?'

'He had to be put down. He broke a leg.'

The pounding in Jim's ears threatened to block out her words. How could Goodfellow be dead? He was at Munmurra grazing in the paddock behind the stables. He'd groomed him only a week ago. Goodfellow sired Jefferson four years ago.

'He's buried under the fig trees.' She gestured to the front of the house.

Sucking in a deep breath Jim continued to stare, mesmerised. 'He's a beautiful horse.' His father's dying words echoed. *I did something I'm not proud of. Right the wrongs of the past before they shatter your dreams.* 'What happened to him?'

'There was an accident. He reared and threw my mother, badly injuring her. We never knew exactly how the accident occurred. Papa held our stud master responsible. When they found Mama she was insensible. She'd cracked her skull. Goodfellow's leg was broken. He had to be shot. Papa lost his horse, his wife and his son in a matter of days.'

And my father lost his life's work into the bargain, but not Goodfellow. How could two stories differ so? His father owned Goodfellow. Kilhampton had transferred the injured animal to him, in lieu of wages. After his wife's accident he no longer intended to run the property as a stud. Jim's mind spun. For a moment he was tempted to tell India his real name. How connected their families were. Maybe with two heads together they could solve this strange puzzle.

'This is the studbook.'

He swallowed the bitter taste in his mouth and turned from the portrait.

'I found it this afternoon.' India moved the pile of paperwork and revealed the leather-bound ledger.

The picture was so clear. His father in front of the fire, a pencil in his hand, entering the names of the horses. He'd repeat them, labouring over the spelling. The smell of the yellowing paper was as familiar as bread and butter pudding, the crackle of the fire in the grate or his mother's gentle touch.

His fingers itched. India held, in her hands, the very reason for his return to Helligen. If he found a deed of sale he could prove his ownership; he could dispute India's story. Goodfellow had not died. Was not buried underneath the wretched fig trees. He cast a look out the window at the sinister buttress roots nursing untold secrets.

He forced a casual note into his voice. 'When was the last mating on the property?'

'Over ten years ago. We've sent some animals out since then but nothing on the property.' She rifled through a series of papers on the desk and produced a smaller book, resting it on top of the studbook. 'Father sold three of the stallions while Violet and I were in Sydney and several of the mares and their offspring.'

Jim ran his hand across his chin and studied the book. It was exactly the same as the one he'd found in the old office that he'd tucked at the bottom of his saddlebag. Would a record of the sale be here? Forcing his mind back to India he said, 'It doesn't leave you with a lot of choice. Which horses do you intend to use?'

'I was hoping you could help me with that.'

She pulled a chair from the corner of the room and sat down, then gestured to another chair.

'May I look?' His voice snagged on the words as he waited. Had she noticed his shaking hands, his eagerness?

India slid the ledger onto the corner of the desk and opened it. His father's neat cursive script and meticulous figures filled the pages. He craned across the desk. Nothing that resembled a deed of sale or transfer. His hopes plummeted.

'If you turn to the back of the book it's all listed there.' India flicked the pages. She started as his wrist brushed against her arm, and then she pulled back and walked to the window leaving him alone.

His thudding heartbeat drowned out the hiss of the lamp. He flicked to the back of the book where the spider-like lines indicated the ancestry of each of the mares and stallions. The faded writing blurred. He would abuse this trust she'd placed in him. This may not be the sales record but it would show Jefferson's lineage.

Oblivious to his rising excitement she stared out the window, her eyes fixed on the night vista. The lines of neatly inscribed names: sires, dams and offspring burned like a brand in his mind. He turned to the very back of the book. Somewhere in this tome lay the information he needed and once he'd found it his job would be done. He could fulfil his father's dying wish—and, if truth be known, his own dream.

Flicking from the front to the back of the book he cross-referenced the entries until he found Goodfellow's name. Sire, dam, grand sire, grand dam. He ran his fingers down the names. The founding stock of Australia. The horse was a wonder. To think Kilhampton had wanted him destroyed. Why would he part with an animal like that?

'Have you come to any conclusions?' India spoke from across the room. 'I would like to begin breeding as soon as possible and ensure spring births next year.' She wandered back to the desk and trailed her long fingers along the tooled leather.

Dragging his mind from the past he concentrated on her words. 'We will check all the females and I suggest we divide them into groups with a male. Paddock mating might be better. It places less stress on the males and the younger fillies will feel less threatened in the company of the experienced mares.'

'That sounds perfect. We'll start tomorrow.' She yawned.

Disgusted by his duplicity, he took the opportunity she offered. 'Why don't you leave me here to go over the records and I'll group the mares and check the lineage. Tomorrow I'll give you a list of suggestions and see if you agree.'

India nodded. 'You're right, I'm tired. It's been a long day. I'll leave it with you. Please turn off the lamp and close the door when you've finished.' She took a step closer and offered her hand then withdrew it as though she thought better of it. 'Goodnight Jim, and thank you.'

No. Thank you.

As the door closed behind her Jim returned to the ledger. If he found the deed of sale and transcribed Jefferson's heritage he would have all he required. Jefferson would race in the Melbourne Cup in November.

Eleven

The moon cast a silvery shadow across the smooth surface of the water. Not a breath of air stirred the massive fig trees standing guard over the house, their buttress roots anchoring them deep in the soil. A phalanx of bats flew across a beam of moonlight and India started at the shadows they created on her bedroom floor.

Jim's presence kindled as many shadows as the bats. Memories of the past and the brief but tantalising possibility she could succeed in the future. She still cherished the dream Papa would return home and Mama recover sufficiently to take part in everyday life. Who didn't dream of recreating their happy childhood?

The fact Mama had spoken to her yesterday rekindled her hopes; it must be a sign of improvement. She'd seen Jefferson and confused him with Goodfellow but she had at least taken notice, responded. That alone was a sign of change.

A movement caught her attention on the edge of the dam, larger and paler than any bat, and she drew the curtain further back. Breathing heavily on the glass she rubbed at the condensation with the heel of her hand then squinted out the window. A ghostly figure astride a horse swept the perimeter of the lagoon, first walking, then cantering.

Not tonight, please, not tonight.

India raced across the hallway to her mother's room. Not stopping to offer the usual courtesies to gain entry she flung open the door. Emptiness greeted her. The forlorn bath chair sat by the window guarding Oliver's empty cradle; the curtains drawn back and a pale patch of light illuminated the carpet.

'Mama! Anya!' She charged through to the adjoining room. Anya's single bed stood pristine and abandoned.

Cold fingers clutched at her stomach as the silence stretched and filled the empty room. She dashed back into the hallway and down the stairs, choking back a sob. A thin sliver of light radiated beneath the library door. Jim must still be in the house.

She tiptoed outside, across the courtyard and into the stables then ran down the aisle checking each bay. The two young stallions peered over the half-doors as she bolted down to the end of the aisle. Jefferson stood in the end stall eyeing her progress with a look of confusion. The mares stood in their stalls, heads turning and ears pricking at her intrusion. The final door swung free—Aura, her mother's buckskin was missing.

India grabbed a rope bridle from the tack room and slipped it over Cirrus's ears. Ignoring the whinnied objections of her stable mates India hurried the horse through the doors. Once outside she hitched up her skirt and straddled Cirrus bareback. The clatter of hooves on the flagstones broke the silence and she offered a silent prayer that Jim would be too absorbed in the ledgers to leave the library.

The driveway wound around under the fig trees to the front of the house. The lagoon glimmered silver and the tussock grass glittered, throwing spiky silhouettes on the still water. Coming to a halt she scanned the edge of the lagoon and searched the shoreline.

Nothing. No sight or sound of Mama.

Driving her horse into a canter she skirted the water following the well-worn path. As she rounded the corner Cirrus lifted her hooves high, refusing to move faster than a walk on the soft spongy ground.

At a stand of contorted tea-trees she slipped to the ground. An unnatural stillness loomed shroud-like and chilling.

'India.' A voice cut the darkness. Not harsh. Soft and sensible, painstakingly calm. She swallowed and sucked a breath into her starved lungs.

'Be still. She is safe.'

India shuddered, the words so close yet no visible sign of anyone.

'I am here. Stand still.'

She stopped, the voice a reminder of her youth and the cool hand that soothed her brow and chased away the nightmares. 'Anya. Where are you?'

'Stop and wait. Watch.' Exuding serenity Anya stood statuesque beneath the tea-trees.

She squinted in the direction of Anya's pale fingernail and the long slim arm she pointed across the lagoon.

'She is safe. Watch and wait.'

Unable to resist the habit of a lifetime she followed Anya's directions. Amongst the grasses framing the lagoon Mama moved, leading a horse so pale it almost glowed in the dark.

'What is she doing?'

'What she does every night. Searching. Hoping. Wishing. Praying. It's her way to heal the hurt nestled in her soul.'

Tears clustered behind India's eyes as the shadow trailed through the grasses. 'Oliver's not there.' She shuddered as a cold breeze swept her skin.

'Yes, but where there is hope there is life. And without hope your mother would be long gone.'

'She must come home. Go inside. She'll catch a chill, fall again and hurt herself.' Her words caught in a sob.

Anya's comforting arm wrapped around her shoulders and pulled her close. 'No. This is what she must do until she has no further need.'

'But the doctors said …'

'The doctors are fools. A broken heart will mend in its own time. Not with medicines or intervention. Just patience.'

'Does she do this every night?'

'Not every night, but often. And tonight is special.'

'Why?'

'She believes he has returned to help her.'

India rubbed at the frown creasing her brow. 'Jim?'

'Who knows? Does it matter? What your mother believes is what matters. If she believes and she can solve her heartache, so be it.'

India dropped her reins and sank onto a severed tree trunk. She rubbed at her temples; the pounding in her head made thought impossible. 'I don't understand.'

'No-one understands the mind. And a broken heart even less.'

'What if she hurts herself?'

'That won't happen. She is strong and she is sensible. Except in this one matter.'

'I see her every day and she is none of those things. She's weak, a delusional invalid.'

'You see what she chooses to show you.'

'I am her daughter.'

'Yes, you are her daughter, her firstborn, but you are not the child of her heart. That child lies buried beneath those fig trees. Until she is certain he rests in peace she will keep searching.'

India shook her head. Nothing Mama had done for the past fifteen years made any sense. Not since the day she'd fallen from the horse and lapsed into a coma. Or was it when she'd awoken and discovered her beloved son had died? Did she know her daughter was the last person to touch his warm breathing skin, the last to kiss his sweet cheek? The one responsible.

Quietness drifted across the lagoon, moments, maybe hours passed. Anya's hand rested warm and firm on her undeserving shoulder, keeping her safe or holding her captive. What did it matter? She couldn't change the past. When she thought she could bear it no longer the white-clad figure remounted. Mama skirted the lagoon before heading back to the outbuildings.

'It's time to leave. She will sleep now.'

Speechless, and with her legs shaking, she struggled back along the track in Anya's wake. By the time they reached the stables a light burned in Mama's window and her silhouette hovered staring out into the night.

Bidding goodnight to Anya, India stabled Cirrus and made certain Aura was back in her stall. Jefferson stood munching a mouthful of lucerne, a self-satisfied gleam in his eye.

Twelve

By the time India awoke the sun streamed across her counterpane. She rubbed at her eyes, scratchy and sore from lack of sleep. She'd lain awake half the night, tossing and turning like *The Princess and the Pea*, consumed by thoughts of Mama and her increasingly strange behaviour, her reaction to Jim and Jefferson's arrival, her nightly sojourns.

As the sky began to lighten she'd fallen into a deep, dreamless sleep that had left her head thick and her body heavy. She reached for the small pot of tea on her bedside table. It was cold to the touch. The day for a new beginning and she'd overslept—a fine example of responsible management.

She struggled from the bed, poured cold water into the china bowl on the washstand and splashed her face. Then raked her fingers through her long swathe of hair and pulled it back into a twisted rope that she knotted with a piece of ribbon. As she turned to the mirror she pinched her pale cheeks and smoothed her rumpled eyebrows.

Why pay so much attention to her appearance? She shrugged at her reflection then reached for her clothes. She'd be riding again today. She tossed her skirt aside and pulled on the crumpled gauchos and loose shirt from yesterday. With one last look in the mirror she picked up the tea tray and made her way downstairs.

The empty kitchen proved her tardiness. By now Peggy would be tending her vegetable garden and planning the day's meals. Jilly would be scrubbing up a storm in the copper and Jim … goodness only knows.

Voices from the mating yards behind the barn drifted across the empty courtyard as she rounded the corner of the stables. The sight of Violet perched on the top bar of the post and rail fence stopped her in her tracks. Dressed in a deep purple riding habit with a small matching hat festooned with a waving peacock feather, she trilled and tweeted her encouragement while Jim ran his hands over the fetlocks of one of the young stallions.

At the sight of the incongruous picture India smothered a groan then slipped through the gate. She rested her hands against the fence next to Violet. 'Good morning. You're up early.'

Violet's face shone, the light sparkling in her eyes and all signs of yesterday's tantrums passed.

'Good afternoon. You've been missing all the fun.' She swung her legs up, displaying a matching pair of suede boots laced to the ankles and gave a small kick of excitement. 'Jim's putting Maestro through his paces. He cuts a fine figure, doesn't he?'

Maestro would make a fine sire. 'He's well bred. He has his sire's stamina.'

'Do you know Jim's family? I thought he'd answered your advertisement in *The Maitland Mercury*.'

India snorted and shook her head. What a foolish mistake to imagine Violet would be interested in a horse. 'I was referring to Maestro.'

Violet covered her rouged lips with her hand. 'Silly me! Jim is, however, a fine figure of a man. Don't you think?' She fluttered her darkened eyelashes. 'Do we know his family? Are they wealthy?'

Getting Violet away from Sydney had done nothing to distract her from her never-ending search for a mate. 'I doubt it. Otherwise he'd be running his own stud, not working here.'

'Hmm. You're right.' With a disparaging look Violet dragged her gaze from Jim and blinked, twice. Her eyes widened and her mouth dropped open. 'What in heaven's name are you wearing?'

India smoothed her hands down the faded felt encasing her thighs. 'My gauchos. I'll be riding again today.'

'Surely you don't still wear those laughable things. They belong in the dressing up box with all the other bits of rubbish Mama and Papa brought from the Americas.'

India fingered the well-worn material. The memory of Jim's raised eyebrows and appreciative stare from yesterday, so at odds with her sister's look of disdain, made her smile. 'I find them more practical for working and besides, I chafed my legs yesterday.' She bit down on the inside of her lip. How foolish to mention that. Next Violet would be asking her when and she couldn't explain the events of last night. She'd managed so far to keep Mama's nightly ramblings secret from Violet. Until she had the chance to discuss them at length with Anya no-one need know of her concerns over Mama's sudden increase in activity.

'It's entirely your own fault because you insist on riding astride. It's so unladylike and very unhealthy. Miss Wetherington would be horrified.'

'For goodness sake, Violet, we're not taking the air in Hyde Park. We're two hundred miles north of Sydney in the middle of a property the size of a small country. We make our own rules here.'

'*You* certainly do that.' Violet rolled her eyes and pulled a face distinctly at odds with her manicured appearance. 'Thank you for reminding me.' She slid down from the fence rail with remarkable agility and minced across the yard.

India dropped her head onto her folded arms. No matter how good her intentions she managed to brush Violet the wrong way every time she spoke to her. Her sister would never feel at home here. The prospect of her returning to Sydney filled India with delight—if only she could find a way to arrange it.

Lifting her head she turned her attention to Maestro who stood placidly while Violet ran her hands over his body. No doubt Jim was delighted with the picture of perfection Violet presented.

A high-pitched giggle brought India up sharp. With her feathered hat in her hand Violet waved her arm across the stallion's line of vision. His eyes rolled in terror. He reared. Violet emitted an ear-piercing shriek as Maestro's flaying hooves dangled above her head. Jim yanked on the lead rope, turned the animal and wrangled him to the ground. Without a word he led the spooked horse away from the jumble of purple velvet thrashing in the dust.

Violet's screeches rose to a crescendo. The stallion reared again. India vaulted the fence. This time Maestro's lashing feet hovered over Jim's head. She crouched and hauled Violet to her feet and dragged her back to the fence line. Her hand clamped her sister's gaping mouth then she pushed her between the rails and followed.

'Let me go!' Violet's fists pummelled India's chest as she scrabbled to find her feet.

Ignoring Violet's thrashing arms and continued screams India half-dragged half-pulled her across the yard. She deposited the enraged bundle with a thud on the seat outside Jim's cottage.

'Sit down and be quiet. You're not hurt.' Her heart thumped as though it would jump out of her chest. She squeezed her eyes shut, blotting out the picture of Violet lying in a bloody mess in the dirt. 'Whatever possessed you to get into the yard and wave that outrageous hat in front of Maestro? You know better.'

Violet screamed and embarked on a fresh bout of sobbing.

Folding her arms India drummed her booted foot in the dirt. Past experience told her Violet would settle faster without a sympathetic audience.

Within a few moments her sister's shoulders relaxed. Her sobbing ceased and her eyes appeared behind her splayed fingers. 'Where's Jim?'

'I have no idea. Repairing the chaos you created with your little display, I expect.'

'Right here.'

She spun around. A hot flush streaked up her neck. 'I'm so sorry. My sister … Is Maestro all right? Are you?'

Jim's mouth quirked and his face broke into his all-encompassing grin. His eyes crinkled and the golden flecks danced. 'Maestro is fine and so am I. What about the young lady?' He peered over her shoulder at Violet, tilting his body close to her. His heat radiated against her body and his lovely masculine scent of fresh air and leather enveloped her. His breath fanned her cheek, making her sway. Her hands rose of their own volition and rested on his broad chest. Through his soft shirt the steady rhythm of his heart reverberated against her palms.

As though scalded, colour flooded India's face. The man would think her a hussy, a wanton flirt, and Violet ...

She wrenched her hands away and whipped around to face her sister. As she took a step back to regain her balance, her shoulders came to rest against the firm bulk of Jim's chest. Her sudden gasp coincided with the touch of his hands against her upper arms as he steadied her. His fingers lingered, sending her heart into the oddest pattern. Every coherent thought vanished and her knees buckled. He held her firm and, incapable of supporting her own weight, for a split second she relaxed against him. A smothered groan rumbled in his chest, vibrating against her spine.

'Well, well.' Violet's words branded her befuddled senses.

India tottered forwards, attempting to stand without Jim's support. Her pulse pounded in her ears and she blinked away the haze before her eyes.

Violet's narrowed gaze raked her from head to toe. 'It would appear I've been pipped at the post, yet again.'

Sucking in a deep breath India drew back her hair. She had to get a hold of her senses and return to some kind of normality. She opened her mouth to speak.

Jim was faster. 'I'm not sure I understand.'

'Narrowly beaten yet defeated,' Violet said with a quirk of her lips. 'I wasn't aware you two had an understanding.'

India moistened her lips as the implication of Violet's words sank in. She swallowed. *Nor was she.* She shot a backwards glance at Jim feeling like a child caught with her fingers in the honey pot. Only the slight reddening of his cheeks and the sparkle in his eyes gave any indication her proximity affected him.

Violet sniggered, a staged noise belonging in the theatre. 'Does that mean you will be declining Mr Cecil Bryce's offer?'

India snapped her gaping mouth closed and glared at her sister. 'You don't know what you're talking about.' Spinning on her heel she marched across the yard, every nerve ending aflame.

Violet was impossible. Maestro might have kicked her head in and all because she'd behaved like a trollop trying to attract Jim's attention. Her sister's involvement in any matters outside the house would be limited and she would arrange for her to return to Sydney as soon as circumstances allowed. She stomped into the kitchen seeking Peggy's tea and comfort.

Thirteen

Jim studied India's ramrod back as she stalked away. The two sisters had their volatility in common although it was the first time he'd seen India lose control. He rather liked it. It hinted at a fiery streak in her nature he hadn't imagined. He understood and shared her passion for horses and the wasted possibilities for Helligen. What he didn't understand was the charged atmosphere he'd created by touching her. She aroused such a protective streak in him and his first thought when Maestro reared wasn't for Violet's safety but India's. Only when Maestro settled did he consider Violet.

From the moment he arrived India had fascinated him. If he wasn't so hell-bent on discovering the truth about Goodfellow he could imagine a hundred ways to explore the strange connection they had. The memory of her lithe body astride her horse stirred him as much as the feel of her in his arms. He shook the thought away. *Lust, most likely.*

'Are you going to help me?' Violet's strident tone set his teeth on edge and drawn from his contemplation of India, he turned around. She stood, one hand supporting her weight against the brick wall of his cottage while she fumbled with her ridiculous footwear with the other hand.

'What's the problem?'

'I need some assistance returning to the house. As you can see the heel of my boot has broken.' She lifted her skirt a little and as no doubt intended he glimpsed a flash of ankle.

'Take it off. It's not far to walk back to the house.' He headed off to the stables, his annoyance increasing with every step. The morning had all but passed and he'd made no progress.

'I hoped I might lean on you.'

A loud sigh escaped. 'Very well.' He returned and offered his arm.

The annoying woman draped herself around his neck. 'It would be so much easier if you could carry me. I fear I may have sprained an ankle.' She gave a pathetic hop and collapsed against him.

Gritting his teeth Jim swept her up into his arms. The feather on her hat tickled his nose as he adjusted her purple-clad body before striding across to the stables.

Violet gave a little giggle and snuggled closer. 'I expected you to take me to the house.'

Her cloying perfume made his nostrils twitch and he fought a sneeze. 'I'm taking you to the house. However, I need to secure the gates on the stalls before I leave the horses.'

'How silly of me. I'd forgotten the horses.'

'It appears to me you may have completely forgotten how to behave around horses—if you ever knew,' he finished with a grunt. Her weight was nothing but her nearness and the way she clung to him made him want to slap her away like a buzzing mosquito. He dropped the hand supporting her back and unlatched the outside gate.

Violet lifted her other arm and wrapped that too around his neck. 'This is such fun. I feel like a damsel in distress rescued by a knight in shining armour.'

Ignoring her ludicrous comments he marched into the stables beneath the hayloft. Jefferson lifted his head and instead of his usual welcoming whinny flashed the whites of his eyes then turned and offered his rump.

Jim continued down the aisle to Maestro's stall. The colt reared as they approached, his ears pricked and his eyes rolling as he backed away. Realising his mistake Jim walked to the end of the aisle and deposited Violet on a pile of straw.

'I was just beginning to get comfortable.' She dropped her arms and sat adjusting the mangled feather on her hat.

'Sit there and don't move.' He tossed the words over his shoulder as he returned to the aisle to secure Maestro.

'I will not move one inch until you return.' Violet leant back and stretched her legs out, looking for all the world as if she were reclining at a picnic.

'Why not stay in Sydney? Why come back here if you hate it so much?' The words poured out of his mouth. He didn't want to encourage her or engage her in conversation. He wanted her out of his hair and out of his stables. The thought caught him by surprise. Out of *his* stables. Whatever was he thinking? Given a further opportunity to check the ledgers for the proof of sale and Jefferson's heritage and he'd be on his way.

'My return is India's fault. If she'd accepted the perfectly reasonable marriage proposal she received neither of us would be in this preposterous position. Cecil Bryce is quite prepared to offer financial assistance to get Helligen back on its feet so the property can be sold. India and I could live in the lap of luxury in Sydney. She will marry Cecil in the end. This personal crusade to restore Helligen is a nonsense.'

Her eyes narrowed as he approached.

'And I suggest you drop any insane notions you might have of romancing my sister. She is spoken for.' Violet sat back with a satisfied smirk on her face.

Jim snapped his mouth closed and stared at the girl. 'I am not *romancing* your sister, as you put it. I'm here for one reason and one reason only. Once I have what I came for I will leave.' He ran his fingers through his hair, squeezing his skull. He'd said too much.

'You will leave?' A frown puckered her flawless forehead. 'India is under the impression you're here to stay. Of course, when she marries Cecil it will make no difference to your position. I feel certain we could arrange to keep you on. I can put in a good word for you.'

'We'll see.' Jim covered his confusion with a forced smile. 'Let's get you back to the house.' Slipping one arm behind her back and the other beneath her knees he swept her into his arms again. Wasting no time he strode across the flagstones to the house.

'Can you take me into the kitchen?' Violet asked. 'I think Peggy needs to see to my ankle. I can't imagine being able to walk unaided for another week at least.'

He nudged the kitchen door open with his shoulder.

India and Peggy sat at the kitchen table, their heads close together. They lifted their faces in unison.

'Don't you dare bring that peacock feather into my kitchen, young lady. It's bad luck.'

Jim chuckled. It appeared animals and cooks alike knew more than he did.

'Peggy, I've hurt my ankle. Jim helped me. Can you strap it for me?'

With his arms full of purple velvet and peacock feathers he hovered in the doorway. Neither Peggy nor India appeared the slightest bit disturbed by the possibility Violet was injured, in fact a smile quirked the corners of India's lips. Violet had taken him for a fool.

Peggy stuck out a pudgy finger. 'Throw that hat down outside.'

The peacock-feathered hat fluttered over his shoulder and landed with a gentle plop on the stone flagging outside the door.

'Put her down.'

He lowered Violet to the ground. With an anguished cry she struggled across the floor and sank onto the chair Peggy held.

His stomach churned at his own gullibility as he stormed out, leaving the women to their own devices.

'Now, what's all this nonsense, young lady?' Peggy's gruff voice mirrored India's own feelings. As always Violet had succeeded in turning the morning into a circus and it was time to make an end of it.

'I fell and twisted my ankle when that horse attacked me.'

'Don't be so foolish. It was your own stupid fault. If you hadn't been primping and preening in front of Jim it wouldn't have happened.'

Peggy peeled off Violet's stocking, tut-tutting as she twisted her ankle from one side to the other. 'I can't see very much wrong with it.'

'It hurts and it's not fair. So unfair. Everyone does everything the way India wants it done. Even Jim is falling all over himself, salivating like a dog the moment he's anywhere near her. It's as though I don't exist.' The palm of Violet's hand slammed down on the table with a sharp crack. 'And I don't even want to be here.'

Peggy dropped Violet's ankle none too gently to the ground. 'I don't think your foot needs binding but your mouth certainly does.'

Violet's lip curled into a smirk, the kind that always spelt trouble. 'I've had a long chat with Jim and he's not labouring under any misapprehension anymore. I've told him all about India's engagement.'

'I'm not engaged.' The words spluttered from India's mouth.

Ignoring her, Violet continued. 'And I've told him we'll be going back to Sydney.' She folded her arms. 'He said he didn't care because he wasn't expecting to stay long, just until he found what he came for. So think again, big sister. Not every man falls at your feet.' Violet as good as crowed as she stood and marched through the door, her ankle miraculously healed.

'I think it might be more sensible if I sent Violet back to Sydney. She's dreadfully unhappy. There must be someone she can stay with, an old school friend, an acquaintance of Papa's. As soon as I next see him I'll discuss it. I can't live like this and you shouldn't have to either.'

And she didn't want to deal with Violet anymore. She wanted to sort out the tangle of emotions wrapping tendrils around her heart. The way she'd felt when Jim held her close, his warmth, and the sparkle in his eye and the dimple in his cheek when he smiled. The palms of her hands still tingled from the glow of his warm skin. She smoothed them together, trying to recreate the sensation of his beating heart. If they'd been alone he might have kissed her. She ran her tongue over her lips imagining the touch of his mouth on her skin. A rush of heat traced a path down her body and her breasts peaked.

'India?'

'Hmm?' She wriggled, the cotton of her blouse rough against her skin. Skin that prickled and shivered with an unnatural sensitivity.

'India!'

Turning to Peggy she plastered what she hoped was an attentive smile on her face.

'What did Violet mean when she said Jim would leave once he found what he came for?'

India shrugged her shoulders, not wanting to entertain the thought of Jim leaving, not for a long time, if ever. 'I don't know. Just more Violet nonsense. Do you think I should persevere with this idea of mine? Violet would be better off in Sydney. I could go down to Sydney and see Papa, if he's not away.'

'India, this is important.' Peggy's round face squeezed into a frown. 'Violet said Jim wasn't expecting to stay long. Just until he got what he came for.'

'I've absolutely no idea, Peggy. I've more important things to worry about.'

'Like your feelings for the man?'

India sat bolt upright, colour flooding her face anew. 'What feelings?' she lied.

'The other comment might be Violet nonsense but she's hit the nail on the head about Jim. I don't think I'd put it quite so crudely, nonetheless the pair of you can't take your eyes off each other. What's going on?'

'Nothing's going on.' Nothing except the delicious feelings his closeness brought. 'We have a working relationship that requires us to spend time together. I won't deny the man is attractive but I'm not harbouring any pent-up desires or emotions.' Her untruth sat between them, knotting her insides. 'The fiasco with Cecil Bryce was bad enough.'

'He's twice your age and ugly as a dead fish. Jim, now he's different. I've seen the way your eyes sparkle when he's near, and what about the other night in the dining room? The two of you sitting there, holding hands, looking like a couple of lovesick calves.'

'We weren't holding hands. If you must know he was comforting me.'

'Oh, comfort. Is that what it's called these days?'

India pushed back her chair. This conversation could wait until her thoughts aligned and her emotions were under control.

'And now I suppose you're going to flounce off like your sister, are you? The truth a bit hard to handle?'

'No, I'm not going to flounce off.' India ignored the second half of Peggy's question. She had no answer. 'I have every intention of behaving like an adult.'

And that required some serious decisions. Employing Jim was the best move she'd made, and in some strange way the focus of her life had shifted with his arrival. Now she could see what had to be done, and Violet got in the way of her progress. Her goal of entering a horse in the Melbourne races was no longer a pipe-dream. All she wanted to do was concentrate on her plans. Once the mares were bred there would be a twelve-month hiatus while they waited for the births. She could attend to all of her other problems then. Right now the stud was important and she needed help from Jim. She turned on her heel. She would go back to the stables and pick up where they'd left off before Violet's ludicrous outburst.

Fourteen

Jim pulled the crumpled piece of paper from his pocket and hunkered down outside the stable to study the notes he'd made. He'd always known Jefferson's quality. The studbook proved Goodfellow's lineage back to the very first thoroughbreds imported into Australia. No wonder the horse had such stamina and perfect conformation. Jefferson would make a formidable stud sire, never mind racehorse. What a legacy to inherit from his father—all he had to do was locate the paperwork and prove his ownership of Goodfellow.

He needed the deed of sale! If there was such a thing. His father said Kilhampton gave him Goodfellow, in lieu of wages. There had to be papers to prove it. No-one gave away a horse of that breeding. His father told him Kilhampton wanted Goodfellow shot. He'd convinced him there was a chance to mend the animal's broken leg and Kilhampton had told him to take the animal.

Leaning back against the wall he resurrected the memories of the night they'd left. Bundled into the back of the dray with his brother. His mother at the reins and his father … he frowned. Where was his father when they left? They'd stopped and made camp very late at night, then stayed for several days in the bush sleeping under the dray. When his father reappeared he said they would be living at Munmurra and he'd driven the dray after that. Had he taken Goodfellow to Munmurra first and then come back for his family?

Pushing up, he scuffed along in the dirt. Fragments of the past rose and fell like ghosts, taunting him with half-remembered phrases and snatches of conversation. Together he and India could piece it all together.

He took only two steps before he remembered—India didn't know who he was. He'd used his mother's family name when he applied for the job. So keen to find the papers he hadn't thought through the ramifications. And now another mystery twice as complicated loomed. Who owned Goodfellow? Too many deaths, too long ago. His mother had carried the secret to her grave and it seemed his father had too.

The Kilhamptons were to be the tool he used to achieve his aim, and instead he found he liked India—more than that, he admired her. He'd imagined she would be like Violet, a spoilt society daughter of the squire. Not a determined woman who shared his interests and dreams. She was nothing he expected.

'Here you are.'

He jumped up, shading his eyes as he squinted into the beam of sunlight, unsure if his imagination had conjured her. As his eyes adjusted his stomach clenched. She lifted her heavy hair from her shoulders in the special way she had. With the light behind her he could see the outline of her body through her shirt, her raised arms accentuating her lithe figure.

'I'm sorry my sister caused so many problems. It's not her fault. She's at sixes and sevens with the world and doesn't know what she wants.' India moistened her lips, an apologetic smile building.

Stepping closer he returned her smile. Her eyes flickered and darkened. He all but saw the spark of desire jump from his taut body to hers. She shivered and then her shoulders dropped and she took his outstretched hand.

His fingers tingled. The scent of spring flowers, honeysuckle perhaps, wafted in the gentle breeze. He ran the pad of his thumbs over her palm, delighting in her responsive tremor, then lifted her hand to his lips and pressed a kiss against the warm soft skin of her wrist.

A blush rose, staining her throat and tinting her cheeks. He slid his arm around her waist and drew her to him. Without hesitation she rested against him. He lowered his head, their lips touched and she gave a tiny sigh. The warmth in her eyes answered his unspoken question. It was what she wanted.

She pressed her body against him, breasts soft against his chest, her hands around his neck. Her mouth tasted of honey and sunshine, the touch of her lips sweet and so full of promise.

With every movement his blood surged and pounded. He spread his hands down her back feeling the responsive play of her muscles. She gave a delightful shiver as he clasped her closer.

A picture of her lying in the straw, her beautiful hair fanned out around her face sent a wave of anticipation streaking through him. When her hands reached for his shoulders and she pushed him back he snapped to his senses. How close he'd come to losing control! He gulped back his desire. 'Forgive me,' he murmured, tasting the scent of her as he fought for control.

'Why?' Her breath fanned his skin. 'I came to apologise to you for Violet's behaviour and now I have proved myself as wanton as I thought her.' Her eyes laughed up at him. 'I think perhaps I was jealous when I saw her in your arms.'

'There's no reason for you to be jealous, believe me.' Loath to let her go he cradled her close to his chest. The truth of his words reverberated through him, his honesty startling him. What did the past matter? Without a shadow of doubt his future rested in his arms.

Her satisfied sigh filled the sunlit stables and Jefferson whinnied in response.

'I think perhaps Jefferson agrees with me.' Taking her hand he led her to Jefferson's stall and slid the bolt on the door. 'Shall we ride?'

'I'd like that.'

He reached for the bridle and slipped it over Jefferson's ears, warmed by the knowledge she watched his every movement.

'I'll go and fetch Cirrus.'

'That's not my plan. Will you ride with me?' More than anything else he wanted her body against his and this was the perfect way to achieve it.

She darted a glance over her shoulder, then shrugged, a twinkle of laughter lighting her eyes. Taking her smile as agreement he led Jefferson outside and mounted, then reached down with his hand. As lithe and graceful as the trapeze artists he'd seen at the shows she swung up in front of him. He turned Jefferson to the gate.

It was the most natural thing in the world to be astride the big bay stallion cradled in Jim's arms. Jefferson carried them both with ease, his steady gait and flawless motion lulling her.

They followed the path around the lagoon. The ibis foraging in the shallow waters turned beady eyes on their progress then unconcerned resumed their search for titbits. As they crossed into the bushland Jim pointed to a large goanna sunning itself on the hard-packed dirt. It turned its head and gazed with unblinking eyes, then gave a sideways dart and scuttled up the straight, tall trunk of a spotted gum.

'Shall we go to the river?' Jim's warm breath tickled her neck. She turned her head and he brushed back the hair from her face. His fingers wandered light as a feather over her cheek and along her lips. Sighing in pleasure she rested against his chest, frightened that words would break the idyllic peace.

In the distance the river wound its lazy way through the grassland. The fertile river flats provided more feed than Helligen's dwindling herds required. As a child she had ridden this path with Papa much as she did today. Safe and secure astride a large bay stallion. The rhythm of the horse, the sun beating down on her cheeks, the warm breeze and the scent of eucalyptus were as familiar as the surrounding landscape.

'Papa,' she'd said, but he hadn't replied. 'Papa?' His head had moved, leant closer, but not a flicker of attention. His eyes held a faraway look, his mouth pulled down, grim, and a tear tracked his tanned cheek. She'd been too young to recognise a man consumed by grief. 'It's too late. I've lost everything,' he'd said.

She'd had no idea what he'd lost or how, but knew she wanted to help him find it. Before she had the opportunity to respond he'd tightened his arms around her and Goodfellow had flown down this very track to the river.

'Jefferson could be Goodfellow,' she murmured.

Jim tightened his arms around her. 'What about Jefferson?'

'He could be Goodfellow, Papa's horse. The one in the painting in the library.'

His body tensed behind her. 'What makes you say that?'

'They are so alike. Not just to look at, their gait and conformation are the same.'

'Many stallions have the same characteristics.' The clipped words made her turn her head. His lips formed a thin line and his gaze darted from her.

'Not when you really know a horse. I rode with Papa, as we are doing now, almost before I could walk. It broke my heart when Goodfellow was shot.' She swallowed the catch in her breath. Such a long time ago and still it caused her pain. The lump of granite between the fig trees was all that remained of the wonderful horse that symbolised all Papa's dreams for their future.

Against her back Jim's heart thudded, no longer in time with Jefferson's stride but faster than before. Heat radiated from him making her shirt stick to her back. She arched her back to let the breeze cool the space between them. 'Shall we walk for a while?'

Jim pulled on the reins and Jefferson halted.

The river drew her gaze, the afternoon sun making her thirsty and hot. She remembered paddling her feet in the cool water, chasing the dragonflies as they danced and skimmed across the tranquil surface.

She slid down and searched the river. 'There's an old jetty just down there.' She pointed out the crumbled timber remains where Papa taught her to fish. 'We can sit and cool our feet in the water, and I'd like a drink.'

'I expect Jefferson would as well,' Jim said.

The lush grass swayed around them as they ambled down to the sleeping river. The warm sun beating down on her back lent an air of indolence and languor to her movements. The crooked jetty reached out into the river and a gentle breeze stirred the surface of the water. Jim dismounted and released Jefferson. He clasped her hand as they strolled through tussocky grass to the riverbank.

He dropped down off the bank onto the small half-moon patch of sand then stretched up his arms to her. 'Jump.' Flecks of sunshine sparkled in his eyes.

Throwing aside her inhibitions she launched into the air. For a moment she flew, a glorious sense of abandonment. Then his strong hands encircled her waist and he caught her. He spun her once before lowering her to the jetty.

'I'll pull your boots off.'

'I can do it.'

'I know you can. I want to.' He settled the sole of her boot against his chest.

Her gauchos slid up revealing her knee and she clasped the worn felt against her leg. Staring deep into her eyes he ran his hands slowly up the soft leather of her boot until they rested on her bare knee. 'Stay still.' His hands ran back down her calf making her muscles tighten. He tugged at her heel until the boot slipped off and he tossed it on the sand.

The quirk of his lips set her pulse racing and then he offered his hand and asked for her other foot. She held it up and the second boot followed the first, only this time he didn't release her leg. His hand remained warm and firm around her calf then trailed slowly down to her ankle and cupped her bare foot.

The jolt to her senses made her gasp and she moistened her lips then wriggled as a flush of heat blossomed on her cheeks. With a grin he released her foot, tugged his own boots free and pulled his moleskins up above his knees. 'Come on. You wanted to cool down.'

She toppled into his outstretched hands and he lowered her into the shallow water. The delicious coolness eased the heat coursing through her body. She bent down, cupped her hands and splashed water all over her face.

Jefferson found his own way to the river. On the other side of the jetty he snuffled and snorted, sucking up the water.

'He's always liked water.' Jim split his attention between the antics of his horse and her burning face.

'I do, too, especially on a day like this.' A day she would be more than happy to repeat again and again. Jim's easy company both soothed and excited her. It made the afternoon stretch and instilled a peace and serenity she hadn't known she craved.

As if reading her thoughts he slipped his arm across her shoulder and pulled her into the security of his body. She tipped her head back and stared up at him.

His hazel eyes widened and he lifted his hand. One fingertip traced her mouth. Her lips parted in a gasp. More than anything in the world she wanted him to kiss her again. Digging her toes into the sand she pressed onto tiptoes and dropped a kiss on his lips. The hard muscles under his shirt bunched, holding her firm, drawing her even closer.

His hand swept around her cheek, trailing tentatively down her neck beneath the collar of her blouse, lower and lower. She clenched her fists tight, squeezing the soft chambray of his shirt against the unaccustomed frisson of pleasure that rose in her.

His lips moved against hers until her mouth opened and his tongue plunged deep, dancing, tempting and teasing, promising delights she could only imagine.

When his hands threaded through the tangled mess of her hair and pushed it back from her face a groan escaped her mouth and she arched against him.

'Come with me.' He covered her fist with his large hand, spreading her fingers wide. With their hands interlocked he led her from the water back to the dry sandy beach.

Still clasping her hand he pulled her down beside him then raised her fingers to his mouth. His tongue traced a path across the lifeline on her open palm. 'I wish we had a whole lifetime ahead of us,' he murmured, raising his head.

Deep within her, muscles clenched and released, setting up a pulse as ancient as the land, thrumming and throbbing beneath her skin. No stranger to the mating rituals of the farm she knew they'd reached the moment where she must make a decision. Did she want to let it pass? A lifetime of regret yawned in front of her and in a heartbeat she made her decision.

Placing her hands on his shoulders she eased him from her. His hands fell and a shadow crossed his face, replaced in a second by acceptance. Pinning his gaze she tugged her shirt from her waistband and slid her fingers to the buttons, undoing the first, then the second. His eyes darkened and his tongue snaked across his lips as he sat wide-eyed, stiller than the sandstone rocks lining the riverbank.

As her fingers slipped from the last button she shrugged her shoulders free, smiling as a low groan escaped Jim's lips. Her nipples peaked and tingled in response. He stared, admiring her nakedness, then leant across to kiss the skin at the base of her neck. He ran his finger down her cleavage and cupped one upturned breast. Her loud gasp filled the space between them as he bent his head and pressed his warm lips to her nipple.

Clasping the back of his head she pulled him closer, wriggling in anticipation, wanting more, wanting him.

He lifted his head; his eyes were closed, his breathing ragged.

'Don't stop,' she whispered.

'I must.' Threading his fingers through her hair he pulled her face closer to his and dropped a lingering kiss on her lips. 'Now. Because if I do not I will ravish you within an inch of your life.'

A giggle worked its way between her lips. 'I think I might like that.'

An apologetic smile broke across his face. 'And so would I, more than you can imagine, but now isn't the time or the place.' He slipped her arms back into the sleeves of her shirt and buttoned it with as much tenderness as he would for a child.

He laid her down again and stroked her hair back from her face, fanning it out around her head until it mingled with the grass beneath them. 'I've imagined this,' he whispered, trailing his finger across her flushed cheek. His hazel eyes were clear, his expression sombre. Her heart raced and she ached in places she'd never imagined would crave a man's touch.

She raised her hand to his face, wanting his lips on hers again, his warm hands on her skin. She slid her fingers into his thick hair, feeling the contours of his head. Her thumbs circled at the base of his neck and ran up until they met the ridge of a scar. 'What's this?'

He shrugged and trapped her hands, lifting them from his head and clasping them in his.

'Tell me how your family came to be here.' He released her hands.

India leant back on her arms, pushing back her desire, disconcerted by his mercurial mood change. 'Papa and Mama always dreamt of owning a property, somewhere they could call home and put down roots. They acquired Helligen just after I was born.' Little more than a babe in arms they'd brought her here, to the home Papa had found to nurture and build his family, his empire.

Jim rolled over onto his back and pillowed his head on his arms. 'Who did they buy it from?'

'I don't know. The man who owned it had to sell to cover the debts he'd incurred during the depression in the forties. Papa bought it lock, stock and barrel. Most of the workers stayed on. He'd never owned a property and he needed their expertise. Over the years the property prospered, Violet was born and then my brother, Oliver …' India stalled; she didn't want to spoil the pleasure of the afternoon with her sorry family secrets. Letting out a huge sigh she shook her head. 'It's a sad tale no-one wants to hear.' So many hopes, all broken. Shattered dreams, such a series of misadventures. 'That's why I am so determined to restore the property. In some way perhaps I can bring back the happiness my parents dreamt of.'

Jim sat up and dropped his arm across her shoulder, squeezing gently, encouraging her.

'Soon after my brother was born my mother went out riding, against Papa's wishes. They'd waited for a son for so long. Mama wasn't young and she'd had a difficult confinement. Goodfellow was Papa's horse. He was headstrong and skittish. Mama had ridden him a hundred times, but she was weak after months abed. Our stud master saddled him for her. When they found her she'd cracked her head, lost her senses. She has no memory of the accident.'

'The lady in white.'

'I'm sorry?'

'The lady in white. I saw her on my arrival. She was searching for someone. What happened to your brother?'

Goosebumps flecked India's arms and she rubbed at them. Mama's words now made sense. Why hadn't she realised before? Mama hadn't seen Goodfellow. She'd seen Jefferson. 'My brother died.' Tears scuffed behind her eyes; she couldn't say more. To talk about Oliver and how he'd died was too painful, too difficult. 'When my mother recovered her senses her baby had gone. It broke her heart and caused her such melancholy she never recovered.' Try as she might India couldn't stop the tears pouring down her face. How she wished she hadn't left Oliver alone, had picked him up, not tucked him tight and left him. No matter how many times she remembered those awful months, relived the events, the raw pain never diminished. In one fell swoop everything had gone and they'd lived in the shadow of that day ever since.

India's agony was palpable. There was no way he could alleviate her pain as much as he wished otherwise; however, the story he'd heard, told by his father, wasn't the same. His father hadn't saddled Goodfellow, hadn't even been in the stables the night Mrs Kilhampton had gone out riding. He'd been asleep by the fire in the cottage. When Kilhampton challenged him there was nothing he could say to convince him of the truth. In his grief Kilhampton had ordered his father and the family off the property and, according to his father, allowed him to take the injured Goodfellow in lieu of his wages. The two stories simply didn't make sense. Didn't tally.

Completely at a loss Jim stared out across the river. He was a fool. In coming to Helligen under false pretences he perpetuated the lies that had destroyed his father. It was time to rectify the situation and discover the truth. 'Let's get you home. Today has been a difficult day. Tomorrow we'll start afresh and restore Helligen.'

India's wan smile twisted his heart. 'I'd like that. If I could make the property prosper, breed a champion, maybe Papa would come home and we would all be happy again.'

He helped India to her feet and they retraced their steps, Jefferson nudging his back as if prompting him to speak, to tell the truth. Ask the questions. How could he do that without causing India more grief?

Fifteen

Peggy's feather duster flicked across the surfaces in the library like a dragonfly over water. Dust motes danced in a shaft of sunlight, bathing her in a shower of gold so she resembled a fairy godmother bestowing magic.

'There you go, my big boy.' She flicked an imaginary speck from the portrait over the fireplace. 'You were one mighty fine horse. Shame, shame.'

'When did you start working here?' India asked. It was difficult to imagine the place without Peggy as she was the focal point of Helligen; even Violet went to her with her troubles. She filled so many roles: cook, cleaner, nursemaid—even mother. She'd been more of a mother to both her and Violet than poor misguided Mama.

'After the accident, when the Cobb family left. Mrs Cobb was the cook and Mr Cobb ran the horses. Your father was in a right mess when they left and Mrs Bagnell from the village sent me up here and told me to offer my services. Best thing I ever did. Mind you, that was in my younger days. I was a tad more energetic then.'

'But you never married?'

'No, I never married. I had a beau there for a while but he took off to the goldfields full of high hopes and blarney. Said he'd be back when he made his fortune. I haven't seen hide nor hair of him since.'

'That's sad. Don't you wish you had children?'

'Got children, haven't I? Got you and Violet.' She ran the duster over the two matching candelabra on either end of the mantel.

'Not while we were at school.'

'True. There were holidays, and Anya needed a lot of help with your mother in those days.'

'I think Mama's quite a lot better. I just wish she wouldn't ride out at night.'

'Time heals.' Peggy resumed her dusting with a burst of vigour.

'She spoke to me the other day.'

The feather duster stopped in midair and Peggy spun around. 'She did?'

'Mmm. She said she'd seen Goodfellow.'

'What, him?' She gave the portrait a dismissive flick. 'He's dead and buried under that there rock. Doesn't sound like she's getting better to me.'

'I think she became confused. Remember Jim said he'd seen a woman riding around the lagoon on the evening he arrived? Mama must have seen him. Jefferson's a lot like Goodfellow.'

'Aye, he is that.' Peggy picked up a handful of loose papers and shuffled them into a neat pile. 'Haven't you got work to do? I thought this was your day for catching up.'

'It is.' India sighed. She'd prefer to be outside with Jim, maybe taking a ride down to the river again. 'Jim's setting up our first pairing.' The thought sent a tremor of excitement rippling through her. 'The paperwork is going to have to wait. I've backed myself into a bit of a corner. I hadn't thought out the routine well enough. Out of the twelve brood mares I only have eight I can use with the young stallions—the others are all related.' She followed the lines in the studbook. 'I need another unrelated stallion. I'm going to have to buy services from one of the other studs. That's going to take time and put me behind schedule. I planned to have the paddock full of foals by August next year.'

'You're talking to the wrong person. I don't know nowt about this breeding lark.'

'It's just like people, Peggy. You can't marry your uncle.'

'Oh no! You wouldn't want to be doing that. Makes for weak babies.'

'Exactly, and we don't want weak foals.'

Receiving no answer India looked up. Peggy's duster hovered around the portrait, her head cocked to one side. 'You *have* got an unrelated stallion on the property, you know.'

India frowned and looked at the portrait, then closed the studbook with a snap. She shot out of the chair and grasped Peggy in a bear hug. 'You're right! I have. Jefferson.'

A big grin split Peggy's face. 'See, I'm not as 'alfwitted as I think I am.'

'No, you're not, not at all. I'll have to pay him.'

'Who?'

'Jim.'

'You're going to have to pay for any animal if it's not your own, and that Jefferson he's 'ere right now.'

Turning over one of the unpaid bills India licked her pencil and sketched a few notes on the back. 'Peggy Dickson, you are a marvel. I don't know what I'd do without you.' She planted a firm kiss on Peggy's pink cheek then made for the door.

It was the ideal solution. Jefferson was a great horse, with speed and stamina, perfect conformation. She capered across the courtyard and coasted to a sedate walk as she rounded the corner to the mating yard.

Jim leant against the fence, his broad shoulders straining his shirt. Inside the mating yard Mistral and Maestro circled each other. There was a lot of tail flicking and nose rubbing going on but not much else. She dropped her hand onto his arm, loath to speak and disturb the two animals.

Jim turned. His smile sent a warm shiver through her. Something in her tummy twisted as she looked into his eyes.

'Morning beautiful,' he whispered. 'Looks as though this might be our first success.'

She nodded. 'Can we talk? I've had an idea.'

He tipped his head in the direction of the cottage. 'Come and sit down over here. I'll make us a cup of tea. Nothing's going to happen for a while yet.'

Leaning with her back against the warm sandstock wall India fiddled with the scrap of paper, re-reading and checking her plans.

'There we are.' Jim handed her an enamelled mug. She put the paper on her lap and took the tea.

He sat so close she could feel the warmth of his thigh through the thin cotton of her skirt and smell his heavenly scent of leather and soap. And a tang of lucerne, she discovered as she pretended to inhale the steam from her tea.

'Well? You've had an idea,' he said.

Dragging her mind back to her plan she turned to face him. 'I have a problem and I think you can solve it for me.'

'I'll do my best.' His green-gold eyes twinkled, flecks of amusement dancing in their depths.

She handed him the piece of paper. 'I've been working out the breeding lines. I have four related mares and no unrelated stallion. I don't want to run the risk of interbreeding. I'm going to have to purchase four outside services.'

'That's a nuisance.' He studied the paper. 'You could approach Munmurra or one of the other Hunter studs. We'd have to take the mares to them. They won't send a stallion here.' He scratched his head. 'You'll be lucky if you can get them bred to anything worthwhile this spring. You might have to wait until next year. I could have a word with Munmurra and see if they can help.'

India's lips twitched as she waited for him to finish, itching to blurt out her perfect solution.

He frowned at her and then a grin split his face. 'But you've got an idea.'

He read her so well. 'How do you know?'

'Because you're not very good at hiding your emotions. It's easy to see what you're feeling.' He clasped her hand sitting in her lap and squeezed.

The colour flamed across her face and she snatched her hand back, spilling her tea. Plonking the mug down on the ground she took three deep steadying breaths.

'And when you're embarrassed you close your eyes and take deep breaths.'

'I'm not emba—'

'I'm sorry that wasn't fair.' He ran his finger down her cheek. 'Tell me about your plan.'

Dragging her hair back from her overheated face she twisted it out of the way. 'I want to use Jefferson over those four females.'

'You want to do what?' Jim stared at her, his mouth gaping wide.

A trickle of unease worked its way across her shoulders. 'I'll pay you for the services, whatever is a suitable fee.'

'No!'

The force of his refusal split the air and he surged to his feet, sending his mug of tea rolling across the dusty ground. It clattered to a halt against the wall of the cottage in a soggy puddle.

India peered at him. Two spots of bright colour stained his cheeks and he shook his head slowly from side to side.

'Why not? It's the perfect solution. Jefferson's not infertile, is he?'

'No. I've never tried him. I doubt it. There's nothing in his bloodlines to …' His voice trailed off and he scuffed the toe of his worn boot in the dirt, studying the puffs of dust with a fierce concentration.

'Then why not?'

She stood and tried to make eye contact with him. He stared down at the ground. Hard furrows creased his brow as though something hurt. He let out a shuddering sigh and glared at her. 'Can't you take no for an answer?'

'I can. It's just that I don't understand why.'

'You wouldn't.' He stormed into the cottage and slammed the door.

India sank back down onto the bench and rested her head back against the rough wall. It didn't make sense. Surely it wouldn't harm Jefferson. And she was quite prepared to pay Jim a fee. Picking up the mugs from the ground she settled them on the bench and peered through the window into the front room. Two overstuffed chairs flanked the fireplace but there was no sign of movement in the cottage. With a shrug she wandered over to the stables.

Jefferson stood in his stall munching on his morning feed of lucerne. He was a magnificent animal. He couldn't be infertile. She stretched out her hand and smoothed the soft velvet of his nose. He snuffled in appreciation then turned back to his breakfast. She would have to think again. So much for Peggy and her great ideas.

—

Jim pushed himself up out of the chair and shivered. The sweat had dried on his skin, leaving him cold. Not only his body, his mind as well. India's suggestion made his flesh creep. She couldn't use Jefferson. He was related through Goodfellow to all her mares. It had never crossed his mind she would ask that of him. What else could he have said? For a moment he'd been tempted to tell her the truth. Tell her why he'd answered her advertisement. Tell her he'd come to check for Jefferson's lineage and find the deed of sale for Goodfellow. There were too many unanswered questions. Why was Goodfellow supposedly buried out under the fig trees? He wasn't dead. He was at Munmurra grazing happily in a paddock, a bit long in the tooth but a long way from dead. Was that what his father had meant when he said he'd done something he wasn't proud of? Had he taken Goodfellow without permission?

Maybe his dream of racing Jefferson in Victoria was far-fetched and unrealistic, but he wouldn't give it up. Not until he'd exhausted every opportunity. He'd nurtured the idea like a wounded beast for too long. It was his one chance to make something of himself, and he'd promised his father he would put matters straight. Besides, he had to have the papers if he was going to stand Jefferson at stud or enter the horse in any worthwhile race.

Then there was India. When he'd first arrived at Helligen his intention had been to make the most of the situation, take what he wanted and leave. He owed the Kilhamptons nothing. They'd sent his father to an early grave, but India … India had possessed him like some enchanting sprite. Not only was she the most beautiful woman he'd ever seen, she tugged at his heartstrings. She had guts and determination, and such vision, and most of all they shared a common goal that reached across their families' history.

India trailed up the stairs. Yesterday, for the first time in her life, she'd missed her afternoon visit with Mama, her mind too full of Jim. She'd tried to kid herself into believing it was because of the horses and paperwork and getting the property back on its feet. It wasn't. Everything she did centred on Jim and being with him. When she wasn't with him all she did was think about him, or if there was anyone to listen, talk about him. He'd slipped into every corner of her mind.

'Good afternoon, Anya. I've come to see Mama and tell her about my day.'

The door opened fully. 'And about yesterday as well, I hope.'

India grimaced, accepting the rebuke, then entered the room and halted. Instead of the usual semi-darkness the open curtains allowed a ray of afternoon sunlight into the room. As always her mother sat in her chair gazing out the window, one hand resting on the empty cradle.

'Hello, Mama.' She bent down and dropped a kiss on her mother's cheek. To her surprise she turned her face and the glimmer of a smile traced her pale lips. India glanced up at Anya and raised her shoulders in question. 'You're looking well today, Mama.'

'We've been watching the animals in the yard,' Anya said.

'Oh.' If only she could ask her mother for advice. She knew more about horses than Papa did and for years had managed the stud with Thomas Cobb before her accident. All that knowledge locked up and forgotten. Such a waste.

'He's like his father.'

India started. 'I beg your pardon, Mama?'

'He's like his father,' her mother repeated, turning her face back to the window.

Frowning at Anya, her heart rate kicked up a notch at the thought of Oliver. How could a five-week-old child resemble a grown man? This was the second time her mother had engaged her in conversation and at first she'd thought it heralded a change for the better. Dwelling on Oliver was not an improvement; it was a backward step. 'His father?' She covered her mouth wishing she hadn't spoken.

Receiving no reply India retreated to her usual routine. 'We've started the breeding. Soon we will have foals in the paddocks again. Won't that be lovely?'

'Just like old times,' Anya said with a smile, smoothing the hair back from Mama's forehead.

'I have a problem. I can't mate four of the mares because they are too closely related to the sires we have. I'll have to get an outside service.'

'Goodfellow's offspring.' Her mother nodded her head knowingly.

'That's right.' Her heart leapt—this was almost a conversation. Certainly the closest she could remember.

'He's like his father. So like his father.' Her mother's eyes fluttered closed.

She turned to Anya and raised her eyebrow again. What had happened?

'She's sleeping now.'

India studied the rhythmic rise and fall of her mother's chest; as always Anya was right. Mama had fallen asleep. 'She seems different. A little better?' she whispered.

Anya shrugged her shoulders. 'It is difficult to tell. She watches from the window. The new activity, the new man …'

'Do you think it's confusing her? Perhaps we should make sure we're out of sight.'

'I think it is good for her. Brings her mind to the present.'

'But she's talking about Oliver so much.'

'No, I don't think so.'

'Saying he's like his father.'

'She is not talking about Oliver, she is talking about the new man and his horse. Remember, she said she saw Goodfellow.'

India rubbed her temples; the pounding in her head made it difficult to concentrate.

'Go now, India, and let her sleep.' Anya held open the door.

She crept from the room and sank down on the top step of the staircase, cradling her head in her hands. If only Jim had agreed to use Jefferson everything would be so much simpler. With a huge effort she pulled herself upright and drifted down the stairs and into the library.

Perched on the corner of the desk she ran her fingers over the worn leather of the studbook. Another day wasted! She'd made no progress and was back where she'd started earlier this morning. Goodfellow stared down at her from the painting, the supercilious expression on his arrogant face mocking her.

She opened the book, flicked through it in a desultory fashion watching the years float by. One of the last entries was in May 1850: *Goodfellow covered Storm.* Just before he died. It was correct because Storm's foal was on her breeding list. Running her finger over the spider-like writing she searched for a solution. Somewhere in this book lay the answer. What had Mr Cobb done? Had he imported sires? She turned back through a few more pages. The notes solved nothing. Over the years she'd tried so hard not to blame anyone but there was no doubt Cobb was the wretched man who'd caused all the heartache they'd suffered. If only he hadn't allowed her mother to ride out that fateful night, life would be so very different.

'Tosh!' She closed the book with a snap. Wallowing in self-pity would solve nothing. Maybe Violet was right, perhaps they should return to Sydney. The thought of handing over responsibility for this mess to someone else grew more inviting with every hurdle. Had she taken on more than she could manage?

'What are you doing?' Violet appeared in the doorway. She drifted into the room and sat in Papa's leather chair, rocking to and fro like a little girl on a seesaw.

India swallowed the scream building in her throat. She couldn't explain the confusion to Violet. She didn't understand it herself. 'I'm looking.'

'Looking at what?'

'I'm looking at the old studbook trying to decide what to do with the horses.'

'Leave them here for Jim and come back to Sydney. That's what you should do. He can manage the property, he's quite capable.'

'I can't do that! I made a deal with Papa. A year. I've already gone against his wishes by employing Jim without his consent. You know how he feels about outsiders on the property.'

'Oh, what? Because Mama had an accident and he blames the stud master for it and Oliver's death. Look, it wasn't a very nice thing to happen, I'll grant you that. I'd love to have a brother. Let's face it, you wouldn't be wearing that laughable attire and trying to pretend you can do a man's job if we had a brother to help. But hundreds of people lose a baby and there's no rhyme or reason. One minute they're asleep in the cot and the next minute, poof—' she snapped her fingers and India's skin went cold, '—they're dead.'

It took a long moment for India to regain her composure. The mention of her little brother lying tucked in the cot, with his bright eyes and the beginning of a smile on his cherubic face, would always bring tears to her eyes. 'Try and show some compassion. There's much more to it as you very well know.' So very much more but nothing Violet would remember or understand.

'Anyway, Peggy sent me in here to get you. She says you're not eating properly and she's worried about you. We're in the kitchen. Come along.'

India clambered to her feet and put her arm around Violet's shoulders. 'Thank you. It's good to have a sister.' She gave her a hug. Constantly blaming Violet for her own woes would solve nothing.

'You've changed your tune.'

'You're behaving like a grown-up instead of a spoilt child. It makes it easier.'

Violet let out a yelp of fury and chased India through the walkway to the kitchen, narrowly missing Jilly carting a basket of washing out to the garden. They barrelled inside and came to a skidding halt.

'Peggy! Peggy! Where are you?' Violet peered into the pantry then the scullery. There was no sign of the promised meal although the table was set. The silence was broken only by the loud tick of the clock in the usually busy room.

'She's not here. Where's she gone?'

'I don't know. I'll go and check outside. You go and ask Jilly.'

India left the kitchen with her skin prickling. Peggy was nowhere to be seen. Three white bed sheets billowed on the clothes line and Jilly stood pegging out more. The gate to the vegetable garden was closed. None of the usual activity in the stables; the mares were all out grazing. The mating yard stood empty. Shivering, she ran into the stables.

'Oh Miss India! Thank 'eavens. I was sent to saddle a horse for you,' Fred said.

'Saddle a horse for me? Why?'

'It's Mrs Kilhampton. She's taken off. Anya and Peggy can't find her. Mr Jim, he's taken Euros but he's real worried because Jefferson's gone and he thinks Mrs Kilhampton might be riding him. He's a mighty stroppy horse for a lady, 'specially a lady who's like Mrs Kilhampton. Sorry miss, no disrespect meant.'

India swallowed, trying to marshal her thoughts. She'd never heard Fred speak at such length and it sent shivers down her spine.

'Go and get Aura for me and bring her back as fast as you can.'

Taking the ladder to the hayloft at a run she clambered right to the top and onto the piles of stacked hay. From the highest air vents she had a complete view of the property. Breathing heavily she peered out through the slatted timber. On the far side of the lagoon Anya and Peggy made their way around the shallows, each holding a long stick, pushing aside the tussocky grass and prodding the water. Surely they didn't think her mother had fallen into the water.

She dismissed the idea and squinted out beyond the lagoon to the paperbark forest. If Jefferson had thrown Mama he'd be running free. For a moment her heart snagged as she saw a flash of bay. The rider came into focus; Jim appeared to be riding in ever decreasing circles, covering the uncultivated area between the river and the paddocks.

'Miss, I'm here.' Fred's voice floated up the ladder. She slithered down and launched herself onto Aura's back from the sixth rung of the ladder.

Fred whistled between his teeth. 'Bloody hell!'

'Fred.'

'Yes, miss.'

'You are to stay here.'

'Aww, miss.'

'Stay here with Miss Violet in case Mama comes back. If she does, tell Violet to take her back to her room, sit her in her chair by the window and stay with her. Do you understand?'

'Aww, miss.'

The arrangements were the best she could do. Wheeling Aura around she left, ignoring Fred's plaintive moans.

As she headed down the track she scanned the undergrowth for any sign of her mother. After the other night Anya and Peggy would be at the lagoon.

History was repeating itself. Flashes of that fateful day flickered behind her eyes. Papa out searching. Men with staffs prodding the lagoon as Peggy and Anya were today. It couldn't happen for a second time and Jim … poor Jim must be beside himself. His beautiful horse. What if something happened to Jefferson? She shuddered.

After an eternity she rounded the bend in the track and the river came into view. The river where she and Jim had—she shook the thought from her mind and concocted a string of ludicrous promises about looking after Mama, spending more time with her, paying more attention to her, ignoring Jim and the strange sensations he aroused. Beyond the old jetty she spotted him cantering across the paddock with his loose, easy grace. Her heart lifted at the sight. She was no longer alone. With his help Mama would be found.

'Jim! Jim!' She waved her hat in circles high above her head. He spotted her in an instant and spurred his horse into a gallop. They met in the middle of the paddock where the long grass swayed around them like a receding tide.

'Any sight of her?'

Jim shook his head.

'Jefferson?'

He shook his head again.

'Jim, I'm so sorry. I know how much Jefferson means to you.'

'It's your mother we must worry about.'

He pointed to the paperbark forest. 'When I first arrived on the property I saw her over there.'

'That's near where she had her accident.' The knot in India's stomach wrenched tighter.

They spurred their horses across the paddock to the tangled mess of trees where a wallaby track snaked in and out of the clumps of low trees and bushes.

Jim lifted his hands to his mouth. 'Cooee! Mrs Kilhampton …' His voice rang out and seconds later the echo bounced back from the distant sandstone hills.

India screwed up her face. Would Jim's calls panic Mama, or encourage her to respond?

'Not a good idea?' he said, reading her expression.

She shrugged her shoulders. 'I honestly don't know. I doubt she'll respond. However, she's been talking to me on and off for the last few days so it's possible.'

They halted the horses and he called again, his deep voice resounding through the trees.

The same wavering echo was the only reply.

Walking in single file down the narrow track India scanned either side of the forest for any sign Mama had cut off the track. There was nothing. Her stomach sank. Heavens! She may not even be on this track. She may be facedown in the river or the lagoon. 'Jim, I think we should go back. I can't imagine her coming all this way.'

'One more try.' He lifted his hands to his mouth. 'Coooeeee! Mrs Kilhampton!' Jim's voice rang out loud and clear then the fading response bounded back. With a disappointed shake of his head he wheeled his horse around and they retraced their steps.

'What next?'

'I don't know.'

'The river?'

'Yes. The river.' Despite the heat of the midday sun India shivered.

'Cooee! Mr Cobb! Cooee! Mr Cobb!'

'What was that?' Jim swung around in the saddle. 'Over here. We're over here.'

Mr Cobb?

Jefferson broke through the trees and galloped towards Jim. India's mouth gaped. Her mother, eyes blazing and a huge smile wreathing her face, reined Jefferson in with an enviable amount of skill.

'Mr Cobb. I'm so pleased I've found you.'

'Mrs Kilhampton. We feared the worst.' Jim slipped from his saddle and reached for Jefferson's bridle. His hand soothed his horse's foaming mouth as he scanned the animal for injury.

Mr Cobb?

Sixteen

Jim's shoulders dropped and he sucked in a deep breath as he ran his hand over Jefferson's neck and muzzle. Keeping a firm grasp on the bridle he shot a look down the animal's flanks. Unable to see any injury to horse or rider he moved to the offside. Nothing. In fact the woman sat as though born to the saddle, except there was no saddle.

'Mama!' India's voice rose above the heavy breathing of all three horses as she slipped to the ground. 'Are you all right? What are you doing out here? So far from the house.'

Mrs Kilhampton tossed an impatient glance at her daughter and urged Jefferson forwards. Jim clamped his hand around the bridle. Now they'd found her he wouldn't let her out of his sight again, or for that matter Jefferson.

'One moment, please.' He tried to keep his tone even and offered a tentative smile, mindful of the way she'd fled on the first day. She shivered like a frightened filly as India's screeches rose, resembling her sister in the mating yard.

'India, why don't you go back and tell Anya and Peggy we have found Mrs Kilhampton.'

'Jim! You …'

'Now! I have this under control.' He locked her gaze. She would do as he said.

'India, do what Mr Cobb said.'

'Oh Mama, I … Mr Cobb?' she questioned again.

'Stop arguing, child. Do as you're told.'

With an enormous huffing sound India remounted then threw him a bemused glance over her shoulder and headed back down the track.

Jim exhaled a slow, shuddering breath.

'Thank goodness you came, Mr Cobb. I knew you would. We remembered exactly where to go but I rather hoped you would find us.' She patted Jefferson's damp neck. 'He's a wonderful horse but then you knew that from the outset, didn't you? You have such an eye for an animal.'

His mind circled, trying to make sense of her words. She must have mistaken him for his father. He doubted India realised Cobb was his rightful name, or how Mrs Kilhampton would know. Right now it was the least of his concerns. He had to get her back to the security of the house, and if it meant pretending to be his father then so be it.

And Jefferson. Jefferson was obviously doing a very good imitation of pretending to be *his* father. If the bloody horse could do it then so could he. Slipping a lead rope from his saddle Jim moved to clip it onto the bridle.

She jerked the reins, pulling Jefferson's head around. 'I don't need that, for goodness sake.' She edged the horse past him on the track. 'You of all people know how well I ride. You taught me all sorts of tricks.' She pulled her bare feet up onto Jefferson's back and dropped the reins, her arms spread like a butterfly's wings.

'Mrs Kilhampton, please.' *Jesus Christ!* If she fell history would repeat itself, and heaven only knew what Jefferson would do if she did as she threatened and stood. The possibility of another accident, more blame and another injured horse made his blood run cold.

She tossed her head and shot him a tedious glance before sinking back down and bolting down the track.

Jim sprang into the saddle and followed, his eyes trained on the swathe of grey-blonde hair hanging down to her waist. He'd known as soon as he'd seen India that these two women were somehow related.

As the track opened out he pulled alongside Jefferson. The horse turned his head and looked at him, snorted and continued on his way with a delighted prance. Almost as though he was enjoying being the centre of attention.

'I knew you'd come back.'

Jim sucked in a breath. 'Let's get back to the house and see what Anya and Peggy know,' he said, hoping it was the right response for the poor woman forced to wander the property searching for her dead child.

The look she flashed him was so like India's his stomach turned. 'Good idea, Mr Cobb. You can always be trusted to come up with the perfect solution.'

Jim returned her look with a tentative smile and scanned the open paddock searching for India. She was nowhere in sight. With any luck she'd found Anya and Peggy and they were heading back to the house. Quite what he'd do when he got there he didn't know. In fact, he had no idea about anything. Mrs Kilhampton's effusive greeting and friendly smile were at odds with all he knew. Surely she wouldn't treat the man responsible for her family's misfortunes with such confidence. She'd greeted him like a long-lost friend and she appeared to have no difficulty in talking to him. Hardly the relationship one would expect between the lady of the house and the hired help.

For the remainder of the ride she sat seemingly lost in her thoughts, occasionally glancing up to the sky or over her shoulder, but not speaking. As Jim mulled over the strange situation his mistake became clear. When his family had been sent packing from the property Mrs Kilhampton lay as good as dead. She knew nothing of their departure. Had anyone bothered to tell her that his father was no longer working on the property?

The gate and Fred came into view and Jim's shoulders dropped the moment they entered the home paddocks. Fred swung the gate and made to speak. Jim raised his hand and shook his head. For once the boy did as he was told, closed his mouth and the gate in matching movements, then followed them up the track on foot.

Once back at the stables Mrs Kilhampton dismounted and Jim led Jefferson into the stall. She began to walk away then turned and picked up a biscuit of lucerne hay. 'He likes a reward after a ride.' She scratched Jefferson behind his ears and dropped the hay into the stall, then drifted off towards the house.

'Bloody hell.' Fred appeared at his elbow. 'That was weird.'

'On this occasion,' Jim said, 'I think I agree with you. Can you see to these animals? They both need a good rub down and so will Aura. Miss India is back, isn't she?'

'Yep.' Fred tossed his head in the direction of the kitchen. 'She's with Peggy. Peggy said she was spitting feathers. Had to have a cup of tea. She'd come over all unnecessary.'

Jim slumped down on a mound of straw. He'd just about come over all unnecessary too, and once Mrs Kilhampton was safely back in her rooms he'd have some questions to answer, that was for sure.

So be it. It was time to come clean and tell India the truth, admit his association with the property and explain why he was there. Today's events had lost him the luxury of picking his moment. He wandered outside and stuck his head under the pump, then shook himself like a dog. The water sprayed out around him making a circle on the dusty ground, just like it had when he was a kid.

He'd miss the place. It was in his blood as much as Jefferson's, however there was little he could do about it. The saddest part of the whole mess was he'd never stand his horse at stud or see him race at Flemington.

Determined to get the whole horrendous debacle over and clear up everything once and for all, Jim made for the kitchen. He had a need to know India was safe, to see her and, if truth be known, hold her in his arms. The likelihood of that ever happening again was receding faster than an odds-on favourite.

Without bothering to knock he walked into the kitchen. Peggy sat crumpled at the kitchen table, her face red and flustered, and Violet hovered around her like a persistent fly offering damp towels and cups of tea.

'Is India about?'

'She's upstairs with Anya, settling Mama down,' Violet said without even looking in his direction.

No offer of tea was forthcoming so he hung in the doorway unproductive, useless and unwelcome. After a few moments Peggy lifted her head and looked at him shrewdly. 'So are you going to spill the beans?'

Violet froze and her eyes narrowed as she squinted at him.

'I need to speak to India.'

'Before you do, young man, let me tell you a few things. First and foremost I've thought there was something a bit dodgy about you from the moment you walked in. Far too familiar and far too at home.' Peggy tipped her head to one side in a bird-like fashion. 'What have you got to say about that?' Her chin jutted.

Peggy was a bit too knowing for her own good. He had no recollection of her working at Helligen when he was a child; however, she didn't miss a trick. He'd never have got away with his ruse for so long if Peggy had been around when he and his family left. 'What I have to say needs to be said to India before anyone else.'

'I'll go and get her,' Violet jumped in, her eyes wide with a curiosity he'd rather not have to deal with.

'I'd like to speak to her on my own.'

'Oh, you would, would you?' Peggy said, putting two and two together and coming up with fifty-four.

'I owe it to her.'

The latch on the door clicked as India pulled it tight and turned the heavy brass key. Until Anya returned she couldn't run the risk of her mother wandering off again.

Questions jostled for space in her head. Her mother's disjointed sentences and illusions of the past were just too confusing. If only she'd been older and had a better memory of the days before and after the accident.

Obviously Mama was still living in the past. Her words made little or no sense. To think that Jefferson was Goodfellow was, in a way, understandable. The two horses were very similar. When had she last seen Goodfellow? Not since he'd thrown her. He was shot while she was insensible. Buried at the same time as Oliver. Too many deaths. Too many losses. No wonder Papa hated the place. More than anything else Mama's strange reaction to Jim nagged at her. She'd called him Mr Cobb and seemed so familiar with him, so at ease, so calm. A different woman. She shook her head. The idea Mama was recovering was a myth; she'd crawled further back into the past and now would probably never regain her senses. Anya needed to be with her. Where was she? Usually the most diligent of nurses, she'd vanished.

The kitchen was the obvious place and as she walked downstairs the sound of voices drifted through the walkway. The door stood ajar. She reached for the handle and paused.

'He is the spitting image of his father.' Anya's words brought her up sharp. 'Alike as two peas in a pod. And about the same age he was when we first arrived here.'

'I don't understand.' Violet's petulant tone drifted under the door and India pressed closer. She didn't understand either.

'Then there's the horse. I would have thought it was Goodfellow if I didn't know any better. Just like that portrait in the library.'

'So what are you saying?' Violet interrupted.

'Violet, be quiet. Let Anya speak. She knows more about this than anyone else.'

'It is not my place to discuss Miss Laila's situation.'

'Anya.' Peggy's tone indicated her frustration. 'I've respected your refusal to discuss things for a long time. None of my business what happened here before I arrived, but things have changed now and I need a bit of background if I'm supposed to do my job.'

'And I have every right to know, she's my mother.'

Anya's sigh was so loud India heard it, then there was the scrape of a chair, and she craned closer to the door.

'Miss Laila tried and tried … baby. Mr Kilhampton … she was always outside working with the horses, working with … put a stop to it … doctors said she must stay abed … Oliver born … Thomas Cobb … spitting image of his father …'

Anya's dulcet tones were barely audible and Peggy's grunts and groans punctuated the fragments of conversation. Unable to stand it a moment longer India threw open the door. Peggy and Anya lifted their heads in unison and their mouths gaped.

Not so Violet. A brilliant smile crossed her face and she sank down onto the chair and folded her arms. The atmosphere crackled like dry grass underfoot in a drought. The colour rose to Peggy and Anya's cheeks. Violet smirked and licked her lips—the cat had unearthed a rat's nest.

'Well?' India asked.

Peggy recovered first. 'Would you like a cup of tea?'

'Not at the moment.' India eyed Anya. 'Mama might like one when she wakes, however before you take it up, Anya, perhaps you and Peggy could tell me what's going on.'

'Glad your mother's home safe. It was a worrying time.' Peggy bustled around the stove clanging and clattering as she filled the kettle then emptied the freshly brewed teapot.

The sound of Anya's indrawn breath skirted the table. 'We were discussing Mr Jim's horse. Your mother is very taken with him.'

Violet shuffled, her mouth opening and closing like a gaping fish.

'So it would seem.'

'Oh, for goodness sake!' Violet knocked her chair flying. 'India needs to know the truth. Stop prevaricating and tell her what's going on.'

'Thank you, Violet. It's about time I had a little support from you. Now, ladies?'

Anya and Peggy exchanged embarrassed glances. Then Peggy sucked in a deep breath and said, 'Anya thinks Jim is the spitting image of the old stud master, Mr Cobb. The one who let your mother ride out that night, the one your father sacked because he was responsible for her accident. There. That's all there is to it.'

It was enough. Now her mother's words to Jim and the way he'd ignored them made sense. But how could he be the son of Thomas Cobb? His name was Mawgan. Jim Mawgan. He'd signed the letter that way, told her that when he arrived.

Her heart plummeted somewhere down near her boots. What would Papa say if he found out? Their agreement would be out the window so fast and she'd be bundled back to Sydney to marry that buffoon, Cecil Bryce. Something she did not want to do. She couldn't believe he wanted her to marry such a pompous idiot.

Cecil didn't make her breath quicken or her heart pound. Indeed, Cecil Bryce was the polar opposite of Jim.

Something in Violet's eyes told her she'd missed some finer details. 'Right, Violet. I want to know exactly what you think the truth is.'

'It's not what I *think* the truth is. It's simply the truth. Your stud master, the very attractive and oh-so-nice Jim Mawgan, isn't who or what he says he is.'

'You don't know that for certain.' Violet couldn't be right. How could Jim be the son of Thomas Cobb, and if he was, why would he want to work on the property?

'I suggest you ask him. I don't know why he's sneaked back in here under false pretences but you know as well as I do, the Cobb family are responsible for this whole horrid mess.' She waved her hand around. 'The entire family were told to go and never to set foot on the property again.'

'Mama's accident wasn't Jim's fault.' Why was she defending him?

'No, but it was his father's fault. If he hadn't saddled Goodfellow and allowed Mama to go riding that night she would never have fallen. Everyone knew perfectly well she wasn't capable. It was too soon after the birth. She'd been confined to her bed for the best part of a year. She could hardly walk, never mind ride. Even I know that.'

India collapsed into the chair, her head spinning. If it was true, Jim had answered the advertisement under a false name. He'd known all along about the place. My God! Her heart almost stopped beating. What could have happened when she'd left her mother alone with him? A flush of heat scored her body. And the way she'd fallen into his arms like a strumpet. Was that part of his plan, too?

'I don't understand how you can defend the man.' Violet had read her thoughts.

India groaned aloud and dropped her head into her hands. Anya patted her shoulder making unsuccessful soothing noises. 'He does look very much like his father. He was a very attractive man as I remember, tall and virile with a wicked sense of humour. He always made your mother laugh. They were inseparable, working away together. And that horse of his might as well be Goodfellow reincarnated. That is what's caused your mother's behaviour.'

India stared up into Anya's eyes unable to frame an answer.

'Papa's going to be livid,' Violet said, a delighted grin splitting her face. 'You'll be dragged back to Sydney with your tail between your legs. I told you. You're wasting your time. The place is doomed—we're all doomed if we stay here. Leave it to Papa to sort out. He'll sell the property and you can go and marry Cecil.'

India pushed up from the table. 'We'll see.'

'Everyone will see.' Violet hummed a few bars of Handel's 'Wedding Anthem'. 'I can't wait to get back to Sydney. I love a wedding.' With a twirl she left the kitchen with Anya following hot on her heels.

Peggy placed a mug of tea on the table in front of her and she wrapped her hands around it, trying to draw some comfort from the warmth.

'I'm sorry, love. If I'd thought about the consequences I would have kept my mouth shut.'

'It's not your fault, Peggy. It's mine. I should have checked into Jim's background more thoroughly and not been swayed by his charm.'

'And good looks.'

'And good looks,' India admitted with a rueful smile. 'I suppose I shall have to tell him to leave the property. Violet's right, Papa will be livid when he finds out. He holds the Cobb family responsible for shattering all his dreams—even Oliver's death.'

'Well, that's a nonsense. It wasn't Cobb's fault Oliver died. Maybe for your mother's accident … who'd let a sick woman only weeks out of childbirth ride a bloody great stallion like that?'

The vision of her mother astride Jefferson flashed through India's mind. These days there was nothing wrong with her physically; she rode as well as she always had. It was the broken skull and consequent brain pressure that had taken its toll. The best doctors in the colony had attended her and they all said the same. A coma as a result of head injury, nothing else could be done. And before Jim arrived her mother had been quite content to ride one of the mares. Why had she been drawn to Jefferson? Because he was the reincarnation of Goodfellow?

Seventeen

Jim pulled the currycomb through Jefferson's coat making it gleam like burnished copper. He found solace in the motion and the company of the horse. Last night he'd tried to see India, to speak to her, but he'd had no luck. Peggy had met him at the kitchen door with a face as dark as thunder, handed him his dinner and sent him packing. For the first time since he'd arrived at Helligen they'd treated him as the hired help. He gave a rough snort and Jefferson responded in kind.

He *was* the hired help. Just as his father before him. People of his background simply didn't spend their time hobnobbing with the Kilhamptons of this world. They moved in circles he couldn't even comprehend, dined with the rich and famous, the pillars of Sydney society. He'd got too close and now he was paying the price. Sent away before he could solve the mystery surrounding Goodfellow, or find the deed of sale.

Jefferson's ears pricked and he turned his head, his nostrils flaring. Jim followed his gaze, hoping it was India although the horse didn't react to her in that way.

'Good morning, Jim.' Violet sashayed down the aisle towards the stall.

Jefferson snorted and backed against the wall, the whites of his eyes shining.

'Easy boy.' He pushed past his horse and closed the stall gate before Violet got any closer. 'She has the same effect on me, mate. I'll get rid of her.' He snapped the padlock on the stall, and pocketed the key, unsure whose safety he wanted to maintain. 'Violet.'

She raised her eyebrows at his deliberate lack of courtesy. He was over her pretensions and if he wasn't going to be around any longer then why grovel? The Kilhamptons could take their social airs and graces and stick them where they belonged.

'Jim, I wondered if we could have a word. There are a few matters which may be to your advantage.'

Now she had his attention. His heart gave a leap. He wouldn't put it past her to have examined every paper on the property. She had enough time on her hands.

Silently Jim held open the door and extended his arm, indicating the seat outside against the wall.

'Thank you.' The coquettish smile she threw at him made his blood run cold and when she reached for his arm her cloying scent wafted around him in a suffocating cloud. She sat then patted the bench next to her.

He perched on the far end and stretched his legs out in front of him, trying to assume a relaxed pose. It was so far from the truth. He couldn't trust the woman for a moment. Every move she made was for her own good. He examined the toecap of his boot, his nerve endings prickling as he waited for Violet to speak.

She cleared her throat. 'Jim. It's not my place to tell you this but …' Her eyelashes fluttered.

'Get on with it.' He clamped his teeth together counting the stitches on his boot.

'I don't believe India has been entirely honest with you.'

He pushed upright and stared at her. India hadn't been honest with him? Surely it was the other way around. Moistening his lips he continued to play Violet's game, all the while imagining turning his back and walking away. 'Really?' he prompted.

'Bear with me. I have to go back a bit. It's important you have the whole story.'

Every bone in his body screamed at him to leave. Get up and walk away. Talk about it with India, not her sister. If only he could let go of his desire to see Jefferson race, and the memory of his father's words. *Right the wrongs of the past before they shatter your dreams.* Somewhere in the piles of ledgers and notebooks lay the answer to the mystery and Violet might know exactly where. 'I'm listening.'

'After my mother's accident and Oliver's death Papa was devastated. He blamed Thomas Cobb for all his misfortunes. He lost all interest in Helligen. The doctors told him nothing could be done for Mama other than giving her time and patience. He tried and it made no difference. It was as though overnight Mama ceased to exist. She was dead to him. At first we stayed here. It was like living in a graveyard. India and I had to tiptoe through the house, and even when Mama began to recover she shunned us. The doctors said her mind was stuck in that one week of her life. She didn't speak or leave her room. Only Anya could offer her any solace. Her illness sucked the heart out of Papa. Finally when it became obvious she would never recover he arranged for some men from the village to oversee the place and Anya and Peggy stayed here with Mama. He took India and me to Sydney. We lived in Sydney and went to school. Then, when India finished she was presented to the governor and became the toast of the town.'

He could imagine that, see India sweeping across a dance floor on the arms of her escort, jewels sparkling at her throat, her eyes flashing as she flirted behind a fluttering fan, bright with excitement. His gut twisted. 'Then why did she come back?'

'A very good question and one I have asked time and time again. Cecil Bryce proposed to India. He's mad for her and he's a wonderful catch. He and Papa have common business interests and he is prepared to help finance Helligen until it can be sold. India refused. She said it wasn't fair to Mama. That this was her home and it belonged to our family. She and Papa had the biggest of arguments. She said he was perfectly happy to leave Mama here to run the property before her accident, so why couldn't she do the job. They came to an arrangement. India has twelve months to resurrect Helligen. If she can do that then she and Mama can stay here. If not, the place will be sold.'

Violet stood up and wandered down the aisle between the stalls, almost as though she was thinking, planning what to say next. Then she turned and marched back, standing in front of him with her hands on her hips.

'I hate to see you wasting your time, Jim. The horses will be sold. If Mama's health is improving she would be better in Sydney where she can receive the best medical treatment. India will end up marrying Cecil. She's in love with him. It's just her misbegotten belief Mama is happier here.'

'And what do you want, Violet?'

She sat next to him and turned, her eyes cold and hard like amethyst chips. 'I want my life. I want to go back to Sydney. That's nothing new. But in this instance I'm thinking of you, not myself.'

He doubted it. Nothing he had seen in Violet in his short time at Helligen made him believe she spoke the truth.

'In fact, I'm thinking of everyone. Mama, Papa, India. And you, Jim. Even Peggy and Anya.'

'And India is in love with this Cecil Bryce bloke. She doesn't want to be at Helligen?' He didn't believe it. India didn't belong in Sydney. She had dreams. She wanted to breed horses, buckskins, and racing champions.

'Oh yes. She's in love with Cecil. Of course she is. He's charming. He takes her to the theatre, to the opera, buys her expensive gifts. He has the most beautiful house, in Potts Point. He's introduced us to his wonderful circle of friends.' She lowered her voice. 'They are all men of standing, of distinction. Papa would never permit India to stay here or marry outside her class. We are a family of distinction and have standards.'

What rubbish! The picture Violet painted was as far from reality as his hopes of racing Jefferson. India loved her horses, and loved the life at Helligen. She'd never be happy in the city.

'She does like the property,' Violet added, perhaps noting the look of scepticism on his face. 'And when she marries Cecil, if Papa decides not to sell, it could become the perfect place for house parties and holidays. We've talked of building a tennis court. Mama could visit and maybe stay if the doctors thought her able. India would still be able to visit once in a while.'

Jim stood up and brushed his trousers. 'You've given me a lot to think over. Thank you for being honest.' The lie slipped easily from his tongue. An art he'd developed, it appeared. More than anything he needed to talk to India.

Violet held out her hand, waiting for him to help her to her feet.

Gritting his teeth he offered his assistance.

'Thank you, Jim. If there's anything more I can do please don't hesitate to ask. Trust me. I do have your best interests at heart.' She threw him a tight smile and left.

The last pile of ledgers landed with a thump on the timber floor. India sneezed as the dust flew into the air, bringing with it the scent of the crumpled past. She combed her fingers through her hair and pulled it back off her neck with an impatient shrug.

She would solve the mystery of Jim's association with Helligen no matter how long it took. And when she had proof she'd challenge him and see if he lied as easily then. She heaved the books onto the desk and opened the top one. Oliver was definitely born in April 1850—it was engraved on his tombstone under the fig trees and tombstones didn't lie. He was five weeks old when Mama had her accident. The answer must be here. Papa's journals were as comprehensive as his business records and ships' logs: purchases, sales, profits and losses. Everything recorded, even the weather.

The first two books offered little other than to confirm all she already knew. Daily life mapped out and marked as though it was yesterday. *Clear skies, wind from the northwest. Goodfellow released with four-year-olds. Cobb keen to try paddock mating. Fencing completed.*

She flipped back a few pages, revisiting the past with terrifying clarity as it unfolded before her eyes. *Cobb boy fell from cottage roof. Doctor Pullem attended. Seventeen stitches.* An army of ants marched the length of her spine. *Cobb boy.* Her fingers itched. Down by the river. Tracing her finger over the raised scar tissue beneath Jim's thick hair.

Closing the book with a crash she fumbled for the next journal. A fine gold chain acted as a bookmark, weighted in place by a small golden cross that dangled below the pages. *Oliver's birth.* She began to read the words, her eyes filling with tears at the joy pouring from the page. *My darling Laila, a son at last, our future. The living, breathing manifestation of our eternal love.*

The writing blurred and two large tears splashed onto the yellowed paper. Blotting them with her sleeve she watched the writing fade. Fade like Papa's dreams. How could the man who had written these words have deserted his sick wife and left her alone for all those years?

The book fell to her lap. What good did it do raking up the past? Perhaps she should simply go to Sydney, see him and admit to her foolishness. He would have to be pleased Mama was better. Maybe he'd come home.

Through the window the fig trees caught the evening breeze and the surface of the lagoon rippled. Two black swans glided to the centre. Their red beaks picked up the streaks of the sunset as they bobbed their heads in their own strange mating ritual, their long, slim necks forming the shape of a heart.

With her eyes still on the swans she turned the page then peered down. A splattered ink line scored the pages, the paper raised and torn from the pressure of the nib. The handwriting heavier, more determined, the single line formed a scar beneath the sentence on the otherwise empty page.

It is done. Goodfellow shot. Cobb's final act. May he rot in the hell into which he has placed me.

India gulped back her horror and ran her thumb over the writing. The bare bones of the story she'd heard before, but never with such vehemence, such raw pain and anger. The next page was blank, and the next.

'India, there you are.'

She turned her head, her shoulders slumped, tired beyond belief. 'Violet?'

'You look busy.' Violet wrinkled her nose. 'What are those dusty old tomes? They smell dreadful.' She reached out and India clapped the ledger shut, narrowly missing her sister's fingers.

'Just the old record books. I'm trying to make up my mind what to do.' In that instant everything became clear. She would go to Sydney and ask her father for advice, and convince him to come home and see for himself how much better Mama seemed.

'And?'

'I'm going to go to Sydney and speak with Papa.' Her voice belonged to someone else.

The snap of Violet's hands made her jump and she blinked to clear the misty fog clouding her eyes. It was the only solution.

'Wonderful. When are we leaving?'

'Not we, just me.'

'No. I'm coming too. Don't imagine that you're going to go swanning off to Sydney without me.'

'I need you to stay here, with Mama.'

'Mama has Anya, and Peggy, she doesn't need me.'

India ignored her sister's comment. If she rode to Morpeth alone it would be quicker. Violet would have baggage and demand the buggy, all manner of fripperies. Alone she could pick up the morning steamer and be in Sydney by noon.

'What about Jim?'

'What about Jim?' India countered.

'Aren't you going to get rid of him now you know who he is?'

'No. I'm not leaving you all here with only Fred.'

'You were quite happy for us to be here with *only Fred* before Jim came.'

'That's different. I was here.'

Violet made a sound that was somewhere between an expletive and a sneeze. 'I'm not staying. I'm coming to Sydney.'

'Please. Just for once do what I ask. I need you to stay here. With Jim here you'll be fine. I want to talk to Papa, and see what he suggests.'

'I know exactly what he'll tell you—get that man's son off the place. He ought to leave the property. What will happen if he goes while you're away?'

'Violet, calm down. If he leaves you'll manage. If there's a problem you can't cope with, you can call on Tom Bludge or any number of the men from the village. Peggy knows where to find them.'

Eighteen

Like cold porridge, the stew Peggy had sent over stuck to the roof of his mouth. Three times he'd attempted to speak to India and on each occasion Peggy had put him off. When he'd sneaked around the verandah like some prowling pickpocket she was deep in conversation with Violet in the library. What he wanted to say wasn't for her sister's ears.

He threw the remnants of his meal to the chickens and took the tray into the scullery. If India wanted him to leave then he would, but he wouldn't take Violet's words at face value. India might very well intend to marry the Sydney bloke, but he wanted to hear it from her own lips. There was also his need to explain why he'd come to Helligen in the first place. He owed her that.

By now she might be on her own and he could take his chances. If he walked away without Jefferson's papers then so be it, but the mystery surrounding Goodfellow still intrigued him. Both India and her mother would want to know the truth. Added to that, India deserved to know why he'd refused to let her use Jefferson over her mares—interbreeding at its worst.

Lost in his thoughts he found himself beneath the fig trees. The sun had set and in the pale twilight the rock the Kilhamptons believed marked Goodfellow's resting place glinted. He squatted and ran his hands over the granite boulder and studied the flat patch of undisturbed grass upon which it rested. The cold, hard surface told him nothing and he sat with his back against the stone, staring out over the lagoon.

The moon rose and the wind dropped so an eerie stillness settled over the house. What secrets it held!

'He's not there.'

He jumped to his feet and spun around. Laila Kilhampton stood gazing down at the rock, the pale moonlight giving her skin an ethereal glow. He shivered, unsure if his mind was playing tricks on him. Her cool hand reached out to him, confirming her existence.

'Mrs Kilhampton.'

'Come sit with me. It is not a place to be alone.'

He followed her to the stone bench between the trees and sat down next to her.

'He's not here and I can't find him. I've looked. I look every day.'

Jim's mind spun. What did you say to a woman who had not accepted the death of her child? If he mentioned the boy by name she may become agitated again. Right now she appeared calm and benign; he might be able to coax her back to her room.

'I hoped you'd found him,' she said.

'I'd found him?'

'When you came here. I thought you'd brought him home.'

Jim cast his mind back to the day he'd arrived. She'd said nothing before to indicate she thought he'd found her child.

'Your secret is safe with me, Thomas Cobb. It always has been. Remember, we had an understanding.' Her cool hand rested on his arm sending his mind spiralling out of control.

'Alexander isn't aware. I understand. No-one, least of all you, could have put a gun to his head.' She twirled the chain she wore around her neck.

Put a gun to his head? She imagined his father had killed her child? No wonder they were bundled off the property so fast. Why in God's name had Kilhampton done nothing about it?

'He's a magnificent animal.'

Jim dropped his head into his hands and let out a long shuddering breath. It wasn't her son she was talking about. It was Goodfellow. The implication took a moment to sink in. She'd mistaken Jefferson for Goodfellow. If he could convince her Goodfellow wasn't dead she'd understand that he sired Jefferson. The proof he needed. The papers. How to delve deeper without upsetting her? He took a gamble.

'He is a magnificent animal,' he agreed, forcing a calm tone into his voice.

'I'm so pleased you have brought him home, Thomas. Home where he belongs.'

'I am not Thomas Cobb, Mrs Kilhampton. I am Jim, James Cobb, his son.' There, he'd said it. Holding his breath, he waited for her response.

She tipped her head to one side and raised a hand to his cheek. 'Of course you are. Thomas would be much older now. We're all much older now.' Her hand fell back into her lap and she studied the granite boulder. 'Then Goodfellow is much older. It wasn't Goodfellow I rode?'

He shook his head and smiled. She appeared to understand his words, but still the fear he might upset her held him back. 'You rode Jefferson, my horse. Goodfellow is his sire.'

'Oh!' Her hand covered her mouth. 'I did it again. I took your horse. I should never have taken Goodfellow. Is your horse injured?'

'No, Jefferson is fine. Remember, India and I found you and brought you home.'

She nodded, then a pensive look crossed her face. 'I wish India was here, now. She would understand.'

'Shall I fetch her?' He'd like to see her, too.

'She's left.'

'She's left?' Jim leapt to his feet, searching the darkened windows. No light shone from the library or from her bedroom. Mrs Kilhampton's startled cry made his mistake obvious. He'd moved too fast, upset her. A wave of panic surged through him. What if she ran away, or worse, took one of the horses again. He looked around. Where were Anya and Peggy? Did they know Mrs Kilhampton had left her room? Even Violet would be a help.

Her hands covered her face and her shoulders shook as he sank beside her once more. He wrapped an arm around her shoulder and pulled her close. The scent of dusty rose petals enveloped him, so unlike India. Where had she gone?

She dropped her head onto his shoulder and let out a trembling breath. 'She's gone to Sydney to see her father. To tell him we must sell Helligen. I don't want to leave. Oliver is here.' She lifted her head. 'See. We buried him there. My poor, poor baby. Alexander said Goodfellow was with him. He's not. I know he's not. Thomas couldn't shoot that horse. He loved him. He didn't tell Alexander. He was too angry, too upset. Alexander blames your father and Goodfellow for my accident.'

The keening sound reminiscent of that first day ricocheted through his ears and he held her firm. He rocked her and bit by bit her cries ceased. For a long time they sat entwined, almost like lovers, as the moon rose and bathed them in its alabaster light. After a long silence he made up his mind. 'I know where Goodfellow is.'

She lifted her head, her face streaked with tears, and pushed back her hair. 'I've been looking for so long. Where is he?'

'At Munmurra. My father took him there when we left. He's an old horse but he's well. He sired Jefferson a few years ago. That's why you mistook Jefferson for Goodfellow. They are so alike.'

A frail smile hovered around her lips at his words. 'Just like you and Thomas. You comfort me as he did. Strong and calm. Can you bring him home?'

'I can do that,' he said.

'What about Thomas? Will he come home?'

Oh God! This was the final straw. To have to tell her his father was dead. Not another death. Just when the woman was regaining her senses.

'Come, let me take you inside.' He rose and held out his hand, hoping she'd forget about his father.

She didn't. 'Thomas is dead, isn't he?'

'Yes, he is.' What else could he say? Please God don't let her ask for details. Don't expect him to tell her how he died a broken man, unable to forgive himself for the sin he'd committed.

'And that's why you came. Why you came back. To put it right. He would want that.'

How well she knew his father. 'Yes, he wanted that. He said he'd done something he wasn't proud of and I should right past wrongs …' The quaver in his voice built and the tears scuffed behind his eyes. 'I had hoped to find the deed of sale for Goodfellow so I could register Jefferson to race.'

She must have heard because she took his hand. 'Come and meet Oliver.'

The hairs on Jim's arms prickled as she led him a few paces to the right of Goodfellow's granite slab. A small Celtic cross sat facing out towards the lagoon.

'This is where Oliver rests.' She smoothed the stone with her hand. 'He was our angel. We'd waited such a long time. He was too special to stay with us.'

Lost for words Jim stood, head bowed while she kissed her hand and smoothed the stone once more. She'd always known where her baby lay.

The blow almost bent him double. She hadn't been looking for her son. India, Anya, and Peggy—they were all wrong. For all these years she had searched for Goodfellow. Goosebumps covered his skin. The time had come to bring the old horse home, back where he belonged.

'I'll fetch Goodfellow.' The rightness of it sat well in his chest and the radiant smile she bestowed on him proved he still had the ability to make at least one person in the world happy. 'Meanwhile, let me take you upstairs. Anya and Peggy will be worried.'

'Oliver and I will sleep well tonight knowing Goodfellow is coming home.'

Jim led Mrs Kilhampton through the silent house to the foot of the carved staircase.

'Good night, and thank you.' She rested her pale hand on the banister. 'You are a good man, and I'd expect nothing less from Thomas's son.' With a nod she drifted up the stairs.

Once her bedroom door clicked shut he left the house. A light shone under the kitchen door and he knocked. 'Peggy?'

Receiving no response he pushed the door open.

Peggy sat at the kitchen table, a pot of tea in front of her and her legs stretched out towards the range. 'What do you want?'

'To talk.'

'It's not me you owe an explanation to.'

'I'm not going to explain anything to you. What I have to say is for India's ears. Where is she?'

Peggy wrinkled her nose. 'Not much of your business really.'

'It's a lot of my business. How's she getting to Sydney?' Jim screwed up his eyes. Mrs Kilhampton was right. India had left. He'd feared as much. 'When did she leave?'

'A while back.'

'And you and Anya have been discussing the matter ever since, which would account for the fact I found Mrs Kilhampton wandering around outside in the dark again.'

Peggy dragged herself out of the chair. 'Anya went back upstairs a good half hour ago.' Her face flushed at his criticism. 'Where is she this time?'

'I saw Mrs Kilhampton back to her room. Now, where's India, and how is she planning to get to Sydney?'

Peggy looked him up and down and her eyes narrowed. 'She's ridden to Morpeth. Getting the morning steamer to Sydney.'

'Thanks,' Jim said as he spun on his heel and left Peggy to her pot of cold tea.

Nineteen

The ostler accepted the pound note India held out with gleaming eyes.

'I expect to be back within the week and I will want some change, plenty of change. In the meantime, and in case I am longer than I intend, this should cover the expenses.'

The man tugged his forelock. 'First class accommodation. Don't you worry. Your horse will be fine, Miss Kilhampton. Give my regards to your father.'

With her small carpetbag grasped in her hand she made her way through the courtyard in search of a room. This time tomorrow she'd be in Sydney. The prospect didn't fill her with any great sense of excitement or achievement, more resignation than anything else. Payment for her foolishness. Swept away by the charms of a man she didn't even know. Taken for a fool. She deserved everything she got. If nothing else she had proved one thing. Her mother may have been capable of running Helligen but she was not.

A young girl dressed in a mob-cap and pristine white apron greeted her as she entered the inn. 'Ma'am.' The girl bobbed a curtsy. 'May I help you?'

'I'd like a room for the night and I wish to purchase a ticket for the steamer to Sydney tomorrow morning.'

'I'll just get Mrs Jones. Will your husband be along soon with your baggage?' The girl cast a sideways glance at the small carpet-bag in her hand.

India gritted her teeth. 'No. I'm travelling alone.' Even the little maid thought she needed a husband. Like Violet she'd think her insane to reject a life in Sydney with the likes of Cecil Bryce in preference to a property, a herd of horses and a dream.

It took an eternity for the older woman to appear.

She too bobbed a curtsy almost as ingratiating as the ostler's forelock-tugging. 'Ah, Miss Kilhampton.' The maid received a heavy cuff across her broad backside. 'This is Miss Kilhampton, Jane. She'll be going to Sydney to meet her father and her lovely husband-to-be.' She dropped her voice and with a conspiratorial wink asked, 'How *is* Mr Bryce, and your father?'

'Very well. Have you a room?' she asked, unable to keep the shrewish note from her voice.

'Of course, of course.' The woman bustled behind the counter and produced a large key with intricate swirls and a pink ribbon. 'Show Miss Kilhampton to the front room, Jane, and hurry up about it.'

Walking up the stairs was a nightmare; her feet dragged, her head ached and she couldn't summon an ounce of enthusiasm. What she wouldn't give to be back at Helligen. Tossing the notion aside she lifted her chin. Confess her sins, sort out the blasted mess, and with any luck she'd be allowed to return home.

After a disturbed night plagued by thoughts of Jim and the chaos she'd created, India struggled out of bed and peered across the dusty street to the wharf. The first streaks of dawn lit the hills beyond the town and the steamer sat puffing and smoking ready for the journey to Sydney. The accustomed sight of the busy wharf soothed her, boats coming and going, unloading their cargo and taking more on. She dressed and made her way through the inn to the wharf.

Passengers lined up to present their tickets at the *Waratah's* gangplank. The journey took close to six hours with a stop in Newcastle for breakfast before the trip down the coast. Familiar with the rancid smell below decks India opted to sit and wait until the majority of the passengers embarked, and then she'd travel up in the fresh air on deck, as far away as she could get from the sickening fug and the crush of people.

Lost in her thoughts it took a loud yell from the man standing at the gangplank to rouse her attention. A red-faced official manhandled a fellow off the ship amid much whistle-blowing and huffing and puffing. Nothing like this had ever happened before and she'd made the trip so many times. She stood to get a better view. The offender hurtled onto the wharf and thumped against the wall before sliding to the ground and landing on his backside with a resounding thump. She peered down. 'Jim!'

He pushed his hair back from his face and threw her a wry grin. 'If I'd known you hadn't gone aboard I could have saved myself a lot of discomfort.' He rubbed at the seat of his trousers as he stood.

'What are you doing here?' Was he going to plead his case, ask her not to tell her father? Perhaps, heaven forbid, he was going to use her foolish, foolish lapse against her. Threaten to tell the world of her wanton ways. Tell them how he'd duped her. How she'd fallen without a second thought for his winning ways and his flashing smile. The heat rose to her face as she remembered his hands on her body and how she'd begged for his attentions.

'Your mother didn't tell me you'd left until late last night.'

'Mama?' What had he told Mama? Why had he spoken with her?

He nodded. 'It's a long story. I need to speak to you.' His face was drawn with tiredness and dark circles underscored his eyes.

She blinked slowly, resisting the temptation to fall straight into his arms and beg him to take her home. The very reaction that had her in this awful mess in the first place. The prospect of talking to Jim, even sitting next to him, terrified her and weakened her resolve. She sucked in a deep breath and sank onto the bench. 'I have about ten minutes before I leave, though I'm not sure you can tell me anything I don't know.' She already knew how gullible she was, how she'd fallen for his lies. How he wasn't who he said he was. That was all that mattered.

When Jim sat down beside her the warmth of his body through his dusty moleskins seeped into her skin. She shuffled along the bench to keep a safe distance between them and concentrated on the mundane parade of people lining the wharf. There were a lot of people around them, saying goodbye, greeting friends, family, and lovers.

He laid his arm along the back of the seat and turned to face her. 'You're angry.' His low, intimate voice wheedled its way to her heart. 'I don't want you to marry Cecil Bryce. I don't believe Violet when she says you're in love with him.'

'And I don't believe you, Jim, or anything you say. You lied to me.' She hadn't lied to him. He had lied to her. She must keep that at the forefront of her mind.

'I'm not Jim Mawgan. My name is James Cobb.' He ran his hands over his eyes before scrubbing at his face.

So, he'd admitted it. For a moment she wanted nothing more than to clasp his warm hand. Tell him she didn't care who he was, where he came from or where he was going, as long as he stayed. Why couldn't he have told her from the very beginning? It was outrageous. How could she still see this man as attractive when he threatened everything she held dear? It wasn't only her heart at stake. It was her family. She mustn't think of herself. No matter what her body told her, the strange little bumps and swirls in her belly, Mama, her family and Helligen came first. She let out a long drawn-out sigh. 'If I'd known who you were from the beginning I would never have let you set foot on the property.'

'I'm aware of that. It's why I had to lie to you.'

'Had to lie? No-one *has* to lie.' Had he lied to her when he took her down to the river, cradled her against him? She crossed her arms and pulled the jacket of her travelling suit tight across her chest. She'd seen him as a hero, her saviour, and a chivalrous man of honour. What a fool she was.

He had the grace to hang his head. A damp lock of hair behind his ear covered his scar and her fingers still itched to explore it. *Cobb boy, seventeen stitches.* Would she never learn?

'Tell me to go and I will.' His voice was gentle, almost tender.

She couldn't do it. Until she spoke to Papa they had unfinished business. 'You may stay at Helligen until I return. I'll be back in a day or two.' Of that she was certain. Papa would jump up and down, carry on, then send her back. He'd insist the house was closed and her mother and Anya dragged back to Sydney. The only person to benefit was Violet. The prospect was too dreadful to even contemplate and there was no alternative.

With a rough, rasping sound he cleared his throat.

What was he going to say? That it was all a stupid prank, or worse—goodbye? 'I don't want to hear any more. I need to discuss the matter with Papa.' He would flay her alive when she told him who she'd employed. She had no intention of telling him she might have fallen in love with the man, no intention of telling anyone, ever.

Jim didn't reply. Despite the surrounding hullabaloo they could be sitting isolated on the old wharf at Helligen—but for the swirling fog of emotion. She didn't know what to say to him to explain how disappointed she was and how much he'd hurt her. Shattered was closer to the truth.

The steamer sounded a loud whistle from its stack pipe, saving her from herself, and she made her decision. His eyes had lost their golden sparkle and his whole body was encased in an aura of anguish and dismay. Why hadn't he told her the truth? Why was it so important for him to be at Helligen? Too many unanswered questions. Too much for her to deal with. Too many people's happiness at stake.

She gave Jim one last, long look. The whistle sounded again and she stood up, smoothing the immaculate skirt of her travelling suit. 'I have to go, Jim. We'll discuss this further when I return, after I have spoken to Papa.' *If you're still there and if he doesn't chase you off the property with a loaded shotgun.*

He stood next to her and placed his hand on her arm. She stared at his lean brown fingers, wanting to grasp them tightly and bring them to her lips.

'This has nothing to do with you and me, but everything to do with the past and our families,' he said.

How she wished she could believe him. But for her family, for the past, she might indulge her fantasies, forget that he'd lied to her and run away with him, and never return.

'My responsibility is to my family.' She shook her head. 'I must go.' She shrugged off his hand and picked up her carpetbag. 'Goodbye.'

Her muscles cramped as she walked the few feet to the gangplank and when she stepped up her ankle twisted. He was there, reaching for her elbow, holding her fast and keeping her safe. Once she established her balance he gave her elbow the tiniest squeeze as if to encourage her, then dropped his hand. She walked aboard unable to look back.

About twenty people sat crammed on the long bench seats.

'The ladies' cabin's aft.' One of the crew indicated through to a door at the far end of the cabin. The fetid air seeped through to coil and swirl around her.

She shook her head and clamped her lips together to control the rush of nausea. Instead she made her way to the centre of the deck where the engine formed part of a platform connecting the two paddle boxes. Dropping her bag she cast a quick look over her shoulder and searched the wharf.

He had gone.

She sank onto the pile of crates stacked against the engine house and forced her concentration to the far bank of the river. She wouldn't look back again, didn't want to know if he waited on the wharf, and didn't dare to hope.

The town clock chimed five and despite her first class ticket she chose to stay on the open deck, relishing the harsh reality of the wind and the cold dawn air.

The sun was high as the steamer made its way through the Heads and into Sydney Harbour. As much as India preferred to take the Great North Road and ride, in an emergency this was a far quicker and easier route to Sydney. Within an hour she'd be in the opulent offices of Kilhampton & Bryce at the Quay. A far cry from the wide open spaces of Helligen. Now she'd arrived the idea of sharing her responsibilities and concerns with her father comforted her. Even Cecil might be a help. Peggy did her best but it wasn't her place. And Violet—well—she let out a puff of breath in competition with the smoke stack. Seeing Violet happy would be the only good thing to come out of this whole mess.

Relying on the familiar routine she disembarked, shunning the attention of the barrow boys and drivers waiting at the wharf.

She sidestepped the puddles and stacked cargoes and entered the imposing three-storey brick buildings flanking Circular Quay. As she walked through the bustling offices faces turned and followed her passage between the multitude of desks. When she reached the polished timber door bearing a brass plaque announcing Kilhampton & Bryce, she knocked.

'Enter.'

Swallowing the lump of disappointment in her throat she turned the handle. If only it was Papa's voice. It would be so much easier to confess her foolishness to him alone.

'India, my dear. What a delightful surprise.' Cecil crossed the room and took her hand between his and squeezed, forcing her fingers into a tight bundle. 'Come in, sit down. This is quite unexpected. Is Alexander expecting you?'

'No, I have just disembarked. I took the *Waratah* from Morpeth this morning.'

'You must be exhausted. Let me call for some tea, or would you prefer coffee?'

'Tea would be lovely, thank you.'

While Cecil bustled out calling to his assistant, India arranged her skirts and sat studying the paintings on the walls in an attempt to take her mind off her problems. Clippers racing across the ocean, their sails billowing in the wind, waves whipping their bows; despite the intrinsic beauty of the scenes she'd replace them with the rolling paddocks and the lagoon at home in an instant. She removed her gloves and studied her work-worn hands. What would Jim do? Return to Helligen and stay until she arrived, or leave before he had to confront Papa? As much as she knew she should put Jim behind her she couldn't let go. He drew her like a dusty moth seeking light.

'Some tea shortly. I've sent a boy to fetch your father. He arrived back yesterday, but he's still aboard *The Cloud*.'

India dropped her hands into her lap. 'I didn't know he was away.'

'He was planning to return to Helligen tomorrow, but a few problems with Customs House over our latest shipment of silk from China have delayed him.'

India didn't know whether to be pleased or angry. If she'd known he was about to come home she wouldn't have rushed to Sydney. However, it wasn't just Papa she'd come to see, it was also Cecil. Once and for all she would quell the absurd notion that she should marry him. He was nothing to her, and it was unfair to him to let him believe that once she'd stretched her wings and had her chance she would settle into life as a Sydney matron. Besides, the man who had played her for a fool had stolen her heart.

He pulled his chair a little closer and leant towards her. 'I am so delighted to see you.' Wrinkles fanned out from his eyes as he gave a benign smile. 'You must stay in town for a while. I want to show you off.' He reached out for her hand and she buried it in the pocket of her skirt, and then removed it, regretting her reaction.

'How is the lovely Violet?'

'Violet is very well. She'd prefer to be in Sydney though. I asked her to stay at home and keep an eye on things.'

'Ah, yes.' Cecil gave a knowing nod. 'Your mother. Poor dear, is she any better?'

India brightened and sat up, pleased the conversation had turned from Cecil's patent admiration. 'I think Mama is a little better. She appears to be taking more interest in the world outside her room.' Just how much interest and why, she wouldn't share. Explaining to Papa that Jim's appearance had sparked a very definite improvement in Mama's demeanour would be hard enough. Her shoulders dropped.

'My dear, you must be so tired after that horrid journey on that smoky little steam kettle. Your father will be along shortly and you are most welcome to stay with us at Potts Point. Mother would be thrilled to have your company.'

India stifled her gasp of dismay with a yawn. Tea parties on the lawn, visits to the dressmaker, mindless conversation and preening girls intent only on snagging the richest husband they could find. She should have allowed Violet to come after all.

With a bang the door swung open to reveal her father, tanned and strong, dressed in breeches and sea boots and one of the soft cotton shirts he favoured.

'India! What are you doing here?' He swung his arms wide and she collapsed into his embrace, his familiar scent of sandalwood, salt and fresh air wrapped around her and sheltered her. She rested her cheek against his shirt and closed her eyes in no doubt that she had made the right decision. His wisdom and strength would help resolve the massive mess she'd created.

'Is everything all right? Your mother?'

Determined not to cry she pulled back and nodded up at him. His weathered face crinkled into a smile and he dropped a kiss on the top of her head. 'So what brings you to Sydney? I was looking forward to seeing you, although I expected to wait until I got to Helligen.'

'I need to talk to you.'

'Here's your tea, my dear.' Cecil fussed over a fine bone china teapot on the round side table. 'The best imported variety courtesy of Kilhampton & Bryce, Purveyor of Fine Goods.' He gave a throaty chuckle and poured a cup.

Papa winked and led her back to the chair.

'You drink your tea. I'll be back in a moment and I'll take you to the ship. I've had some improvements done and my cabin is really quite luxurious. A far cry from the old days.'

'India will be staying with Mother and myself, at Potts Point. We've already discussed the matter.' Cecil's florid cheeks darkened a shade. 'She will be well chaperoned.'

In reply Alexander Kilhampton raised his untamed eyebrows. 'India, where would you like to stay?'

She shrugged her shoulders and sipped her tea, revelling in the luxury of leaving the decision making to someone else.

'In that case, why don't we go to *The Cloud* now and you can have a look around and tell me all your news. Cecil, we may avail ourselves of your generous offer later in the evening.'

Cecil grunted and pulled his pocket watch from his waistcoat. 'It's getting late. Mother will want to inform the servants.'

The sheer pleasure of handing over responsibility to Papa threatened to swamp her. She sipped her tea and leant back in the chair.

'In that case we won't inconvenience you. I'm sure India will be more than comfortable aboard ship tonight, otherwise we will take rooms at The Royal.'

With a grunt Cecil stuffed his watch back in his pocket. 'Tomorrow, perhaps. I do have an important meeting later this evening with members of the assembly. If you'll excuse me, Alexander, Miss India.' As he took her hand and bowed over it his moustache tickled the skin of the back of her hand. She had to make certain Papa understood she could no more marry Cecil Bryce than she could give away her life at Helligen.

Once Cecil departed India wiped her hand on her skirt and picked up her teacup.

'Drink up.' Papa smiled. 'I can't wait to show you the improvements.'

Twenty

Halfway between Morpeth and Helligen Jim veered off the track and followed a wallaby trail in the direction of the Hunter River. He yawned as Jefferson ambled along the narrow path. After his madcap ride to Morpeth the previous night he was in no hurry to return to Helligen, although he couldn't shake his feelings of responsibility for Mrs Kilhampton. Strangely, he relished the prospect of discussing Goodfellow with Kilhampton when he returned from Sydney, but he'd be no use to anyone if he collapsed from exhaustion.

Ahead the river drifted wide and lazy through the cleared river flats and he headed for a stand of trees in the distance. Both he and Jefferson needed a drink and an hour's rest should see them on their way refreshed.

Under the shade of a sprawling gum tree he dismounted and unsaddled Jefferson. Together they made for the riverbank. He crouched and cupped his hands, sinking them into the cool water before splashing his face and drinking his fill. Jefferson, free of his saddle and bridle, performed his usual snorting and snuffling antics in the shallow water.

Jim left him to it, moved up the bank and lay back, one arm folded behind his head, staring up at a solitary white cloud drifting above the hills. Munmurra lay about thirty miles to the west. It would be so easy to return and put the last weeks behind him, admit he'd been chasing rainbows and that his dream of owning a stud of his own one day was as likely as finding a pot of gold.

He rolled over onto his stomach, his gaze following the hills in the distance until he picked out the tree line behind Helligen, a little closer to the northwest. The smell of the river and the warmth of the sun brought back the memory of the press of India's body when they rode together, the touch of her lips when he'd kissed her. Every time he saw her he wanted to reach out to her, reassure her. Behind her determination and courage he could see the grief etched into her soul, as though she held herself responsible for her family's despair.

He stretched his back, ignoring the stab of guilt. There was no escaping the fact he'd used India as a pawn in his search. If Kilhampton had been at Helligen the likelihood of his ruse being accepted would have been far less. He was a dead ringer for his father—it was simple luck no-one on the property recognised him earlier. His subterfuge left a sour taste in his mouth; lying didn't sit comfortably with him and now he'd left it too late.

His promise to Mrs Kilhampton niggled at his mind. He intended to honour it and one day soon take Goodfellow back to Helligen. It was a fitting end to his foolish quest. Without the deed of sale his father could be branded a horse thief. It must have weighed on his mind otherwise he wouldn't have asked him to set the record straight.

The horse, despite his age, was quite capable of making the trip. Besides, he had more questions to ask Mrs Kilhampton about his father, and when India returned with her father he had every intention of demanding answers. Whether they'd answer them was another matter, but there was more to the story of Goodfellow and Helligen. India had accused him of lying—what had the Kilhamptons been doing, for goodness sake?

Jefferson stuck his wet nose into his hair and snorted until Jim rolled over. He scratched him behind the ears. The perfect stallion he'd reared from a foal. Such conformation, such stamina, and now he'd never have the opportunity to see him race. It was a bloody good job his father had taken Goodfellow away instead of allowing the trigger-happy fool to wreak his vengeance on the poor animal, otherwise Jefferson wouldn't exist.

Someone had to know the whole story. The horse snorted and tossed his head in the direction of the hills, to the west where the sun was beginning its descent.

'No, we're not going to Munmurra, not just yet.'

Jefferson whinnied and ambled off along the riverbank. After about twenty paces he stopped and looked back, then kicked up his heels and took off down the track.

Cursing, Jim leapt up and sprinted after him. Something must have spooked the animal. As he rounded the bend in the river he found Jefferson waiting under the shade of a tree eyeing him.

'What's your problem?'

The horse gave him a long, considered look and turned his head once more to the west.

'I told you we'll go soon. When India returns we'll get Goodfellow and take him home.'

Jefferson shook his head and snorted, unimpressed by the response he'd received.

'We can't …' Why the hell couldn't they? Returning to Helligen via Munmurra would mean an extra day. No more. Then, when India got back she'd see Goodfellow with her own eyes and understand the reason for his subterfuge. At worst, Kilhampton would order him off the property. Tell him to pack his bags. That was going to happen anyway. At best, India would understand. And Mrs Kilhampton would be happy.

Jim looked the stallion in the eye. 'Stay there.' He ran back to collect his saddle from under the tree.

Once astride Jefferson and heading west a weight lifted from his shoulders, replaced by a calm certainty. He'd be back at Helligen by tomorrow evening with Goodfellow. It was where the animal belonged and at last his father would rest easy. Mrs Kilhampton would no doubt be overjoyed to see the horse and when India returned … when India returned he would put everything straight.

Twenty-One

India leant back against the bulkhead and pulled her knees up to her chin, hugging her shawl around her shoulders to protect herself from the stiff breeze whipping across the harbour. The rock and sway of the ship reminded her of a simpler time, a time before heartbreak and disappointment stalked the Kilhamptons. She was born aboard *The Cloud* and took her first steps on the rough timber of the decks. The carefree life of freedom and adventure was one Papa still relished.

'It's wonderful to have you in Sydney again. You can't imagine how I miss you and your sister.' His pose was so familiar. Erect, hands behind his back and his legs braced against whatever the ocean might throw at him. His large, strong hands rested on the smooth wheel, his eyes scanning the waterways. Even though they were at anchor his senses were alert to the slightest movement. Perhaps Papa didn't belong at Helligen, maybe her dreams were misplaced. He appeared so at ease captaining his ship.

'Why did you buy Helligen? Why didn't Mama stay aboard with you or live here in Sydney while you were at sea?'

He turned with a quizzical expression on his face, his lips twisting in a half smile as though he found pleasure in the memory. 'It was an old dream, forged long ago. We both wanted more than we'd had for our children, you and Violet, and life aboard a ship, no matter how beautiful …' His voice trailed off as he cast his eyes up the tall, straight mast to the immaculate furled sails. '*The Cloud* is not the life for a family.'

'But nor was Helligen.'

'Helligen was everything we dreamt it would be and when Oliver was born …'

The memory of the words in his journal knifed through her mind.

He swallowed his grief. 'We had everything.'

'Until Mama's accident and Oliver's death.' Speaking failed to alleviate the tightness in her throat. She had to shoulder some of the blame. She clutched her arms tighter around her body and swayed with the motion of the ship.

He nodded. 'Your mother's accident should never have occurred.' Papa's jaw tightened. In the past the conversation ended here. They had never discussed Oliver's death or the events that led up to Mama's accident.

'Tell me again what happened.' India embarked on forbidden territory, the subject taboo as far back as she could remember. Now there was more at stake and perhaps she was selfish, but if she had to give up Jim for her family she had a right to understand the reason.

He grunted. 'You've heard it all before. Your mother fell in love with that wretched stallion. She was determined to ride him, breed from him. She and the Cobb fellow hatched some foolish plan. They were going to breed the finest racehorse in the world.' He swung the wheel, his face etched with pain. 'From the moment she set eyes on Goodfellow she was besotted.' He turned from her, his shirt taut across his broad shoulders as he stared over the water.

Her dream was no different to Mama's. She wanted to breed the finest racehorse, too. She wanted to plead with him, beg him to continue. 'Papa?'

After an uncomfortable silence he twisted and faced her once more. The look in his eyes sent a stab of guilt through her. 'She spent all her time out in the paddocks, riding, working with that wretched man. That's what caused the string of miscarriages. Damn it! I wanted, we both wanted, a son. The doctors said the only way was for your mother to spend her time confined to the house, no riding, a life of calm and peace. I returned home and managed to convince her she should leave the place to Cobb and the band of labourers we had on hand. Wait until after she had given birth. She did. And Oliver was born. The culmination of all our dreams.'

Papa's jaw tightened and he compressed his lips. The agony in his face made her heart bleed. She stood up and moved closer to him, but he held up his hand, stilling her.

He swallowed and continued. 'The doctors recommended light exercise, a short walk every day, and they promised she would recover her strength. Then five weeks, just five weeks after Oliver's birth, Cobb lured her back out and almost killed her! He had my strict instruction she wasn't even to be in the stables.'

Raw anger, untempered by time, boiled to the surface. The colour rose to his face and he slammed his fist against the bulkhead. What hope had she of convincing him Cobb's son belonged at Helligen, that he was the man for the job?

'He didn't even accompany her. Just let her go.'

A picture of Mama only a few days ago flashed before her eyes—astride Jefferson, bareback, wheeling to a halt on the narrow bush track as competent as any stockman.

'When I discovered she'd gone we sent out search parties. Cobb had the audacity to pretend he had no knowledge of the incident.

She couldn't have even mounted the animal without assistance. He stood seventeen hands! A man's horse. A stallion.'

Mama was far from an incapable or novice rider. She'd managed to mount Jefferson without any help only the other day. Did Papa have no knowledge of his wife's capabilities? India studied his face, weighing up the possibility of continuing the conversation. It was as though there was something just inches from her, something slippery that she couldn't quite grasp.

'When you found her …'

'Cobb found her. Is it essential we go down this track, India? I don't see what bearing it has on matters today. The past is just that—past. Leave it where it belongs.'

India's temper flared. It might be the past but it still affected her every waking moment, her whole existence. She had too much to lose and a debt to pay. This time she wasn't prepared to give up without a fight.

'It's not in the past, Papa. Violet, Mama, you and I—we all live in the shadow of this every day. I want to understand.'

'There must be a reason for this sudden interest.' He turned and fixed her with a stare, the same stare that halted her in her tracks as a child. 'Well? Is there something wrong with your mother?'

'No, there's nothing wrong with Mama. In fact, she seems better, brighter. The renewed activity, the prospect of new foals and …'

'And?'

Colour flooded her face. 'The new man I employed has a stallion and she's captivated.'

'Captivated? By the man or his stallion?'

India puffed her cheeks then let out a long slow stream of air, trying to dissipate the heat in her face. It wasn't her mother who was captivated by the man, far from it.

'I think you'd better tell me the whole story.'

'So do I. Will you listen and not lose your temper?'

'I don't like the sound of this. I can't promise I won't be angry. I will, however, listen until the end.'

India sucked in a breath. 'I put an advertisement for a stud master in *The Maitland Mercury* in your name.' Without giving Papa the opportunity to interrupt India took a quick breath and continued. 'Jim Mawgan arrived. He seemed perfect for the job and I employed him. He's strong and capable, has a way with horses and a great understanding of my … our needs.'

'You sound like your mother.' There it was again, the oblique reference to something more than she'd expected. She raised an eyebrow and he closed his mouth, lips pursed.

'Everything went well. That's when Mama began to take an interest. She watched all the activity from her window.' India swallowed back the whole truth about her mother's nightly sojourn; she'd get to that later. While she had Papa's attention it was better to move on and leave out the finer details. 'It turned out Jim Mawgan, as he'd introduced himself, was in fact James Cobb, the son …'

All sound disappeared, no splashing of waves against the ship, no screeching of gulls, just a solid and agonising void. A shadow fell across Papa's face, a mixture of pain and loathing that quickly turned to downright anger.

His bushy eyebrows shot together and a deep frown creased his forehead. 'I know who he is,' he spat through gritted teeth.

She ploughed on regardless. 'You told me I had a year. A year to make this work until I had to consider marriage.'

'I didn't expect you to advertise for a marriage partner.'

'I didn't.' She slammed her hands down on the deck and jumped to her feet facing him. 'Why do you think I'm interested in the man for anything other than his capabilities?' Who was the liar now? 'You promised you'd listen.' The plaintive note in her voice made her cringe.

'I'm not having him on Helligen. I will not have any member of that family anywhere near my property or my family. They as good as destroyed us. Cobb's last act was to put a bullet through my stallion's head. It was a fitting end. I only wish he'd turned the gun on himself.'

'You don't understand. Jim is not his father. Thomas Cobb is dead. You can't blame the sins of the father on the son. It says so in the bible. His son is a charming, capable young man with a great knowledge of horses. He has the most beautiful stallion of his own, so like Goodfellow. I would like to use him for some of our mares. I'm sure he'd throw buckskins.'

'And he has you wrapped around his little finger, just like your mother.'

'No, he does not have me *wrapped around his little finger.* I believe he's the best man for the job.' And the only man she'd ever wanted.

'He is not, and neither was his father. I will not live through this again. Thomas Cobb ruined our family, destroyed my wife, your mother. I will not have his son doing the same to you. Don't you understand there's more at stake than your infatuation with this man and his horse? If you say you want to take responsibility and manage Helligen then you must understand what that entails. An entire community is reliant on your success. If you're not up to the job then the property must be sold. Either get the man off Helligen or I will.'

'You promised me a year and I'm not prepared to let him go. He *is* the best man for the job. Regardless of whose son he may or may not be, I want him at Helligen.' There, she'd said it. Forget Jim's lies, his ulterior motives, she wanted him at Helligen and she wanted more time to explore the strange connection they had.

'Then you have a further decision to make. Your family, or the family who destroyed all I held dear. We return to Helligen as soon as possible.'

Twenty-Two

Jim opened the wooden gate and ran his fingers over the carved words—*Helligen Stud.* He led the two horses through and shut it firmly behind him. This was his final opportunity and he would make good his promise to his father. He would right past wrongs. Return Goodfellow to his lawful owners and move on. The old horse raised his head and breathed the air. Jim's heart lifted. Helligen was in his blood and he suspected in Goodfellow's, too. He kicked up his heels as if to urge Jefferson on and tell him fresh water and a biscuit of lucerne waited just around the corner.

'Hey, Mr Cobb, sir. We've been wondering when you'd be back—' Fred's eyebrows disappeared into the shock of hair hanging over his forehead and he let out a low whistle. 'Who's that?'

'Goodfellow. Jefferson's sire. I told you—Jim. Cut the Cobb and the sir bit.'

'Yes sir, Jim.' Fred walked around the back of the two horses, an appraising grin on his face. 'That's what I call a horse. And he throws true. No doubt he's Jefferson's sire. The missus was right.'

Jim grunted. Now he'd arrived the wisdom of his idea rankled. Supposing Mrs Kilhampton became upset when she saw

Goodfellow. Maybe the truth was more than she could bear. She might collapse into a decline. Then India would never forgive him. His stomach churned and he pulled the horses up sharp before he rounded the corner of the barn.

'Let's put them in the barn, Fred, not the stables. I don't want them near the other animals yet. They'll need a good feed. It's been a long trip for the old boy.'

'Doesn't look as though he's suffered much to me.' Fred opened the wide double doors.

The light streamed in through the gabled windows illuminating the timber interior.

Jim glanced around and inhaled. 'The barn's looking good, Fred. Been keeping on top of things?' He handed Goodfellow's reins to the boy.

'Thought you might promise me another ride.' He threw a wink.

Cheeky bugger. 'We'll see. There might be a few people lining up before you.'

'I'll give them both a rub down. Peggy's in the kitchen. Better go tell her you're here otherwise you'll miss out on your tucker.'

Jim's feet dragged as he made his way across the courtyard. Without India the place had lost its sparkle, or perhaps his mood had something to do with it. The problem was when and how to tell Mrs Kilhampton that Goodfellow was back. With Fred and Peggy's big mouths it wouldn't stay a secret for long. He pushed the door to the kitchen wide, unsure of the reception he'd receive.

When Peggy turned around to see who dared cross into her territory her face broke into a welcoming smile. 'You're back. About time too. Mrs Kilhampton's asking after you.'

Jim pulled off his hat and scratched at the road dirt on his face. 'I thought I'd get a mouthful when I got back here.'

'You might have done except she's been busy telling us what a wonderful man you are. Want a cuppa?' She turned the teapot three times and poured him a cup. 'And how you're going to lay all the ghosts to rest.'

'And which ghosts would those be?' Jim asked as he stirred sugar into his tea.

'Mrs Kilhampton's ghosts. The ghosts of the past. Helligen's ghosts. They're one and the same.' She shrugged her ample shoulders and pulled a large baking tray from the oven. The meat hissed and sizzled and the smell of roasted beef filled the kitchen making Jim's mouth water. 'Wait until after dinner. Go and see her then. Have you brought the horse back?'

'What horse?'

'Goodfellow, of course. When you didn't turn up yesterday Mrs K told Anya that's where you'd be.'

Jim nodded. 'Can't keep much a secret around here, can I?' A weight lifted from his shoulders. It was good to be himself again and not some trumped-up imaginary character. There would be no more secrets. 'I'll go and get washed up.'

'Eat in here. We need the company.'

Jim threw her a grin. 'I'd like that. Rattling around in that cottage on my own was beginning to make me feel like the Ghost of Christmas Past.'

'Christmas isn't far off. Got a few bits and pieces to sort out before then. Haven't even started my Christmas cake yet. Off you go. Won't be long.'

Jim ran his fingers over the date engraved on the lintel, just for luck, and pushed open the door to the cottage. Home. The thought caught him by surprise. This would always be the home of his heart, whether or not he could stay. The sooner India returned the sooner he could lay all his cards on the table.

The pump performed its usual antics and he kicked it until it spluttered and delivered. With the road washed off and a clean shirt he headed back to the kitchen relishing the prospect of Peggy's beef. On the way he stuck his head around the corner of the barn and checked Goodfellow and Jefferson. Side by side in the two stalls like doppelgangers they turned to greet him, satisfied gleams flickering in their eyes.

'Stay there until tomorrow, boys, and then you can have a romp in the paddock.'

He latched the heavy doors on the barn and as he turned a bilious pink vision strutted across the grass. With a cry it lifted its skirts and flew across the yard.

'Jim! You're back. I'm so pleased to see you.'

He braced himself against Violet's effusive welcome. Would he be subjected to Violet the Flirt, or Violet the Tantrum? Neither character presented itself as she slipped her hand through his arm. 'Dinner's ready. Peggy said to come and get you.'

Somewhat taken aback by her cheerful reception Jim tucked her arm into his. 'And what's been happening while I've been away?'

'Not a lot, not a little. India's in Sydney seeing Papa. Oh! You know that, don't you?' She shot a glance at him from under her lashes and gave a little smirk. 'Mama has taken on a new lease of life. She's been telling us stories about you as a little boy.'

A snake the size of a diamond python uncurled in his belly as he waited to hear what she had to say.

'All about how you fell from the roof and split your head open and had to have it sewn back on.'

His spare hand ran through his hair, fingering the scar behind his ear. 'So long as it's not all bad.'

'She said she expected you to bring Goodfellow back and that's why you've taken so long.' Violet stopped and made to turn. 'She's so excited. Have you brought him home?'

How had Mrs Kilhampton known he'd gone to fetch Goodfellow? At the risk of being accused fanciful, it was almost as though she had some communication with the animal. As if she'd known all along he would return. No wonder she'd been so determined to find him.

'He's in the barn with Jefferson.'

'Can we go and see him?' She pulled him around in a circle.

'Not right now. They've both had a long day. I don't want to disturb them.'

'You do have him, don't you?'

'I've got him.'

'Thank goodness for that. Short of going and digging up his grave—' she gave a delicate shudder, '—I wasn't sure whether to believe Mama or not. Anya swore it was true and so did Peggy.'

'How would they know?' he asked, curiosity coiling inside him.

'Just because that's what Mama said. She's been so completely different since you and India left. It's as though she's thrown off the past. She's quite animated. She's even wearing a different dress. I can't remember the last time I saw her in anything but that billowing nightgown affair. She's, well, she's almost normal.'

The python in his belly settled as they made their way across the courtyard. At Mrs Kilhampton's bedroom window the curtains blew in the evening breeze although there was no sign of the usual hovering silhouette.

'Fred and Jilly are joining us. Anya has taken Mama's tray up and told her you're back. She wants to talk to you after dinner.' Violet dropped his arm and waited for him to push open the kitchen door. He covered a smile as he held the door back and she swept into the kitchen. He rather liked Violet this evening.

She still had all her Sydney airs and graces, but there was a little more humanity about her.

'There you are,' Peggy said, flicking her cloth as she put the last of the heated plates onto the table. 'Just in time. It's ready.'

Once he sat at the familiar scrubbed pine table Jim was truly home. He studied the diverse group. He wasn't the only person who was affected by that night so very long ago. The events had spread their tendrils far and wide. If his mother hadn't left, Peggy wouldn't be here. Violet might well have grown up and become a different person and India—what he wouldn't give to have her here beside him now! He could sense her presence in every stone and every blade of grass on Helligen. She belonged here as much as the swans on the lagoon or the goanna that stalked the river track. Her eyes reflected the clouds before rain and her hair the dappled sun as it danced on the gum leaves. How he missed her.

'With a sigh like that you sound as though you have the weight of the world on your shoulders,' Peggy said. She stabbed a large piece of roast beef with a serving fork. 'Is the food not to your liking?'

'No, it's perfect, as always. I was wondering when India would return.' He lifted a piece of Yorkshire pudding to his mouth. It smelt of home, comfort and tradition, yet it didn't fill the void in his heart.

'Who knows?' Violet said, shrugging her shoulders. 'It depends on what Papa says and what she decides to do about Cecil Bryce. She should marry him. It would make life so much easier.'

Peggy slammed down the carving knife and fork. 'Don't you start that again, miss. You know perfectly well she isn't the slightest bit interested in that fish-faced old fool. The only person who's interested in him is you—and that's only because of his money. Why don't you marry him?'

Violet smirked. 'He doesn't even know I exist and besides, he's far too old for me.'

'He's far too old for India, too.' Peggy curled her lip and then flashed Jim a meaningful look. 'What she needs is a man with plenty of energy who shares the same interests and passions as she does.'

'A man of her own class. One Papa approves of.' Violet's triumphant grin was a stark reminder of everything he was up against. How he wished he'd prevented India from getting on the steamer at Morpeth.

'There's nothing anyone can do until India gets back and that all depends on where Mr Kilhampton is. He could be in Timbuktu for all we know.' With a deliberate scrape Peggy pushed back her chair. 'And that's that. Clear the plates, Jilly. Who's for apple pie?'

With his stomach comfortably full Jim rocked back in the chair and stretched out his legs. Peggy was right. Until India returned there was nothing he could do. He'd promised he would stay, and besides, there was a chance Kilhampton would return with her. There were a few things he'd like to say to him. He owed an explanation to India, too. There was no chance Kilhampton would sign over Goodfellow, but there was an outside possibility he might be talked into signing stud papers for Jefferson.

'Thanks for the meal, Peggy.' Jim stood up. 'I want to go and check on the horses.' He tousled Fred's hair. 'You can have my extra helping of apple pie.'

'Cor, thanks, sir.'

'Jim.'

'Sir Jim,' Fred said with a cheeky grin.

Jim rewarded him with a cuff around the head.

There was no moon and Jim picked up the lantern outside the kitchen door and lit it. Inside the barn it would be pitch black and he wanted to give both of the horses a good look-over, especially Goodfellow. It had been a long day for the old boy and he hoped he wouldn't find any injuries.

The huge double doors creaked as he swung them open and stepped inside. An air of peace and calm pervaded the entire space. The elegant detailed roof trusses soared above him, creating a cathedral-like splendour. When he'd left Helligen as a boy the building was unfinished. Just a frame and a roof used for hay storage. In the intervening years it had been completed, a right and fitting place for two such magnificent animals. He lifted the lamp, illuminating the centre aisle. The stall gates threw a slatted pattern across the hard-packed dirt floor. Jefferson whickered and Jim lowered the lamp and made for the back of the barn. As he approached the stalls the sound of hushed voices wafted into the space. Goodfellow and Jefferson lifted their heads in unison and acknowledged his arrival.

He took a guess. 'Good evening, Mrs Kilhampton.'

Two heads appeared over the stall gate.

'And Anya.'

'Thank you for bringing him home to us,' Mrs Kilhampton said. 'I've known all along one day he'd return to us. I felt it here.' She lifted her pale hand to her chest. 'No-one would believe me.' Having given Goodfellow another pat she slipped out of the stall and offered her hand. 'Thank you.'

The fragile bird-like bones belied the strength in her hands, hands that could control Jefferson, and his sire. What a mass of contradictions this woman was, just like her daughter. 'It's my pleasure, he belongs here. As soon as we entered the property his ears pricked up. I couldn't slow him down. He wanted to come home.' The rightness of his words sank into the churchlike stillness.

She inclined her head in agreement. 'Perhaps now what I say will not be taken as the foolish ramblings of a hysterical female.'

Anya tutted in the background while Mrs Kilhampton's lips twisted in a sad smile. Did she believe they had treated her that way?

He sat down on the stack of hay and Anya joined him. Mrs Kilhampton hung over the gate stroking Goodfellow's muzzle and crooning to him. The old horse's eyelids closed in delight as her hands ran over his ears. 'It wasn't your fault, was it, boy. That big black snake spooked us.'

Jim turned to Anya and she covered her lips with her finger to silence him.

'You saved my life, rearing and stamping on the snake.' She turned from the stall. 'When I looked back I fell.'

'You broke your skull,' Anya said. 'We thought we had lost you.'

'I woke up and everyone had gone. Oliver, Goodfellow, Thomas. Everything had changed.' Her voice caught. 'Everything I held dear. My life was over.'

Anya moved like a shadow until she stood next to the distraught woman and could wrap her arm around her shoulder. 'Not of your making.'

'I shouldn't have taken Goodfellow without telling Thomas.'

Jim stilled, and Anya looked at him.

'I tried to explain to Alexander. He didn't understand. He thought I was distressed over Oliver. My baby died and my heart broke. But it wasn't Thomas's fault.' She turned her tortured face to him. 'Not your father's fault. I took Goodfellow out of my own accord.'

'Did Mr Kilhampton sign Goodfellow over to my father?' There! He'd asked the question he'd wanted to ask from the moment he'd seen the portrait of Goodfellow.

She shook her head, her long hair flying around her face. 'I don't think so. I don't remember.' Her hands turned palm up and she shrugged her shoulders. 'Anya?'

'Mr Kilhampton told Thomas Cobb to shoot Goodfellow and bury him under the fig trees and get off the property. Your mother left and took you and your brother and your belongings. Your father stayed to finish the job, his last task at Helligen.'

Jim's heart sank. Kilhampton hadn't given his father Goodfellow in lieu of wages. He had taken him. 'Why were you so certain Goodfellow wasn't buried under the fig trees?'

'He was a good man, Jim. He loved those horses like he loved you. They were a part of his family. He couldn't have shot Goodfellow any more than you or your brother. The horse was like a son to him.'

His father may have been a good man, but it was beginning to look as though his search for a deed of sale was nothing more than a wild goose chase. If Kilhampton hadn't given his father Goodfellow and he'd spirited him away then the answer was clear. His father had stolen the animal.

I did something I'm not proud of. Right the wrongs of the past before they shatter your dreams. The full impact of his father's words made his blood turn cold and his heart pound. By stealing Goodfellow his father had ruined any opportunity for him to fulfil his dream. He would never see Jefferson stand at stud or race because he'd never be able to produce his papers. Jefferson was the product of a mating with a stolen animal.

'Goodnight, Jim. Thank you for bringing Goodfellow home where he belongs.'

He inclined his head as the two women left the barn, the taste of bitterness thick in his mouth. He swallowed. The anger left him as quickly as it had come. There was nothing he could do. In inheriting Goodfellow he had assumed the responsibility to right past wrongs, as his father had said, or live with the consequences. He would have to face Alexander Kilhampton.

Twenty-Three

India slipped from the saddle and took in the vista before her. 'We've had rain.' She unlatched the gate and swung it open to allow her father to pass. 'I've been gone less than a week and the paddocks have greened up.'

'It doesn't take much. It's good land.'

As she remounted she cast a sideways glance at Papa. He sat relaxed in the saddle and his eyes roamed the property, missing nothing. Why he would even consider selling the place was beyond her. If he didn't want to live here, why couldn't she? Giving up and running away wasn't something she wanted to consider.

The long meandering driveway wound its way to the house, always her favourite approach. The post-and-rail fences marked the paddocks and the cattle grazed contentedly in the afternoon sun, their coats gleaming. To her right the mares wandered along the river flats but there was no sign of the stallions in the adjacent paddock. Whether Jim had continued with the services in her absence she would find out when they arrived—if he was still on the property. The thought of him leaving turned her stomach. Had he honoured his promise to stay until she returned? More than anything else she wanted to believe in him. It was six days since she'd left him on the wharf at Morpeth. Papa's business in Sydney had taken longer to conclude than either of them expected, and while he was tied up at Customs House Cecil squired her around town. If nothing else it proved one thing—a cosmopolitan life was not for her. The thought of living in Sydney left her cold. Despite Mrs Bryce's best intentions the interminable round of morning calls and tea parties drove her to distraction. The only event to prove other than inextricably boring was their trip to the Sydney races.

While still not as structured and sophisticated as the Victoria Racing Club, Randwick proved to be a worthy track. The promise of a new autumn carnival gave her hope of seeing a Helligen horse make a name—if she could convince Papa not to sell. Their few desultory discussions on the occasions they found time to dine alone were unsatisfactory. He drew the line at making any decisions until he was back, simply repeating his statement that she'd have to make a choice between her family and Jim. He was so adamant; no member of the Cobb family would set foot on the property. Fifteen years was a long time to carry a grudge against one man and his family.

'Nearly there,' she called over her shoulder, and unable to contain her impatience a moment longer she dug in her heels and galloped up the driveway.

Clattering to a standstill in the courtyard she searched for any sign of Jim. The courtyard sparkled. Rain had given new life to the daisies blooming in the old barrels. Peggy's vegetable garden sported a new trellis and her scarlet runner beans were once more restored to their former glory.

'Fred!' She led Aura over to the stables and swung the two stable doors open. She wanted Papa to be impressed with the welcome he received, the air of efficiency and prosperity. It was important he should see from the outset that she was capable of running the place, and the difference Jim's presence had made. 'Fred! Where are you?'

She tethered her horse and set off in search of him. As she rounded the corner to the kitchen she heard a high-pitched giggle and ground to a halt.

Violet straddled the fence sporting a pair of gauchos and boots, with a cabbage palm hat stuck on her blonde ringlets at a rakish angle. Jefferson stood in the middle of the yard with Fred balanced precariously, his knees high and his body bent forwards and Jim ... Jim straightened up and met her eyes.

The breath disappeared from her lungs as though she'd been thrown. He removed his hat in a salute and smiled with such pleasure she forgot everything, and ran. He reached the gate before she did and his strong arms swept her into his embrace. As he lifted her from her feet and spun her around and around the familiar scent of horses, leather and home enveloped her.

Once he'd ground to a halt and relaxed his arms he let her sink to her feet. His heart thudded in time with hers and she rested her cheek against his rough work shirt for a moment before he held her away from him.

'You're home.' His smile sparked the dimple in his cheek.

'At long last. I feel as though I was away forever.'

His eyes glittered and the corner of his mouth tweaked as if he had a special secret, and then he said, 'I want you to come and meet someone.'

As he led her through the gate into the small yard she remembered seeing Fred astride Jefferson.

'India, this is Goodfellow.'

Speechless, her mouth gaped. The huge stallion resembled Jefferson, the colour and markings identical. He stuck his nose into her hand and she fingered the grey whiskers sprouting on his muzzle. Something in her chest cramped and twisted as she ran her hand down his long neck.

How could it be Goodfellow? He lay beneath the fig trees with Oliver. *May 16th, 1850. Goodfellow: 17 hands bay stallion: black points: broken hind leg: shot …* 'Goodfellow is dead. How? Papa will be—'

'Papa will be what?'

'Papa!' Violet vaulted off the fence and barrelled into her father's arms.

Over the top of Violet's head Papa spotted Goodfellow. His jaw dropped and a frown puckered his weathered forehead. A look of confusion flashed across his face, followed by disbelief, and then his eyebrows pulled together and his mouth dropped again. He as good as tossed Violet aside and stumbled across to the fence, crumpling like an old man against the rails as he studied the horse standing amiably in the yard.

Everyone stood in a frozen tableau waiting for his response.

'Papa, I …'

He gave a shudder and with a look of pain let out a huge sigh, turned and stormed across the courtyard and into the house.

Violet grabbed India's arm, her fingers bruising her skin. 'Let him be. It's a shock. A shock to us all—except Mama.'

'Oh God. Mama?'

'She's fine. Better than she's ever been, in my memory anyway.'

Violet's words swirled around her. Her eyes blurred and she sank onto the ground, her legs no longer capable of holding her upright, her mind jumbled, full of confusion and conflicting emotions.

Jim's shadow fell across her, blocking the heat of the sun and making her shiver.

'Fred—' his voice came from a great distance, '—sort things out. Put Goodfellow in the barn with Jefferson and see to the other horses.'

India closed her eyes and dropped her head between her knees, concentrating on the insurmountable task of dragging air into her lungs.

'Violet, could you go and organise a cup of tea for India? I'll bring her to the kitchen in a moment. I expect Peggy knows your father is back by now.'

India grimaced as she waited for the waves of nausea to pass. Her father was no doubt at this moment on his way to see her mother. A scene she couldn't even imagine. 'How? How?' She crooned as she rocked to and fro. Whatever had possessed her to delve into the past? Not more heartbreak. She should have left life as it was. All this upheaval and confusion only made matters worse. Why did she ever imagine she could make life better? How could Jim have known all this time that the grave in front of the house was a sham? How could he have looked at the portrait in the library and said nothing? Would his lies never end?

When his arm wrapped around her shoulder the tears began, great gulping sobs shaking her whole body, rendering her incapable of thought. He pulled her against him and smoothed her hair from her face saying nothing. What could he say?

How long he held her there in the dirt of the yard she had no idea. Slowly the breath returned to her body and her world came into focus. 'Jim, I—'

'Don't talk, not yet.'

His strong arms held her firm against his chest until the light began to fade and the cold seeped from her heart into the marrow of her bones. With infinite care he helped her to her feet. 'Are you ready now?'

She swallowed the last remnants of her sobs and shrugged him off. 'I have to see Mama and Papa.'

'You don't have to do anything until you're ready.'

Oh, but she did. There were so many things she must do. First and foremost she must discover the truth. 'Why is Goodfellow here? I thought he was dead. We all thought he was dead.'

'He has been at Munmurra all along. My father didn't shoot him. He took him away, healed him. Goodfellow sired Jefferson.'

Of course, he sired Jefferson. How could she have missed it? She must have been blind. On their ride together down to the river she'd even commented on how similar the two animals were, how much it reminded her of riding with Papa and he'd brushed her comments aside and then they had … Oh God! What had she done!

'Why didn't you tell me? Why did you keep it a secret? Why … oh, *the studbooks*. You weren't interested in Helligen, or the job here. And that's why you refused to let me use Jefferson over the mares, because they're related.' How many lies had he told? How much had he kept from her? And she'd fallen for every single one of them, and worse, him! She had believed herself to be in love with the man and he was nothing more than a scheming fraud.

She shrugged his hands off and steadied herself against the fence line. Tears still blurred her eyes and as she dashed them away she stared into the empty yard. She could almost have dreamt the whole thing. Only a smouldering pile of horse dung indicated a horse had once stood there. A horse she'd believed dead.

'India, let me take you inside. To Peggy.'

She lifted her head and looked him up and down. The dark wing of hair falling across his forehead, his strong, warm arms with the sleeves of his shirt pushed up above the elbows. Her gaze travelled to his face and his eyes, dark and unfathomable. The eyes of a liar.

From the outset she had been taken in by his attention and his concern and while he smiled and kissed her, toyed with her affections, he hid his true motive.

'India?'

She kept her eyes averted. Her heartbeat thundered in her ears. 'I have nothing to say to you. Leave the property.' Papa was right; she should never have allowed him to remain at Helligen. Never advertised for a stud master. *What a fool.* She turned her back on him and walked away, across the courtyard, her boots scuffing in the dust, her breath growing short. She kept her head up and her shoulders back— Miss Wetherington would have been proud of her—and she didn't stop. Didn't look behind her, didn't even take the one last glance to imprint on her mind the man who had played her for a fool.

It wasn't until she reached the welcome protection of the walkway that she broke into a run. Her cheeks bright with shame, her body hotter than in any moment of the passionate embrace she'd shared with Jim. With a muffled scream she clutched the smooth cedar banister and mounted the curved staircase, stamping on every tread until she reached the top.

The door to Mama's room stood open. How she longed to throw herself into Mama's arms, seek the comfort she hadn't known since she was a small child. To sob and sob until she had no more tears. But it was a luxury she had never been permitted, not since her mother's accident, not since the Cobbs had ruined her life, ruined her family's life. Everything Papa had said was true. No member of the Cobb family belonged here. She'd been blinded by her loneliness and entrapped by a fraud and liar.

Throwing open the door to her bedroom she staggered over the threshold and collapsed onto the bed, shading her eyes from the brightness pinpointing her foolishness. Curled tightly into a ball she hugged her knees to her chest and buried her face into the pillow, away from prying eyes and the awful realisation she'd been duped. The tears fell. Tears of remorse, despair, embarrassment and, worst of all, shame.

Twenty-Four

Jim gripped the roughened rail. Only the tiniest shiver in her shoulders indicated she was doing anything other than crossing the courtyard. When she'd greeted him he'd seen the joy shining in her eyes. He hadn't imagined it. What he didn't understand was the transformation in her face when she saw Goodfellow. And then the shutters had come down. Closing him out.

Nothing had gone the way he intended. He bunched his fist and slammed it into the timber. He didn't understand. Mrs Kilhampton had been overjoyed to see Goodfellow. Whereas India and her father had responded as though he'd committed some dreadful crime.

'You all right there?' Fred's head appeared around the stable doors. 'What d'you want me to do with the horses? Back in the stable?'

Back in the stable? How the hell did he know? Given the opportunity he'd wind the clock back and try it all again. 'You clear up.' His father wanted him to set the record straight; all he'd succeeded in doing was stirring up the past and opening old wounds. All because of some misbegotten desire to race Jefferson and stand him at stud.

When he'd walked back through the gates with Goodfellow he truly believed he was putting the past behind him and moving on. The look on Mrs Kilhampton's face when she'd seen Goodfellow made it all worthwhile and now in one fell swoop his good intentions lay trampled in the dirt.

'Leave them in the barn, Fred. There won't be any more rides today.'

'As you wish. I'd be expecting a summons from the master if I were you. Cor, he looked as though he'd seen a bloody ghost.'

Mr Kilhampton had. The enormity of the chaos he'd evoked settled across his shoulders, weighing him down.

As he crossed the courtyard a curtain twitched in the window above. Mrs Kilhampton watching? What was India doing? The possibility of simply walking out the gate and leaving became more and more enticing by the moment.

Within the barn the cool half-light soothed him as he settled the horses and checked the locks on the stalls, then instead of hanging the bridles on the gates he looped them over his shoulder. The last thing anyone needed right now was Mrs Kilhampton taking either Jefferson or Goodfellow on one of her surreptitious rides.

He lifted the heavy latch and closed the barn doors and made his way back to the cottage. A cottage he wouldn't be occupying for much longer. It was time to move on. Time to accept he had failed.

The old ledger from his father's office still sat on the table between the two chairs. He dusted it off and took one final look at the spidery hand before snapping it shut. It had proved nothing. There was no record of any sale because his father had stolen Goodfellow. Taken him in the dead of night like a common thief.

Making a final round of the cottage he threw his clothes into his saddlebags then went through the stables to the old office. He had no need of a light; the pathway had once again become as familiar to him as his own hand. He pushed the door open and made his way through the discarded odds and ends to the desk and deposited the book in the drawer, pushing it firmly closed.

Tomorrow, once he'd explained everything to Kilhampton, he would head off. Goodfellow was home—granting his father's last wish. The only thing he'd managed to achieve. He'd like to ask Kilhampton to acknowledge Jefferson as Goodfellow's progeny, but under the circumstances he didn't think he'd get a favourable reaction.

'Mr Jim, sir.'

'Jim, Fred. Jim.'

The boy jumped from one foot to the other, his face as red as a beetroot.

'What is it?'

'You're wanted in the library.'

Jim raised his eyebrows in question.

'No idea, Peggy sent me across to get you.'

He straightened his shirt and wiped his boots down the back of his trousers to brush off the worst of the dirt. His mind was made up. He'd level with Kilhampton. Tell him the story right from the beginning. Once the initial shock was over the man would have to be pleased his horse wasn't buried under that bloody great lump of granite, and he would understand that his father had taken the animal because he believed it was for the best. Then they'd take it from there.

The back door of the house was open and he walked through into the hallway. The dining room stood empty and a puddle of light spilt from under the library door. He glanced up the stairs. No sign of India, or Violet. The house was as quiet as the mausoleum Violet believed it to be.

Ignoring the knot in his stomach he approached the closed door and rapped loudly.

'Enter.'

The door squeaked as he pushed it open. Goodfellow glared down at him from the portrait on the chimneybreast. Kilhampton sat, his hands folded across his stomach, legs stretched out in front of him in the leather chair Jim had occupied a few weeks before. A single lamp illuminated the room, shining on the stack of studbooks and ledgers piled on one side of the massive cedar desk. A wave of shame swept through him. Private papers he'd rifled through without any thought other than his overriding determination to prove Jefferson's lineage.

'Good evening, sir.' The *sir* caught in his craw. His use of the word served only to emphasise where the power rested in the relationship.

'Sit.' As a greeting it didn't bode well. Kilhampton nodded to the chair across the desk from him.

'Thank you.' As Jim sat he searched the man's face for some indication of the way the conversation might progress. As much as India and her mother shared their looks there was nothing in Kilhampton's face that indicated his relationship to India. The man's eyes were the deepest blue, cold like the ocean's depths, and his skin as weathered as old leather. That was the only thing that signified the difference in their age. Even sitting behind the desk power radiated from the man's body. In his shirtsleeves his heavily muscled wrists and corded hands paid testimony to an active life. This was not a man who spent his days taking life easy. This was a man in his prime, a powerful man, equally at home in a Sydney drawing room as a dockside tavern.

The uncomfortable silence stretched and Jim shifted in his chair under Kilhampton's cold blue scrutiny.

When he could stand it no longer he leant forwards. 'I would like to explain about my return to Helligen.'

Kilhampton didn't move a muscle. 'Go ahead,' he said.

The man wasn't giving him an inch. Why hadn't he thought this conversation through? From the moment he set eyes on Kilhampton in the courtyard and watched his reaction to Goodfellow he knew this confrontation would come. He swallowed and the sound echoed in his ears.

'I saw the advertisement in *The Maitland Mercury* and thought if I returned and spoke with you we could sort out the papers for my horse, Jefferson.'

Kilhampton's eyebrows raised then his eyes narrowed.

'I want to race Jefferson, stand him at stud.'

'I'm not interested in your horse. I'm interested in mine.'

Jim let out a long slow breath. Now he'd broken the stalemate perhaps a rational discussion could proceed. 'Goodfellow?'

'Goodfellow.' Kilhampton's eyes flickered to the painting and then shot back to glare into his face.

'I am not Jim Mawgan.' It was as though he had a handful of straw and each slippery piece refused to sit in line with the others, slipping from his grasp each time he tried to realign them. 'I came here—'

'Under false pretences.'

'Yes, but—'

'Under an assumed name, with an ulterior motive.'

'My father … Thomas Cobb.' It was as though his father's name removed the last remaining vestige of control Kilhampton had exerted to this moment. He slammed his hands down on the desk and stood, towering over Jim. 'You and your father are fucking horse thieves and I'll see you both hang for it.'

An icy calm settled on Jim as he contemplated Kilhampton and his admiration for his father increased. He had stood against him. Defied him. He may have lost the battle in his own eyes, but Jim had every intention of fighting it to the end. His father might not have been proud of what he did yet he had, against the odds, done what he believed was right. In the same way he'd returned Goodfellow because he believed it was the honourable thing to do. 'You may see me hang for my father's actions, Kilhampton, but he is beyond even your reach. He's dead.' Jim leant back and folded his arms. Probably not the wisest track to take, but he no longer felt like an emasculated schoolboy.

Kilhampton sank into his chair, and pushed it back from the desk. A sliver of light fell across the darkened room from the lamp, illuminating a pair of black leather boots and dark trousers. There was someone else in the room. He shuffled higher in the chair and flicked a look back at Kilhampton who slumped with his eyes downcast and his head resting in his scarred hands.

Straightening his back Jim squinted into the corner where a wingback chair was flanked by heavy drapes. The man's face was in shadow and he sat as still as one of the portraits on the wall.

Kilhampton lifted his head and Jim turned his attention back to him.

'I instructed your father to shoot Goodfellow and bury him.'

Jim nodded.

'What happened?'

'To be honest—'

'That might make a change.'

'I don't know. My memory is hazy. My mother, my brother and I left Helligen.' *Were chased off the property in the middle of the night, thrown out of our home, sent packing.* 'We camped in the bush for several days and finally my father arrived and said he'd found another job and we would be living at Munmurra. When we arrived Goodfellow was there. His leg was broken and my father believed he could mend it.'

'Your father is a horse thief. And you're guilty by association, benefitting from stolen goods. Next you'll be telling me you own the horse.'

'I was under the impression my father owned the horse. He said you'd given Goodfellow to him in lieu of wages.'

'A liar, like his son. And a horse thief into the bargain. If your father is dead who owns the horse now?'

'I do.' As the words slipped from his mouth his mistake registered. The man in the shadows stood as if on cue.

Kilhampton followed suit. 'Constable, arrest this man. He's a self-confessed horse thief.'

Twenty-Five

India sat up and pulled the blanket tighter around her shoulders. Through her frosty bedroom window the cold grey light hovered on the horizon. Out beyond the paddocks the tussock grasses would be pearled with ice and the water birds would be stirring. That she'd slept for so long beggared belief.

She swung her legs over the side of the bed and examined her pale feet. At some stage last night she must have removed her boots and her riding habit because she wore only her chemise. No wonder she was cold. She walked to the window and rubbed the heel of her hand across the chilly glass and peered down into the courtyard. Today she'd have to face Papa and give a detailed account of her foolishness, then tell Jim to leave.

What a mess she'd made. To be so gullible. If only—there could be no if-onlys. She would never be able to believe anything Jim might tell her, never be able to look at him without remembering the way she'd thrown herself at him. A poor, lonely girl falling at the feet of the first man who'd paid her more than a passing glance. No. That wasn't true. Cecil, plenty of men in Sydney had paid attention to her. None had made her blood sing or her heart pound like Jim.

Somewhere downstairs a door banged and the first sounds of morning broke the night's silence. She pulled on yesterday's clothes and dragged on her riding boots then tiptoed into the passageway, down the stairs and out to the kitchen. Searching for tea and the home truths Peggy would deliver.

'It was a right proper shindig, Peggy.' Fred's outraged tone filtered down the walkway. 'They took him in a cart. Wouldn't let him take that horse of his. Not either of them. Made him climb up in the back of the cart. All trussed up like a chicken, he was. Cuffed and chained.'

She pushed the door open. 'Peggy?'

'Come and sit down, love. There's something you need to know.'

Fred shuffled his feet then thought better of it and sped off out across the courtyard without a backward glance.

'I don't want to sit down.' She held her hands out to the stove searching for warmth, unable to meet Peggy's prying eyes.

'Then I'll make a pot of tea.'

'I'm not sure I want tea, either.' She couldn't remember the last time she'd eaten, and the prospect of even tea made her stomach turn. How long since she'd been in Sydney? When she still believed the only battle she fought was acceptance for the man she'd absurdly thought she loved.

'Yes, you do.' Peggy pulled one of the chairs closer to the range. 'Sit here and put your feet up. It'll warm the cockles of your heart.'

'Peggy, just tell me. What was Fred talking about? It's Jim, isn't it?'

'It's Jim. Your father called in the constabulary. They took him away last night, to the Maitland lock-up.'

'Whatever for?' Her voice cracked. 'What has he done—you don't go to gaol for using an assumed name. Half of Australia would be behind bars if that was the case.'

'It's a bit more than that, love. Here.'

The cup rattled in the saucer as she took it. She put it down on the top of the range and picked up the cup alone, holding it close and letting the fragrant steam warm her cold face.

Peggy cleared her throat.

'Come on, Peggy. Spit it out.'

'Your father's had him taken into custody for horse thieving.'

'Horse theft!' How could he do that? The only thing Jim had stolen was her heart, not any of the horses. 'When? When did this happen?'

'Last night. Your father locked himself in that library of his and the next thing anyone knew he'd got that jumped-up pompous old fool Tom Bludge from the village with him. They talked for a while then he sent him off. We didn't know nothing until Constable Coxcomb turned up with his band of merry men.'

'Why didn't someone tell me?' All the while she'd languished in her bedroom like a grieving maiden and slept the night away. 'Where was Violet?'

'It was Violet what found out.'

India slammed down the teacup. Papa must have planned this from the outset. She cast her mind back to their trip from Sydney. When had he had the opportunity? She pushed open the door.

'And where do you think you're going?'

'I'm going to talk to Papa and find out what he thinks he's doing. He can't have someone arrested because he doesn't like his name. Jim hasn't committed theft. I'd stake my life on it.'

'Just you wait a minute and do a bit of thinking. First and foremost it's too early. Your father's still abed and the last thing you want to do is go waking him, and besides, I'm not sure there's much you can do about it.'

'Jim's innocent.' No matter how wrong she'd been about Jim, he didn't deserve this. He might not have told the truth about who he was or why he'd come to Helligen, but theft? She was more guilty of gullibility than he was of thieving. Why had she encouraged him? Why had she let him into their lives? 'It's my fault.'

'Not really. He didn't have to answer the advertisement, didn't have to take the job. Didn't have to bring Goodfellow back here, for that matter. He walked straight into a trap if you ask me. Didn't think about the consequences.' Peggy shot her a look, enough to say Jim wasn't the only one who hadn't thought of the consequences. 'His father stole Goodfellow, no ifs or buts about that, and now he owns the animal.'

'He's no horse thief. His father perhaps, but not Jim.'

'And it's a hanging offence.'

'Peggy, this is impossible. I have to talk to Papa. Explain that it was entirely my fault. I shouldn't have been so foolish as to place that advertisement in the newspaper.' *Or to fall in love with the man.* She wasn't about to admit that to Peggy, or anyone else.

Twenty-Six

The imposing gates of Maitland Gaol threw a shadow that penetrated even the depths of the prison cart. Jim craned his head and peered through the narrow slit in the canvas, flexing his cramped muscles and aching shoulders. Massive sandstone walls towered above him. He shrugged, trying to ease the deadening ache in his body. At what point in time had he crossed the line from dutiful son to horse thief? When he first heard Kilhampton's accusation he had expected to laugh it off. He was no thief. Goodfellow belonged to his father. *Your father is dead*, the voice in his head reminded him. And he had inherited Goodfellow.

The truth sat like a solid stone in his belly. No matter what accusations Kilhampton made he couldn't think of his father as a thief. But … there were no 'buts' in the law. He knew that well enough. As unpalatable as it may be to admit, his father had stolen the animal. In the face of the law it was irrefutable and he'd walked straight into the trap by delivering Goodfellow to Helligen. Gaining from stolen goods? He'd heard the muttered conversation between Kilhampton and the bloody constable.

The cart ground to a halt and the back door flew open. Jim blinked against the hovering lamplight.

'Down you get and no funny business.'

He shuffled along the timber seat and launched himself onto the hard-packed dirt, staggering as he landed. The heavy chains destroyed any sense of natural balance he may once have had. Out of the cart the full impact of the towering sandstone walls hit. Caught like a rat in a trap. There would be no escape. The wind howled like a banshee, whipping his hair into his eyes and cutting through his shirt.

'Foul bloody night. We're not hanging around. All yours.' The constable pushed him at the turnkey with a sniff and disappeared into the darkness. The cart rattled back towards the gates and they clanged shut.

A jab in his kidneys propelled him across the courtyard to a massive door, padlocked and bolted. The turnkey swung a heavy chain up from his waist and inserted a key into the lock. He turned it with a clunk then drew back the bolt and released the door. A sound far louder than the screeching wind assaulted his ears and the hairs on his neck quivered. The shouts of men, defiant whistling, and women. Women's voices. Singing. The cries of children. A hell on earth.

Led through another doorway and into a corridor lined with solid timber doors, Jim gritted his teeth and fought back the desire to pull away from the sour-smelling gaoler. They passed at least a dozen more tightly sealed doors with small barred windows before the turnkey jabbed him again. Taking it to mean they had arrived at their destination Jim stopped. The tunnel of the dark corridor stretched ahead and behind him. The clamouring noise shot through with the howling whistle of the wind drummed inside his head.

The key twisted in the padlock and the door swung open with a metallic grind. Plunged into an eerie gloom, he was trapped in a tiny space between the putrid gaoler and a barred gate. He waited, hands hanging by his sides, the metal of the cuffs cutting into his wrists while the door behind him was locked once more. In front of him was another door of iron bars and through it a damp, dank smell wafted, a mixture of festering humanity and bodily fluids.

The turnkey fumbled with another lock and the barred gate swung open. A final shove and he toppled onto the ground. He crawled around in time to catch the turnkey disappearing then stilled. Alone in the darkness. The fetid air coated his tongue. Below the constant whistle of the wind and the muted noises of the prison, the rasp of shallow breathing sounded. Not the regular breath of sleeping men but a tense silence, as if something held its breath and waited in the shadows.

A sudden longing for the fresh clean air of the bush swept him. Another door clanged shut. His eyes adjusted to the darkness; a pale slant of moonlight shone through the two barred windows high above his head, throwing a pattern of bars across the dirt floor. He turned, scouring the recesses of the cell. Huddled mounds became visible. He eased down onto his haunches in the centre of the cell, filling the only space that guaranteed he wouldn't sprawl across one of the blanketed bundles. Four mounded shapes, one propped in each corner, with heads resting on knees, arms pulled tight around their legs as though they were gargoyle cornerstones, part of the solid walls.

His chains rattled as he eased the blanket around his shoulders and hunched down with his legs crossed, listening to the rasping gasps, picking out the individual breathing patterns. He measured the size of the cell. No more than three paces by four. Above him iron girders reinforcing the ceiling ran the length of the cell.

A long slow exhalation and a movement. From one shrouded bundle a face appeared, eyes dark as Hades; cheekbones bleached white by the moonlight above a bushy beard. 'You're in the way. Back against the wall.'

The sound took him by surprise. He twisted around. Back against the wall, where?

'There something the matter with you?'

He shook his head and pushed onto his knees, shuffled across the floor useless as a baby with the weight of the chains, until he reached the wall beside his hollow-eyed companion.

'Sort the links out. It'll give you enough play to sit. You'll get used to it soon enough.'

He shot a glance across the cell at the man lounging against the opposite wall and took heed of his words.

'What've they got you for?'

'Horse thieving,' Jim muttered. He fiddled with the rusty chains until he could turn and take a closer look at his cellmate. A long beard covered the lower half of his blackened face and his straggling hair hung almost to his shoulders. 'You?' He received no response. How long would this last? The turnkey hadn't taken his name, hadn't recorded his arrival. What about sentencing, facing a court? 'So what happens next?'

'Either you prove your innocence or you'll be committed to stand trial at the next quarter sessions. If you're lucky you'll get bail or they'll keep you here in the interim.'

Proving his innocence was a long shot. There was no escaping the fact his father had stolen Goodfellow, no matter which way he looked at it. By virtue of his father's death he now owned Goodfellow. What in God's name had possessed him to take him back to Helligen? If he hadn't done that the worst thing Kilhampton could have done was kick him off the property. 'That's a long shot.'

'Guilty or not? No point in sitting around waiting to see what happens. You need someone to speak for you.'

'No, I didn't do it, but I'm responsible. It's a long story.' A long story that still made little or no sense. It had spiralled out of all control and he was being sucked down into the vortex of the past, made to pay for events that had occurred when he was no more than a child.

'You're going to have a lot of time on your hands to sort your story out. Magistrate ain't due for another two weeks. Is the animal branded? Local?'

Jim nodded. 'Stud stock, local, branded.'

'You're history. Ten years at best. More if you've crossed someone with any clout.'

Oh yes, Kilhampton had clout. He had no doubt about that. And contacts.

'Count your blessings. They did away with the death penalty for horse thieving a few years ago. Not for the likes of me. Or them.' He indicated to the other three corners of the room with a wave of his hand. Who were these men? Why were they here? Bushy hadn't given away any details, no names, and no crimes. They all looked as though they could handle themselves and none of them appeared intimidated by their incarceration or their plight. No longer huddled shadows beneath the blankets the men stared back at him, their pale faces clearly visible now his eyes had adjusted to the gloom.

'What are we going to do about him?' The bloke in the far corner tilted his head and all but spat the words at Jim.

'Bloody lousy timing.'

'Piss weak.'

The phrases batted backwards and forwards, the underlying tension tighter than the chains around his wrists. He shuffled further back against the wall and attempted to pull his arms from under the blanket.

Bushy's hand snaked out and tweaked the blanket free.

'You're not chained?'

There was a general rustle and three other pairs of hands lifted and turned. None sported the iron bracelets that chafed his skin. It didn't make sense. Nothing made sense.

The man closest to Bushy heaved his stubby body vertical then lumbered three paces across the room until his shadow loomed across Jim's body. With his face almost pressed into the man's festering crutch he craned his head back. The meaty hands above him brandished a weapon. His heart rate kicked up. A heavy chisel. The scars of cuffs were clearly visible on the man's brawny wrists.

'Well?'

He was a sitting duck. Was the bloke threatening him or offering to remove his chains?

He took a punt and held his arms up. What had he to lose? These men had worked out a way to do without their cursed irons and he wanted the same.

'Not so fast. What do you reckon, boys?'

'We got two choices. Leave 'im trussed or take the risk.'

'Keep him tied. He can't interfere then.'

Interfere? What would he interfere in?

The third man uncoiled himself, long and sinewy with bunched and corded muscles, not an ounce of fat. 'Or offer him a chance?' A chance? A chance at what?

'Too much risk. Who the hell is he?'

'James, James Cobb.' He clamped his lips closed. What was the matter with him? Helligen manners had rubbed off on him. This was no civilised meeting; he'd answered no advertisement though it was where it had landed him.

'No names.' Bushy turned to him, and then nodded up at the two men. 'Give him a go. He's got no bloody chance. Horse thief'll go down for ten at least.'

'Pfft.' A globule of spit flew through the air and landed with a soft thud on the dirt in the centre of the cell. The fourth man threw back his blanket revealing a pile of worn and rusted implements at his feet, a small bow saw and several cold chisels. 'Keep bloody talking and we'll be out of time.'

Bushy heaved to his feet with a resigned sigh. 'You've got a choice. We leave you chained and go about our business or you take your chances with us.'

A chance at what?

'He'll have to come with us otherwise they'll have us pegged.' Stubby hauled the chain upwards, wrenching Jim's arms above his head.

'Jesus, you can be fucking dense sometimes. They're going to know who's shot through the minute they open the cells up.'

Swimming through the impenetrable fog that had clouded his mind since the constable had bundled him into the cart, Jim sifted through the garbled words. The only conclusion he could draw was the turnkey had thrown him into a cell where he'd interrupted an escape attempt.

'Are you in or not?' Bushy's remark confirmed his suspicions.

What had he to lose? Stay and he'd have a long wait for the magistrate and then no chance in hell if Kilhampton pulled the full force of the legislature down on his head. Run and maybe, just maybe he'd have the chance of clearing his name, prove to Kilhampton his intentions were honourable. And India. He still owed her an explanation. Had she known? Had she watched from the security of an upstairs window while they bundled him away? Relieved to be free of the man who'd lied to her.

He pushed the thought away and held his wrists higher, his mind made up. 'If you're getting out of here, I'm in.'

'No guarantees.'

'No guarantees.'

'We'll get rid of these chains then you can make yourself useful.' Bushy wiped the back of his hand over his hairy lips and stepped back. 'You got something there to do the trick?'

The fourth man, a giant, produced a heavy metal chisel and hammer.

'Blacksmith reckons he's the best in the colony at removing irons. Put your wrists down on the ground.'

Jim lowered his arms and looked away. One slip of either of the two lethal tools the blacksmith brandished and he'd be minus a few fingers or have his wrists slashed. He tensed as the giant raised the mallet above the chisel then held his breath. The force of the blow ricocheted up his arms making his teeth rattle. Two more swipes and the chains were gone. Meaty fingers clasped his wrists and the bow saw bit into his flesh as it ground across the rusty metal of the cuff.

'What's the go?' he choked out in an attempt to draw his attention away from the stench of mangled flesh, his flesh.

'Just do what you're told. And keep your mouth shut.'

In response he offered his other wrist and watched as the saw bit through the metal.

'Want these for a souvenir?' the blacksmith asked as he lifted off his second cuff.

Jim shook his head. 'You can have them and thanks. Thanks a lot.'

With the chains and cuffs gathered in one hand, the blacksmith loosened a sandstone block from the wall and slipped the chains and one chisel onto a pile in the cavity. 'Leave no trace. Might do some other poor bugger some good.' He replaced the block and ran his large hand over the wall, checking the alignment.

Jim twisted his wrists and flexed his fingers. The sudden lack of weight seemed odd. He'd worn the cuffs for less than twelve hours and already he'd become accustomed to their presence. The thought made him shudder. What would it be like to be sentenced to work in chains, wrists and ankles restrained, for years? Would the chains become an accepted item, like shoes or a hat? He wasn't about to find out. He was well out of the place.

'I owe you. All of you.' He squinted at the mismatched assortment of men crammed in the small space then settled back against the wall to wait, his head propped against his knees. Soon enough dawn would come and his fate would be set. Given his time again would he have played it the same way? Had he not travelled to Morpeth a couple of months back and picked up his repaired boots wrapped in a single sheet of *The Maitland Mercury* he wouldn't be sitting in a cell contemplating the prospect of escape with a motley crew of gaolbirds.

Boots or no boots, gaol or not gaol, he wouldn't have given away the opportunity to return to Helligen, to lay the old ghosts to rest. His father could rest easy now. Goodfellow was back where he belonged. Alive, very much alive, not buried under some granite slab along with a thousand heartbreaks and half-truths.

His only regret was India. For a short time he believed they were destined to be together—separate souls swirling aimlessly in the heavens, finally drawn into each other's sphere by some unknown force.

Lost in thought the weight of Bushy's hand on his shoulder almost sent him through the roof. A dirty and rather smelly hand covered his mouth. 'Ssh!' He shrugged it off.

Through the barred windows high above his head the sky lightened to that peculiar lilac grey that heralded the first spark of dawn. Around the cell the blanketed forms unravelled, grasping saws, chisels and random tools, now weapons, in their hands. Jim forced one foot in front of the other, trying to ease his muscles and restore the blood flow to his cramped limbs.

Bushy stretched to his feet, reached into his pocket and pulled out a key. He slid his hand through the metal bars on the first door and lifted the padlock. With a twist and a jiggle the lock snapped open and the door swung free. The door the turnkey had locked. He moved to the second door and sank to his knees, ran his fingers below the metal reinforcing bar and pulled the hefty chain and padlock aside. He lifted the chisel and inserted it into a hole and proceeded to work his way along the timber, until he lifted free a panel to reveal a gaping hole about eighteen by fifteen inches, open to the corridor.

Jim stared. He'd walked through that door only hours before and it had appeared solid. No wonder the strange breathing pattern he'd heard and the tense sense of hostility as he'd entered the cell. His arrival had interrupted their preparations. 'How?' He clamped his mouth shut.

'Five o'clock turnkey'll get the boys up on cook's duty. Makin' the hominy for breakfast. We'll spring him before he unlocks their cells. Tie him up and make our way outside. Rest of the place'll be quiet as a grave. There's a ladder waiting by the cookhouse. Over the wall, down the other side and God willing, we're out.'

Jim massaged the throbbing flesh on his wrists. Over the walls, the sandstone walls.

'Main thing is to move as fast as we can.'

The words swarmed in his head. Out. Out of this godforsaken hole.

'Sure you're in? Makes no difference. Leave you here trussed up with the turnkey and you can deny all knowledge. Or come with us.'

His heart lifted for a moment and then sank. All well and good if they were successful. What if they failed? Did he really want to be clobbered with escape as well as horse theft?

'You're the last one up the ladder but it'll give you the chance to make a bolt for it.'

He hesitated too long.

'Make up your mind. Otherwise you'll be sitting festering here until they decide to pull you up in front of the magistrate. Ten years. No less. Stud stock, branded. Not a hope in hell.'

'I'm in.' What had he to lose? Nothing. If he was going down for ten years then an attempted escape would make little or no difference, and there was always the possibility they may succeed. 'And once we're on the outside?'

'Got horses lined up. You'll be on your own then. Only got four sorted. Weren't expecting an extra.'

Not so good. The gaol sat in the midst of East Maitland surrounded by houses and businesses. The sun would be as good as up by the time they cleared the wall.

'Double with me,' Bushy said over his shoulder. 'I'll see you to the outskirts of town then you're on your own.'

The outskirts would suit him well enough. If he cut across country he'd be back close to Helligen by sunset. *Then what?* He'd get Jefferson, leave Goodfellow and think about the rest. Kilhampton could lay no claim to Jefferson. There was no proof Goodfellow had sired him other than their uncanny similarity and there were no papers to prove it. Maybe it was a good thing.

The men stood and Jim followed suit then turned to his hairy-faced companion. 'Now?'

'Yep. It's time for a bit of fresh air.'

Keys rattled in the thick air. They stood by the outer door, tense and silent, ears straining for any unexpected sound. Bushy bent down and one by one they crept through the hole in the door out of the cell.

At the far end of the corridor a light flashed behind the barred window as the turnkey fumbled with a firestick. The bolt grated and the door groaned and swung open. The turnkey stepped inside.

Bushy and the sinewy bloke grabbed him by the arms. He had time to utter one mangled cry before Bushy stuffed a handful of rags into his gaping mouth.

'Stay still and you'll come to no harm.' Bushy nodded and the blacksmith tied the turnkey's hands behind his back with twisted strips of blanket, then his legs before knotting the whole lot together. Rummaging around his waistline Bushy produced the turnkey's set of keys then dumped him, trussed like a chicken, in the corner.

He peered through the door and then raised his hand, beckoning them to follow into a small walled yard.

The moon rode high in the predawn sky, casting an iridescent glow across the compound. Nothing moved. Last through the door, Jim closed it and shot the bolt home then followed the four men along the walls and around the back of the cookhouse. Chained against the wall stood two ladders. His heart sank—neither appeared long enough to allow access to the top of the walls. So much for the great escape plan: thwarted before they'd even started. His confidence was restored as Bushy produced the turnkey's bundle of keys and inserted one into the lock. The padlock sprung open and the blacksmith interlocked the two ladders, one atop the other against the wall.

In an instant the shadowy forms scooted up the ladder. Bushy sat astride the high compound wall and unwrapped a strip of blanket rope from around his waist. One by one the three men lowered themselves over the wall and disappeared from sight.

'Too bloody late to change your mind now. Come on.'

Without a second thought he scaled the ladder and sat astride the wall facing Bushy.

'Grab the rope and down you go.'

'What about you?'

'Got it covered. Yes or no?' Without waiting for an answer he pushed his hand hard against Jim's shoulder. 'Last chance. Go!'

Jim clamped his hands tightly around the blanket rope and pushed his feet back from the wall. His arms all but wrenched from his sockets as he scrambled against the wall. A hand clasped his ankle, pulling him down. He kicked out and heard a muttered curse then his hands slipped from the rope and he hit the ground with a thud. The air whooshed from his lungs and he lay curled in a heap in the dust, his hands covering his head as one of the horses pranced aside.

Looking back up the wall he saw Bushy lower himself, feet pressed against the wall. There was a groan and a clatter, the rope dropped five feet and Bushy landed on the ground agile as a cat, followed by the makeshift rope.

'No time,' Bushy hissed, brushing his arse and clambering astride one of the horses. 'Haven't got all day.'

Jim struggled to his feet. The four mounted men stared down at him. What now? On horseback they'd have half a chance, on foot he'd be back inside in minutes. Was Bushy good to his word?

He leant down and offered a hand. 'Up behind me. I presume a bloody horse thief can manage.' Grabbing the proffered hand with both of his he swung up onto the horse and they clattered down the empty street.

Jim flashed a look back over his shoulder. Light blazed above the main gates, illuminating a group of men spilling helter-skelter out of the gaol. They set a thundering pace, heedless of the noise of the horses' hooves. In a matter of moments they had left the town behind.

The countryside surrounding Maitland was a bushranger's dream. Jim ducked his head as they passed beneath low hanging branches following the twists and turns of a wallaby track.

A few isolated farmhouses lay scattered on the surrounding hills. After an hour of hard riding the raggle-taggle group slowed and made their way to the creek, the horses' foaming breath making large white clouds in the early morning air.

Jim slid from the back of the horse. It was a mottled badly conformed animal with a broad deep chest and spindly legs, but it had done sterling duty carrying two men at such a pace.

'Thanks.' He held up his hand to Bushy.

'Think nothing of it. What are your plans?'

Jim shrugged his shoulders; he hadn't had time to think further than this moment. The escape had come as such a shock and simply hanging on behind Bushy for the madcap ride had left him little time to dwell on the future. One thing was certain. He needed a horse. Travelling with these men would slow them down and put them in unnecessary danger, besides, they owed him nothing. They'd done more for him than they needed. 'I'll leave you here. I know the area so I'll cover it on foot until I find a horse and then decide where to from there.'

Bushy leant down and clapped him on the back. 'Once a horse thief ... You're welcome to tag along a bit longer, though it'll slow us down.'

'You've done enough. I'm fine from here.'

'Then in that case we'll be making a move. If you come unstuck make for St Albans and ask for Molly's daughter.'

He lifted his hand in farewell as the four men disappeared around a bend in the track and vanished from sight. Only a random bird call and the rush of the creek over the stones broke the silence of the bush. He sucked in a lungful of freedom and let out a sigh, then found a fallen tree trunk and settled behind it in the sunshine.

Helligen lay about ten miles to the west. If he followed the creek it would lead to the river and thence to the back paddocks of the property. In four hours he could reach the lagoon. He'd wait for sunset and make his way to the barn; Goodfellow wouldn't like being left behind, but he had no other option. All he needed was his saddle, bridle and Jefferson. His saddlebags and belongings he would forgo. Helligen would be the constabulary's first call.

When Jefferson was discovered missing Kilhampton would know who was responsible, but no-one could level horse theft at him for taking his own animal. Besides, with escape under his belt as well they had enough on him. Then what? Munmurra was out of the question. All his plans for the future skittled. From now on he would think his plans through and weigh the consequences. One lesson he'd learned over the past weeks. Queensland beckoned, or Victoria, the goldfields. It was madness to go back to Helligen but he was unable to resist. He needed a horse and there was only one he wanted and one he was entitled to. Jefferson was his and he intended to claim him. Goodfellow belonged at Helligen and that's where he would live out his days.

The opportunities were endless. In the meantime he'd enjoy the sunshine, relax and avoid thinking of what might have been.

Twenty-Seven

The grandfather clock in the hallway struck ten as India knocked on the library door. Receiving no answer she pushed the door open and stuck her head around the corner. Lost in thought Papa stood gazing out of the long window to the fig trees and beyond.

'Good morning, Papa.'

He gave a slight shudder and turned, his face grey and grim, and India's stomach sank. He looked about as approachable as a red-bellied black, ready to strike at a moment's notice.

'May I speak with you?'

His grunt of agreement did little to encourage. She sat in the chair facing his desk, a prisoner in the dock awaiting his wrath. She deserved it. Jim did not. He should not be in the lock-up for a crime his father committed. No matter how he had presented himself, what name he'd used, he was not guilty. When the so-called theft took place Jim was no more than a boy. How could he be held responsible for something his father had done?

After an agony of delay Papa turned from the window and collapsed into his seat on the other side of the desk. For a moment she had a vision of Jim sitting in the same spot poring over the studbooks. The knowledge she'd given him free access to all of the stud records made her hands clammy and heat climb up her arms. How could she have done that? She had no right to the responsibility of running Helligen.

'Well?'

'I don't know where to start.'

'At the beginning, I suggest.'

'I've come to apologise.'

'Hmm?'

'The situation in which I placed our family. It is my fault entirely. I made a mistake.'

Papa nodded in agreement, no smile, just a curt nod.

She rushed on. 'However, Jim's not a horse thief. He shouldn't be in gaol and he shouldn't be held accountable for a crime committed over fifteen years ago when he was just a boy. You have to drop the charges and have him released.' There, she'd said it. Her shoulders sagged and a little bit of the tension trickled away. She shuffled back in the chair, clasped her hands in her lap and waited.

Goodfellow peered down at her from the portrait. It was a remarkable likeness, she could see that now. How she could have missed the similarity and not recognised Jefferson was beyond her. Then again most, if not all, of her behaviour in the last months defied description. The persistent flush rose to her cheeks and she beat it back, pushing thoughts of Jim and the river aside.

Papa steepled his fingers and stared across the desk. 'Do you have any idea what you're asking?'

Of course she did. She was asking him to have Jim released from gaol. Not to hold him responsible for a crime he hadn't committed. She wasn't asking for Jim to stay at Helligen, in fact she never wanted to set eyes on him again knowing she'd been played for a fool—but she didn't want to see him hang. 'Horse thieving is a hanging offence. He doesn't deserve to die.'

'You've been talking to Peggy,' Papa said with the first glimmer of softening in his harsh features.

'Yes, I have. Peggy told me Jim had been taken away last night. No-one else saw fit.' She couldn't resist the last barb and regretted it the moment the words left her lips.

His brow drew together in a familiar scowl, the one capable of making her stomach sink and as a child had heralded all sorts of horrible punishments. 'Only Sydney's Supreme Court is entitled to award the death penalty. The punishment for horse and cattle theft is a prison sentence. I somehow doubt the common little horse thief will be dragged to the gallows, as much as I would wish otherwise.'

'Papa!' The noose loosened around Jim's neck. 'You cannot wish any man dead.'

'I can, I have and I did. Unfortunately God intervened and beat me to it.' A dreadful look flashed across Papa's face, an absolute leaching of all colour, his eyes glazed and dulled, fixed in the past.

Whatever was he talking about? 'I'm sorry?' She had to concentrate. Her mind kept slipping back to Jim. If he received a gaol sentence, how long would he be incarcerated, and where?

'Thomas Cobb is dead. He died before his son saw fit to pay us a visit. It was his death that inspired your stud master to begin his misbegotten quest.'

That's right. She knew that. Jim had told her right at the very beginning his father had died a few months back. He hadn't lied about that. 'His father was a stud master who worked for some of the more reputable studs in New South Wales. Jim grew up around horses.'

'Indeed. Helligen amongst them,' he said drily. Her face flushed again as he pinpointed her gullibility. 'Didn't you think to ask him where?'

No. She hadn't thought to ask him where, instead she'd told him everything there was to know about Helligen and her family. 'Oh Papa, I have been so very, very foolish.'

'You have and now I think it's time for you to tell me about the rest of your foolishness. Shall we start at the beginning?'

The look of compassion on Papa's face swept away any doubts. 'I should never have placed the advertisement without asking you first.' Her words tumbled out, jumbled and confused. 'I wasn't thinking straight. I was so keen to …'

He walked around the desk until he stood in front of her and took her hand in his, patting and soothing. His eyes searched hers. 'Of course you were, my poor girl.'

'I should never have … I just wanted everything to be as it was. Full of laughter and love, not misery and memories.'

Perhaps it was the haze of shame that made her accept responsibility for the chaos she'd caused; it certainly wasn't the outrageous feelings Jim had inspired. He had duped her, tricked her and lied to her. She covered her cheeks with her hands, hiding the putrid beetroot colour. Never could she look at him again. How could she have been such a fool? She dropped her hands into her lap, her face no longer burning. A cool calm certainty told her she must make amends.

Papa sat on the corner of his desk. 'This is what I have decided.'

With a demure expression on her face she waited for the axe to fall. If only she'd thought things through and hadn't jumped in full of enthusiasm and determination. She had played straight into Papa's hands. A year to prove herself—she hadn't even reached the halfway mark.

As she ruminated on her plight there was a brief knock on the door. Papa lifted his head and a guarded smile drifted over his face. 'Laila.'

'Mama.' Surprise made her voice catch. Mama's pale grey silk dress swished as she crossed the room. She stared all the while at Papa with the strangest look in her eyes.

'Come and sit, you will tire yourself.' Papa led her to the wing-back chair by the window. India stared open-mouthed at the transformation a few short days had wrought. Mama's long hair was drawn back off her face and her carriage was poised and upright.

'Thank you, Alexander. I will sit, not because I'm tired, but because it's time you gave me the opportunity to speak. Anya tells me Jim was taken away last night, at your behest, to Maitland Gaol.'

'Don't concern yourself, my dear. I have everything under control.'

'I am concerned. You have accused him of horse theft. He's not a thief any more than his father was.'

Papa's jaw clenched and his shoulders tensed. 'You know nothing of the situation. Please, I beg of you, let me handle the matter.'

'Jim brought Goodfellow back to Helligen because I asked him.'

India attempted to smother a gasp and failed. Mama looked up at her and smiled. 'I have always known Goodfellow did not lie beneath the granite monstrosity you saw fit to place beside Oliver, as I also knew Thomas Cobb could not have shot Goodfellow.'

'How did you know?' India couldn't keep quiet a moment longer.

Papa took several steps away from Mama, his face darkening. 'I rest my case. The man was a horse thief, however I didn't imagine he'd committed the crime with your consent.'

'Oh, Alexander. You're jumping to conclusions. Let me speak and let India hear the truth. It's time to heal past wounds. Her life hangs in the balance because of something that happened half a lifetime ago.'

In a strange way it was right Mama should be the one to understand her feelings. She settled back into the chair. Papa stood with one arm resting on the mantel. He tossed a glance up at the portrait above the fireplace and then back to Mama.

'For all these years you have laid the blame for my accident on Thomas Cobb's head. Said he allowed me to ride Goodfellow that night. He didn't. I did it of my own volition.'

'I thought you had no memory of the events.'

'That's right. I *had* no memory of those events, but when I looked from my window and saw Jefferson it was as though a fog had lifted and I began to remember. At first I thought it was a dream. For so long I had been searching for Goodfellow. I knew if I could find him he would be the key to unlock the past.'

'You were looking for Goodfellow?' India asked. 'When you went out at night?' The enormity of Mama's statement ripped the ground from beneath her feet. All this time she, they, had thought her mother searched for her dead son. That one fact, her failure to comprehend Oliver's death had convinced the doctors she'd lost her senses. The sound of Papa's hand slamming down on the mantel made her jump.

'I have had enough of this. Are you telling me you have been riding again, Laila?'

'Alexander, will you hear me out or will you let a man go to the gallows because of your pigheaded attitude?'

'He won't go to the gallows,' Papa mumbled through lips rigid with frustration. 'Continue.'

'For over a year everyone had fussed and pampered me. Kept me abed all the time I was carrying Oliver.'

'It was for your own safety. I couldn't lose you … the string of miscarriages all because you insisted on working in the paddocks with that man. I wanted a son.' Papa's hand slammed down again, rocking the skeleton clock beneath its glass dome.

Her mother's plaintive cry was almost a wail. India recoiled. What had she done? She'd opened up even more heartbreak and all because she hoped to heal? What a diabolical disaster.

'Yes, I was determined to give you your heart's desire. A son to carry your name and rule the perfect kingdom you'd created for us, your family. Everything we hadn't had as children.'

India's throat tightened. Papa stood and peered down at Mama. His eyes narrowed, almost as though he didn't believe what she was saying. Mama offered a timid smile. 'I sneaked out of the house, as I have done so many times. I needed to feel the wind in my hair and the freedom. You had your ship. For months I had only four walls and Anya. The accident was my mistake and my foolishness. It was God's will we lost our beautiful son. It was never Thomas Cobb's fault and his son shouldn't pay.'

A tear rolled down India's cheek and she brushed it aside. It was as though she stood in the audience in one of the Sydney theatres watching a great melodrama unroll, but this was no narrative. It was her family. And Mama and Papa had no knowledge of her own role that night.

'It would appear both of you wish to take responsibility for the Cobbs' failings. None of what you have said leads me to change my opinion. Thomas Cobb stole Goodfellow.'

'And what about Jim?' Mama asked.

'I will consider Jim's plight. Leave him in gaol to ponder his actions for a few days, kick his heels. It'll do the boy good. The magistrate won't be around for another two weeks.'

Papa's comment echoed her own sentiments, as long as Jim wasn't to hang. 'Will you withdraw your charges?' Pushing the issue wouldn't help but she had to know.

'Against my better judgement, since both of you wish it so.'

Her heart soared. Papa liked to make deals, make arrangements and once made he stuck by them. That was part of the reason she was confident her year at Helligen would run its course. She still had time to rectify her earlier mistakes and with Jim off her conscience she'd be better able to do that.

'However, I'm putting a condition on it.'

'Condition,' India squeaked. What did he mean, condition? The ground beneath her feet wavered and she eased back into the chair.

'I will withdraw the charges against James Cobb on the condition he gets the hell off my property and out of my life. None of the Cobb family will ever set foot on Helligen again.'

India swallowed. It was to be expected.

'And Goodfellow?' Her mother asked the question in the forefront of India's mind.

'Goodfellow stays here where he belongs.'

'But you will allow Jim to take his own horse, Jefferson?'

'Again, against my better judgement. It's obvious to anyone with half a brain who sired that animal but there are no records to prove that. The animal goes with him.'

Her breath escaped in a shivering sigh and when Mama's hand came and rested on her shoulder the tears welled in her eyes. Whether from the unaccustomed gesture of understanding from a woman so long locked in her own world, or relief, she wasn't sure. Jim would be gone, it was for the best, and her life would resume the pattern she had so foolishly disrupted by her ill-advised advertisement. Helligen would live again; with her mother's help they could breathe life into it and maybe, just maybe her dreams would not die.

Papa walked to the fireplace and stared up at the portrait of Goodfellow and turned back. 'I have one more condition.'

One more? What else could he possibly want from her, from her mother?

'This nonsense is over. I will find someone to manage the property until I can find a buyer.'

'But—'

He raised his hand, stopping her words.

'I made enquiries before we left Sydney.' He raised his bushy eyebrows and glared down at her, emphasising her inability. 'India, you and Violet will travel tomorrow to Morpeth. Fred will take you in the buggy. Cecil has agreed to meet you there. He'll escort you back to Sydney.'

Her mother's fingers clenched against her shoulder. 'What about Mama?'

'Your mother and I will remain here until a new manager is installed and then return to Sydney where she'll be assessed by the doctors.'

'Mama?' Her mother's face was blank as she stared out the window, out beyond the manicured lawns to Oliver's gravestone.

'It's a matter for us to discuss. In the meantime I suggest you go and break the news to your sister. I have no doubt she will be thrilled.'

Violet would indeed be thrilled. The prospect of Sydney, the interminable drawing rooms, Cecil's cloying attention and worse, if it was possible—his mother. A fitting punishment for her foolishness? Papa's words in Sydney reverberated in her head. *A choice between James Cobb and your family.* There was nothing she could do but make that choice and live with it. She had brought this down on her own head. She was responsible, a greater responsibility than anyone imagined.

Twenty-Eight

Violet twirled through the house like a dust storm, clattering and banging as she added to the oversized pile of trunks and hatboxes collected at the bottom of the stairs. India sidestepped them and placed her single carpetbag alongside.

'Is that all you're taking?'

India sighed and shook her head. 'I have clothes in Sydney.' She couldn't pierce the cloud that hung over her. She should be pleased Papa had at least agreed to withdraw the charges against Jim, even if he wasn't to know of it for another week or so. And the transformation in her mother should surely have given her some pleasure. How long had she wanted Mama to take an interest in life, be a part of the family? Now all she felt was a vague sense of annoyance. As though there were still obstacles cluttering her path.

'I cannot wait to get back to Sydney.' Violet rammed her purple hat onto her head and adjusted the peacock feather in front of the mirror in the hallway. 'I would rather stay at Potts Point than reopen our house. The Bryces' mansion is absolutely magnificent and the gardens a dream.'

And that was the crux of her distress—the Bryces, Cecil, and her failure to resurrect Helligen. She'd wasted her opportunity and the possibility of ever presenting Papa with the Melbourne trophy. The closest she'd get would be to bet on someone else's horse, and with the way her luck was going she wouldn't manage to pick a winner. The peacock feather was the culprit. Hadn't Peggy said it was bad luck to have them in the house? For goodness sake, what was the matter with her? 'Take the peacock feather outside. Peggy will be livid.'

'No, she won't. She's far too excited for me. She says it's the best possible thing that could have happened and I deserve to be in Sydney.'

Despite her malaise India's lip twitched. Peggy didn't mean her comment in quite the way Violet had interpreted it. No doubt, Violet was the winner in the situation. Who would have thought a foolish advertisement in a newspaper would have provided her with her longed-for release?

'I am absolutely convinced I will strike up some friendships in Sydney in a matter of days. I'm sure not all of the girls from my time at Miss Wetherington's can have snaffled themselves husbands. I do believe there are some new plays at the Prince of Wales theatre and in another month or so, the first of the balls. Oh, my gosh! Do you think I might be presented to the governor? Would Papa permit it?'

'I don't see why not. I was.' Not that it was an experience she would ever want to repeat. All the gewgaws, baubles and inane tittle-tattle.

'Of course, I will need an entirely new wardrobe. These old rags—' she kicked the pile of trunks, '—will just have to do for the time being. Where is Fred? We'll be late into Morpeth and Cecil will be wondering where we are.'

Violet's prattle swirled and dipped around her. Thank goodness she was riding. Perched between Fred and Violet in the buggy all the way to Morpeth would be more than she could bear.

'There you are, Fred. Hurry up and get this loaded, it's time we were leaving.' With a wave of her gloved hand Violet turned on her heel and drifted off in the direction of the buggy, leaving Fred to wrestle the accumulated baggage out of the house.

'Violet, I think we should go and say goodbye to Mama and Papa.'

'I've already done it. Do hurry.'

India walked down the hallway. Once she'd made her farewells there would be no going back. Her feet dragged. If only there was another way. It was as though Papa had forced her to trade her freedom for Jim's. *An eye for an eye* … She knocked on the library door.

'Enter.' As ever the terse command made her stomach flinch as she pushed open the door. The sight that greeted her wasn't what she'd imagined. Her mother sat in the winged chair, her legs crossed at the ankles and resting on a small footstool. Papa had dragged his leather chair around, loosened his cravat and removed his jacket, and his feet were resting on his desk. Shrouding her look of surprise she walked in and dropped a kiss on her mother's head.

'Violet and I are leaving now for Morpeth.'

'Goodbye, my darling. Have a wonderful time in Sydney. I'm sure Cecil will look after you both admirably.' She couldn't be certain, but she thought Mama met her gaze with a gleam of sympathy in her eyes, as if aware of her reluctance to leave.

'Your father and I have a lot of catching up to do. He'll be down in Sydney soon and, who knows, I may even accompany him.'

Papa nodded in agreement. 'I've received word from Cecil that he'll be in Morpeth this evening to meet you. Go directly to the Rose, Shamrock and Thistle. He has already set in motion the matters with our Sydney house. You'll be pleased to know you won't have to stay too long at Potts Point.'

'Yes, Papa,' she replied in a dutiful voice. It would appear Violet had already been appraised of all the arrangements—maybe Papa no longer deemed her the more capable sister. However, the news that she'd be subjected to Mrs Bryce only briefly was a small bonus.

Papa stood and escorted her to the door. 'Take care, and I'll see you soon.'

'Goodbye, Papa.' For a split second she had the urge to drop a curtsy, as she would have done as a young child. Bringing her hand to her lips she blew a kiss to Mama and closed the door behind her.

The bags had disappeared from the hallway so she made her way to the kitchen. Saying goodbye to Peggy would be harder than farewelling her parents. As happy as she was to see her mother so much more … alive, Peggy had been the centre of her life for too long and she'd miss her more than she dared imagine.

In the warm, cosy kitchen a tantalising waft of apple pie hung in the air. 'I've come to say goodbye.' She threw her arms around Peggy's ample waist and received a floury hug in return.

'You take care now and don't you worry. It will all turn out for the best. That boy won't be languishing in that gaol for much longer, I promise you that.'

'I hope you're right. Jim doesn't deserve to be imprisoned, even if it's only for a short time as Papa says.' As much as Jim's deception irked her she couldn't see a man imprisoned for a crime he hadn't committed. No-one should have to pay for another man's sins. Thomas Cobb had stolen Goodfellow. Jim had simply inherited the horse.

Peggy fixed her with a steely stare. 'I guess Jim would feel a lot happier if he knew his stay was only temporary.'

'If only there was some way of telling him.' Peggy was right. Jim's stay would be far more tolerable if he knew it was only for a few days.

'So Fred's taking you to Morpeth, is he?' Peggy rubbed her hands together, her head tipped to one side in a habit she must have picked up from the curious willie wagtails that inhabited her vegetable garden.

'I'm riding. He and Violet are travelling in the buggy.'

'So they'll be taking the turnpike road. No cutting across country like you did when you went last time?'

India narrowed her eyes. 'I presume so.' Since when had Peggy developed an interest in the roads? On the rare occasions she left Helligen it was to take a simple walk to the village.

'The road goes through Maitland, doesn't it?'

'It does.' Perhaps Peggy was planning a trip; once Mama and Papa went to Sydney her workload would be cut in half.

'Peggy, we're going. I've come to say goodbye.' Violet hovered at the door. 'But I can't come in and kiss because I have arranged my hat, besides, I don't want to greet Cecil smelling of apple pies and kitchens. I'll just wave from here. Hurry up, India. We're ready.'

Peggy lifted her hand and Violet disappeared. With a sigh India turned to follow.

'You'll be travelling right past Maitland Gaol, won't you?' Peggy asked.

India stopped in her tracks and turned back to Peggy. 'Yes, yes we will.'

And then Peggy's strange behaviour became clear, making her heart leap. She gave a quick wave and offered an enormous smile. 'And thank you, Peggy, thank you for everything. I hope to see you before too long.'

Her heels rang as she crossed the flagstones. Should she or shouldn't she? Fred held her horse and she stepped onto the mounting block, eyeing the saddle with displeasure. It was the perfect symbol—side-saddle. Perched on the horse with little control, cramped in an unnatural position giving no pleasure to rider or mount. That's what Sydney would be like. A prison. Jim wasn't the only one incarcerated. Neither of them had any hope, or could see the end of their sentence. The least she could do for Jim was give him hope. Let him know his sentence would be lifted when her father saw fit. He'd be free to take Jefferson and resume his life. His father's debt to the Kilhamptons paid.

Everyone deserved hope. She would leave Fred and Violet to continue on their way and stop in Maitland. The gaol would surely give her a moment or two with Jim, or at least pass a message to him. It would take the buggy far longer to reach Morpeth than it would take her on horseback, even riding side-saddle. She'd catch up with Fred and Violet long before they reached the Rose, Shamrock and Thistle, long before Cecil docked and no-one would be any the wiser.

Anticipation fizzled and bounced with every prance of her horse. Her skin stretched tight, as though at any moment her excitement would burst free and sprinkle like raindrops over her head. When Peggy had reminded her of the route they would take it all became clear in her mind. As though the final pieces of the puzzle had fallen picture-side-up, ready to slot into place.

Papa might think it fitting punishment for Jim to languish behind bars for a week or two, but he didn't deserve that. And besides, she had a moral obligation to ensure the man she'd employed was safe before she set off for Sydney.

'Fred! Whoa up! I need to talk to you.' The dust thrown by the buggy billowed around her. Why Violet would prefer to travel perched like a bird in a gilded cage was beyond her. She sneezed as Fred pulled back on the reins and brought the buggy to a grinding halt. From the flushed look on his face it was obvious the pleasure of driving Miss Violet was almost as high on his list of priorities as being a jockey. She smothered a grin.

'I'm going to ride ahead. I have a couple of messages to deliver for Papa in East Maitland.' That wasn't exactly an untruth. Telling

Jim he would not be prosecuted was a message from Papa, just not one he'd asked her to deliver. More of a half-truth really. Not a lie. 'You go ahead and I'll catch up with you before you even reach Morpeth. If not, I'll see you at the inn.'

'Miss India, that's not a good idea. I promised Mr Kilhampton I would escort you both to Morpeth. You're under my care. I'm responsible. Mr Kil—'

'Fred. I'm not asking. I'm telling. I've ridden to Morpeth many times on my own and survived. I'm sure it won't be a problem. I'll see you at the inn.' The boy was getting ideas above his station. Ever since Jim bribed him with a ride on Jefferson he'd cast himself in a role way beyond stable boy. 'I'll see you soon, Violet.' She dug in her heels, giving her sister no opportunity to express any opinion, then veered off the road to follow the rough track that skirted the town.

The gaol dominated the landscape, leaving no doubt as to the direction she should take. Massive sandstone walls held it firm, perched on top of the hill; a solid building made from Hunter sandstone. The slate roof glinted in the afternoon light. Large and oddly handsome, vertical iron-barred windows sat at equal intervals along the walls. Jim languished somewhere behind those bars. She couldn't wait to see him and tell him the news. The peculiar golden flecks in his eyes would flash and his grin would spark the dimple in his cheek.

The gates appeared ahead of her, an imposing entrance for such a hellhole. She dismounted and tethered her horse to the convenient rail. Within moments a small door opened in the studded wooden gates and a man's head popped out. 'What?'

She swallowed, ignoring his terse greeting. 'I'd like to speak to someone in authority. I have a message for one of the prisoners.'

'No admittance today except on official business.'

What was the fool talking about?

'Gaol's closed.'

How could the gaol be closed? What rubbish! 'This is official business. I have a message concerning one of the inmates with regard to his sentence.'

'Nope. Not today.'

'I beg your pardon?' She pulled herself up to her full height and peered down her nose. If she could imitate Papa's quelling glare the man might take more notice. 'I am India Kilhampton of Helligen. I have a message from my father regarding the prisoner Jim Mawgan.' She paused as a frown crossed the man's face. He disappeared from the small door and she peered through. Inside the small gatehouse he stood scratching his head, studying a piece of paper pinned to the wall.

'Well?'

He unlatched the main door and swung it wide and without a second thought she stepped over the threshold.

'Oi! You can't come in here.'

'I'm here now. Jim, Jim Maw ... James Cobb.' She'd blundered. 'His real name is James Cobb.'

The man's head shot up and he turned and looked her up and down with a rather ratty squint. 'James Cobb, you say.' He sniffed. 'You better come with me.'

With a tight smile she stepped to one side to allow the man to lead the way. This was more like it. How foolish of her to forget that Jim Mawgan was nothing but a fantasy. It was James, James Cobb. The name had a solid ring.

The ratty man slammed the main gate and slid the large bolt across, locking out the real world. 'This way.'

From inside the compound the substantial buildings gave the impression of vast strength. The huge sandstone blocks dovetailed into each other forming an impassable barrier. Escape would be impossible. The walls were as high as the roofs of the buildings inside the compound, and thicker than she'd ever seen before. The hairs on her arms stood to attention as they walked past a caged but thankfully empty exercise yard. They skirted sheds, storehouses and rejected sandstone blocks. To her right she picked out a timber structure that had to be gallows. She averted her eyes, pushing aside the picture of Jim swinging in the breeze. It might be time to revise her opinion of the restraints Sydney would impose on her—they were nothing compared to incarceration behind these walls. A door swung open across the yard bringing with it the sound of wailing voices and crying children. 'Are there women and children imprisoned here?'

The turnkey looked her up and down as if assessing her rationality, then raised a bedraggled eyebrow. 'Women commit crimes too.'

Yes, he was probably right, but she didn't want to dwell on it. And children. Why would there be children?

'Through 'ere.' He led her into a small room. Benches lined the walls and on the opposite side was a heavy timber door, cut into it a small opening covered with metal lattice. The turnkey approached the window and stuck his face up to the grid. She couldn't catch his mumbled words, but it took only a second before he turned and made for the door.

'What should I do?' she asked his disappearing back.

'Wait here.' He slammed the door behind him.

India cast around the small room looking for something to take her attention and found nothing. She tapped her foot and counted the seconds as they passed. This wasn't working out the way she'd intended. If she had to wait much longer Violet and Fred would reach Morpeth before her and, heaven forbid, Cecil might decide to send out a search party. She had to have at least another hour or two of daylight. It was difficult to tell now she was within the confines of the gaol. Once darkness fell she'd have to think twice about riding alone. She stood up and knocked on the door where the turnkey had mumbled in conversation. Receiving no response she knocked louder, then stamped her foot. Behind her the door ground open and she turned. A corpulent, red-faced gentleman filled the doorway. His black jacket and matching trousers marked him as a man of more significance than the turnkey, despite the stains splattering his yellowed shirt.

'Miss Kilhampton, I believe.' He took a step towards her. 'It's a great honour to make your acquaintance. I've had the pleasure of your father's company on several occasions in Sydney.'

Her heart sank. Why in heaven's name had she embarked on this ludicrous goose chase? She did not want Papa brought into the conversation any more than was absolutely necessary. Pulling herself up to her full height she peered down her nose at him. 'And you are?'

'Alfred Braithwaite, the governor of this fine establishment. I believe you're enquiring after one Jim Mawgan.'

She nodded, the knot in her stomach twisting a little tighter. The man had a sly cast to one eye and he smelt musty, as though he lived underground.

'We have no prisoner of that name.'

No prisoner? What did he mean?

'Or is there some confusion … James Cobb?'

The ratty little turnkey was just as shrewd as he looked and had reported her confusion over Jim's name. She licked her lips. How to respond?

'Well, who is it?' the governor barked.

She took a step back to escape his intimidating presence and the waft of unwashed armpits and alcohol seeping from his portly body. 'James Cobb.' Somehow saying his name aloud boosted her confidence and she straightened her spine.

'In that case, I cannot help you.'

Deflated once more she stared at him. 'Why not. I know he's here. Accused of horse theft.'

'Was, my dear, was.'

Was? The word screeched through her head. *Was! The gallows.* Was she too late? Had they hung him or taken him away? Not Sydney. Not so soon. He can only have arrived last night, less than twenty-four hours ago. Papa said they would keep him for at least two weeks until the magistrate arrived. 'Where has he gone?' Ignoring the stench she took a step closer to the man with her hands outstretched.

He lifted his arm and she slammed her hands behind her back.

'I have no idea. I thought you might be able to enlighten me?'

'What do you mean, you have no idea? He is under your care, is he not?'

'He was. Until he and four others escaped this morning. The constabulary is out now. No doubt they will round them up before long. Would you care to wait in my office?'

Escaped! Wait in his office? No chance. She skirted him, step by careful step with her eyes fixed firmly on the door. *Jim had escaped.* A thrill shot through her at his daring, and subsided equally quickly. Now he truly was a wanted man.

'Not so fast, my dear.' The overweight oaf lumbered back, blocking *her* escape route. 'I have a few questions first.'

The memory of the women's voices in the compound echoed in her mind. What law had she broken? Could he restrain her? Throw her into a cell until someone, anyone, came to her rescue. No-one knew she was here. *Oh God.*

'You called the prisoner Jim Mawgan. It would appear you know something we're not aware of.'

She shook her head. 'A mistake, a simple mistake.'

'I would like to remind you that aiding and abetting an escaped prisoner carries a sentence in its own right.'

She sank down on a convenient bench as her legs turned to jelly. What a foolish mistake she'd made. James Cobb had escaped, but she'd given his name as Jim Mawgan. With those two words she'd flagged him as a man with something to hide.

'I'm enquiring after James Cobb. I have a message from my father, Alexander Kilhampton. He intends to drop the charges he levelled against Jim Mawgan.' Goddamn it. What was the matter with her? 'James Cobb.'

'I see, however the prisoner is known to you as Jim Mawgan?'

'Jim is simply a childhood name, a pet name,' she stammered, pulling words from the air. She had no idea. No idea until recently that he hadn't used his real name.

The governor interlocked his sausage fingers and twirled his thumbs. 'I see.' He rocked on his heels as he studied her. 'I presume then you're well acquainted with the prisoner?'

'Yes, yes I am. He worked for me, for my father, until—'

'Until your father had him committed for horse theft.'

This was getting more and more complicated by the moment. If Jim had escaped then she was wasting her time. She could hardly give him a message that the charges had been dropped. 'Since he's no longer here …' She rose to her feet, eyeing the door, envisaging the narrow corridor she'd walked down with the turnkey, the trip across the compound, the gallows, the heavy gate, and her horse on the other side of the walls. No. She didn't have a hope in hell. She would have to brazen it out. 'There's little I can do to assist you. I shall bid you good evening and be on my way.' She reached around him for the door handle.

His hand landed on her wrist, hot and sweaty on the strip of bare skin above her gloves. The hairs on the back of her neck quivered and rose.

'Perhaps you would care to accompany me to my office and we can discuss this in greater detail. As I said, the prisoner has escaped and any information you can provide about his possible whereabouts would assist us greatly.'

His piggy eyes glinted with something more than concern for an escaped prisoner as he cleared his throat and sent a waft of warm alcohol over her face. 'My office.'

It wasn't a request. 'I'm afraid I haven't the time. The hour is late and I'm expected in Morpeth before nightfall. Should I not arrive ...' India let the threat hang in the air. Should she not arrive, what would happen? Would Fred come looking for her? He was no match for this pompous fool. And Cecil. If she called upon him it would leave her in his debt. He would delight in rescuing her and she'd pay for it until her dying day.

'Should you not arrive ...?' His eyebrows rose and the beginning of a leer lifted the fleshy folds surrounding his eyes.

She dredged up as much righteous indignation as possible and peered down her nose. 'Are you insinuating you intend to keep me here against my wishes?'

'My dear, of course not. However, as you are aware, the light is fast fading and it would be irresponsible of me to allow you to travel unaccompanied to Morpeth. I would be remiss in my duty.'

She stepped nimbly away from him. There was nothing for it. Cecil was the only answer. 'My father's business partner, my fiancé—' that would please Violet, finally admitting she needed the wretched man, '—will be more than happy to come to my aid. Please send a message at once and tell him I require his assistance.'

'And he is?'

'Mr Cecil Bryce of Kilhampton & Bryce, Sydney. I feel sure you have heard of him?' She raised an eyebrow hoping the oaf understood her veiled threat.

'Ah yes, indeed. Mr Bryce.' He crossed the room and rapped on the small window.

'Percy. Open up.'

The window opened. 'Sir?'

'I need a message taken to Morpeth, immediately, at once. Paper, pen and organise someone to deliver it. Now my dear—' he turned back, '—what shall we say in this missive?'

A very good question. *Dear Cecil, please come and rescue me from yet another ridiculous situation I've landed myself in.* That wouldn't do at all. Cringing, she said, 'Please ask him to come to the gaol and escort me to Morpeth.'

'As you wish.' He gave an inappropriate, almost jovial smile. 'I shall arrange that and in the meantime you can enlighten me about the prisoner and his likely whereabouts.'

'I don't think there's any information I can give you.' There was certainly nothing she wanted to tell him and she had no idea of Jim's intentions. Whatever had possessed him to escape?

'Let's make ourselves more comfortable in my office while we wait for Mr Bryce.'

She lowered her eyes and acquiesced. There was little else she could do. He spent a few more moments at the barred window then opened the door and escorted her out into the corridor. There was no doubt about the lateness of the hour; leaving the small room the corridor yawned dark and foreboding ahead of them. He reached for a lantern hanging outside the door and held it aloft then led the way deep into the bowels of the gaol.

'My offices are at this end of the building, away from the caterwauling of the prisoners. A constant reminder of the riffraff we have to deal with is difficult to tolerate. I would not wish to subject a lady of your breeding to such horrors.'

The riffraff? Horrors? Where had Jim been imprisoned? How could he have escaped? The walls were at least fifteen feet high.

The corridor ended and the governor led her across a compound. 'The walls are eighteen feet high.' He pointed through one of the barred windows to the massive sandstone blocks entrapping them. 'Escapes rarely succeed. We will have the offenders back here within a matter of hours, of course.' There was something in his tone that made her doubt his blustering. If that were the case then why would he be interested in any information she could give?

'Here we are.' He led the way through the door into a well-appointed room dominated by a large polished desk with bulbous legs. 'Please make yourself comfortable. I'm certain Mr Bryce will not be too long. Morpeth is a mere five miles hence.' He shot her a look from under his uncontrolled brows, as if he disputed the veracity of Cecil's existence. 'Can I offer you any refreshments?' He gestured to a silver tray on which a half-filled cut glass decanter sat beside two well-used glasses.

Her stomach churned at the thought. 'No, thank you.'

'If you'll excuse me, I feel the need for a little something. It has been an interesting evening, has it not?'

Gritting her teeth India refrained from uttering a word. Anything further from interesting she had yet to imagine. It had been a nightmare, and worse still another of her own making.

The governor settled back into his chair and twirled the amber liquid in the glass before taking a somewhat noisy slug. He smacked his lips then placed the glass with exaggerated care on the desk and pinned her with a cold-blooded gaze. She must take care and keep her wits about her.

'If you could just fill me in on a few details I'm sure it will assist our efforts to secure the prisoner.' He rifled through a pile of papers on his desk, pulled one out and scanned it.

The prisoner. Jim was not a prisoner. Papa was dropping the charges.

'You say your father, Mr Kilhampton, intended to drop the charges against James Cobb? I have nothing to that avail in my paperwork.'

'My father realised his accusations were erroneous.' If he insisted on sounding like a court reporter from the newspaper then so could she. 'He intended to come to Maitland himself and ensure the charges were dropped. Since I was passing he asked me to inform Mr Cobb to … to prevent him being unduly concerned until his release was secured.' There, that didn't sound bad.

'And your father employed Mr Cobb to work on his property?'

'No, I … yes. He advertised for a stud master and Mr Cobb answered the advertisement and secured employment.'

'So your father has returned from Sydney and is now residing at Helligen once more.'

'Yes, he's residing at Helligen at the moment.' That was closer to the truth. To admit that she, a mere woman, had been running the property would no doubt make the situation appear even more peculiar. Where was Cecil? For a man who prided himself on his ability to sort matters this time lapse was impossible. The clock struggled its way past the hour, each and every second ticking in her head. For the first time in her life she would be pleased to see Cecil.

'It states here that James Cobb was in possession of a horse, Goodfellow, belonging to your father. I take it that is no longer the case.'

'It was all a misunderstanding. Goodfellow is at our property and, as I said, my father intends to drop the charges.' How many times did she have to say it?

'Ah! Intends. I see.' He took another sip. 'In that case, when Mr Cobb escaped he was still under the charge of horse theft.' He refilled his glass and drummed his fat fingers on the side. 'And you have no idea where Mr Cobb might be?'

She shook her head although she knew exactly where Jim would go. Back to get Jefferson—she'd put money on it. Jefferson meant more to him than his freedom. He would leave Goodfellow but not Jefferson. The horse was all he had. And when Papa found out he was back on the property? A cold shudder traced her spine. She had to get back there. She couldn't go to Sydney until Jim was safe. Why had she agreed to leave?

'A thief generally returns to the scene of his crime.'

The words hung in the air. The wretched man was a mind-reader. 'I have absolutely no idea what you mean.' She scrabbled for something more. 'He has *not* committed a crime. He is *not* a horse thief.'

She almost missed the knock. Before the governor had time to open his mouth again the door flew open.

'India. Thank goodness.'

She leapt up and almost threw herself into Cecil's arms. Never, never in her life had she been so pleased to see anyone, least of all Cecil.

'Mr Bryce.' The governor lumbered to his feet, his hand out-stretched and his face wreathed in a sycophantic smile, a far cry from anything she'd been privy to.

Cecil pulled himself up to his full height, which was in fact quite imposing, and peered down at the governor. She took a step closer, surprised by her need to seek Cecil's protection.

'I hardly think this is a social occasion.' Cecil ignored the governor's outstretched hand. His inane grin dropped along with his hand and India restrained a cheer.

'Quite why you saw fit to detain Miss Kilhampton is beyond my comprehension. I shall be taking the matter further, have no doubt of that.'

A degree of spluttering filled the room, almost covering Cecil's words. 'Come, my dear. Let me get you home.'

Home. For a moment hope blossomed. *Home.* And they might get there before Jim ran into Papa. Cecil ushered her out the door without a backward glance and marched her across the compound.

The shadows cast by the gates had lengthened and she drew closer to Cecil's side, resting a hand on his arm. He tucked it under his elbow and she shrank against him, comforted by his presence.

'Violet is at the Rose, Shamrock and Thistle. We really can't leave her alone any longer. It is hardly suitable. The mistress assured me she would act as chaperone but I'm unconvinced. Violet would tempt any man. I took the liberty of bringing Fred with me.'

The ratty man at the main gate appeared from his hidey-hole, took a quick glance at the grim look on Cecil's face and swung the gate open. Swaying against Cecil she almost collapsed in relief at the sight of Fred lounging against the buggy, with her horse tethered behind munching on a bag of something delicious.

Cecil handed her up into the buggy. 'Let's get back to Morpeth now, Fred, quick as you can. Miss Violet will be worried.'

'Yes, sir. Mr Bryce, sir.'

India collapsed against the padded seat and let out a long slow breath. The afternoon had not been one of her finest. At every turn some evil bunyip stretched out a toe and tripped her, and then before she had time to get back on course something else cropped up.

Her most pressing need now was to return home. How to convince Cecil of that? He had played an admirable role as rescuer, but the prospect of Jim returning a wanted man, in search of Jefferson, sent shivers scuttling down her spine. Papa would not be impressed.

'Not long now, my dear, a few miles and then we will have you safe and sound at the inn. We'll take the steamer to Sydney as planned in the morning. By tomorrow afternoon we'll be ensconced at Potts Point with all this nonsense behind us.'

Nonsense! Wasn't he even going to ask her what she'd been doing at the gaol?

'Miss Violet was really worried when you didn't catch up with us before Morpeth.' Fred answered her question. *Violet!* Of course, she would have taken great delight in apprising Cecil of her version of the situation. India could almost hear the conversation, the sighs and raised eyebrows, lowered lashes and coy smiles.

'Cecil.'

'Yes, my dear.' He gave her arm another soothing pat.

'Thank you so much for coming to my rescue. I feel a complete fool.'

'Think nothing of it. Your father would be horrified if anything happened to you on my watch. I'm only pleased we resolved the situation so easily. These pompous fools always crumble in the face of authority.'

The only problem being the situation was not resolved, and she had to find some way of persuading Cecil that she must return home. Travelling to Helligen tonight was out of the question. Tomorrow, however, was a distinct possibility.

Twenty-Nine

'I think it's an absolute disgrace, India, that you can throw our plans into such disarray.' Violet tossed her head and stepped up into the buggy. 'Papa will flay you alive. Cecil is a paragon of virtue to tolerate your tantrums.'

India didn't deign to answer. She'd exhausted every last ounce of her energy convincing Cecil they should return home. It was only when she played her trump card, burst into tears and suggested she, and by association Cecil, might be implicated in Jim's escape that Cecil had crumbled and agreed. He'd drawn the line at allowing her to travel alone with Fred though. Why, she had no idea. She'd made the trip unaccompanied more times than she could count. Something about responsibility and appropriateness.

'India, do you still insist on riding? I'm sure we can make room for you.' He shifted along the seat closer to Violet.

From her vantage point in the saddle Violet's little quiver of delight as Cecil moved closer was more than obvious. India ignored it. Let Violet play her games. The thought of marrying Cecil made her physically sick. It would mean trusting him to take care of her, losing control, conforming. There would be no more freedom to spend days at Helligen. The look her mother had given her and the touch on her shoulder had exuded such sympathy and understanding she'd dared to dream that she might, with Mama's assistance, escape her sentence. It would require time and gentle progress to build the bridges that illness and guilt had shattered. Marriage to Cecil would prove an impenetrable barrier.

Since his masterful rescue last night Cecil had been more than attentive to her every need; however, she was in grave danger of suffering an attack of the vapours for the first time in her life. Riding would give her a better chance to breathe and scour the countryside. She had no doubt that Jim would make for Helligen. Jefferson would be his only concern. If she could find him and manage to convince him not to return while Papa was at home, then perhaps she could bring Jefferson to him.

The miles disappeared beneath the horse's hooves along with her hopes. Jim wouldn't travel the road. On foot he'd stick to the trails and tracks, out of sight … unless he'd managed to acquire a horse. Or steal a horse!

As the shadows lengthened the hills above Helligen appeared on the horizon and India reined in beside the carriage. 'I will ride ahead and alert everyone to our return.'

Cecil leant across Violet. 'I don't think that's a very sensible idea, my dear. Would it not be better if we present a united front to your father? I feel sure you will need my support. I shall speak to him man to man. Make him understand the need for our return. Convince him you have only gone against his dictates because of the dire circumstances in which you found yourself.'

This was exactly what she'd feared. 'I am quite capable of presenting my own case, Cecil, thank you.'

Violet compensated for her shortness by resting her hand on Cecil's sleeve and giving him an understanding pat, reminiscent of the kind one would offer a faithful hound. 'India, that's unnecessarily rude. Cecil is trying to do his best for you. Don't be so churlish.'

Not bothering to respond India brought her crop down on her horse's flanks and took off with Violet's cry of disgust echoing in her ears. She didn't look back. She'd got herself into this situation and she would be the one to take the matter up with Papa. Not Cecil.

She crossed the river and entered Helligen through the back paddocks, gulping in the sweet fresh air. It was such a relief to be home. She could breathe again. Think again. And think she would have to do before she faced Papa. She picked up the driveway below the mares' paddock and slowed to a trot only when she reached the fig trees flanking the house.

The courtyard was empty save for the kookaburra that offered a raucous welcome from his perch on the open stable door. A string of washing billowed in the breeze and white butterflies flitted around Peggy's cabbages, searching for crevices to lay their eggs.

She dismounted and loosened the girth before allowing her horse to drink, then tied the slip rope to the hitching post. The buggy could not be far behind and Fred could deal with everything when he arrived. She had other things on her mind. Who first? Papa or Mama? Better still, Peggy. An easier reception would give her time to collect her thoughts and find out how the land lay.

As always, the kitchen door stood ajar. Peggy's ample rump welcomed her. Head as good as stuck in the oven, her muffled mutterings peppered the warm air.

'I'm back.'

'Sweet Mary and Jesus, you made me jump.' Peggy straightened up, almost dropping the tray of scones in her hands. 'What are you doing here? I imagined you arriving in Sydney. Swanning around Potts Point with the upper crust.'

India unhooked her hat from around her neck and dropped it onto the table. 'It's a long story.'

'Nothing changes. What have you done this time?'

'It's not so much what I've done but what Jim's done.'

'Oh, not again. That man's more trouble than he's worth.' Peggy wiped her hands on her apron. 'Tea?'

India nodded. She'd made the right decision. Tea and comfort, then she'd face Papa. She pulled out her favourite chair and sat at the table, elbows resting on the weathered surface.

'Well?' Peggy asked, spooning leaves into the big brown teapot.

'I went to the gaol.'

Peggy flashed her a look from beneath her eyebrows and reached for the kettle. 'You spoke to him then, told him.'

'Not exactly.'

The water hissed and spat and most of it ended up in the teapot. Peggy plonked it onto the table and reached for two cups. 'I'm waiting. Spit it out for goodness sake. I can't stand the suspense.'

'He wasn't there.'

'Wasn't there? But Mr Kilhampton hasn't left the place to get the charges dropped. He couldn't have sent anyone, either. I would have known. Fred was with you. And Tom Bludge has been sleeping off the devil's own hangover. He couldn't have put one foot in front of another.'

'Exactly.' Her face flushed. If it were so difficult to tell Peggy, how on earth would she face Papa? 'I sent Fred and Violet ahead to Morpeth and went to the gaol. As you suggested.'

'Me? I did no such thing. Just said it would be nice for him to know the charges weren't hanging over his head. I didn't expect you to go there. Thought you'd send Fred or something.'

That thought hadn't even crossed her mind. If she was honest she'd rather hoped she might see him. 'I went. When I got there I asked to see Jim and—'

'Jim? He was arrested as James Cobb. You didn't—'

'Yes, I did.' She hung her head. 'I didn't even think.'

Peggy pursed her lips and gave the teapot three aggressive twists. 'And …'

'I ended up seeing the governor.'

'The governor. The governor of Maitland Gaol.' Peggy shuddered. 'Foul place. Nasty man, I've heard tell.'

The sounds of the wailing women echoed in India's ears. 'Yes. Yes, it is.' She had to spit it out. Get it over and done with. In some strange way she was pleased Jim had escaped. At least her foolishness hadn't made it worse. Not yet, anyway. 'He'd escaped.' There, she'd said it.

'Oh Lordy. What did he go and do that for? How? No-one gets out of that place. The walls are six feet thick. I saw the blocks they quarried from round Morpeth way. Huge, they were. How did he get out?'

'I don't rightly know. The governor implied he wasn't alone.'

Peggy tut-tutted the tea into a cup; added milk and two large spoonfuls of sugar, then pushed it across to India. 'Not a nice place. Gaols aren't. My mother came here on one of them convict ships. The stories she used to tell. And the chains. Manacles. They chain them like dogs, you know. Worse than dogs, big steel collars.'

Now for the rest. 'It was awful. I could hear the women wailing and children crying. The place was like a vision from hell. Something from *Gulliver's Travels*. I thought he was going to keep me there.' She hiccupped back a sob.

'Drink your tea. It'll make you feel better.'

Sniffing at the steam she flattened her fingers around the cup and sipped the comforting brew. 'I had to get Cecil to come and rescue me.'

Peggy rocked back and let out a long drawn-out sigh. 'Oh. And I suppose he did, since you're here and not locked up. I bet that went down like a sack of potatoes.'

'Actually, he was kindness itself. He took me back to the inn. We all spent the night there. Violet was insufferable, but in the end I managed to talk Cecil into coming back here instead of taking the steamer to Sydney.'

'Cecil Bryce and Violet are back here? Where are they?'

'Probably entering the courtyard as we speak. I rode ahead. I wanted to let you know and maybe get to Papa before Cecil had the opportunity. I'd say that's the final death knell to my chances of ever running Helligen.'

'We'll see, we'll see. Drink up.' Peggy followed her own instructions. 'And do we know where Cobb is?'

India shrugged her shoulders. 'No idea. I'd put money on him coming back here. He won't leave Jefferson. It's just a question of how long it takes him. Whether they catch him.' And put him in irons and send him God-only-knows-where to serve out a hefty sentence for escaping. 'They have gallows in the compound at Maitland Gaol.'

'Ssh. Now. We'll worry about that later. Right now we've got to decide what to do with that sister of yours and Mr Cecil Bryce. That puts my menu up the spout. Jilly!' Peggy bustled out into the scullery. 'Go and prepare the guest room for Mr Bryce, right now. I want clean sheets and the place perfect. We don't want to give him any chance to complain.'

Jilly's eyes expanded to the size of saucers and India offered her a watery smile as the girl bobbed a curtsy. Serve her right for eavesdropping. Now her curiosity would be killing her.

'Off you go, girl. No time to waste.'

'And you, missy. You get yourself out there. Make sure Violet goes straight to her room and show Mr Bryce to his. Your father's locked in that library of his and that's where we want him to stay. Once you've done that, go and have a word with your mother. She needs to know what's going on.'

'Mama?' Not Mama. What would she say? *I've come to tell you about my day.* She couldn't. 'I can't, Peggy.'

'Yes, you can. And yes, you will. Your mother is in a much better place since that wretched horse came back and we all know she can wrap Mr Kilhampton around her little finger. Go on. Off you go. Soonest said, soonest mended.'

'Least said, Peggy, least said.'

'Not in this case, my girl. Off you go and take your medicine.'

India gulped back the rest of her tea. Life without Peggy would be intolerable. She threw her arms around Peggy and dropped a kiss on her soft cheek. 'Thank you, Peggy. I don't know what I'd do without you.'

'Humph! Get a move on.' A pleased flush stained Peggy's cheeks making India want to cry. From this moment on she'd remember just how much she owed Peggy. She was her rock. Right from the moment she'd walked up the path from the village and picked up the job after Mama's accident.

As she returned to the courtyard the buggy appeared around the bend. Fred brought it to a halt and Cecil tumbled out and offered Violet his arm; she smiled prettily as he handed her down. Violet was so much more suited to Cecil. She thrived on his attentions whereas they drove her to distraction. He wasn't a terrible man. Just not for her. She didn't want to be mollycoddled like some hothouse orchid; she belonged here, at Helligen, where she was needed.

'You made good time.' Violet adjusted her hat with one hand and held tightly onto Cecil's arm with the other, almost as though she would never, ever let him escape.

'I took a shortcut through the paddocks. I've had a word with Peggy. The guest room is being prepared for Cecil. Can you show him up there? Peggy's busy in the kitchen. We've disrupted her menu.'

'I certainly hope not,' Cecil said. 'I'm looking forward to a hearty country meal.'

'I'm sure Peggy will manage. I'm going to go and see Mama, unless you'd like to, Violet?' She couldn't resist the jibe.

'Oh goodness, I couldn't. Just look at me covered in the dust from the road. I shall see Papa at dinner. Maybe Mama will join us. Can you let them know Cecil is here?'

India curbed a grin. 'Yes, I can do that. You make sure Cecil is comfortable and I'll see Mama.'

'It sounds like a perfect solution to me. Come along, Cecil. We'll use the front door. I won't subject you to the back entrance.' Violet's heels click-clacked along the verandah and she disappeared around the corner with Cecil in tow.

'Fred.'

'Yes, miss.' Fred had a new tone in his voice. It sounded as though the last few days had made him grow up a bit.

'I can leave you to sort everything out here, can't I?'

He gave her a curt nod, turned on his heel and then turned back. 'Miss?'

'I have to go and speak with my mother,' she said, impatient to be gone. Surely Fred wasn't going to offer her some advice.

'Mr Jim, miss. He will be all right, won't he? I don't like to think of him chasing across the country with a bunch of ne'er-do-wells. He's not like that. It's not where he belongs. He should be here, on Helligen with Jefferson and Goodfellow.' He scratched his head. 'He'll come back, won't he? Come back for Jefferson. He'll leave the old boy, but he won't leave Jefferson. He's proud of that horse.'

Well, that made two of them. She wasn't alone in her belief Jim would return. 'He may well do that, Fred.'

'And if he does, miss. I won't be telling nobody. 'Specially not Mr Kilhampton. I promise you that.' Fred turned on his heel to walk away then whipped around and glared at her. 'He shouldn't have called the constables. That was a downright mean trick to pull. Mr Jim didn't steal that horse. His father did. He can't be responsible for what his father did. Half the country would still be in chains if that was the case.'

He had a point there. A very good point. Hundreds of sons and daughters of convicts had made their lives a success, and she'd never heard of any held responsible for their fathers' crimes. 'If Jim turns up you let me know, Fred. And in the meantime, look after the horses. Jefferson especially.'

'I'll do that, miss. I'll do that.' He doffed his cap. 'Can't stand around here gossiping. Man's got his work to do.'

'Indeed he has, Fred. And thank you.'

She tossed him a smile and left him to his work. He was a good kid. And he was right. Jim couldn't be held responsible for any crime his father had committed. After all, he'd brought the stolen goods back to their rightful owner. It wouldn't stand up in court. Any judge worth his salt would throw it right out. And she had every intention of speaking up, even if it meant incurring Papa's wrath.

She walked under the covered walkway and through the back door to the main house. As always she paused at the bottom of the stairs and ran her hand over the smooth cedar banister, inhaling the lingering scent of beeswax and lavender. After a moment she lifted her skirts and ran up the stairs. For the first time in her life she couldn't wait to see Mama, to admit to her foolishness and share her burden. Peggy said she was 'in a better place'. What did that mean? Goodfellow's return had made such a difference to Mama's outlook, even Violet thought so. She knocked on the door mouthing the same old refrain. Habit got the better of her as the door opened and Anya's face appeared. 'I've come to see Mama and tell her of my day. Days, actually, Anya.'

The door swung open. The curtains billowed in the breeze and a patch of sunlight illuminated the jewel-coloured carpet on the floor. The bath chair had gone and the bed was made, pillows plumped and the pristine white coverlet glowing. She spun around. 'Mama!'

'India. How lovely. What do you think?' Mama turned from the mirror, her grey-blonde hair catching the light in a series of intricate braids that pulled back from her face and collected in heavy strands at the nape of her neck. She looked so … well, she looked beautiful.

'I feel quite like a young girl again. Do you remember when I used to braid your hair? You hated it! I used to sit you on the kitchen table and Peggy would bribe you with biscuits to make you stay still. Your hair was always such a tangle. We have thick hair. You've inherited that from me.' She patted the sides of her head and turned this way and that.

'It looks lovely, Mama.' Their eyes caught in the mirror, grey reflecting grey. She'd never noticed how alike they were.

'But wait a moment. What are you doing here? I thought you'd gone to Morpeth with Violet to meet Cecil. Anya?'

Anya nodded. 'Yes, they went to Morpeth.'

'Then why are you back here so soon? Why aren't you in Sydney?'

'That's why I came to speak to you.'

'Oh, and I thought it was to tell me about your day.' Mama's look, reflected in the mirror, showed no sign of confusion. How long had she hidden behind the wall she'd built to save herself from day to day reality?

'Cecil and Violet are back here as well. I was hoping you would join us for dinner.'

'I think I've made myself presentable for dinner. What do you think, Anya?'

'You are always presentable in my eyes.'

'Enough of this nonsense.' Mama turned to face her. 'Sit down, there on the bed, and tell me what you're doing back and about Cecil and Violet. I don't want to cause any problems.' Her lips twitched as though she knew every bit how difficult Violet could be.

'I took matters into my own hands.' It was so important to get this right, so important the story Mama related to Papa didn't inflame the situation. Papa must understand what she had done and why. 'Papa said he would drop the charges against Jim and I wanted him to know so that he had some hope. I called into Maitland Gaol.'

'And because you wanted to ensure Jim had survived his ordeal.'

'Yes.' She inclined her head. She couldn't meet Mama's eyes. Instead of seeing past her they now bored into her very soul, as though her mind was an open book.

'When I got there, Jim had gone.'

'Your father's message must have reached the gaol quicker than we expected.'

'Gone *before* the message reached the gaol. He'd escaped with some other men at first light and they were out hunting them down.' Like dogs on a kangaroo hunt. Running them down. Her stomach churned and she bit down on her lip.

'I see. And Cecil brought you back here. He ignored your father's wishes and came back here. You must have been very persuasive. I don't expect Violet's happy.'

'Yes, I was. And no, she isn't.' Surely she could get away with not admitting she'd called upon Cecil to rescue her.

'And why is it so important that you come back here?'

Her mouth dropped. *Why was it so important?* Jim was being hunted across the country. He still believed a sentence hung over his head. Anything could happen to him and Mama wanted to know why it was important.

'I need Papa's help, your help. We must find Jim. I know Papa doesn't want him on the property, but we must return Jefferson to him. He brought Goodfellow back. He cannot be held responsible for something his father did. I must know he's safe.'

'Ah! Now we get to the truth.'

'It's all the truth. Jim has committed no crime.'

'You seem to have changed your tune, my darling. Before you left for Sydney you wanted no more to do with the man.'

India reached for her face as the colour flooded her cheeks, making her skin prickle and her collar too tight. Her mother was right. Jim lied. Not Jim. James! He inveigled his way onto the property. Pretended to be someone he was not. Didn't even use his own name. And kissed her, made love to her. Who had done that? Jim Mawgan or James Cobb? How could she care for a man who had used her, lied to her? But she did. 'I may have been wrong,' she mumbled into her hands.

'It seems your father and I have a lot to talk about. Go and get changed. I'll find him and we shall all meet in the dining room.'

Thirty

The sky hung dark and heavy and the wind picked up, bringing with it a hint of the wetlands. No better than a wild animal pursuing his quarry, Jim broke into a run. The wide lagoon came into view, flat and dark, reflecting the gathering storm—a far cry from the golden vista that had greeted him on his arrival, an eternity ago.

A pang of disappointment shafted through him. Had he taken the time to think through his foolhardy plan the outcome might have been so different. He wouldn't be sneaking around, a sentence hanging over his head, stealing a horse that was rightfully his, from under the nose of the man who had already accused him of being a horse thief. The irony of the situation didn't escape him. Imprisoned for horse theft and this was the closest he'd come—stealing his own horse.

Arriving on the foreshore of the lagoon he found a sheltered spot amongst the trees and settled down to wait until the sun set and he could make his way to the barn unobserved. At least now he knew what he was up against. The risk he was running. No wonder his father was keen to right past wrongs. Guilt alone must have driven him to his early grave.

The possibility Kilhampton may go further and accuse him of benefitting from stolen goods niggled at him. Jefferson was the product of a service by a stolen animal. If Mrs Kilhampton had sanctioned his father's actions it might have been different. When his father spirited Goodfellow away she lay half dead, unable to condone his actions. The waters were muddied by so many different versions, different perceptions. It was unlikely he would ever know the truth of the events that night. Fifteen years later and the consequences still dictated every facet of his life. What he wouldn't give for the opportunity to talk to his father one more time.

One by one the windows of the house lit up. He followed Peggy's progress—first to the dining room, then her shadow crossed the hallway and a second or two later a light flickered in the library. No doubt Kilhampton would be poring over his papers and organising everyone's lives.

A little later her shadow passed the upstairs windows and two bedrooms blossomed to life. Not Mrs Kilhampton's room, that was around the back of the house overlooking the courtyard, as was India's. Violet's room. But who else? What business was it of his?

Peggy returned to the dining room, setting the table for the evening meal, he guessed. His stomach rumbled—some of Peggy's roast beef and Yorkshire pudding wouldn't come amiss. The likelihood of him ever being an invited guest, even a tolerated one, was long gone. What of Mrs Kilhampton? Despite the conversation they'd shared and her patent joy at the return of Goodfellow she'd done nothing to support his cause, and neither had India.

Twilight spread its diffused palette across the landscape, lengthening the shadows, telling him it was time. He skirted the fig trees and took the back path to the barn where with any luck

Jefferson and Goodfellow would still be stabled. If not, he'd have to cross the courtyard and run the risk of being spotted.

The wretched mopoke owl hooted an alarm as he slipped between the shadows, but it went unheeded and he edged his way to the double doors of the barn. As he reached for the latch the door swung free. He'd been off the place for two days and already Fred had returned to his slapdash ways. When he got his hands on the boy he'd tan his backside. He shook his head at his own foolishness. He wouldn't have the chance. The strange sense of responsibility he felt for the place irked him. He'd be sorry to leave. Perhaps he might have done better at the beginning walking up to the gate and announcing his arrival, and to hell with any advertisement. If he'd known Kilhampton hadn't been on the property he would have considered it. Then India wouldn't be able to level her accusations of lying. The sticky strands of the tangled web had reached out from every corner and lured him in.

It was too late now to do anything about it. His dreams of racing Jefferson were over. It would be enough simply to turn his back on Helligen and ride away. Put the past behind him and start anew.

Inside the barn, amid the warm sweet smell of hay and dung and the welcoming darkness, he breathed more easily. A sense of peace washed over him as his eyes adjusted to the darkness. He gazed up at the high raked ceiling soaring above and his pulse settled to a more regular pace. The horses watched from their stalls, ears pricked, aware of the promise of change. One of the soft-eyed buckskins whinnied as he approached, putting her face forward for a rub.

The shadowy outline of Jefferson's head moved, noting his arrival, nostrils flared in welcome, and Goodfellow turned to greet him too. He reached out and offered his hand. The velvety nose touched his skin, telling him how much he'd been missed.

Jefferson backed gently away from the gate to allow him to enter the stall. When he swung the saddle onto his back he shifted a little as he always did. Jim growled in response. This was no time for games. Resorting to soothing endearments, he slipped the bridle over Jefferson's head.

'I wasn't expecting you so soon.'

The hair on the back of his neck stood to attention. He dropped his hand and turned. 'Mr Kilhampton!' Soothed into a false sense of security he hadn't noticed the man sitting on the bench opposite the stalls.

Kilhampton eased to his feet. Their eyes met and shoulders tensed. Like a looking glass Kilhampton's stance mirrored his own. Weary, despondent and suspicious.

'They released you.'

'Released?' No, not released, escaped. A cold hand squeezed his heart. He clamped his mouth shut. There would be no more lies.

'You've come for your horse?'

'I have.' He sensed the slightest quiver in his voice and swallowed it down. Now wasn't the time for self-recrimination.

'I take it you will be leaving mine.' Kilhampton's words were clipped, tight with sarcasm, chasing away any hope of reconciliation.

'I came for *my* horse. Jefferson.'

'Not a thief like your father then?'

'My father was not a thief.'

'He stole *my* horse.'

'He rescued your horse from an untimely death.'

The air crackled. As the pause lengthened Kilhampton let out a long shuddering breath and with it the overpowering stench of alcohol, enough to knock a man down.

Jim shot a look to the bench. A bottle sprawled empty on the ground, the cork thrown aside. He turned back and caught Kilhampton's momentary stagger.

'Thomas Cobb destroyed my life.'

This time he didn't answer. It was not the time or place to indulge a drunken man's insinuations. He needed to get the hell out of the place before a band of constables arrived to drag him back to the gaol.

'The wretched man even visited her when she was abed and gave her daily updates.'

Jim slipped the latch and led Jefferson out of the stall. The sooner he put Helligen behind him the better. He didn't want to hear any more accusations, indulge in any further exchange. His time here was over.

'I'm talking to you, boy.' Kilhampton weaved in front of him, head lowered, fists clenched.

Boy! Jim ground his teeth together and flexed his fingers.

Anger radiated between them, a tangible presence swirling in the cosy humidity of the barn, sucking away the air.

'My father did what he thought was best.' He wouldn't take the bait, be lured by Kilhampton's vicious tirade.

'Took what was rightfully mine.'

That old chestnut again. How long would it go on? 'Goodfellow is back now, where he belongs. I lay no claim to him.'

'I'm not talking about the bloody horse.' Kilhampton swung a kick at the stall door. 'Intolerable situation. Cuckolded in my own house by the stablehand.'

Jefferson backed away, ears pricked and the whites of his eyes brilliant orbs in the half-light. If only he could do the same. The man was mad.

'He took my wife, took my son. Destroyed my family.' With a guttural groan Kilhampton staggered back until the backs of his knees hit the bench.

Feigning a disinterest his heartbeat belied, Jim led Jefferson back into the stall, murmuring a selection of soothing words. Whether they were for the horse or himself he had no idea. *Took his wife? His horse, yes. But his wife! Cuckolded by the stablehand. His father and Mrs Kilhampton?* Kilhampton was beyond drunk.

'He tempted her with his ideas, wheedled his way into the very fabric of her life, until she was consumed by the desire to win. She lived and breathed nothing but the horse and a ludicrous dream of the racetrack.'

Jim exhaled. Perhaps not cuckolded in the true sense of the word. Just the ravings of a drunkard. He latched the stall gate behind him. Kilhampton sat, his head bent, clasped in his big brown hands. *She lived and breathed nothing but horses and the dream of the racetrack.* He might have been talking of his daughter, of India, with her wild dreams and passionate ideas. Ideas and dreams that matched his own. 'My father was committed to Helligen, committed to your family. You threw him off the property, and blamed him for your misfortune.'

'He *was* responsible for my misfortune.' Kilhampton let out a hollow laugh. 'My stallion wasn't the only thing of mine he stole. He stole my wife. And now you turn up and try to prise my daughter away from me. Take your blasted horse and leave before it's too late.'

Kilhampton lurched to his feet, missed and sprawled face down in the dirt. Jim shook his head. There was little else he could do but leave before it became too much, before he learned something about his father he didn't want to hear, before he retaliated. Oh, but the truth tantalised him; he needed to know. Another jagged piece of the puzzle, with edges as sharp as a cutthroat razor, thrown at him and yet he must walk away.

He reached down to help Kilhampton to his feet.

Kilhampton's fist came from nowhere. Bone connected with bone. Pain exploded in his head. Through a reddened haze Jim saw Kilhampton stagger back against the barn wall, his eyes wide and staring. He shook his head and launched. Head down. A bull charging.

His weight barrelled him against the stall. A rush of air whooshed out of his mouth. Clutched in some parody of an embrace he raised his hands, fingers spread, and pushed Kilhampton off. *Just far enough. Call a halt. Stop this insanity.* Now was not the time. Nothing good could come of it.

A sharp crack. The bunched fist slammed into his jaw. A warm rush of blood filled his mouth and he spat it away. 'Stop. This will solve nothing.'

Bathed in sweat, Kilhampton's chest heaved. 'I should have given that to your father.' He stepped back, taunting him, egging him on. No longer drunk but tense, poised, ready to strike. He lunged again.

Wild punches rained down on him peppered with a stream of shipboard oaths. He was a fool. This was no old man. This was a seasoned fighter, survivor of a thousand dockside brawls. Jim bent over to catch his breath. He'd left it too late. Drips of his sweat soaked into the dirt floor. He couldn't fight the man. This was India's father. He turned away.

A punch slammed into his kidneys. His body screamed in pain. Sweat stung his eyes, a flash of light. Self-preservation won. He twisted, his temper red-hot at the injustice. He slammed his fist into Kilhampton's gut. The man dropped to his knees before him. Hands clutching his stomach. He returned the man's cold stare, ignoring the blood as it oozed from his lips and dribbled down his chin.

'Enough!' Jim pulled up his shirt and mopped his face.

'Enough.' Kilhampton groaned. He shuffled until his back rested against the wall and pulled his knees up to his chest, his breath a rasping, ragged wheeze.

Dear God! All he needed was an accusation of assault to add to escape and horse theft.

Kilhampton coughed and spat a bloody globule onto the dirt floor. 'I'm getting too old for this.'

With a sigh Jim sank down opposite him, his legs like jellied eels, shivering in time with the pounding in his head. 'I'll be out of your hair in a moment.'

'Don't you want to know about your father?'

'Some things are better left unsaid.'

'Too many things have been left unsaid. None of this would have happened if people had spoken.'

He didn't want to hear about his father. It was bad enough to know he'd stolen Goodfellow; anything else was better left buried with him. 'I've heard enough.' He pushed to his feet, sucking in a deep breath to test the pain spreading up from his kidneys. Jesus! The man packed a punch.

'Sit down. Is there anything left in that bottle?' Kilhampton gestured to the upturned bottle on the ground.

'No.'

'Shame.'

So he could fight like a navvy and drink like one too.

'I owe you an explanation.'

'I don't think you do.' Another lie. It dripped off his tongue like the blood filling his mouth. Something passed down from father to son. Like Goodfellow and his long legs. Chalk it up to expediency. His head throbbed like the very devil. The pain from his kidneys filled his chest. If he'd known the man could fight he wouldn't have been so hesitant, or dropped his guard. Same things he'd done more times than he could count since he set foot on the place.

He slumped back against Jefferson's stall and closed his eyes. Just a few more moments and he'd take his horse and leave. Surely Kilhampton had finished with him now. He needed to put a good fifty miles between himself and Helligen. This would be the first place the constabulary would look.

A beam of light turned the blood behind his eyelids to red, then a cool hand on his cheek made him open his eyes. He licked at the congealed blood on his lips and tried to bring the dark, shadowy face into focus.

A damp cloth dabbed at his face and the stringent smell of neat alcohol burned an acrid path up his nostrils.

'Rest easy. It is not so bad.'

Whose voice? A woman. Not India. Anya.

'Oh Alexander. What have you done?'

'Men's business. Leave it be, Laila.'

Red faded to pink, light seeped in beneath his lashes. He peeled one eye open. The sliver of light grew. Kilhampton looked like a dog's breakfast, blood across his mouth, his voice slurred. Maybe he'd defended himself a little better than he thought. Then why did he hurt so much? He sucked in a deep breath and pain knifed through him—a broken rib.

'Look at the pair of you. Two squabbling children. Now, what has happened?'

Anya's cloth continued to dab at his face. He was better off than Kilhampton. His wife glared down at him, hands on hips, more like a fishwife than the invalid lady of Helligen. 'You promised me there would be no more brawls, no more drinking. Your dockside manners do not belong here.'

Beneath the smeared blood Kilhampton's face flushed red and he winced. 'And you promised you'd learned your lesson. No more mad gallops and no more contact with the Cobb family.'

At the sound of his name Jim pushed aside Anya's hand and struggled upright. Were Kilhampton's drunken accusations familiar to his wife? More than the ravings of an irate, disappointed man?

Anya lifted a tin mug to his lips and tipped it. Water trickled down his chin. Listening was more important. Water could come later. He pushed her hand away.

'Thomas was a scapegoat. You held him responsible for all our misfortunes. It's always easier to blame someone else.'

'Was Oliver my son?' A ponderous, expectant silence hung like a cloud.

Mrs Kilhampton pulled back her hair from her face, her gesture so like India it made Jim's heart cramp. 'Oliver is dead.'

Kilhampton dragged himself to his feet, arms hanging loosely by his side. 'Was Oliver my son?'

Jim's breath snagged as Mrs Kilhampton stepped towards her husband. His stance was the same as it had been before he delivered the blow that felled him. Would he hit his wife? He pushed back against the wall and tried to lever himself to his feet.

Anya's hand rested on his shoulder and nudged him back down. 'Ssh. Do not interfere. It is long overdue. They must sort this thing alone.'

'He'll hurt her.'

Mrs Kilhampton would tuck quite neatly under her husband's arm yet she faced him, legs astride, her head tilted in defiance as she glared up at him.

'She is strong.'

'She's an invalid.'

'She has a broken heart, not a broken body. This is the final act of a long tragedy.'

'Do you still doubt me?' Mrs Kilhampton's hands came once more to her hips.

In the face of her bravery he felt weak. He had pandered to Kilhampton and his histrionics, brought the beating upon himself. Anya was right. Mrs Kilhampton was strong, like her daughter.

Jim tensed as Kilhampton took a step closer to his wife. All sound faded, breaths held as though everyone—Anya, the horses and most of all, Mrs Kilhampton—waited for the answer.

'I don't doubt you. But why? Why throw away all we had?'

'That I didn't do alone. We did it together.' She took a step forward and rested her tiny hands on her husband's chest. 'As we have always done everything.'

Anya sucked in a breath and a tentative smile lifted the corners of her lips.

'Oliver was your son. No-one else, ever. That night, Thomas told me I couldn't ride, that you said I was to stay away from the stables. I waited, waited until he'd gone into his cottage then I slipped out and took Goodfellow. I wanted to ride. To feel the wind in my hair. For months and months I'd been imprisoned in the house. Kept in that dark stuffy room by you and the doctors.'

'You were not imprisoned, never imprisoned. I wanted what was best for you. I couldn't lose you.' Kilhampton's arms wrapped around his wife and he pulled her against his broad chest.

Anya's hand slipped under Jim's arm. 'Come. It is time to leave.' She eased him to his feet.

The lump in Jim's throat outweighed any ache in his body. 'I must leave.'

'You will go nowhere tonight other than your bed in the cottage.'

'Jefferson. He is … I must …' He swayed. Blood pounded in his head, drumming out all sound. There was a sharp snap as his head met the wall and the ground spiralled up to meet him.

Thirty-One

'I must say that was the most delightful piece of roast beef I have tasted in a long time. My compliments to your cook, Mrs Kilhampton. I wonder if you realise just how lucky you are. My mother has the most terrible trouble with domestics. She finds it almost impossible to retain staff longer than a matter of weeks. But then again, that is Sydney where I suppose the demand is a little greater.'

Cecil droned on and on. Mama gave a polite nod and tweaked her lips offering a shadow of a smile, her eyes fixed somewhere beyond the tall windows. She was listening, of that India was certain. The expression on her face wasn't the vacant look of the past; she wasn't hiding behind any veil of misery, but there was a large possibility she wished she were elsewhere. Who wouldn't?

Violet wouldn't. She lapped up what she no doubt viewed as a refined and sophisticated atmosphere permeating the dining room. She patted her pink lips with her napkin and placed it onto the table, then turned to Cecil. 'You deserve the very best we can offer. Nothing can repay you for your kindness and the lavish attention you have showered upon us. And you were so brave, rescuing India from that nasty, nasty gaol.'

'Please my dear, it was nothing.' His back straightened. 'I'm only sorry your father hasn't been able to join us.' With a perplexed frown he stared at the empty chair at the head of the table and curled his lip, as if unable to believe Papa had the audacity to miss such an important occasion. 'I do hope he is not indisposed.'

Mama lifted her head then, and her eyes flashed with something that looked remarkably like a warning. Her attention hadn't been elsewhere; she just hadn't deigned to respond to Cecil's blathering. Whatever had happened between Mama and Papa? Had Mama spoken to him about the visit to the gaol? Was Papa so angry that he wasn't even prepared to sit down at the table with them?

'My husband has important business to attend to. He … I might see what has delayed him, if you will excuse me. Peggy will be along in a moment with the dessert. Please continue without me. India, ensure our guest has everything he needs.'

Cecil rose as Mama left the table. She swept out of the room without a backward glance in a rustle of lavender silk. The transformation was remarkable. With her hair coiled into an elaborate chignon and pearls dangling from her ears she would grace the smartest salons in Paris. In a matter of days she had shed her melancholia like a caterpillar's cocoon and become a creature of beauty and elegance. Faint stirrings surfaced of a long forgotten figure, buried in the mists of childhood. Long before Violet was born. Violet! Whatever must she think? A mother she had never known.

The door clicked shut and India glanced down the table. Violet wasn't the slightest bit interested in Mama. She and Cecil were deep in conversation. From the fluttering eyelashes and ripe pouts Cecil was no doubt piling on the compliments, and Violet lapped them up like a thirsty kitten. She was so much more suited to the role of wife.

Maybe it would be better to simply tell Cecil she wouldn't marry him. Didn't he deserve to hear it from her mouth? It wasn't as though they were actually betrothed, it was more of an understanding. He'd given her no token of his esteem; there had been no announcement, no promises. They hadn't discussed wedding plans. It was all just presumed. Oh, how she would love to scream!

A series of rattles and squeaks heralded the arrival of Peggy and her trolley. If only she could leave the table, follow Mama and discover what had happened. It was an agony. Within a moment the table was cleared and a large summer pudding took centre stage.

'You'll be serving this, I take it. Or would you like me to do the honours?'

'I can manage, thank you, Peggy. Did Mama say how long she would be?'

Peggy frowned and shook her head, then shot a surreptitious look at Violet and Cecil. Whatever was her problem? A silver dish overflowing with whipped cream appeared on the table then Peggy bustled out.

'Violet, would you like some pudding?' Serving spoon poised India waited, and waited, until Violet turned her pink flushed cheeks.

'Oh! I don't think so.' She gave her waistline a delicate pat, drawing Cecil's gaze. Once she'd achieved her aim she smiled. 'On second thoughts, why not? Peggy makes the most divine desserts, Cecil. I have no willpower. I can't resist.'

'It would seem the household is full of divine delights.' He ran his eyes over Violet then dragged his attention back, sending a shiver of disgust skittering across India's skin.

She had to tell him. 'We have Peggy to thank for that.' The ridiculous conversation was enough to drive a sane person round the bend. Couldn't Violet manage to come up with anything of significance? She'd been fortunate to have an education and besides, under those china doll ringlets was a mind as lethal as a hunting trap. 'The delights have more to do with Peggy's garden than anything else.' She sounded like a disgruntled harpy. If only she'd followed Mama from the room.

'The woman is a treasure. I have no idea how she manages the workload.'

India had no idea how Peggy managed everything she did, either. She had a finger in every pie and if the look on her face before she left was anything to go by, something more than summer pudding was cooking. Where was Papa? And why had Mama left in such a hurry?

'Cecil?' She gestured with the serving spoon. She should have allowed Peggy to serve the pudding. The berries oozed across the plate like drops of jewelled blood and onto the pristine white tablecloth.

'Thank you. Berries. Delicious. My mother would give her right arm for a cook like Peggy.'

Neither the prospect of a recap of Mrs Bryce's domestic problems nor the picture of her minus an arm appealed. Although anyone's desire to escape from Mrs Bryce's Potts Point household was quite within her comprehension. She hated the stuffy formality of the place. A shiver trickled its way across her shoulders as she passed the plate to Cecil. He ladled a generous portion of cream on top and licked his lips before shovelling a sufficiently large spoonful into his mouth to make his cheeks balloon.

The serving spoon slipped from her fingers and clanged as she attempted to replace it on the plate. She took a sip of water to settle her stomach.

Violet looked up with a frown. 'Are you all right, India? You look a little pasty.'

Ignoring Violet's comment India took a deep breath. 'Cecil?'

He raised his head and gave a grunt. A blob of berry-stained cream sneaked out of the corner of his mouth. His Adam's apple bobbed beneath the wrinkled skin of his neck. He swallowed and licked his lips.

'I have to speak with you.'

'The time is ripe.' He wiped his mouth on his napkin and placed it on the table, then sat back with his hands laced over his ample stomach. 'Yes, my dear.'

This was worse than talking to Papa. India patted her cheeks, her cool fingertips easing the heat in her face. She had to do it. She sucked in another breath. 'Cecil, I can't marry you.' She'd done it. It wasn't terribly difficult. The words had been stuck in her head for so long she must have been practising in her sleep. She lifted her head. Violet's mouth gaped open, and then a slow smile tilted the corners of her lips and she looked at Cecil.

A sound, a cross between a harrumph and a sigh slipped between Cecil's lips and he shook himself, ever so slightly. 'My dear, I am of course mortified, however …' His words trailed off and he shot a surreptitious glance at Violet.

'Did you actually have an arrangement, or was it simply presumed?' Violet drew the word out and finished with a small click. She stared at Cecil, nowhere else. *The cat!*

'Presumed. I think that might be the word,' Cecil said, a flush tinging his bulbous nose, or was it a berry stain? 'While I find you the most desirable of creatures, India, and I can understand why any man would simply be head over heels in love with you, I have to admit my affections lie elsewhere.' He grasped Violet's hand, which was waiting in just the right place.

Laugh or cry? She'd been rejected, supplanted, pushed aside by her little sister. *What a relief!* She rested her elbows on the table and dropped her head into her hands, masking the smile creeping across her face.

'India, I'm sorry if we have upset you.'

India peered through her fingers.

Violet sat with her head tipped to one side and she glowed, positively glowed.

India let out a small sigh and her shoulders slumped.

'Are you sure you're all right?'

Thank you, Violet! Thank you. 'Actually I'm feeling a little unwell. Possibly all the sun today.' Her hands muffled her words.

'Oh dear, I warned you riding was not a good idea. The sun can be quite overpowering at any time of the year.' Cecil's chair scraped against the timber floorboards.

Oh God! He was going to come and comfort her. Taking the lifeline Violet had thrown before it was snatched away, India pushed her chair back from the table. 'If you'll excuse me, I will arrange for Peggy to see to your needs and retire.'

'I shall be more than happy to keep Miss Violet company.' Cecil hovered, caught somewhere between sitting and standing, rather like a chicken trying to lay an egg. 'Can I escort you?'

'No, I'm perfectly fine, thank you. Please enjoy yourselves.' Drawing on Mama's example she swept from the room masking her huge sigh of relief. Determined not to give the game away and run or crow with delight, India counted her measured paces until she passed through the back door and out under the covered walkway leading to the kitchen. She'd done it! It was so easy. All that time, Violet had planted the idea of marriage in everyone's head and it had grown, blossomed, flourished like the weeds around the water troughs.

'Peggy! Peggy! You'll never guess what has just happ ...'

A team of possums might have ransacked the kitchen. Dirty saucepans and serving plates covered the table. Dishcloths and napkins lay strewn across the floor. The kettle shrieked on the range top and Peggy was nowhere to be seen.

'Peggy!' India stood in the middle of the room resisting the temptation to stamp her feet and cry even louder. Jilly appeared carrying a large enamel bowl, threw her a brief nod and filled it from the steaming kettle. 'Jilly, what's going on? Where's Peggy?' A cauldron of curiosity bubbled inside her. Something was up.

'I'm right here. Stop fussing.' Strips of torn sheeting hung from Peggy's plump arms and her hands clasped several bottles and a large jar of comfrey salve.

'Peggy?'

'What! Can't you see I'm busy? What are you doing here?'

'I came to ask you to take coffee to Violet and Cecil in the sitting room and to tell you—'

'Doesn't it look as though I have enough to do instead of pandering to those two peacocks?'

'How can I help?' Her news would have to wait.

'By getting out from under my feet.'

'Peggy! I need to know what's going on. Tell me.'

'Here, take this, and make yourself useful.' Peggy snatched the bowl of steaming water from Jilly and thrust it into her arms.

The heated enamel scalded her fingers and she dropped it onto the table.

'Use these to hold it.' Peggy handed over the strips of sheeting. 'Now take the whole damned lot over to Anya in the cottage.'

The cottage. What was Anya doing in the cottage? 'Why?'

'Just for once in your sweet life do what you're told. I'm too busy to argue.'

India wrapped the strips of sheeting around her hands and picked up the bowl again.

'And don't forget these.' Peggy held out a bottle of laudanum and a large jar of her comfrey ointment.

'What's that for?'

Peggy wedged the bottle and jar under her elbows. 'Now get a move on and don't spill anything on that dress. I'll never get the stains out of that watered silk.'

India shouldered her way out of the door and stood for a moment, waiting for her eyes to adjust to the darkness. Someone was hurt. Papa? No. He'd be in his room upstairs if he were injured, unless … *Who would be in the* … Her heart skipped, not one beat, about six. Disregarding Peggy's instructions about slopped water India ran across the courtyard to the cottage.

There was no sign of any activity outside the cottage, nevertheless, as she drew closer the merest strip of light spilt from under the door, a faint yellow tinge seeping out, leading her on. To knock or not? She couldn't. Her hands were full. It had to be Jim. She batted the thought away. *Don't jump to conclusions. It will only come to crying. Damn Peggy and her platitudes.*

It must be Jim. Who else would be there? She lifted her foot and slammed it against the door. Pain ricocheted up her shin. Stupid, stupid evening slippers. Oh for riding boots. All these frills and fripperies didn't belong at Helligen. If it was Jim and he was in some way injured he might not be able to get to the door.

She placed the bowl down on the seat then wriggled and squirmed until she managed to get the bottle of laudanum and the comfrey ointment out from under her arms unbroken. As she unpeeled the sheeting from her hands the door opened.

'Anya!'

'Ssh! Have you got everything?'

She closed her mouth and nodded.

'Quick. Come inside.'

Anya picked up the bowl without a second thought for the heat while India collected the sheeting and bottles and followed her inside.

The dark chill was oppressive. No fire burnt in the grate and the only sign of movement was the flickering candlelight dancing on the walls in the first room. She followed Anya through the door, her heartbeat hammering in her head.

A body lay sprawled across the bed, wrapped in a faded patchwork quilt, the face in shadow. 'Anya?'

'Ssh. He is out cold. It is better he stays that way. First we will clean up the mess.'

'Mess?' Her voice was no more than a feeble squeak.

'Yes. The mess men make when they brawl.'

'Men. Brawl. Which men? Who? What happened?' It had to be the men Jim had escaped with. They must have decided he was a liability and set upon him in the bush. How had he got here?

'Your father looks just as bad.'

'Papa?' Papa had gone to Jim's rescue, and was injured as well. 'Where is he?'

'Your mother is dealing with him, in the house. At least she was until she had to attend Violet's dinner party.'

That's why Mama appeared so far away. 'Is Papa all right?'

'He is a sight better off than this one. It is time a man of his age learned to control his temper. And stayed away from the bottle.'

Nothing made any sense. 'Anya?'

'Help me.'

Any doubt that Jim lay beneath the stained quilt vanished as Anya lifted the corner. Thick congealed blood smothered his face, his eyes were swollen shut, blue and bruised, his eyelashes spiky, glued together. His lips split, distended, spread across his poor face. A groan sounded in the small room. He hadn't moved. Had it come from her mouth?

'India!'

That voice. The voice of her childhood. She snapped back to the present. 'Yes,' she gasped.

'Breathe. I need your help.'

She sucked in a gasp of the cold air. 'What shall I do?' How had it come to this? What had she done?

'Wring out the cloths in the water before it gets cold.'

Anya tucked the quilt around Jim's lower body. 'We must keep him warm. The shock will harm him more than his injuries.'

She passed a warm, damp cloth across his prostrate body. Anya placed her hand on his forehead, her long fingers dark against the awful whiteness of his skin. With infinite care she pressed the cloth against the congealed blood around his eyes.

'Wring out another one and lay it across his forehead.'

Her hand shook as she brushed back the dark wing of hair from his forehead and lowered the cloth, easing it across his stretched, swollen skin. 'Whatever happened to him?'

'Your father. Flexing his dockside muscles.'

'Papa?' *Papa wouldn't do a thing like this. Call the constabulary, have Jim arrested, see him carted off to gaol. But this?* 'Papa wouldn't do this.'

'Believe it.'

India took the bloodstained rag from Anya and dropped it into the bowl, then passed another. She laid it against his cheek, and then a second and a third until his face was wrapped like an Egyptian mummy. 'Will he survive?' She squeezed her eyes closed.

'I have seen more terrible wounds,' Anya said.

Bile rose and filled her mouth. She had too. Mama with her head bandaged, lying prone in the bed, the dark stain of blood oozing through the bandage. The shadowed lamp. The brooding stillness. Oliver's incessant wail reaching an ear-splitting crescendo. She'd pushed his tiny arms beneath the blanket then pulled it up, tucked it tight around his thrashing body. Too tight. And left him, alone, all alone. The guilt slammed down on her. Too tight. He hadn't drawn another breath.

She flashed her eyes open. Anya peered across Jim at her, frowning. She was angry. She knew. Anya knew her secret. She'd known all along.

'India. More cloths.'

More cloths. The water swirled. Pink, like the first rays of sunrise staining the dawn sky. She wrung out the rag and passed it to Anya, swapping it for the next batch.

'Will he die, like Oliver?' She clapped her hand across her mouth to block the smell of Jim's blood invading her nostrils. 'Loosen the quilt. It's too tight.' Her fingers snatched at the faded material of the quilt, ripping it from the wadding as she tried to pull it free of Jim's body. He needed air. He wasn't breathing. She rested a hand on his chest. No movement. She wrenched the quilt back and stared down at his body. *No movement. Dead. Dead like Oliver.* What had she done?

Slap! Her head snapped back. Her cheek stung and her eyes watered.

'India!'

She blinked against the tears. Anya replaced the quilt, tucking it in again, tucking it tightly. Jim shuddered and his chest heaved. He uttered a long, low groan and his head rocked from one side of the pillow to the other.

Anya lifted her hand and rested it on the pulse point on his neck, his skin doughy beneath her fingers. 'He is not dead. Be calm.'

Tears splashed against her hand. Not sobs, just tears.

'Let them fall. It is time.' Anya dabbed at Jim's face. The blue stain of bruises. The reddened mark of knuckles. Papa's knuckles.

She let out a long shuddering gasp and snatched some air.

'Better.' Anya wiped the last remaining traces of dirt from Jim's swollen eyes. 'He will not die. Sore, very sore. Sleep and patience will heal him.'

'I didn't mean to, Anya. It was his crying, the noise. He wouldn't stop. And Mama. I thought he would disturb her. I thought she would die. And then … and then—'

'Hush. You did not kill your brother. When you left he slept, the beautiful baby. Too beautiful for this world. Sometimes that happens with babies. The angels come and take them.'

All this time she'd thought she … *He was sleeping … The angels took him*. 'I didn't kill him?'

'Listen to me. You did not kill Oliver. He died sleeping.'

'But I wrapped his blankets too tight.'

'No, you did not.'

'But Mama, she knows I killed him.'

'Your mother has never believed that, India. Never even thought it. You must ask her yourself. Do you understand?'

India sank onto the edge of the bed. Anya lifted her palm from Jim's forehead and rested it in her lap, then she turned back to her cloths.

She hadn't killed Oliver. She wasn't responsible for Mama's misery, Mama's sickness. Her shoulders slumped, relieved of the weight she had carried for so long. 'I have always thought I killed Oliver. That I caused Mama's sickness. Papa's misery. Made him leave us.'

'And that is why you tried so hard for Helligen, to repay your debt?'

Anya knew. Anya understood. Why had she never thought to talk to her before? The one person who had always been there. 'Anya, were you there when I was born?'

'I have been with you since the very beginning. I took you from your mother's womb. You are named for my country.'

Jim stirred and Anya's response was cut short. India wanted more but she'd have to wait. His eyelids flickered and he groaned. It started as a rumble and built, lifting his chest when he drew in breath. His hands flailed and she held him still, covering his swollen knuckles with her hand. He must have defended himself, hit something, someone. 'How bad is Papa?'

'Not so bad. Your mother and Peggy can manage.'

How had Mama sat through dinner all that time knowing … 'Anya, when did this happen?'

'We found them brawling in the barn. Both of them exhausted. Both of them black and blue. He did not win.' She tossed her head in Jim's direction.

'I should see Mama, make sure Papa is all right. Shall I get more water? Anything?'

'There is nothing more to do. He doesn't need Peggy's laudanum. You stay here. I shall go and see how the other brawling boy fares.'

Anya pulled a candle from her pocket and lit it from the spluttering mess on the side table. 'There are more candles in the front room. And blankets, too. It will be a long night.'

She collected the bloody cloths and dirty water then faded into the shadows.

India stood and smoothed the bedclothes, tucking them around Jim. All that time, almost all of her life she had believed she'd killed her brother, and Anya said she hadn't. Would it have made any difference? Would she have returned to Helligen if it hadn't been for the sense of obligation, the debt she owed? Of course she would. Helligen meant the world to her. It was in her blood, it was so much a part of her.

At last Jim rested. He was the one good thing to come from the whole sorry affair. Without her guilt Jim would not have walked onto Helligen, not answered her advertisement. She would never have known him, or unearthed the family secrets that bound them. She had a lot to thank him for. When he woke she would do just that.

Thirty-Two

He didn't move one inch. He couldn't. Not a muscle. Any stirring, even a shallow breath, sent pain lancing through him. A cool draft drifted across his face, stinging. His eyes refused to open.

A sliver of flickering light played across his vision, tinged pink by the skin of his eyelids. Why couldn't he open his eyes? Something cold against his face. Dampness. A trickle of water touched his lips and he tried to grasp it with his tongue. Thick, four times its normal size, it filled his mouth like a mound of stale bread. Another drop, then another. *Cool. So cool. More.* He opened his mouth wider and a finger traced his lip, trapping an escaping drop.

Concentrate. Jefferson. He'd saddled him. *The barn. Kilhampton.* He had to leave. *Get up.* He flinched, pain flashed through him. His head throbbed to the beat of thundering hooves.

A gentle weight pinned him down.

'Stay still. I'm here.'

India? He was hallucinating. *God!* He hurt. He blinked against the growing light and levered his gritty eyelids apart only to be rewarded by another stab of pain piercing his skull. The scent of spring flowers. The trail of hair across his shoulder. Warmth. Her face swam into focus.

So close that if he tipped his head he could touch her, touch her cheek. He closed his eyes and opened them again. She was still there. Eyes as dark as last night's storm clouds. Sparkling jewels in her ears, the pale skin of her throat, the swell of her breasts above the sapphire blue of her dress, so bright it stung his eyes. Presented to the governor. She swept across the floor, her skirt fanning out around her, a swirl of colour. Her head held high. Clasped in the embrace of … *No!* He blinked again. *Don't dwell on it. It is past. Beyond your reach. She belongs to another. Cecil. Kilhampton & bloody Bryce.*

'Jim.' The damp cloth touched his swollen eyes.

He pushed her hand away, leant on one elbow and levered himself upright.

'Jim, lie still. You're hurt.' She pushed him back, her voice the softest whisper.

Hurt. Quite right. Every bone in his body ached. As though an unseen hand had ripped him apart then rearranged the pieces. Some fool who couldn't tell up from down or left from right. He dragged in another breath. Deeper. Testing the pain. A familiar pain. *A broken rib.* Had Jefferson thrown him?

'What happened?' His words slurred, dribbled through fat lips refusing to do his bidding. Refusing to form the words. He was tired, so damn tired. Where was he?

His mother's room. Wrapped in her quilt. A dream. A bad dream. *Sleep tight, Jimmy boy. It will be better in the morning. Morning. No.* He had to leave. *Jefferson.* He groaned, his head pounded. The scent of wildflowers again.

'You were knocked insensible.' She threaded her hair through her fingers, pulling it back from her face. Staring at him with eyes that saw right to his core.

Insensible? Knocked? Who? How? He could fight. Fight with the best of them. Why hadn't he defended himself?

'Papa …'

Papa? Kilhampton. Bloody hell! He slumped back.

'Lie still. You'll do more harm than good.'

Images, flashing too fast. Kilhampton. *Your father stole my wife … and now my daughter. India?* Why wouldn't his lips form the word? Say her name.

'Let me raise your head.' Her soft hand slipped behind his neck. *Impossibly difficult.* His eyes closed. Cool water dripped down his throat. He swallowed, swallowed more. His breath caught. The cough raced through his chest, and dreading the pain he forced it down. He pushed her away.

'Gently.'

His breath exploded. The agony blossomed and burst. India standing by the bed. Frowning. *Don't frown. Smile, India.* He wanted her to smile. To remember her smiling when he left.

The ache settled and he took a tentative breath.

'What happened?' he repeated. 'Tell me.'

'You and Papa fought. Papa …'

Oh God! What had he done? 'Did I hurt him?'

A gentle smile. 'No more than he hurt you. I don't think you even knocked him down.'

He struggled up the bed, pushed down the quilt. 'I have to leave. Where's Jefferson?'

'You can't go anywhere, not like this, besides—' she ran her cool hand over his bare chest, '—you have no shirt on.'

He looked down at his chest. His shirt? Where had it gone? He needed his clothes. They'd be coming soon, looking for him. Not here. He couldn't bring them here. 'My clothes, they're still here. I have to leave.'

'No, Jim, you don't have to leave.'

'But, the gaol. I'm wanted. Just get my clothes, a shirt and Jefferson. I saddled Jefferson.'

Her hand was heavier now, forcing him back down against the bed. The muscles in her arm tightened, filling the blue puff of her sleeve. Her skin was so smooth. He raised his hand and let it fall. Not for him.

'Fred has taken care of Jefferson. Papa dropped the charges.'

Over the wall. Because the opportunity presented itself. Because the prospect of incarceration was more than he could bear. Because whoever said honesty was the best policy was wrong, so very wrong. None of it mattered. Helligen was not for him. And neither was this glorious vision hovering over him, her hand warm against his bare flesh.

'I can't stay, India. They'll come for me. You, your family will be drawn into the mess. I can't do it. I, my father, we've caused enough grief. I must leave.'

'You're not going anywhere. Not now. Not until you have healed. Only the family know you're here. No-one will say anything.' Her eyes darkened. 'Leave when you're healed.'

'Your father …'

'Papa dropped the charges of theft.'

'And now assault?'

She shrugged her shoulders. As if it didn't matter, as if it was nothing that he'd taken to Alexander Kilhampton with his fists.

'I'll speak to Papa and we'll sort it all out.'

The last time she said that he'd ended up behind bars.

'It will be different this time.' She'd read his mind. 'It's almost morning.'

'I'll leave today.'

Her eyes dimmed, and she turned. The outside door opened. 'He's awake.' The tone in her voice was as distant as the space she'd put between them.

'He could do with something in his stomach, then.'

Peggy. Only the family. How big was the Kilhampton family? Who did it include? Its control spread far and wide. The Hunter, Newcastle, Sydney …

'I see you're with us now. Gave us a bit of a fright, you did. You and the master should know better. Bickering like a pair of street urchins.'

Bickering? He shook his head. Nothing made sense. It was more than bickering. 'What time is it?'

'It's morning, still dark. Some of us lesser mortals are familiar with the dawn.'

The gurgling in his gut rumbled upwards.

'When did you last eat?' Peggy appraised him like a joint of meat ready to prod, to test his quality.

He shrugged. 'Can't remember.'

'You stay there. I'll be right back. Fine nursemaid you make, miss, allowing your patient to starve.'

India hovered in the doorway while Peggy trundled to and fro collecting the bowls, bottles and bandages. 'You stay here. Keep an eye on him.'

'I need to go and see Papa.'

'You won't be seeing him for a while. He's sleeping it off. And it's not just the punches. According to your mother he drank enough to fell an ox.' Peggy snorted. 'Looks like he did.' The door slammed behind her, leaving him alone once more with India.

'India? Help me. To remember everything.'

She pulled the timber chair next to the bed, her movements slow. She must be so tired, bone-weary. He should let her sleep, but he had to know. 'I went to the barn to get Jefferson. Your father was there. He fell. I went to help him up. Did I hit him?'

'I don't know, Jim. I haven't spoken to him. Mama found you both, in the barn. Do you remember that?' A frown creased her forehead. 'Why did Papa hit you?'

The fog in his mind swirled and cleared. The vision of Mrs Kilhampton with hands on her hips defying her husband flashed before him. Kilhampton believed his father had stolen more than his horse. Did India need to know that her father believed Thomas Cobb had stolen his wife? Was he going to lie to her again?

She saved him from finding an answer. 'Peggy will be back in a moment. I'll return later. I have things I must do.'

What things? Talk to her father. He struggled to sit.

'Lie down, and rest.' She left in a swirl of blue, as unreachable as a midsummer sky.

Rest. How could he rest? Colours, words, snippets of thoughts all blurred in his mind in a never-ending stream. Mrs Kilhampton and his father, Goodfellow, the gaol, India, the river, the touch of her skin and lies, lies and more lies …

He gave up on sleep and pushed the quilt back. The candle hissed and spluttered in a pool of its own wax. Through the open door he picked out the shape of the easy chair by the fire, imagined his father sitting, recording the day's events. He felt his mother's touch, heard his brother's laugh. This was the home of his childhood, where it all began and where it would end. The end of his dreams. Jefferson would never race. Never stand at stud.

The candlelight faded, replaced by the pale morning sun slanting across the bed. It was time to leave.

'I've brought you something to eat and a visitor.' Peggy elbowed the door open and entered the room, bringing with her the smell of chicken broth.

His mouth watered, then dried.

Kilhampton stood behind her. One arm nonchalantly raised against the doorjamb, as though he hadn't a care in the world. 'We have unfinished business,' he said.

Jim's stomach turned. He wanted no more of Kilhampton and his unfinished business. It was over.

'Let the poor boy have some food before you start haranguing him.' Peggy placed the tray on the small table beside the bed, unfolded a napkin then spread it across his lap.

He searched Kilhampton's face for evidence of last night's debacle. Puffed skin tinged with blue matched his icy eyes and the corner of his lip showed a slight split. There was no doubt he was the victor. He clenched his fist. Why hadn't he retaliated? Because of some misbegotten belief that he might hurt the man? *What a joke!*

'Here.' Peggy pressed a spoon into his hand, forcing his fingers to relax. 'Small sips, slowly.' She gave Kilhampton a withering glance. 'And don't you disturb his eating. You've done enough damage.' With a look to quell the devil she left.

'May I come in?'

Jim nodded. He could hardly refuse. He lay in a bed on the man's property, an accused horse thief, and an escaped prisoner. What exactly did India mean when she said her father had dropped the charges?

'Eat. While you eat I'd like to talk.'

Jim blew on the broth, examining it, trying to convince his stomach it would enjoy it once he got it down his throat, once Kilhampton said what he had to say.

The chair grated across the floorboards as Kilhampton pulled it closer to the bed, then he sat astride it, bringing with him the smell of soap and a new day. 'Can you manage?'

Even if Kilhampton was the last man on earth and he was dying of starvation he wouldn't accept his help. He grunted and swallowed the first spoonful of broth, his throat tight and his stomach rebelling. He held it down.

'When Laila and I bought Helligen your parents were already here. So were you, if I remember rightly.'

Jim nodded. He had few recollections of Kilhampton other than a big man who carried his daughter on his shoulders. More memories of India in fact, but then children always attracted children and the rules and regulations of society didn't impinge on their lives. It was only later when class and rubbish like that labelled you a have or a have-not that it mattered.

'Your father knew it all. Every bit of the property, how it worked, who to call on. I bought the place lock, stock and barrel. I wanted it all for Laila, and India and the sons that would follow. Helligen would be the making of our family. Laila and I started with nothing, two kids shipped out paying for their parents' sins.'

Jim lifted his head. Paying for their parents' sins. How ironic. He wouldn't have picked the Kilhamptons of Helligen as convict spawn. He cast his mind back, trying to envisage a time when free men were in the minority. Transportation had ended over twenty years before. The ships, the business. Kilhampton & Bryce? Violet's affectations. India presented to the governor, the political connections, houses and businesses in Sydney.

'I worked as a barrow boy on the docks.'

Jim swallowed a mouthful of broth, his stomach settling as he ignored Kilhampton's pristine white shirt and neatly tied cravat and concentrated on the fact the man was once a barrow boy.

'Campbell took a shine to me. Offered me a job in his shipbuilding business. I built my first boat with my bare hands. Built it for Laila. We'd been together in the orphanage. Both taken from our mothers at the Female Factory. Years later I found Laila working in an inn at The Rocks. I married her. The cabin on an unfinished hull was our first home. When I'd served out my apprenticeship I started trading, and so *Kilhampton* was born.'

'Kilhampton?'

He gave a smirk. 'Hampton, London, that's where I was born. Kill-Hampton. Forget the past. A new beginning deserves a new name.'

Not even his own name, an assumed name. Good enough for the likes of the landed gentry but not for him. 'And Bryce?' Why was he interested, why did he care? Something in the man's eyes, a determination masked by grief and failure, despite everything he had.

'Cecil brought to the business something I could never emulate. An air of respectability. Not convict stock. A free settler. Money, society, connections. My family would have it all.'

Jim's head reeled. He replaced the soup bowl on the table by the bed and sat up a little taller. Who would have thought … it made no difference. Once free of their dubious background Sydneysiders became the most intolerant self-serving members of society, determined to erase their connections with the past. 'What has this to do with me? With my father?' The remnants of last night's anger swirled inside him, the warmth of the soup flaming the fire in his belly. So the man came from humble beginnings. None of it excused the way he'd treated his father. Treated him.

'Your father was the backbone of this place. And he knew horses. How he knew horses! He picked out Goodfellow, from a disposal sale. Some other Hunter property down the drain because of the depression.'

So casual. No thought for the people whose homes and futures relied on those properties.

'I was jealous of him. He was so competent, it was plain he'd make a better master of Helligen Stud than me.'

He cocked his head to one side—had he heard right? Alexander Kilhampton was jealous of *his* father.

'I returned to what I knew. Trading and my ships. Laila managed the property. She rode well and had an aptitude for life on the land and a love of horses I couldn't fathom. She worked so hard. Together she and Cobb built the stud. He fired her with dreams, dreams I didn't even understand.'

And now Kilhampton's accusations last night made sense. It was an awful thing to believe the woman who held your heart did not love you, did not admire you. Something he was learning very quickly.

'My view of you was clouded by the past. I shouldn't have let it happen. I have dropped the charges against you.'

Thank you very much. Right at that moment he couldn't forgive the man. No matter how the past had clouded his judgement. He shouldn't have levelled the charges against him in the first place. It might remedy the question of horse theft, but what of escape and assault?

'I've sent Tom Bludge to Maitland Gaol. All charges are dropped. The letter says the ex-prisoner, you, left of your own accord. There will be no further ramifications. You were wrongfully detained. It also says you are now here.'

Kilhampton gave the final twist. He'd told them where he was. The constabulary would be here. He might apologise but the man couldn't be trusted further than he could throw him, and judging by last night's experience that wouldn't be very far.

'The letter also says I will offer surety.'

'And I'm free to leave, with Jefferson?' He needed to get this sorted, and soon. He wasn't going to walk into one of Kilhampton's traps again. He cast a look through the open door half expecting to see the pair of black boots, like last time, waiting to cart him off to Maitland Gaol.

'Except for the money you owe me and the fact I cannot offer surety if you're no longer on the premises.'

'Money?' To hell with the surety. Why did he owe money? Had Kilhampton stood bail for him? No. The charges were dropped.

'Yes. You owe me for the service Goodfellow provided that produced Jefferson, your horse. I will not sign a stud certificate unless you pay. You need it, if you still harbour a desire to race him or breed from him.'

With those words Kilhampton resurrected his dream of racing Jefferson and doused them as reality set in. 'I have very little in the way of assets.' How much would Kilhampton demand? How could he hope to find the money? Who had put him up to it? There could only be one person, only one person he'd confided in—and it wasn't India.

'Then I suppose you will simply have to work it out.'

'Work it out?' That wouldn't be so bad. 'Pay you in portions, you mean?' He could return to Munmurra or, better still, another stud. Find a job. If he worked long and hard it was feasible. Jefferson wouldn't race this year but maybe the next, maybe before he was too old. Archer was six when he won the Cup for the second time. Did he trust Kilhampton to honour his commitment?

He had no other option. 'I'll pay you your money. You've got me over a barrel.' He couldn't throw the opportunity, however tenuous, away.

'And where do you think you might gain employment?'

'I'm not sure. I'll find something.'

'Let me know if I can be of assistance.'

Offer him a reference? No chance of that. Jim narrowed his eyes and frowned, the split skin on his forehead stinging with the movement.

'I shall speak with my new manager.'

New manager? A stud master? The job he'd once coveted. Before his foolish quest unearthed a past that reached down over the years and turned his life upside down, dictating his every move.

It pleased him no end to hear Kilhampton groan as he struggled to his feet. Maybe one of his punches had landed square. Shame he'd allowed his conscience to get the better of him.

Swallowing what little pride he had left Jim took the hand Kilhampton stuck out. 'I will pay for the service. And I will enter Jefferson in the Melbourne Cup. Maybe not this year, but soon.'

'Not you as well. What is this passion for the Melbourne Cup? India is besotted by it. Don't we have something in New South Wales that's just as good?'

'Sadly, no. The race is gaining in popularity—there's talk of making Cup Day a public holiday. One day that race will stop the entire country, not just Melbourne.' The enthusiasm lifted his voice and his spirits. There was hope, a future. He would put the past behind him.

'We'll see, we'll see.' And with that Kilhampton left.

Jim sat up and pushed back the quilt. It was time to cut his losses.

Thirty-Three

Concentrating hard India forced one foot in front of the other. Her hand rested on the dado rail along the wall and, as if blind, she used it to guide her through the house. The staircase loomed above her, an insurmountable barrier. She had to find Papa and discover why he and Jim had fought.

A draught from the front door fanned her face, and the first feeble rays of morning light shone pink against the pale walls. She moved closer and peered out at the sunrise. A new day, a new beginning, and she remained trapped in the past. Living a life dictated by events long gone. She rested her head against the cool panes of glass framing the door and inhaled the crisp air. She'd had such plans, so many hopes and dreams. Did she have the energy to fight for them any longer?

She needed to be outside, to walk with the horses, and let Helligen speak to her. For so long her guilt had driven her, given her purpose, and now there was no sense of relief, only a hollow emptiness.

She took the path to Oliver's grave. It began with him; maybe he could provide the solace she needed, show her the way. The sun breached the distant hills, dispersing the soft pink chill of the dawn.

It came as no surprise to find Mama sitting between the fig trees. She lifted her head and patted the seat beside her. 'I like to watch the sunrise here. It's full of promise, a new day. How are you, my darling?'

A sigh bigger than India believed possible slipped from between her lips and her shoulders drooped. She moved closer and rested her back against the timber bench, clutching her shawl against the shivers of tiredness. 'It's been a long night.'

'It has. Anya tells me Jim will recover.'

'Yes, he's awake now. I left him with Peggy. She's more concerned by the fact he hasn't eaten for a couple of days than his bruises. What about Papa?'

'I've seen him in a worse state. He'll survive.' Mama sounded severe, as though Papa deserved his injuries.

'Worse state?'

'He promised me when we left Sydney he would put his dockside manners behind him, as befitted a man of his new standing. It seems his old habits still loiter below the surface. Jim's appearance and Goodfellow's return have resurrected old emotions, and with them his tendency to resort to fisticuffs.'

None of this sounded as dire as she expected. Where were the charges of assault, the threats? 'I don't really know what happened between them. Jim is unwilling to discuss it. Only saying he must leave as soon as possible. Has Papa dropped the charges of theft, and what will happen about the fact Jim escaped from the gaol?'

'I do know the charges have been dropped and your father has spoken in his favour and offered surety. I feel certain that the governor at Maitland Gaol will accept a small financial contribution to spread oil on any troubled waters and the matter of escape will be overlooked. Talk to your Papa later, after Peggy has dosed him with raw eggs and whatever other foul concoction she has up her sleeve to cure a surfeit of rum.'

'Rum!'

Mama nodded. 'A sailor's succour.' She rolled her eyes skywards painting a picture India could hardly imagine.

There were so many things she knew nothing of, so much she wanted to know. The good things and the bad, not masked by the shroud of darkness that had descended with Mama's accident and Oliver's death. 'Did you love Papa when you married him?' Whatever made her ask that?

'There has been no other man for me, from the time we were children. He has always taken care of me, and he has loved me with a passion that he sometimes cannot control.' A smile slid across Mama's face, lighting her eyes.

'Then how, why did he leave you here, alone after …'

'That was of my making. I sent him away. I'd failed him. After Oliver—'

'I didn't mean to hurt him,' India interrupted. 'I'm so sorry.' A large tear dropped onto the back of her hand. 'None of this is Jim's fault, or his father's. None. It's mine. If I hadn't killed Oliver none of this would have happened. I destroyed this family. From the beginning it was all my fault.' Try as she might to explain, her words opened the floodgates and tears dripped from her eyes. They fell, great dark patches against the beautiful blue watered silk of her dress. Peggy would be furious.

Mama's cold fingers dug into the bones of her shoulders, hurting as she twisted her. 'Look at me, India Kilhampton.'

She lifted her eyes, her vision blurred by her tears.

'You did not hurt Oliver. You did nothing to him. It was a sad and horrible time, but none of it was of your making—or for that matter Thomas Cobb's.'

If only it were true.

'Maybe if I hadn't tucked Oliver in so tight, if I'd picked him up. Maybe if I had—'

'India, you were six years old. It was no-one's fault Oliver died. It was sad, heartbreaking and your father and I failed to deal with that heartbreak. It was not of your making. Is this where your notion of restoring Helligen comes from?'

She nodded her head, her secret revealed. 'I just want everything to be as it was, before, before …' More tears splashed down. She scuffed them away, irritated by her weakness.

'It's time for you to stop trying to be all things to everyone. Let the world spin. Sometimes we're thrown more than we can manage, and no single person can make amends. It's time you took a leaf out of your sister's book.'

Violet? Whatever would she want to do that for? 'It is?' She sniffed, looking up.

'Yes. It's time you were selfish and considered your own happiness.'

Her own happiness wasn't something she dwelt on very much, except she was positive it didn't lie with Cecil and a Sydney marriage. She belonged here.

'Firstly, we'll dispense with the idiotic notion that you should marry Cecil Bryce. I have no idea where or how the matter ever became a topic of conversation. I suspect it was dreamt up by Violet. And your father, in the manner of men, made no objection.'

She sniffed again. 'I already have.' In her concern for Jim she had all but forgotten her words to Cecil at the dinner table, and the look on Violet's face. 'He said he was mortified.'

'Oh dear!' Mama sighed.

'But his affections lay elsewhere.'

'Really. I wonder where.'

India had no doubt where. Violet had done an admirable job in the last few days and had cemented herself in Cecil's affections.

It appeared he no longer caused her to shudder, more shiver with delight.

'My poor darling. We need to find you someone who shares your interests, cares about the things you care about. Loves Helligen.' The corner of Mama's mouth twitched almost as though she was teasing. Perhaps it was her imagination? Her heart kicked up a beat or two and she pushed her shawl from her shoulders.

'Do you think it would be difficult to find someone who'd fit that description?' Mama asked.

No, it wouldn't be difficult—she'd done that already. Keeping him was a different matter.

'Jim, perhaps?'

By now her heart hammered so hard the blue silk of her dress rose and fell with each breath. Had she been so blatant? 'How did you know?'

'A mother's intuition, I suspect. An instinct I've buried for a long time. Shall we go and find some breakfast and send Peggy into the lion's den? She can tell us when she thinks it's safe to talk to your father.'

'I'd like that. Jim says he must leave because he has caused enough trouble. I don't want him to go.'

'I know, my darling. He won't leave, not without Jefferson and not before he has spoken to your father. Take yourself inside and I'll go and see how the land lies.'

'I think I'd rather stay out here for a while. I like the peace and quiet.'

'Everything will turn out for the best, I promise.' Mama's lips grazed her cheek. It seemed like the most natural thing in the world and the greatest reward. With a gentle smile she walked down the path back to the house, back to her lover and her husband.

How India wished she could set the clock back, back to a time before the accident, before … just before. And then she paused. If circumstances had been different would she have come to know Jim? Or would he have been relegated to the stable, like Fred, an indispensable but invisible stablehand?

A flight of ibis took to the wing, their shrieks breaking the silence as they soared into the sky. Their white plumage iridescent against the sky formed a perfect v-shaped skein. Everything she held dear was disappearing, like the birds, beyond her reach. She wanted to pull it back, keep it close. She didn't want to leave Helligen, ever. And she wanted Jim to stay. She longed to see him somewhere away from the constant comings and goings of the household, away from prying eyes. She longed for the silence of the river, for that snatched afternoon they'd shared, somewhere to talk without the risk of being overheard. Heaven forbid—she longed for him to hold her again.

No matter what Jim had or hadn't done the thought of never seeing him again, not knowing whether he was alive or dead, how he was feeling, whether he truly cared about her the way she … 'I think I'm in love with him,' she murmured.

'Look who I found.' Mama's voice held more than a hint of excitement and India turned to see her parents walking arms linked and with broad smiles, as though they had come to some agreement, or worse, hatched some plan.

'Good morning, India.' With the exception of a slightly swollen eye and lips fuller than usual, Papa looked much as he always did but for a twinkle in his eye that she hadn't seen for a long time. 'I was wondering if you could spare me a moment. I thought we might have a little chat in the library.'

She cast a second look at him. Papa's immaculate appearance put her to shame. Her dress was covered in blotches and splatters, some of which had to be Jim's blood. Although tempted to decline and plead the need for sleep, or at least a change of clothes, she stood. Jim was more important. If he must leave it had to be with Jefferson, as a free man, with nothing hanging over his head. She owed him that.

'Come along, India. It's still cold out here. You'll catch a chill.' The undertone in Mama's voice brooked no argument and like a recalcitrant child she tagged behind her parents as they strolled together into the house.

Papa settled Mama into the wingback chair by the window and indicated to the small footstool India had favoured as a child. She shook her head. 'I'll sit here.' She perched on the arm of one of the chairs by the fireplace. She didn't want to be cast in the role of child. Those days were over.

She couldn't resist a quick glance up at Goodfellow. He peered down from his portrait with his know-it-all expression. Someone had unscrewed the small silver plate below the painting. The record of death of an animal who was very much alive and munching hay in the barn remedied with a flick of the wrist. If only all the other repercussions could be so easily rectified. She pulled her shawl tighter around her shoulders and laced her fingers in her lap.

'Your mother and I have discussed the situation and with her advice I have decided you should see out your plan and remain at Helligen. I have decided on the new manager.'

Her stomach dropped. How could he deliver such good news and such bad in one breath? She didn't want a new manager. *She* wanted to be the manager.

'I intend to play a more active role.' Papa stretched out his legs and interlocked his fingers across his chest. 'It's all very well breeding a herd of horses, but what are we going to do with them? No business flourishes unless it has aims and aspirations. I shall discuss it with the new manager. We will aim to enter a horse or two in some of these races that are gaining popularity.'

What was he suggesting? Adopting the very ideas she'd put forward. 'Who do you have in mind for the position?' *Tom Bludge?*

Surely not. Someone in Sydney, perhaps. Papa had come to a solution far too quickly. 'I am quite capable of doing the job myself.' She lifted her chin. 'I have … I can … and …' Oh, how could Papa spring this on her after a sleepless night? She had no hope of arguing her case effectively, or Jim's for that matter.

'I have a candidate in mind and an interview to conduct.'

It would be Tom Bludge. What hope would she have working with him? To his mind both women and children should be seen and not heard. It would be impossible.

'Now I take it you would like to apply for the position? None of this one-year rubbish. I'm talking about a commitment.'

Her head snapped up, all thoughts of Tom Bludge vanishing in an instant. *Apply for the position?* She could … she hadn't ever imagined he'd suggest it. In Papa's mind the one year he'd granted her was an arrangement to appease his headstrong daughter prior to her marriage—or so she'd believed. Through the haze of tiredness and confusion the joy on her mother's face became apparent. Papa was offering her the job. She would employ a stud master. She'd done that already and look where it had led. Was he saying she could re-employ Jim? Jim would never agree. Did she dare ask? He might agree. What had she to lose? She chased her scattered thoughts into some semblance of order.

'I would very much like the position—' she sat up a little taller and sucked in a fortifying breath, '—on the condition I can reinstate Jim—James Cobb as stud master.' She waited, the silence crippling. Papa pursed his lips, studied something outside the window, picked up a pencil, twirled it in his fingers, turned to Mama and raised his eyebrows in question. Mama gave an imperceptible nod. Or was that simply her imagination, wishful thinking?

'I suggest you go and discuss the matter with Cobb. See if he's interested. When I spoke to him this morning he had every intention of leaving, returning to Munmurra to see if he could take up his old job, now he no longer has a sentence hanging over his head. Apparently he has a debt to pay. If you hurry up you might catch him before he leaves.'

She snapped her mouth closed before Papa could change his mind and shot to her feet. She must speak to Jim before he left.

Thirty-Four

It was harder than Jim expected, but if he took shallow breaths he could manage quite well. He reached into his saddlebag, pulled out a shirt and eased his way into it. His boots proved more difficult. With a deal of bending and tugging he won in the end.

He cast a glance around the room ensuring he'd left nothing behind, then walked back through the cottage. A final farewell. Not exactly as he'd imagined matters would work out, although considering the alternative he should count himself lucky.

Making his way through the house he checked the windows and doors, quite why he didn't know. The place wasn't his to worry about. He cast one last look at the two chairs in front of the fire, his father's presence finally gone, before he slipped the latch and stepped outside.

As he passed through the door he reached up to the lintel and traced his initials. JMC. James, or Jim, his mother's pet name for him. Mawgan, a nod to her Cornish ancestry. His assumed name had more credibility than bloody Kill-Hampton.

His abiding regret would always be India, leaving without the opportunity to explore the strange and frightening rapport they had. One day, when he had something to offer, he'd return.

If Kilhampton could drag himself up from the gutter then why couldn't he? He was young. He'd find a job, and pay Kilhampton the money for his bloody service if it was the last thing he did. Give it twelve months and he would see Jefferson race, then with a few judicious bets on the racetrack and a lot of luck he'd be set.

As long as she didn't marry that fool Bryce—she couldn't. From all he'd heard Violet would be better suited to the life Bryce offered. India belonged here, on the land; it was in her blood and he knew how strong that pull was.

He slipped his hands through the strap of his saddlebags and hefted them onto his shoulder, batting away the stab of pain in his ribs. There would be no mad gallop with Jefferson today. No fifty miles covered in a day. It would be a gentle journey, along the river. A night spent under a tree and the opportunity to farewell his father. He could rest easy now. Goodfellow was back where he belonged and there was nothing for him to be ashamed of.

The barn doors stood open. The light streaming in filled the high roof with dancing dust motes, twinkling flecks of gold cavorting in the shaft of sunlight. A pile of straw stood by the door steaming into the air. There was no sign of Jefferson or Goodfellow. Fred must have let the horses loose in the paddock. He dropped his bags in the corner of Jefferson's stall and hung his saddle on top of the dividing wall, then set off to collect his horse, the bridle swinging between his fingers.

The spring air carried a hint of warmth. In another two months the Cup would be run. He'd be watching from the hill, not cheering Jefferson to victory as he'd hoped, but soaking up the atmosphere and learning everything he needed to know. Kilhampton would have his money so fast, even if it meant he had to work every hour God sent until he held Jefferson's papers in his hands and could submit them to the Victoria Racing Club.

He skirted the courtyard and the house, not wanting to have to explain himself to anyone, least of all Peggy with her uncanny knack of seeing right through him. It was Violet's coy twitter that caught his attention. 'Oh, Cecil!'

Cecil? Cecil Bryce. It had to be. Kilhampton's words echoed in his head. *An air of respectability. Not convict stock. Money, society, connections.*

Violet and the pompous fool on the wooden bench under the apple tree in the sunshine. What was *he* doing here?

Jim ducked around the corner of the stable block and cast another glance just in time to see India lifting her skirts and running across the courtyard. She skittered to a halt in front of Violet and Cecil, a radiant smile on her face. A shaft of jealousy far worse than any pain from his altercation with Kilhampton stopped him in his tracks as she clasped both Cecil's hands. The buffoon's face turned brick red as she leant in and dropped a kiss on his whiskery cheek. He hadn't wasted much time.

Hands thrust deep in his pockets Jim stomped off. Ten minutes to get Jefferson and he would be out of the bloody place. But for his father he wished he'd never returned to Helligen Stud.

When he reached the first fence he stopped and rested his arms along the top rail. This was where he'd sat with India on that first day as she explained her hopes and dreams. She wanted to breathe life into the place, breed the best horses and enter them on the racetrack. He'd never imagined he'd share a common goal with a Kilhampton. In this very spot he'd said he would help her.

It was obvious she no longer needed any assistance from him. She'd got Cecil Bloody Bryce to do that and besides, there was something more important than India Kilhampton. His pride. He squared his shoulders. He'd almost lost all sense of self-worth and dignity amongst the Kilhamptons. What had possessed him? He'd buried the hunger that burnt deep within him and become enmeshed in their lives. It was over. He would do what he'd promised. Rise above his birth and be his own man, subject to no master. He'd come so close to becoming a replica of his father, suffering at the hands of the Kilhamptons.

Something inside India burst free and she laughed aloud with the relief of it. Cecil and Violet made the perfect couple. Both of them loved Sydney, they would have everything they wanted and so would she. Who would have thought the solution could be so simple?

'I'm so happy for you both. I'll see you later. I have one more thing I need to do.'

'And we—' Cecil grasped Violet's hand in both of his and patted it, '—are absolutely delighted for you.'

'I do think, though,' Violet simpered, 'you should go to your room and get changed first. After all, if you're going to run Helligen you need to look the part. Even your gauchos would be more appropriate than that very dirty, blood-splattered evening dress. I'm sure if you give it to Jilly she can do something with it. Mind you, I have to say the colour suits you. It highlights your eyes.'

'I don't have time,' India threw the words over her shoulder. 'I have to go and find Jim, before he leaves.'

She crossed the courtyard and rapped on the door of the cottage. Receiving no response she tried the handle. The door refused to budge. Frowning, she peered through the window into the bedroom. The faded quilt lay neatly rolled at the end of the bed and there was no sign of Jim. He couldn't have gone. Not yet. Not without saying goodbye.

Running across the courtyard she made for the barn. The doors hung open; a sure sign Fred had let the horses out into the paddocks. That's where Jim would be, getting Jefferson. He wouldn't leave without telling her. Or would he?

She slipped around the back of the stable block and headed for the paddocks. Within moments her sodden slippers slipped and the hem of her skirt clung heavy and dripping to her legs. She hitched the material a little higher. Damn Violet for being right. This was the last time she'd dress in anything but gauchos and boots. She would have several pairs made. The dressmaker could take a pattern from the old ones. She ploughed on, the grass getting longer and damper and making her progress nigh on impossible.

She stopped and pushed back her hair, squinting across the rolling grass into the sun and her heart lifted.

Jim stood at the fence gazing out, down to the river. Even from a distance she could tell he was lost in thought, see in her mind's eye the faraway look on his face. The weight of anxiety she'd carried for days lifted and then came crushing back down again. What would he say? Would he accept her proposition? Would he want to remain at Helligen? He might refuse. After all, he'd only come in the first place to find the deed of sale for Goodfellow and prove Jefferson's lineage. Papa had given him all he sought, or would in exchange for a few pounds.

Maybe the bond they had was a figment of her imagination, or worse, something he'd manufactured to make his task easier. She stopped, suddenly embarrassed and a little shy.

Even though she was at least a hundred yards away Jim sensed her presence. He turned and lifted his hand. A farewell? The bridle swung from his hand, and Jefferson and Goodfellow grazed behind him, oblivious to the tumultuous emotions of mere mortals.

As long as Jefferson remained in the paddock she had time. Jim wouldn't leave without his horse. He might leave without saying goodbye to her, but not without Jefferson. She repeated the mantra over in her head. Perhaps she should just lift her hand and wave. If he wanted to say more he'd call out, walk to her. What if he turned and left? Then she'd never know.

She had to find out. Perhaps he'd had a change of heart since that day on the wharf at Morpeth. He was right—it had everything to do with the past and their families—but that was an eternity ago. Before he'd been accused of horse theft, been carted off to gaol; before he'd escaped, before Papa had knocked him senseless in a drunken rage born of past grudges.

Biting her lip she took one long last look at him and her heart soared. No longer would she be held prisoner by the past; the truth had set her free and the future beckoned. Without a twinge of regret she lifted her silken skirt and flew across the grass.

'Jim! Jim Mawgan!'

Why did she insist on calling him that? Jim Mawgan was no more. A relic of the childhood he'd once cherished. The name belonged to the world of halcyon dreams and foolish ill-conceived plans where there was no class structure, no haves and have-nots, and no Kilhamptons.

Jim Mawgan died somewhere on the floor of the barn beneath the soaring roof trusses that matched his infantile notions of right and wrong. Black and white—a world where there was no grey, no grey like the colour of India's eyes.

Eyes that right at this very moment were gazing up into his face like the precocious child who'd ridden on her father's shoulders, convinced everything in the world existed for her own pleasure.

'What are you doing? You can't leave. Not yet. I have to talk to you.'

'The time for talking is over, India. I've got a lot of miles to cover today and I need to make a move.' He reached for the gate but she beat him to it, insinuated herself between the five bars and his body. Wildflowers, warm summer skies, everything he'd ever wanted and nothing he could have.

'Please, Jim, listen for just a moment. It's so exciting. I've been talking to Mama and Papa and everything, just everything, has changed.'

What could have changed, what could have brought such a flush to her cheeks and a sparkle to her eyes? The prospect of a marriage to Cecil Bryce? He didn't want to hear about it.

'I have a job, not just for a year but forever. I am the new manager of Helligen Stud.' *Wonderful. The perfect wedding present for her and her husband-to-be.* She performed a small pirouette in front of him, her blue skirt billowing around her.

He gritted his teeth. 'Congratulations. I'm very happy for you. I wish you and your husband all the best.'

'My husband? What are you talking about?'

'Cecil Bryce. He looked suitably pleased when I saw you smother him in kisses in the courtyard.'

'Cecil has nothing to do with this. He's here because he brought Violet and me back from Morpeth. I have to admit he was wonderful. When I went to the gaol I thought that I'd made matters so much worse and he came rushing to the rescue.'

'You went to the gaol?' What was she talking about?

'Yes. I wanted you to know Papa had dropped the charges against you. But I was too late, you'd already left.' She stared up into his face, her brow furrowed, and then she smiled.

His heart performed some sort of backflip and he wrestled it back into place. She had gone to the gaol, to see him. To let him know the charges were dropped. She'd cared enough to do that.

'Oh! In all my excitement I forgot to tell you. Violet and Cecil are to be married.'

Violet and Bryce?

'Cecil and I were in total agreement. He was so relieved. He and Violet—'

'Excuse me, India, I need to open the gate. Let Jefferson out. I have to be on my way.' As far away as he could get from Helligen before he made an even bigger fool of himself.

'Jim, listen to me, please.' Her tiny hand rested on his arm, her grip firmer than he imagined. 'I won't be going back to Sydney. I'm going to stay here. Stay and run Helligen. And that's why I'm here. I want to ask you if you'll stay. Do you remember the day you arrived and you said you would help me rebuild Helligen?'

Oh yes! He remembered. He would never forget, but he had no intention of being lured into her world again. A man could take so much, and no more. He didn't want to be beholden to the Kilhamptons, India, her father, anyone.

'We can make it all real. Our dream. Remember we sat here on this fence on the very first day and you said you would help me. Now we can do it. Oh, please say yes. You don't want to leave. I'm offering you the job as stud master of Helligen.'

Stay! How could he stay and recreate the situation that had caused all the problems they'd faced. He would be living his father's life. He didn't want to work for her. He wanted to provide for her, marry her, and be her husband, not her hired lackey. The thought hit him like one of Kilhampton's punches, right in the kidneys, the truth robbing him of breath.

But first he had a bill to pay and there was no way he intended to work for Kilhampton and hand over his wages like a bonded servant. No! As much as it would pain him to leave his pride was more important. Was pride a sin? Did it matter? One more to add to the long list of sins he'd committed. He couldn't do it.

'No, India. I'm leaving.'

He opened the gate and slipped the bridle over Jefferson's head, then eased through the gate leaving Goodfellow hanging over the fence with a puzzled expression on his face.

Not daring to wait a moment longer in case he changed his mind, he set a cracking pace across the paddock, Jefferson trotting by his side in an attempt to keep up. He had to go, leave before he weakened, before he remembered her soft skin, the feel of her in his arms …

'You told me in Morpeth the only thing standing between us was the past.' Her voice, loud and irate, stopped Jefferson in his tracks. Jim tugged the bridle, the horse stood firm. India didn't. Puffing with exertion, or maybe emotion, she caught up.

'The past has been sorted out. Mama and Papa have resolved their differences, put it behind them. Why can't we?'

His temper snapped. 'Why, India? You ask me why? Can't you understand that I want you as my wife? As an equal. Not as your hired hand, someone who answered your advertisement. Filled a vacant position.' There he'd said it.

Her face paled, her eyes widened and she sank down into the long grass, a blue pile of soggy silk. Like an injured bird, head hanging, shoulders slumped.

He couldn't stop. She had to understand. 'Besides, Jim Mawgan answered your advertisement. Not James Cobb. I'm not the person you believe me to be.' His pain made him cruel.

She lifted her eyes, those storm cloud eyes and he waited, chest heaving, for the thunderclap.

'I'll give away Helligen. I'll come with you.'

His breath hitched and he rubbed his face with the heel of his hand. The sheer impossibility of her statement made him want to bay like a rabid dog. 'Don't be ridiculous, you could never give Helligen away any more than I could give away my dreams.'

'I would for you, Jim. I would.'

'Do you know why your father hit me? Do you know why I took the punch? Not for me. For my father. I can't stay. It will simply be history repeating. I have a debt to pay before I can call myself a free man.' He settled his hat on his head and tugged at Jefferson's bridle. 'The past can't be rewritten, but the future doesn't have to be the same. History doesn't have to repeat itself.'

Thirty-Five

History certainly wasn't repeating itself and India could do very little to rewrite it. Hiatus was the best word to describe the situation. Everyone else had moved on to new chapters while she stayed locked in a hell of apathy. Cecil and Violet's wedding and the reception at Potts Point was the most glamorous affair and filled the society pages of *The Sydney Morning Herald*. And then last week they'd departed with much pomp and ceremony on their long-awaited Grand Tour. London, Paris, Rome—Violet was beside herself with excitement. Marriage to Cecil had fulfilled her every dream.

Even Mama and Papa forged ahead, the despondency of the past fifteen years firmly behind them. Mama had received a clean bill of health and had settled into Sydney life. She planned to travel with Papa aboard *The Cloud* on his next trip to the East and Anya would finally get to see her homeland once more. Whereas India remained locked in some well of indecision and waiting. Waiting for the mares to foal, waiting for the foals to grow, and then it would be years before she'd know if she'd bred a racehorse.

'Well, Peggy, it looks as though it's just the two of us. A couple of old women, both of our lovers lost to us.'

'Least yours hasn't gone off in search of fool's gold.' Peggy pushed a plate of oatmeal biscuits across the table.

'He might as well have done.'

'A man has his pride. You wouldn't want him if he didn't.'

'He rejected me.' And Helligen, the very job he said he wanted, and his dreams, their dreams.

'Give it time. Give it time. How much does he owe your father?'

'Thirty pounds.'

'Well, I'm sure he'll come up with it.'

India pulled the pot of tea towards her. No matter what Peggy said it was not to be. There was only one constant in her life—loyal, unchanging and forever forgiving—and that was Helligen. Even Peggy had deserted her, taken sides. A man has his pride! Well, she had pride, too. She'd give Helligen her very best, follow her dream, and if she had to do it alone then so be it.

'Now, what are you going to do about employing some more people? You'll need someone to give you a hand, especially once the foals are born.'

'I could run an advertisement …'

Peggy slammed her hand on the table. 'I'm not living through that all over again. Can't you employ a few more people from the village?'

'I do need some help. Fred has an uncle who's looking for a new position. I'll employ him. And I've decided to send three of the brood mares out for mating. It's just … I don't seem to be able to summon any enthusiasm.'

The best thing about being alone at Helligen was the peace and the quiet. The knowledge that at long last the past had been laid to rest. Old wounds healed and for everyone else the promise of the future. Her dreams hadn't changed. She would do as she always intended and one day present Papa with the Melbourne Cup—not a watch anymore, now they presented a cup. It would sit well on the mantle in the library under the portrait of Goodfellow. A fitting end to a long drawn-out saga.

'I'll go and check on Fred and then do some paperwork in the library. As silly as it sounds now, I rather miss my afternoon visits to Mama.'

'You do that. Me, I've got things to do. No-one's appetite seems to be missing. Shall I lay the table in the dining room?'

'No, it's a waste of time. I'll eat in here with you and Fred and Jilly.'

'Sounds as good an excuse as any. Can't get you out of those work clothes no matter how hard I try.'

India tucked her shirt into her gauchos and threw Peggy a wink. It was as well Violet was no longer around to reprimand her about her attire. She couldn't even bring herself to look at her blue evening dress that Peggy and Jilly had so laboriously restored. It hung in some cupboard along with all her Sydney clothes, consigned to the past, to a time when hope had sparked an odd moment of vanity. She wouldn't wear them again.

The warm summer sun beat down on the top of her head as she crossed the courtyard and made her way to the small yard next to the vegetable garden. Goodfellow greeted her with his usual supercilious stare and tossed his head before nudging at the gate. He had become more of a companion, ambling around after her, picking and choosing his spot in the sunshine and the tastiest treats in the garden.

Really he was too old to ride although a quiet walk would do him little harm. She slipped the rope bridle over his head, pulled her old cabbage palm hat from the peg by the door of the stable, then mounted the old horse bareback. Needing no encouragement Goodfellow followed the path out through the gate and took the track past the lagoon, through the edge of the paperbark forest to the river.

The ibis foraging in the shallow waters turned beady eyes on her progress, more interested in their search for food than a lonely woman invading their territory. As she crossed into the bushland she searched for the goanna, but it had found a better place to sun itself than the hard-packed dirt of Helligen. In the distance the mighty Hunter wound its perpetual, lazy way through the empty paddocks.

The river drew her gaze, to the wharf where Papa had taken her to paddle her feet in the cool water, chase the dragonflies as they danced and skimmed across the tranquil surface. The memories surfaced. Not memories of Papa this time. Jim occupied her thoughts and her dreams.

Safe and secure astride a large bay stallion, the hot sun beating down on her cheek. The warm breeze and the scent of leather, sweat and saddle-soap. All poignant reminders of that one stolen afternoon before the past had caught up with her. Jefferson's steady gait and flawless motion, Jim's warm breath tickling her neck, his fingers light as a feather over her cheek and along her lips. His hard muscles as he pulled her into his arms, holding her firm, drawing her close. A lifetime of regret yawned in front of her.

Goodfellow picked up his pace, sniffing the welcome scent from the river, longing for the cooling relief of the water as much as she did. Summer had taken its toll; the paddocks beyond the lagoon were no longer the verdant green of spring and the ground cracked and crackled as they picked their way along the track. She pulled back on the reins. It was too hot for an old horse, but he had a mind of his own. He broke into a gallop, his mane flicking and the heat from his body permeating hers. Clinging tight to the bridle, and with her legs clamped firmly around his round belly, she gave him his head.

As the wharf came into sight she reined him in and pushed back her hat, wiping the stinging sweat from her eyes. He tossed his head, impatient for the water, for the river.

'Slow down, old fellow. It's not far.'

The sun hung bright in the sky, a shining yellow orb turning the landscape to gold, creating distorted flickering silhouettes and sparkles that danced on the surface. She squinted into the light.

Another horse frolicked at the water's edge. Poachers? Trespassers? She slid from Goodfellow's back and shaded her eyes. The bridle slipped from her hand and Goodfellow, free at last, kicked up his heels and bolted.

The two horses cavorted and capered at the water's edge, mirror images of each other. India scanned the river, the wharf, the tiny half-moon bay, searching for Jim's familiar long, angular shape. God, how she'd missed him. The force of her longing swept through her heated body. It had been six interminable months. She'd forced his memory away, buried beneath hard work and the day-to-day grind. Now it swelled like a tidal wave ready to consume all in its path.

'Jim.' Step by step she made her way to the water's edge, his name a prayer on her lips, an unanswered prayer.

When she looked up Goodfellow stood alone in the shallows. He snuffled and snorted, droplets of water cascading from his mane in the dappled light. No sign of another horse. She shook her head and rammed her hat back down low over her eyes. *Dreaming. Imagining. Wishing. What nonsense!*

Striding across the tussock grass she jumped down onto the patch of sand below the bank and whistled through her teeth. The old horse lifted his head and ambled over to her; she slipped the bridle over his ears and led him back onto the path. It was time to go home.

And that was when she noticed the figure beneath the spreading branches of the red gum, lolling against the trunk, a large bay horse standing untethered by his side. A tantalising shiver covered her skin with goosebumps and her breath caught in recognition.

Epilogue

November 1866
Flemington, Victoria

The horse jumped as the flag dropped. In less than four minutes the race would be over and he wasn't even close to the track.

The caller's voice crackled and died, lost as the crowd roared their excitement. Unable to bear the tension a moment longer Jim whipped off his hat, pushed the chairs aside and vaulted across the benches. He forced his way through the throng, heedless of the cries of offence heralding his mad rush. Past the women in their perfumed finery, past a gaggle of overdressed Melbournians and gossiping socialites, past the punters and the gold diggers waving their race slips, convinced their bet would come in. Didn't they know the odds against winning?

This race was a big ask. The biggest. Only a unique mix of speed, agility and strength would see the winner surge over the line. Not to mention the skill of the jockey. He must time it right; let the horse have his head for the first mile and a half, then use the whip. Any animal worthy of the win had a mind of their own—push them too early and they'd pull up short.

He weaved his way forward, apologising as he went. How could he be so stupid as to lose track of time? The race would be over before he reached the rail. Stretching onto the balls of his feet, he peered over the heads of the thousand-strong crowd lined up at the winning post. Was he heading in the right direction? No point being at the rail if he couldn't see the winner cross dead on. How he wished he'd had the foresight to make it to the stands in time.

With only seconds to spare before the two-mile handicap ended he elbowed his way through, his eyes fixed firmly on the finish line.

Craning his neck he studied the empty track. They hadn't rounded the last. Thank God! A cloud of dust billowed and the horses took the final bend, the roar from the crowd drowning out the caller's words. Where was his horse? What the hell was the jockey thinking? His bet would be down the drain. Straining his eyes to the far inside rail, he focused on the worn track. The crowd bellowed for the favourite as the blur of runners emerged. Four horses running in tandem.

There was no hope. If the horse didn't have the lead he wouldn't run on. He pushed further, clasping the rail, stretching for a better view. The pounding of hooves on the dry track hammered in his chest. The roar from the crowd drummed out all other sound.

As he gripped the rail, his fingers dug into the paint. He eased his way into the narrow space and hooked his toes into the bottom of the rail, lifting above the eager heads, above the hats and shoulders. The smell of freshly mown turf blended with warm perfume, beer and expectation.

The horses bore down fast, the leaders four abreast. As they pulled into the final straight the dust began to clear. A tantalising glimpse of grey and sapphire silks, thundercloud grey. The bay pulled forward, a head or so in front of the pack.

He gripped the rails tighter and clenched his teeth, not daring to draw breath.

'C'mon!' He willed the stallion on. 'C'mon!' He focused on the rhythm of the pounding hooves, saw his horse pull forward to make it a length. The whip flashed down. The horse responded, charging on, stretching beyond a length. Close enough now to see the tilt of his head. He sucked in a gasp of air, relaxed and smiled as the horse's ears pricked forward. He could do it—he had plenty to give.

The stallion surged ahead of his exhausted competition, lengthening his stride, dust streaming behind him. Muscles rippled across his burnished chest, ears flicked back. Almost level with the finish line the thunder from the approaching hooves mirrored his pounding heartbeat. The jockey sat back, gave the horse his head, no need for the whip now. He could do it. His excitement released, bubbling up into a laugh. 'C'mon!'

A bystander turned, eager to share his enthusiasm as he stretched, leaning out over the rail, willing him on. Two lengths ahead, the sunlight rippling across the hindquarter muscles, mane and tail streaming behind him, black as a cockatoo's wing.

The jockey wielded his crop above his head in a victory salute and they stormed home, crossing the finish line three lengths ahead.

Gazing heavenward into the bright blue Melbourne sky he replaced his hat with a flourish and turned to the hill. Across the crowded expanse of spectators their gazes locked. Even at that distance he could see the sparkle of excitement in her eyes, feel the touch of her smooth skin and smell her everlasting scent of spring.

'How's that, sir?' Fred's voice was louder than the roar from the stands, and the punters' winning shrieks filled his ears. Jefferson's hot breath covered his face.

He grinned up at his jockey, the first person at Helligen to acknowledge Jefferson's potential. 'James.'

'Sir James, I reckon, today. Not every day your horse wins the Melbourne Cup.' Fred slipped from the saddle and handed him the reins.

'You take him into the winners' circle. I'll collect the winnings.'

With prize money of over two thousand guineas he'd see his stud secure for many years to come. Not to mention his bet on Jefferson. At ten to one he'd snagged a tidy twenty thousand. 'Get back up there. Today you rode and besides, you're needed for the weigh-in. I'm not giving this one away on a legality.' He pulled a lead rope from his pocket and clipped it onto Jefferson's bridle. 'You've done me proud.'

'Are you sure you've got papers for that animal?'

For a second the past flashed and Jim's heart stuttered.

'Fred Ward and those bushrangers make a habit of racing stolen thoroughbreds.'

He stared into Alexander and Laila Kilhampton's smiling faces.

'Ask my wife about the papers, she's the manager.'

'Not for much longer.' India ran her hand protectively over her voluminous skirts. 'We might have to employ someone to do that job from here on in. I'll have other things on my mind.'

Historical Note

There is a rural myth that the racehorse Archer, winner of the first Melbourne Cup in 1861, walked over 500 miles to attend the inaugural race meeting. It's not true!

Records show Archer was foaled and trained by Etienne de Mestre in Braidwood in southern New South Wales and he didn't walk to the Melbourne Cup.

A sporting newspaper of the day, *Bell's Life in Sydney and Sporting Chronicle*, reported on 21 September, 1861:

> *Wednesday last saw the departure of Mr De Mestre's three nags for Melbourne, and by this time we trust they have arrived in good order. A large number of friends went down to the wharf to see the horses on board …*

And two weeks later, *Bell's Life in Victoria and Sporting Chronicle* announced:

> *The City of Sydney, which reached Sandridge (Port Melbourne) on Saturday last brought the Sydney entries for the Melbourne Cup, viz, Archer, Inheritor and Exeter. Archer is considered the best old good 'un in New South Wales …*

In the nineteenth century success on the racetrack was the most efficient way to prove the strength and stamina of a horse and secure stud services, and many horses arrived at race meetings having travelled long distances.

A famous Hunter horse by the name of Young Dover was frequently ridden from Maitland to racetracks across NSW. He won many races after travelling over 100 miles in one day.

Today the Hunter Valley in NSW is regarded as one of the most important horse breeding areas in Australia, but it wasn't until the 1870s that the first Hunter horse won the Melbourne Cup. Perhaps the reason the Hunter lays claim to breeding the first winner of the Melbourne Cup is that the stories of Young Dover and Archer have melded in the minds of Hunter Valley residents over the years. In some of the more 'historic' watering holes in the Hunter Valley, Archer is still claimed as a Hunter animal.

The Melbourne Cup—the race that stops the nation—is now run on the first Tuesday of November. In the early days it was the first Thursday, and until 1865 there was no Melbourne Cup; instead, the winner received a purse of around a thousand guineas and a gold watch.

For fiction's sake I have adopted the Hunter version of the myth. The Kilhamptons did not exist other than in my imagination, nor did their property, Helligen. It is loosely based on the historic homestead, Tocal, near Paterson in the Hunter, north of Sydney.

Acknowledgements

Writing is said to be a solitary occupation—this was not the case with *The Horse Thief*. So many people had a hand in this story and I am so grateful for their support.

First and foremost Sue Brockhoff who took my garbled pitch at the 2014 Sydney RWA Conference and believed in my story, then Romance Writers of Australia, because without that wonderful organisation there would be no conferences, no pitches and, most importantly, no critique partners.

I couldn't do without my writing buddies—Eva Scott, Ann B Harrison, Joanna Lloyd and Sarah Barrie. Thank you for reading, re-reading, fixing my dilute genes, sorting nineteenth century legalities and putting up with my incessant ramblings. I would be lost without my editor, too. Sharon Ketelaar, please accept my heartfelt thanks for your never-failing patience and vice-like grip on timelines.

I would like to acknowledge Sandra Earle, the event coordinator of Tocal Homestead. Her comprehensive behind-the-scenes tour of the beautifully preserved colonial farm buildings and their fascinating contents made *The Horse Thief* come to life. I recommend a visit if you're ever in the area.

And last but not least, Katy Clymo, thank you for the up-close-and-personal account of the finish line at Flemington.

Acknowledgments

Turn over for a sneak peek.

The
NATURALIST'S
DAUGHTER

by

TEA COOPER

AVAILABLE JANUARY 2018

One

Agnes Banks, New South Wales, 1808

Rose loved Pa's dusty workroom filled to overflowing with notebooks and samples, paints and charcoals. A treasure chest of strange and wonderful objects. A charred boomerang; the tall, tall seed head from the shaggy grass tree; a huge *oh-don't-touch* emu's egg painted with careful patterns, more tiny dots than even she could count. Collected heads of banksia, their knotted faces leering; the beautiful curling tail feather of a bulln-bulln; and in the centre of the worn table her most favourite of all—the mallangong. Once it lived and breathed until Bunji's Pa speared it out in the billabong. Now it sat … pre-ser-ved for all eternity—that's what Pa said. *Pre-ser-ved.* She ran her hand over the dark brown fur and touched its funny little beak.

Pa rose from the chair, his brown face wrinkling as he smiled his special smile. 'Shall we go down to the river, my heart?'

A trickle of excitement ran through her—she'd sat quietly waiting all afternoon for him to say those very words. 'Yes please, Pa.'

'Put on your boots before you tell your mother we are off.'

She rammed her feet into her clodhoppers, leaving the long laces trailing, and hoisted her knapsack carefully onto her back. Pa's supplies were precious. How she loved the wooden box with its tiny blocks of paint and brushes wrapped in fine linen. Pa promised she'd have her own paintbox when she was bigger, all her very own. Now she shared his and she had to be careful, so very careful not to break anything.

The box came from London a long time ago with Pa on the big ship when the colony was blackfellas' country. Now there were people everywhere—mostly convicts with their clattering, clanging chains and long sad faces.

Some days Mam was sad too. She'd stare down the river and sigh as though she'd been waiting a long, long time and every time Pa went to Sydney Town she asked him for a letter. When he shook his head, tears came to her eyes. One day she'd write her a letter so Pa could bring it back; maybe then Mam would smile.

'Mam, where are you? We're going to the river to see the mallangong.'

Mam turned from her seat on the ground, her fingers dirty from scrabbling in the garden where she grew her medicine—herbs that made people well, helped birth their babies, fixed their fevers and healed their cuts and bruises. That made Mam happy but the letter sadness never left her eyes no matter how hard Rose tried to be a good girl.

'Tell your pa not to be late for tea. And don't forget to keep your hat and boots on. The sun's still strong.'

'We can't come home too soon because the mallangong don't play until the sun goes down.'

'You and your mallangong. I'm frightened one day I might lose you. You'll swim away and not come back to me, go and live with them in Yellow-Mundee's lagoon.'

She'd never do that, never leave Pa. Why would she do a thing like that?

'Off you go now. That's your pa calling; he doesn't like to be kept waiting.'

Pa was always saying he had two precious treasures brought to him by the piskies. That made Mam smile. A sad faraway smile. She leant over and brushed her lips against her mother's smooth cheek, wrinkling her nose when the curl of hair, black as black, tickled her face. 'Bye Mam.'

Little puffs of dust rose at her heels and her heart beat in time with her boots as she ran. The rain hadn't come and it was hot and dry and dusty. Down by the river it would be cool, underneath the big gum where the fallen branch stretched its arms into the river. That's where the mallangong dug their burrows in the damp sand.

She skipped down the well-worn path. She was a big girl now and knew the way but still Mam said never go alone, not unless Pa was there. The blackfellas mightn't like it if she did. Mam was a silly fuss. Bunji and Yindi were her friends: they showed her all the secret paths up through the rocks where the grass trees grew and down to the swimming hole where it was never hot. Sometimes they laughed at her when she took off her boots and tried to swim. Not her chemise, she never took off her chemise. Good girls didn't do that. Yindi didn't have to wear boots, or a hat.

A jackass made her jump right off the path and almost fall into the long grass. She waved her fist at him. He didn't care. Just laughed and flew away.

She slowed and scuffed her feet. She hated her boots, hated them more than her apron and her hat. She plonked down onto the ground and reefed them off, tying the strings together and hanging them over her shoulder. Pa wouldn't notice. By the time she got to the river he'd have his easel set and his paints—oh, his paints! No, he wouldn't. She had his paintbox in her pack.

Quick, quick. She must be quick. Her bare feet pattered on the dry earth as she leapt around the tough kangaroo grass. Not much grass now, only the bunches like tiny spearheads. The bulbs tasted delicious—soft and always juicy. Yindi's mam, Yukri, had shown her which ones to pull.

When she reached the big gum tree she skittered to a halt, her heart big and pattering hard. She loved Pa so much. His big strong arms and rumbling voice made her safe. 'I'm here Pa.' She waved and weaved along the track right to the edge of the billabong.

Pa raised his finger to his lips then beckoned. He hadn't set up his easel; he stood staring across the grey-green water. 'There's movement over there. Can you see it?' He took the pack from her back and settled it on the grass, then her boots. He didn't say anything about her bare feet even though his lips made a funny shape as though he was eating his laugh. 'Step lightly now. Shade your eyes with your hand, like this.'

She peered across to the shadows beneath the roots of the big tree. Little ripples broke the top of the water. Then she saw it. A squeal jumped out of her mouth as the sleek dark brown body dived and twisted.

'She's looking for food.'

'Maybe she's got babies.'

'Juveniles. Call them juveniles. See? Just above the waterline.'

'Juveniles.' She wrapped her tongue around the word then squinted hard and moved her hand to and fro. 'Yes, yes there. I can see the hole into their burrow.'

'Good girl. You watch carefully. Tell me what she does. I want to make a record.'

'Can I make one, too? Please Pa, please.'

He twisted one of her curls around his finger and tucked it behind her ear not saying a word about her missing hat. Thank goodness. Mam would be mad. Perhaps the jackass had made off with it.

'Sit down over there and I'll set you up. We must always record our evidence. It's the only way.' He opened his paintbox and took out a piece of charcoal. Only a little bit. It was precious and she mustn't waste it. Then he passed her little sketchbook to her from the pack. Squirming she turned the pages past the first few drawings. They were baby drawings. Now she did better. She could make the mallangong's fur look wet or dry when she mixed the paint. Dark for wet and not so dark for dry and she knew their fingers and their toes—webbed. She knew that word very well. And their bills, like a duck but not really; not hard and snappy like Mam's ducks; soft and bendy.

Pa sat down next to her and his special smell of pipe and grass and scrunched-up leaves made her nose prickle. She turned her head to see his face, his deep brown skin almost like the blackfellas, with big creases around his eyes. He said they came when he was on the big ship and they'd got deeper like the cracks in the sandstone rocks at the swimming hole. Maybe he was getting old. That made her goosey even though the sun was still shining. Bunji's grandfather was old, very old, and he'd died. She'd snuck through the trees and seen the corroboree. Big bonfires, the dancing stomp of the feet making her chest bounce.

'So where is your drawing?'

Chewing her lip, she studied the empty page.

Hands laced, thumbs circling, Pa waited while she drew the outline and shaded it with a crosshatch of fine lines, to bring the mallangong to life, just as he'd shown her.

'I think you've been dreaming. Here's my picture.'

The riverbank, the tree and there the little hole, the door to the burrow and the mallangong swimming through the water fast, so fast it left arrows on the surface. And then another diving deep.

'I didn't see two. Were there two?'

'No, my heart, just one. I wanted to show Sir Joseph one diving down. Why do you think they dive so deep?'

She knew the answer and Pa knew it too but he liked to ask her questions just to make sure. 'They push their bills along the sand at the bottom of the river sucking up the fishes and …' she moved her lips and tongue into place '… crustaceans.'

'Crustaceans, very good. And what are they?'

'Maybe prawns and other shellfish. If they're very hungry mallangongs can eat half of themselves.'

'I don't think they eat themselves.' Pa's big, deep, rumbling laugh made her laugh, too. But then it flew away and she frowned. He was teasing. She scowled back at him. 'He eats half as much as he is heavy. There.'

'That's right. You're such a clever girl. One day you will know all there is to know about these special creatures and I will take you to meet Sir Joseph. You can tell him and his fine friends all about *Ornithorhynchus paradoxus*. Would you like that?'

She mouthed the words, her lips fighting the slippery rhythmical sounds. '*Ornithorhynchus paradoxus*. What's *paradoxus*?'

'It's an old word, from the Latin. Something that is contradictory, against common belief, differing from what people believe is true.'

'But the mallangong is true. He's here, we see him almost every day.'

'Indeed we do, indeed we do.' Pa stared out across the water and tapped his charcoal stick against his teeth, the way he always did when he was thinking.

'Where does Sir Joseph live?'

'In London, in a very fine house.'

London! That meant a ship, a ship with big white sails, not like the lighters that travelled up and down the river with their flapping square of ragged canvas. A voyage across the ocean. As long as Pa was there she might like that. 'Can Mam come too?'

'No, Mam must stay here.'

'Why? That's not fair. She'll be lonely if we leave her.'

'Such a wise head on these young shoulders.' He hugged her close, making his sketchbook fall to the ground. 'You're right. She would be lonely. I was only dreaming.'

'Mam says we mustn't be home too late or tea will spoil.' She bent over and picked up his open sketchbook keeping her fingers right on the edge the way he'd told her, then blew across the paper so the charcoal wouldn't smudge.

He took it from her and gazed out across the river. The sun was setting and the mallangongs had gone home. 'You're a good girl and I love you and your mother very, very much. I will never leave her. Not after all she's lost.'

What had Mam lost? Perhaps she could help find it. Then maybe Mam would smile. Everyone felt miserable when they lost something.

Two

Sydney, Australia 1908

Dust, ink and old paper, binding leather and hushed tones cocooned Tamsin Alleyn in a familiar tranquillity. Beneath the muted hum of the incandescent lights she took a deep breath, her heart hammering and her fingers itching to unwrap the package from London.

'I thought I might find you in here. Why don't you come and have a cup of tea?'

'I just want to open this. I think it's more of the correspondence from London that I requested.' She snipped the string securing the brown paper, rolled it into a ball and deposited it in the desk drawer with a flick. Funding was tight at the Public Library of New South Wales now they were working on the Mitchell bequest and every little bit helped.

'Come along, hurry up.'

She'd spent months writing letters, sending requests to the Royal Society asking for the return of the letters sent to Sir Joseph Banks from the early Australian naturalists. Dear God let her hard work be rewarded.

'Bring your lunch. I've got something I want to talk to you about.' Edna Williams left with a spring in her seventy-year-old step Tamsin envied.

Not game to ask what it was Mrs Williams wanted to talk about she reluctantly left the unopened package and made her way down the corridor and up the stairs. She'd been so pushy about the correspondence, determined the letters should be returned to Australia where they belonged. Besides it had gone some way in dragging her out of the morass she'd waded through ever since she'd sold Mother and Father's house. Not because of the memories, more because there weren't any and try as she might she couldn't feel any connection with the past.

She shouldered open the door to the tearoom.

'I've made you my favourite, a Grey's tea with some lemon.' Mrs Williams patted the chair next to her, her dark beady eyes darting like fireflies around the room and her buttoned boots tapping. 'Do hurry up.' The no-nonsense woman rarely showed a glimmer of impatience yet today her feet were jiggling around like a young girl promised a strawberry ice. She was up to something.

What had she forgotten? The two librarians from the cataloguing department threw closed-mouthed smiles at her, a cloud of bemused expectancy almost visible above their heads. Whatever was afoot wasn't a secret.

'Right. I'm ready.' Tamsin picked up her cup and inhaled the aroma of bergamot. Quite what Mrs Williams could have to complain about she had no idea. Ever since Tamsin had managed to wheedle her way into the job she'd given it her all. Coming at the lowest point in her life, and facing the daunting prospect of having inherited a bundle of worthless shares and a house she couldn't maintain, a salary of ninety-six pounds a year was not to be sneezed at.

'Are you up for a trip? It's fairly short notice I'm afraid.'

'A trip?' A trickle of anticipation worked its way across her shoulders and she concentrated on the slice of lemon swimming on the surface of the tea while she tried to look calm, responsible and professional. Of course, she was. It was exactly what she needed. The last time she'd left Sydney she'd been wrapped in a shawl, clutched in her mother's arms.

'You're the obvious candidate, given all your hard work with the Royal Society.'

Her heart took up an irregular patter. Surely Mrs Williams wasn't going to suggest she take a trip to England. Highly unlikely. The Blue Mountains would do. Somewhere she could shrug off the lead boots that still made every step an effort despite the job of her dreams. She still couldn't believe it. When she'd filled in the application form she'd simply been flying a kite, a badly balanced hastily tacked together kite at that. And she'd landed here firmly on her feet, working in this prestigious establishment with a history dating back to the 1820s. 'Of course I am.'

If she was lucky a trip might get her out of the celebrations at the Missionary Society. Even after all the years it still hurt too much. She hadn't managed to come up with anything to say that would be deemed appropriate. What could she say to commemorate her parents' death? She hadn't seen them since they'd handed her into the care of the Sydney Ladies Academy the moment she turned ten. She had nothing but bitterness to offer.

'It's not too far and you're about the only person who has sufficient understanding of the matter. We can cover the transport and accommodation costs if you're prepared to stay at one of the local establishments.'

It must be something important if they'd managed to find the money for an overnight stay. 'I'm all ears.'

'I received a letter from a Mrs Quinleaven; she lives just outside a small town in the Hunter. She has a book she'd like to donate to the Library. She's getting on a bit and wants to make sure she delivers it before it's too late. She has no faith in the postal service and transport to the area is a little patchy.'

Tamsin pushed her empty cup away tapping her fingernail on the table. 'The Hunter's not too bad. I know the train goes to Maitland. I could do the trip in a couple of days.'

'We might have to consider a travelling companion. Is there anyone you would like to invite?'

Tamsin shook her head. It didn't require much thinking, there was no one she could ask, except perhaps her housekeeper but the thought of any kind of close contact with Mrs Birkenhead didn't fire her with enthusiasm. 'I'm quite able to travel alone. It's hardly very far.'

'You really should pay more attention to these things. It's hardly appropriate for a young lady to be seen travelling alone.'

Tamsin lowered her lids mostly to cover the rolling of her eyes. 'I think at the ripe old age of twenty-five I hardly classify as young. Besides this is the twentieth century, not Regency England.'

'I know, I know. I'm sure you're quite capable of managing. Please don't start on the New Woman claptrap. I'm an advocate, remember?'

'I won't, I promise. Now what exactly is this donation?' A library full of books she could understand but one book? It must be something quite special. She leant forward resting her elbows on the table, her chin cupped in her hands.

'A sketchbook. Detailed anatomical line drawings and water-colours.' Mrs Williams's dramatic pause signalled something more. She lowered her voice and leant closer. 'We think it belonged to Winton.'

'Charles Winton?' Winton the naturalist, one of the first to send Sir Joseph Banks detailed information about the platypus. One of the very men whose correspondence she'd requested from London. 'How thrilling. Where did the sketchbook come from?'

'The usual sort of thing. Been in Mrs Quinleaven's possession for years and she'd never bothered to do anything about it.' Mrs Williams gave a disdainful sniff as though incapable of believing anyone could be uninterested in such a legacy.

'Winton's family?'

'No. No relation as far as we know. A promise she made apparently. I've no idea how it came into her possession.'

'I can go and have a look. If it's authentic it would be a wonderful addition to the letters. As you know I've requested Winton's correspondence in particular. I think that's what's in the parcel.'

'The sketchbook will have to be appraised to certify its authenticity; perhaps the people at the Mitchell, although they have their work cut out preparing for the opening. I'd like you to check for signatures and dates, take a look at the paper type and construction, the illustrations, any clues to previous ownership. You know the sort of thing. And while you're there you might enjoy exploring the area. I believe there have been sightings of the platypus in the local waterways although the exact location might be a bit difficult. A personal view would give you some insight into Winton's letters. Take a couple of extra days. It will make the display all the more relevant.'

Tamsin pushed back her chair. 'It would be an absolute pleasure, Mrs Williams.' She almost bent down and kissed the woman's peachy powdered cheek; instead she grasped her hand and squeezed it, inhaling her dusty scent of rosewater. 'Thank you so much for thinking of me. When would you like me to leave?'

'As soon as possible. Say tomorrow, and stay over the weekend, or longer if you need to. Make it a bit of a break. You could do with one. You've been looking a bit peaky lately. There's a hotel in the nearby town, Wollombi—the Family Hotel, I think it's called. They have rooms and it's very respectable. I've looked up the train times. The Brisbane Express leaves from Central Station. You'll be in Maitland in time for an early lunch then pick up the branch line to Cessnock. After that you're on your own. It's about eighteen miles to Wollombi. There's a regular postal service every afternoon which takes passengers; if not there's bound to be someone who can help if you ask at the station.'

'Perfect.'

'I understand it's very short notice. I wanted to give you first refusal. If you don't feel comfortable Ernest and Harry are willing to go.'

Tamsin shot a look across the room at the two cataloguers trying to prove they weren't hanging on Mrs Williams's every word by pretending to be deep in conversation.

And then she remembered and her shoulders slumped. 'There's just one tiny hitch; it can be resolved with a telephone call. May I use the office?' Not waiting for an answer Tamsin headed for the door barely managing to control her desire to dance across the room. If Mrs Williams got wind of the fact she was supposed to be attending a function at the Missionary Society, Ernest and Harry would be off on the weekend of their dreams and she'd be sipping tea and making polite conversation to a group of starchy matrons who wanted to reminisce about Mother and Father.

She closed the door of the office behind her and picked up the handpiece.

'One-two-five please.' She stared out of the window over the rooftops at the palm trees fringing the entrance to the Botanic Gardens.

'This is Mrs Benson.'

Tamsin stood tall. 'Tamsin Alleyn, Mrs Benson. I'm afraid I will be unable to attend the function for Mother and Father. Please accept my apologies.'

'Surely not. We have several people looking forward to meeting you. They feel they owe your parents so much.'

Tamsin bit back a groan. 'It's inescapable. I've been asked to go and assess a new exhibit for the Library. It's a great honour and if I refuse ...'

'Obviously far more important. You do realise this is a charity event.'

Tamsin rolled her eyes; no matter how hard she tried she couldn't summon any enthusiasm for the society. Everyone presumed she'd follow in Mother and Father's footsteps. She couldn't do it. Their shoes were far too big and uncomfortable. 'I'm terribly sorry. There really is nothing I can do about it.'

'In that case I shall be forced to make your excuses.'

'I'm sorry to let you down, perhaps we can organise another time.' The receiver clattered into the cradle and she swallowed a whoop of excitement before belting back into the tearoom.

'All sorted, Mrs Williams.'